LAND OF WOLVES

Also By TJ Turner

Lincoln's Bodyguard

LAND OF WOLVES

THE RETURN OF LINCOLN'S BODYGUARD

TJ TURNER

OCEANVIEW PUBLISHING
LONGBOAT KEY, FLORIDA

ISBN 978-1-60809-202-4

Published in the United States of America by Oceanview Publishing Longboat Key, Florida

www.oceanviewpub.com

10 9 8 7 6 5 4 3 2 1

PRINTED IN THE UNITED STATES OF AMERICA

To Nancy—my partner in all adventures.

ACKNOWLEDGMENTS

I ONCE HEARD a smart man—Steve Berry—declare that the only thing harder than writing a novel is to write a second one. He wasn't wrong, especially when wrestling with headstrong characters like Joseph Foster and Molly Ferguson. So once again, I find myself indebted to so many who helped this novel come together and make it out into the world.

First, I need to thank Nancy, my incredible wife, who never pulls any punches in her editorial reviews. Thanks also to my children: Cheyan, who keeps me humble with her brutally honest critiques; Jia who thinks that there aren't enough jokes; and Sierra who says she will one day become a much better writer than me. I must also thank my parents, Connie and Jim, for their feedback. Gwyn Sundell also read through the manuscript and forced me to admit that not all *bluffs* are created equal. And of course I need to thank the "Yellow Springs Wine Sipping Club with a Book Problem" who read the manuscript and discussed it with me in between boxes of Trader Joe's wine and fine cheese: Jen Clark, Karla Horvath, Alice Basora, Liz Robertson, Kathleen Galarza, Eden Matteson, and Nan Meekin. Anne Noble missed the wine, but she sent me extensive revisions, all by text message. I also owe thanks to Sharon Short who gave me incredible feedback on my early manuscript, helping me craft an even better story.

I am also forever indebted to Oceanview Publishing for taking a chance on Molly and Joseph's story, and then believing that I could follow it up with the sequel. They have an amazingly supportive team. Thank you, Pat and Bob Gussin, Lee Randall, Lisa Daily, and Emily Baar.

Of course I would never have made it this far as a writer without my incredible literary agent, Elizabeth Kracht (Kimberley Cameron & Associates). She knows just how to push and challenge her writers, and is always looking out for their future careers. Liz, you're a great friend. Thank you!

Finally, the Antioch Writer's Workshop and the Bill Baker Award got me started on this writing career. I never would have gained the courage to call myself a writer without that supportive community of literary citizens.

LAND OF WOLVES

There is a struggle inside each of us—between two wolves. One thrives on justice and peace, the other on anger, fear, and hatred.

CHAPTER ONE

2 MARCH 1874

BREATHING DEEP, I forced the space before my next breath to fall longer. It gave my ears a chance against the stiffening silence. There was nothing. I willed my heart to slow, anything to better hear through the darkness. But no noise reached me—no fall of hooves, no creak from the axles of an old wagon. Each passing night made it harder to bear the delay. By any measure, they were late—too late for my liking.

I leaned against the doorframe. The shaved wood still smelled of pine, and the sap was sure to stick to my clothes. Molly would lecture me again, when next it came to do wash. I had ruined many shirts while building our cabin and a few pairs of pants playing with the children outside. We had been here the better part of a year, passing the winter in town while the Old Man and I worked at the cabin on the days where the wind didn't bite too hard. This country air filled our hearts—a place to heal. But it came with the price of an ever-growing mending pile I left to Molly.

Around me the sounds of night bloomed, and the moon fell in uneven fashion. In its light, the giant oak cast a shadow across a thin trail as it snaked its way through the meadow. The children had forged other paths as well. Their feet plodded the tall prairie grass, cutting deep to reveal the mud underneath, as if a giant knife had scarred the earth. The lights were out at the Old Man's cabin, where Emeline slept sound in her room. She still knew the Old Man as *Uncle Abe*. Someday we would tell her the truth. She visited her mother often, buried a short distance from the oak. I pushed the recollection of that night from my mind. I would never wash the blood from my hands or the taste from my mouth. I drew consolation in keeping my promise to the dying woman. I had watched over her little girl and delivered her safe to her father.

In our cabin, Daniel slept in his small loft—the only room on the second floor. His bouncing amongst the rafters drove Molly crazy, though I regarded it a small price. He adjusted well in this place, accepting Molly and I as guardians after the loss of his family. I imagined Colonel Norris standing alongside the Great Spirit, enjoying the irony in our patchwork family. He had long fought for his Confederacy. Yet a half-bred Indian and the man he had despised most—Abraham Lincoln—were among those who raised his grandson.

Taking in the cool night air was like drinking water from a deep well. As I pulled it into my chest, a call echoed amongst the hills. The locals said there had never been a wolf in the area before, at least as far back as anyone could remember. But every night she tilted her head skyward, paying homage to some ancient wildness. Her song fell upon the land, long and intense. The howl rose and fell, only to start anew. This night she seemed closer, making her way from the rolling hills to the north. No call ever answered. It seemed odd she would be so far east, or alone. The Great Spirit created these social creatures to travel in packs. They taught the first men about loyalty and family. But this wolf had lost her pack, or been forced from it.

Behind me, the loose flooring creaked. I had not finished fastening it down, focusing instead on the roof. We needed shelter from the rain and scorching sun that would come with late summer. We had been here just under a year, yet with the Old Man's help we made tremendous progress. As soon as we could move into the small cabin, Molly insisted we make it ours, even as I finished it from within. She tried to be quiet to surprise me, but her feet fell heavy on the rough-hewn pine planks. Without turning, I spoke before she made it to the porch.

"Thought you'd catch me with whiskey?"

Of late I had done well, though the shakes would not leave my hands. As long as I had no need of a gun or knife, I needed no whiskey.

At first Molly said nothing, wrapping her arms around me as her head buried into my back. She pulled me in, breathing deep in the crisp night.

"I worry that you don't sleep."

"I can't."

"I know."

The remnants of slumber held her voice, muted as she pressed her face against my back. Her forehead filled the space between my shoulders, her breath warm.

"It's been too long," I said. I stared toward the tall oak. "Something happened."

Molly nodded. She abandoned any attempt at excuse. Nothing fit. She knew it as well as I. My mother's last telegram came from deep inside Georgia, five weeks earlier. She sent it after she found Aurora, the little girl I had lost so many years ago. They headed north to us. Molly and I postponed our wedding until their arrival. But the days stretched, and then the weeks turned to a month.

"What will you do?" she asked.

"They could be anywhere. I can start with the telegraph operator, but I don't know if it will be much good."

"You can't go south," Molly insisted. "They know you to be dead—as does the North. The entire country thinks *Joseph Foster* is long buried."

Faking my demise the year prior had been my only manner of escape. It bought our freedom from the Industrial Barons—a consortium of the rich and powerful. They had long run the country through corruption and manipulation. Years earlier, with the great Civil War about to falter and die, I had saved the Old Man from John Wilkes Booth. With that simple action I pushed the Old Man into the hands of the Barons. They used him as political power. Trapped in the White House, he enforced the Draft—a system to supply their factories with free child labor. All the while the last embers of our great Civil War held the South in a simmering conflict.

When the Old Man resigned, clearing the way for President Johnson, it invoked the wrath of the Barons. The new president worked to undo their influence while rebuilding the country. He supported the labor unions and sent the children home. The Barons would love to see me dead, but thus far the assumption of my death had shielded us. No one had come for me.

"What would you have me do?" I asked.

Molly's hands clutched my suspenders. Her nightgown tossed in the light breeze. I knew she longed to pull me to her, to drag me back across the threshold until I stood inside. She would be happy then. And I might be, too. Essary Springs existed as a slice of perfection—deep in western Tennessee. The Old Man lived at the other end of the meadow, and the people here were a rough mountain folk. They paid little notice to the nation's politics. Instead, they elected the Old Man as their mayor without care that he had once been our president. Pure heaven would fall short in describing this place, though the thought of enjoying it eluded me. I needed Aurora—to hold my daughter once more.

No matter how patch-worked our family was, it would never be complete without her.

"I will go to town tomorrow and telegraph Pinkerton," Molly said. "He will have some advice."

I drew her near. She always knew what to do. Allan Pinkerton, the famed detective to the presidents, had employed us both. Only his network of informants and spies reached deep enough into the South. They would be of use in finding my mother and daughter.

"Until then, I know you won't sleep," Molly continued. "I'll put on some tea."

"Lie down, Molly. I shouldn't keep us both awake."

She drew me close once more, resting one hand on the side of my face.

"My bed has been empty for far too long without you. If you insist on listening to the night and that damned wolf, then I will make us some tea. I will not go back to bed alone."

By her footfalls my mind followed her into the kitchen. The cabin had only two bedrooms, a small dining room, and a kitchen. I would build upon it later, or let this one serve as a living space while we crafted a grand house next. But I had made the kitchen extra-large—enough to fit in the cast iron stove that arrived from over the rails. It had taken four of us to haul it inside. I closed my eyes and listened as Molly stoked the coals and then added a piece of wood. She placed the kettle on the top with a clank and set about with the china. I loved the sound of her. After all we had been through—all she had seen—she desired a simple life. This place would heal us, once all the pieces of our jumbled puzzle fell into place.

I moved onto the porch and sat upon one of the rocking chairs the Old Man made for us. He intended them as wedding presents. But night after night he watched us stand upon our front porch and could bear it no longer. He gifted them early. The wood creaked, and the noise of the rockers on the rough planking killed my listening for the night. I would never hear a wagon on approach. Instead, I closed my eyes and waited for Molly. Many nights in the last month I had watched the sun rise and push away the darkness from this spot.

With my eyes closed, I drifted. I floated above the night, letting the howl of the wolf course through me as I rocked. Her voice pitched again, rising, then fading. She lured me toward sleep. A moment longer may have been all I needed, but in mid-song, she stopped. The immediacy of it stood in jarring contrast as the night became silent. Other sounds rushed to fill the void. I started from my chair.

Horses.

Their hoof falls were fast, echoing amongst the trees. At first I thought it a dream. Molly took the kettle from the stove. It steamed but hadn't boiled. She heard them, too. I stood, searching the night. They were coming up the trail and toward the clearing.

"Joseph . . ." Molly called from within.

Stopping at the threshold, I reached above the doorway. I had nailed a crude rack to the wall above the door. It held my Henry rifle. Molly joined me, grabbing the shotgun next to the door.

"Do you think it's—"

"Bad news," I interrupted.

"How do you know?"

"When is good news ever in a hurry?"

"The Barons?" Molly asked.

I shook my head.

"Why not?" she pressed.

I didn't want to frighten her, though it didn't matter. She read the fear on my face, as I did on hers.

"When *they* come, we won't hear them."

I stepped out onto the edge of the porch and strained my vision, waiting for the riders to emerge from the dark.

"All the same," I said. "Go blow out the lamps."

I racked the rifle, cocking the hand-lever under the stock. The metallic sound split the night as the bolt forced a cartridge into the rifle's chamber. When Molly blew out the last of the oil lights, I stepped off the porch into the night.

My advantage would lie in the darkness.

CHAPTER TWO

WITH THE BARREL of my rifle propped against the woodpile, I took deep breaths to steady my hands. They still shook. My mouth dried, as if my lips anticipated the flask. Liquor had always held the fear at bay and, without it, the pounding of my heart made my hands worse. I shifted until certain the moonlight did not cross my body. It concealed me amongst the shadows. My eyes narrowed—anything to gain the advantage if I had need to fire first.

The horses pulled closer. Whoever rode them forced the animals into a pitched run. From the sound, I thought there might be two. But as they emerged from the trail and into the clearing, the hoof falls echoed off the great oak making it hard to tell. They slowed to a trot, and then the noise faded, save the din of their breath as a rider pushed them forward. In the moonlight a man sat atop the first horse. He held one arm outstretched behind holding the reins to a second riderless horse.

"Sheriff Foster! Sheriff Foster!"

The voice came out winded and strained. At once I lowered my rifle and stepped from behind the cord of wood.

"Charley, I'm over here."

The horses started forward again, this time toward the sound of my voice. The form of the rider emerged from the dark. An eagle's feather stuck out from the band around the Stetson hat.

"I can't see you."

"What is it, Charley?"

He guided the horses until they stood nearby. I grabbed the reins of the one he pulled. Charley had worked both into a lather—their hides glistening under the moon.

"What's the fuss, Charley?"

"An Indian woman, she came to town an hour back. I thought of you right away."

The breath sucked out of me as his words struck hard about the gut. I tried to answer, but nothing came. Charley knew I waited for my mother—and daughter. We had talked on it plenty.

"Did you hear me, Sheriff? She's down at Doc Herman's right now. She's in a bad way."

I turned toward the cabin. Molly stood on the porch. Her hand covered her mouth as she stared. The shotgun hung limp from her other hand.

Without saying anything, I stepped forward and handed her my rifle.

"Joseph, I'll . . ."

I didn't hear what she said. Turning to the empty horse, I pulled myself up and barely settled before I dug both heels into the beast.

"Stay here, Charley. I want someone with Molly and the children."

Below me the horse twisted, unused to the weight. As I took up the slack in the reins, I pulled her head until she faced the end of the meadow. With a swat to her backside she reared before falling hard on her front hooves. When she gained her footing, we flew past the moonlit meadow and into the darkness.

I let her find the way. She knew it as well as I, and my vision held nothing on hers in the dark. I spoke in her ear—like my mother used to do when riding bareback to escape the slave catchers. As the darkness of the trail closed around us, I leaned closer to avoid the low branches. Loosening my grip on the reins, I remembered my mother's words in her old tongue. The horse seemed to know, running at her limit through the night. Branches tore at me. My shirt ripped as they tried to pull me to the ground, but she steered me clear. I closed my eyes and spoke, feeling her gait and moving my weight as she needed.

She played her role to perfection, making the fastest descent from Big Pond Hill I had ever seen. We found our way out of the woods and into Essary Springs, then down Main Street. I only grabbed the reins to slow her as we reached the doctor's office. I didn't bother tying her as I leapt from the saddle. The town lay dark and still, and only my footfalls on the wooden boardwalk disturbed the peace. I pushed into the door of the doctor's small office.

Inside, he sat next to his exam table. A sheet laid over her, though not covering her head. Doctor Herman rose to meet me.

"Joseph. I figured you'd be by soon."

"Is she—" I didn't finish the sentence.

He shook his head. "She's resting now, though she lost a lot of blood. I gave her some opium a while back. She'll need more soon."

I started into the room, but he caught my arm.

"I couldn't stem all the bleeding, Joseph."

"I thought you said . . ."

He shook his head again. "This was deliberate—to make it painful and slow. I did what I could, but we would need a real surgeon."

"Then we'll get her on the train in the morning."

"She won't make it through the night. I'm sorry. And likely she won't wake again. There's not much more I can do. I'm a country doctor. I do simple things here."

He stared into his hands before looking back to me.

"This . . . this was evil. They carved on her something awful. Those who did this, they knew how to use a knife. Maybe a good surgeon could have done more, but I don't know."

Fear held me. I had killed so many with my blade. What I sowed came back to haunt me. My stomach turned as I stood over her, watching her face turn cold. I had seen it too many times. The sheet was pulled high under her chin, but left enough folded over to cover her face—in anticipation. Her arms extended to her sides, wrapped in bandages that had bled through. I stepped into the room, just a half-step forward.

"Thanks, Doc," I said.

"Sit with her. If she stirs and needs more medicine, I'll do what I can."

I nodded, and he left me alone.

I took a moment—embarrassingly long. I hadn't seen her in years, not since I went to Washington to enlist. She had kept at her work, ferrying escaped slaves to freedom despite the fighting. It had earned her an audience with the Old Man, well after I had saved him in the theater that night. She seemed smaller now, somehow shorter as she lay stretched on top of the table. Maybe the stories, the ones from the Underground Railroad, made her larger in my mind. Perhaps I stood that much smaller when I saw her last. I forced myself forward until I leaned over her.

Peace held her face. So much so that I stooped near to hear her breathe. Her chest rose and fell, in shallow breaths that arrived in unsteady intervals. More wrinkles set about her face. No one would deny that native blood flowed through her veins, despite the store-bought dress. Even my stepfather, enlightened as he was about the worth of men, referred to us as civilized savages. To him we were a force to tame.

I sat next to her. She stirred as I held her hand. It wasn't enough to wake her.

"*Djòdjò*," I whispered. *Mother.* "I'm here."

The sounds felt awkward, some long cherished memory that I finally spoke aloud. I remembered such little of her native *Algonquin*. She did not stir, even as I caressed her hand. Doctor Herman carried a lamp into the room. He placed it on the table by the head of the bed.

"Did she wake?" he asked.

I shook my head. "Is there any way to rouse her?"

"Not while she's under the opium."

"I need to know what happened," I said.

He stood quiet for a time, a small brown vial in his hand with a metal syringe—more medicine.

"We should try to make her passing comfortable."

"I need to know," I insisted, raising my voice.

"Why would it matter, Joseph? So you could hunt them down? What good comes of it?"

"She had my daughter."

Doctor Herman looked to the vial in his hands. He nodded.

"We won't give her any more then. Wait and see if she wakes."

"Thank you."

He placed the vial and needle on the table near the lamp, and then walked out.

"*Djòdjò*," I said again, this time louder. "I need you to wake. Tell me where to find Aurora."

She did not stir.

I sat by her as the hours passed, the large clock chiming in the front hallway. It marked the progression of night. Every hour playing its music until the first gray light passed through the windows. Her breathing felt shallower. I prayed to *Wakan Tanka*—the Great

Spirit—though I had forgotten the words. I asked for mercy—to bring her back to us. I needed to know. She held the only way to find Aurora.

When next I woke, Molly stood next to me. The morning fell brighter in the room, though a gray pallor still gripped the horizon. She placed her hand on my shoulder. As I stirred, she leaned in and kissed the top of my head.

"I see I have more mending." Her fingers played with a split in my shirt. Below it a red welt had raised at a place where one of the branches had lashed me.

"Anything?" she asked.

I shook my head.

Molly walked out of the room and returned with a cloth. She placed it on my mother's head, wiping gently before letting it lie.

"How did you get here?" I asked.

"I took Charley's horse."

"And the children?" I didn't need to ask. Molly would have it well in hand.

"I left Daniel with Mayor Lincoln. Charley is with them."

I nodded. "You didn't have to come."

Molly leaned over, placing her head on mine.

"Of course I did."

"How will I find her?"

"Aurora?"

I nodded.

"We'll think of something. I'll leave you and send that telegram."

Before Molly left the room, my mother stirred. It wasn't much. I stared, not wanting to move. Molly pulled the cloth from my mother's head after wiping her forehead. Her eyes opened. She appeared confused, her stare falling to Molly, and then me. I stood and leaned over.

"*Djòdjò.*"

She tried to smile, but couldn't make it fill her face as I always remembered.

"Joseph." The sound of her voice held barely above a whisper.

"It's me," I said. "You made it."

Her other hand began to lift from the bed. I grabbed it and raised her palm to the side of my face. She spoke, so soft that I leaned close. The words that came out were not English. For a moment I panicked, not understanding. Then I let the sounds in, repeating them again and again as she spoke, hoping to remember.

She looked at me for understanding, but I feared the words would fall from my memory as I tried to untangle their meaning. I wanted to ask her to speak them again, to say it in English, but even the thought of speaking caused me to lose the sounds. I stumbled over them, saying each out loud this time.

She listened, and then repeated. As she finished, her eyes became glassy. I had seen it before, too many times. I gripped the hand at my face tighter, fighting the mask of death that descended.

"*Djòdjò!*"

It brought her back for a moment. She locked eyes with me and smiled. Then she said something different, hurried and rushed. She looked through me, seeing the world beyond. She tried to smile once more. Her hand at my face clenched—then let go. Her breath fell short and faded.

I leaned in, my forehead against hers. I tried to fight the sobs, not wanting Molly to see me this way. Molly placed a hand on my shoulder, pulling me away to hold me. We stayed like that for minutes, maybe the better part of an hour. I don't know. The clock in the hall sounded, and Doc Herman came in to pull the sheet over my mother's face.

Molly pulled back from our embrace.

"Joseph, what did she say?"

I thought of the words, played them over in my mind, repeating each one.

"Do you know?" she asked.

I nodded. I remembered enough.

"What?"

"Find Aurora and go to the *Paha Sapas*."

"What does it mean?" Molly asked.

"I don't know. I've never heard those words before—*Paha Sapas*."

"She said nothing else?" Molly pressed.

She had said something more. I tried to translate those words, but they filled me with fear. She had grown serious, her voice deeper. In my youth that tone of voice meant words I needed to heed well.

"What was it?" Molly asked. She read my face.

I didn't want to tell her. It would shatter our peace—the perfection of Essary Springs. I looked away, but Molly turned me until I saw into her eyes.

"*They're* coming."

CHAPTER THREE

THE OLD MAN stopped the wagon in front of the station. The afternoon sun hung low. Heaviness still gripped me. The image of my mother lying under that sheet would not shake from my memory. The morning sun had been so bright off the white fabric that it still blazed in my eyes. For so long I imagined what I might say when I saw her again. But I never pictured it in this manner, struggling to understand and with no time to say my peace.

I dismounted from the wagon and the Old Man handed me my bag. It held the few things I would need—a change of clothes and food for the trip. I would head east and then make my way to Georgia where my mother had sent her last telegram. She left nothing else to go on, and Doc Herman estimated that she traveled injured for days. If she had stopped, she might have lived, but then Aurora's trail would be that much colder. She pressed on knowing she sacrificed herself.

The Old Man got down from the wagon while the children stayed in the back. Charley sat with them, holding a shotgun across his lap. Emeline watched. She had grown tall, matching her father's gait. Their contrast never bothered folks here—the darkness of her skin against his. Daniel sat next to her and seemed not to mind that I would be gone for a time. He tried to grab the feather from Charley's hat. They had made it a game, where Charley swatted him away at the last moment.

"I wish you would wait for Pinkerton to respond," the Old Man said.

"Would you?"

He shook his head. "No. I would send you."

"I won't sit here and wait—that's a means to die when they find us. And who knows how far away Aurora will be by then. With my mother . . ." I paused. I couldn't bear to think of the glassy look that came upon her eyes. She saw something in those final moments. It left me sick in the pit of my stomach. "They want me scared. And I will be if I sit and wait. I'm going to find them. I'm going to find her."

"You know that's what they want."

"I do."

The Old Man held out his hand and I grasped it.

"Do be careful, Joseph. The South is not yet healed. There is no telling what you will find there."

I nodded, shouldering my bag.

"I almost forgot," the Old Man said.

He reached inside his jacket and produced a package wrapped in linen, tied by burlap twine.

"I had this made for you. After I gave away the rocking chairs, I thought I might need something else for your wedding. I figured you would use it as we set the fields and such. Now it will have more important work."

Tugging at the burlap, I let the string fall away. When it came undone I held a long knife, sheathed in leather. The smith had forged it in haste, attaching rough Osage handles.

"The only good steel he had came from an old file," the Old Man said.

I pulled on the handle, and the knife came free. The blade still held hammer marks. Little triangular indentations pocked the sides of the blade—from the cutting edges of the old file. The blacksmith heated and reheated the steel, hammering the file into a useful blade. At least the edge looked sharp, and it felt well balanced.

"Thank you."

"It will serve you better than a gun," the Old Man said. "You were always good with a knife."

Though not as refined as the Bowie knife that had sent John Wilkes Booth to his demise—this blade would do the job. I tucked it away, behind my hip where the leather stayed in place inside my belt. Reaching out, I grasped the Old Man's hand.

"You come home to us, like your mother said, and bring Aurora."

"Will you talk to Molly for me? She seemed a might sore this morning as I packed."

"I'll see what I can do. I've never been good with those kinds of things." Then he glanced over my shoulder. "Although, Joseph, you might give it a try yourself."

I turned. Molly stood on the boardwalk. She wore a simple homespun dress, holding her finest bag.

"Molly, we've talked about this."

"We have," she said. "And I decided I'm coming. Mr. Lincoln can no doubt handle two children after steering a nation. And he'll have Charley to help."

Charley tipped his hat at the mention of his name.

"But Charley has the duties of Sheriff while I'm gone. He has enough to do."

"Round up drunks? Find lost cattle?" Molly asked. "It's hardly a job that will tax Charley's time or skill."

"And I would feel better if you had help," the Old Man added. "We will manage here."

Winning such an argument stood beyond my grasp. I had been outmaneuvered. It became clear she had already talked about this with the Old Man. I held out my hand for her bag. At first she refused.

"Are you so stubborn that you will not permit me to carry it?" I asked.

"Are you placing it on the wagon or the train?"

I turned to the Old Man. He had already mounted the wagon. He tipped his hat, and with a crack of the reins, the wagon started forward.

"The train," I answered.

Molly handed me the bag. We walked down the walkway of the station, toward the ticket counter.

"I had not imagined we would leave this place ever, especially so soon," Molly said.

"I know."

I shifted the bag into my other hand and tried to look over my shoulder. Essary Springs had filled, crowded with people. The frontier beckoned. As President Johnson sought to quell the fight in the South, the West cast an undeniable allure. People headed into the wilderness to make their fortune. The newspapers even whispered rumors of gold. And then the mountain men chased those rumors into the Lakota Indian country.

"What is it?" Molly asked.

I turned to the ticket counter.

"It's getting harder to find the outsiders. Even in the last few weeks."

"It will calm again. Things always do."

Molly purchased her ticket and then handed me mine.

"I trust you can find us comfortable seats?" she asked.

"Where are you going?"

"The train leaves in twenty minutes. I will find you," she said, without answering my question.

She left me on the platform and headed toward town. There were only a few stores along Main Street, though I had no idea what she might need. I didn't want to think about it. The night had left me drained—the passing of my mother numbed every-thing. Aurora seemed so far from reach now, as far as she had ever been. I couldn't bring myself to imagine who had her, or what they might do to her. They wanted me, and I would give them everything they wanted—and more.

As I stepped into the train, old habits took over. They drew me some small manner of comfort—something to focus on. I looked for a seat where nothing would escape my notice. I moved a few cars forward, opening the doors and walking through. Most were near empty after dropping their load of pas-sengers. No one wanted to head east—adventure and fortune lay to the west.

When I settled into a seat, I searched out the window, looking for signs. I didn't know for what I searched, only that I had to be careful. My mother's warning lingered. *Who were they and how would we tell?* I had no idea.

Molly found me a short time later. She had a small package, wrapped in brown paper and tied in twine. She took her bag down from the shelf overhead and placed the package inside.

"What did you need?" I asked.

She sat across from me and smiled, though she said nothing. The stress of the night, of venturing into the unknown, it pushed me to the edge.

"What was it, Molly?" I snapped. Anger felt good. In truth, I didn't care what she had purchased.

Molly looked to me for a moment, ever calm, and then back out the window. Her brow furled as she noticed something. I strained in my seat to see behind me, to discover what she watched.

"What is it?" The anger eased, replaced by worry.

"What did you used to say," she asked, "about seeing people multiple times?"

"To see if you're followed?"

She nodded.

"Once is happenstance, twice coincidence."

"And three times?" she asked.

"Deliberate." I looked out the window, turning in my seat to look over my shoulder. "What is it?"

"That man in the Bowler hat and the gray suit."

"I don't see him," I said.

"He watched us at the platform earlier, and then I saw him in town just now."

"That's only twice. Maybe he's traveling."

"His hat," Molly said.

"What about it?"

"The Sears catalog says it is popular back east, especially in New York."

"I don't think that matters."

"Why would there be four of them from New York, here in Essary Springs?"

"Four of them?"

Molly nodded. I strained once more to see. At the end of the platform, three men stood talking. They were not from here— not from Tennessee, not from the West. I had never been to New York, but I could well imagine these men in a large city.

"I only see the three," I said.

"The other one, the man who followed me, he just stepped onto one of the passenger cars." The train jolted as Molly finished talking. Up front, the engine tugged as the steam built, and the whistle let out a long lone howl. I thought of the wolf.

I strained to see out the window once more, trying to find the three men left behind. They walked together, not bothering to tip their hats to a group of women who passed. They did not belong. I turned over my other shoulder to see down the aisle. If the other man had climbed on the train, he couldn't see us. Several cars lay in between. Standing, I held my hand out for Molly.

"What is it?" she asked, as if she had forgotten the entire conversation.

"We're getting off."

"Joseph, I didn't mean it for real. There are many newcomers in town."

"Not like this."

She stared, the defiant look beginning to form across her face.

"The children," I said.

Those were the only words Molly needed to hear. She stood, only taking my hand at the end. Then she reached for her luggage, though I pressed my hand into the small of her back to hurry her down the aisle. The train began to roll, and in a few moments would be moving too fast to step off.

"Joseph, you will not hurry me, and I will not leave my luggage. That is my finest bag."

I removed my hand from her back. When she reached this manner there would be no arguing without conceding some point. Like the time we escaped Jekyll Island. She had insisted on removing her dress to carry through the marsh. Now she pulled the bag down and handed it to me. It nearly pulled me off-balance.

"What could you possibly have packed?"

Molly said nothing. She turned and walked up the aisle, away from where the man in the Bowler hat had entered the train. At the end of the car, she pushed open the door and descended the stairs. A man on the platform extended his hand as she stepped off. I followed her, and once on the platform, I turned to look as the train picked up speed. The man in the Bowler hat walked down the aisle inside the train, searching the faces of the few passengers. It would not be long before he realized we were gone.

I placed my hand on Molly's back and led her toward the nearest alleyway. I didn't want the others to find us—to see that we had stepped off the train. The knife along my hip felt reassuring.

"Did they see?"

I shook my head, still concentrating on the backs of the men walking at the far end of the boardwalk. The giant steam engine strained to gain speed, and we waited until it cleared the end of the station.

"Is it gone?" Molly asked. "What now?"

As the last car pulled out of sight, I took Molly's hand.

"Come. We need to find a horse."

CHAPTER FOUR

MOLLY AND I rode out of town in a meandering fashion on the one horse I found in a hurry. With the saddle not overly comfortable for the two of us, Molly clutched me from behind. She held fast to her bag, even when I suggested we leave it in town and come back for it. She refused.

We were not followed—at least not that I could tell. The daylight waned, and I hoped to return to the cabin before night crashed around us. The horse climbed, winding through smaller trails that would lead us to the Old Man and the great oak. We didn't take the main trail for fear of finding the men from town.

Night had nearly settled when we finally broke through the forest and into the meadow. I steered the horse away from the clearing and into the shadows at the edge of the woods. Halfway around the open grassy area I found what I looked for.

"Why are we stopping?" Molly asked.

I tied the horse a ways behind us so, if he stirred, the trees and deep green of the forest would dampen his noise.

"I want to wait for a time."

Nearby, an old hollowed log sat between two trees. I rolled it over. An oilskin tarp lay underneath. I pulled it from the hollow area of the log and then found a patch of thick sweet grass to lie upon. The place had a perfect overlook to the cabins.

"What is that?" Molly asked.

I motioned for her to lie next to me. Untying the twine that bound the cloth, I unrolled two rifles concealed within.

"You knew we were coming back?" she asked.

"No. But I didn't want to leave my rifles in the cabin, and I figured this might come in use."

Molly lay next to me. My hands worked the mechanism of my Henry rifle—a repeating gun. The other had seen more years, an old Sharps rifle. I had taught Molly on it. Instinctively, she pulled the Sharps to her and began to load it while I put cartridges into the Henry.

"How long will we wait?" Molly asked.

"Until nothing happens."

"That doesn't tell me much, Joseph."

"If I were them, I would come later—once the cabin is dark."

The Old Man's place filled with a soft light. He read late most nights. Molly stayed quiet for a time, arranging the oilcloth so she could lie on it. I tried to relax, to absorb the night around me. But I pictured my mother's face as she spoke her last warning.

"Why would they come here if they think we're gone?" Molly asked. "If they think we're on the train?"

"There were four of them. Only one got on the train. I figure he was sent to watch us. The others . . . they're here for something else."

"Maybe I was wrong about them," Molly said. "Maybe they have nothing to do with this?"

"You weren't."

In truth, I wasn't certain. But I couldn't tell her what Doc Herman said—the evil in what they did to my mother. I had hacked pieces off men to make them talk, but not like that. They cut her with the precision of a butcher, to make her lose blood— her life draining as they tracked her. I had been wrong. This wasn't a challenge to draw me out. She hadn't escaped. They let her go, gave her enough life to reach us and make fear and rage cloud my judgment. I breathed deep, fighting both.

"I'm sorry, Joseph—about your mother. I didn't tell you before."

I shifted to see her. Darkness surrounded us, but her outline came to my eyes despite the lack of light. Her deep red hair remained just out of reach, teasing her face the way it always did.

"Last year when she came to drop Daniel off," Molly continued, "she spent time with us. She was proud of you. She wanted to tell you herself."

I focused on the rifle in my hands, holding back the sobs that had robbed me of my senses the night prior. I hadn't seen my mother in more than a decade. But she loomed so large, as if she watched over me all those years. Now she had gone with the Great Spirit, so far beyond my reach. Her presence no longer guided me, and the path she would lay out for me seemed lost. The sadness pressed in, but I resisted, refusing to let it take grip. I worked the lever on the Henry rifle. The metallic sound of the cartridge loading into the chamber felt good—cold and emotionless. If they came tonight, they would pay. Molly reached out. She found my shoulder. I shifted to grasp her hand. Mine shook as I held hers.

Letting go, Molly reached into her bag and pulled out the package she had bought earlier. Unwrapping the twine and paper, she revealed a bottle of whiskey. It held the rough frontier liquor, brewed in stills hidden in the mountains. She looked at it a moment, then pushed it toward me.

I shook my head. "I don't need it," I lied. I would love the numbness it would bring—to quell the rage and anguish at the same time.

"I can feel it in your hands," she said.

"I'll be fine."

My hands still shook when I tried to do anything fine. The anger, and even the sadness, I held at bay. But if they mixed with fear only the liquor would keep them away.

"Are you sure? I know how hard you've tried. And with your mother . . ."

She let her thought fade, consumed by the night. Instead, she pulled the bottle back and placed it on the oilcloth by her rifle.

We stayed like that for a time—watching the dark descend from the heavens. The sounds of creatures came out, filling the quiet that had held the meadow. Night summoned a changing of the guard. The stars pierced the black cloth above us, and the moon rose, creating shadows at the edges of the fields. My eyes traced the trails the children had made, weaving in and out of the grass. They found the ends of the meadow and then dove back to the interior. They would be disappointed when we plowed a portion to make way for the wheat.

Scanning the meadow, I began to relax. Perhaps the men in the Bowler hats were here only to try their luck out West. With each passing minute I felt more foolish. I wanted to find Aurora—instead I lay in a field in rural Tennessee, seeing monsters at every turn. I started to grab the Henry rifle to help me stand when movement in the grass along the far side of the meadow caught my eye. I pulled my hand from Molly.

"What is it?" she whispered.

I pointed. The grass shifted slightly. I rose to my hands and knees. As the wind picked up, the grass parted again. A dog-like creature trotted into the light. She stood long and lean, her coat dark gray—near black. Sensing the wind, her nose lifted and bobbed to catch the air. She stopped and stared at us.

She had never ventured this close before. I felt certain of it. As she sniffed the night, she stopped, frozen amongst the grass and the light wind. She knew we were there. Even so far away, she could sense it. Her eyes pierced the dark. As the wind picked up, my mother's voice came to me—a noise barely above the wind. It sang in her native tongue, the intonation rising and falling, telling of the two wolves. For the past year I had fed the wolf of peace, wanting nothing more than to settle here and raise our family. I had neglected the other, figuring I had killed enough to make her happy for a long time to come. Maybe I had taken enough lives to keep her at bay until I met the Great Spirit. Yet here she was. This wolf was not cast from her pack—she searched for me.

Slowly she shifted into full view. Raising her head, she started her song, filling the entire meadow with the wilderness. Beside me, Molly raised the rifle. With my hand I pushed the gun down, stopping her just as she drew the sights onto the wolf.

"What are you doing?" Molly hissed. "Look how close she is! She will take our chickens—or come after the children."

I eased back down, lowering my voice as far as it would go. I leaned close to Molly until my breath fell on her neck as I spoke.

"A gun that shoots a wolf will never shoot straight again."

"That's ridiculous, Joseph."

"It's not. She's here for a reason."

"What reason?"

I shook my head. "There's always a reason."

The wolf still stared in our direction. She had stopped her howl, hearing our voices. Abruptly, she looked to the edge of the field where the trail entered the meadow. For a moment she stood frozen, then she bolted through the grass the way she came.

Horses.

This time they came slow, not wanting to make noise. The lights in the Old Man's cabin had gone dark. My feelings of foolishness vanished, pushed aside by fear. I glanced to the whiskey—I didn't need it. I didn't *want* to need it.

Three riders emerged through the night, careful to make no noise. I remembered John Wilkes Booth stepping so carefully in the theater that night. These men approached in the same manner. *Death creeps quietly.*

"Can you take one?" I asked.

Molly nodded. She said nothing. Her body had stiffened, and she reached for the whiskey. She unstoppered it, took a long pull, and then raised her rifle.

"Which one?"

"I'll take the first two when they get closer to the cabin. As soon as I fire, don't wait or they'll spook. You only have one shot. Let your breath out first, then pull."

I steadied my rifle, propping my elbows into the dirt to form a frame. Pulling the stock tight against my shoulder helped, but my hands still shook. I closed my eyes and snapped my head, as if extra concentration could take away the need for the whiskey.

The horses stopped in the middle of the field, and the man at the back pulled a pistol from his belt. The high-polish of the metal caught the moonlight. The length of the barrel did not suit the West, too long for these parts. Men out here wanted as fast a draw as they could muster, not firearms that hung above the mantel as showpieces. These were the men from the station—city men with Bowler hats and little country sense.

The first two dismounted from their horses. The third directed by pointing his pistol. He took their reins so the horses wouldn't run off, and then the two started walking toward the Old Man's cabin. Each drew forth their pistols as well. I waited until they were halfway, then I drew my aim on the second man. Taking my own advice, I inhaled and held it. Slowly I let the breath out. When the last of it eased from my body, I pulled back on the trigger.

The shot broke the night. Instantly the noises around us died, the dark violated by the suddenness of it. My shot went wide. Both men turned toward me, startled. The shaking in my hands had caused me to miss.

"Damn!"

I pushed to my knees, racked the lever under the rifle, and drew my aim again.

Molly fired. The horse under the third man reared before collapsing. I took aim at the second man, slowly taking up the slack in the trigger. The rifle kicked, and the man disappeared in the tall grass as he fell.

The final man shot in my direction. The bullet went high. It hit amongst the trees and branches in the forest beyond. He fired again, the moonlight catching the smoke from his pistol. He stood too far away. I answered with another round, and he stumbled. My hands were worse now as adrenaline mixed with the fear. I had hit him, but not enough to stop him.

The Old Man's cabin door swung open. The man spun in that direction. He didn't have time to get another shot off. The Old Man stood on the porch and leveled a carriage gun at him. The gun kicked, buckshot striking the man in the chest. He fell backwards, covered by the prairie grass.

Molly and I stood. I loaded another round into the Henry in case there were more of them. Then I called to the Old Man.

"It's Joseph."

"Are there more?" he called back.

I held my rifle ready as I crossed the meadow, Molly right behind me. She had reloaded the Sharps.

"I don't know."

Back in the direction of the trail, all stood quiet. I walked to the first man, picking up his pistol. Death had set over his face—the same with the second man. My bullet had found his chest. Molly stood by the felled horse. The other animals had run off. The smell of gunpowder lingered, and I searched toward the wood line. No one else came. The Old Man stepped from his porch and began walking toward us.

"Joseph!" Molly yelled.

I rushed over, with the Old Man and Charley close behind. Molly stood over the last man. He still breathed. Her shot had felled his horse—dropping the animal so fast he became trapped beneath it. A more experienced rider would have bailed from the beast as she reared. These men were not of country stock. His hand flailed, reaching for the pistol on the ground that escaped his grasp.

"Who are you?" I demanded.

His focus held fixed on his pistol, reaching to recover the gun. I kicked it away. Handing Molly the Henry rifle, I cocked the pistol in my hand and leveled the barrel at him.

"Who are you?"

"A messenger." He clenched his jaw, fighting the pain. A vein throbbed at his forehead.

His accent fell thick upon my ears—Irish. A tailor had hand sewn his suit, another trapping of city life. His kettle-black hair competed with the dark of the sky, except for a patch of white perched to one side of his forehead. A matching mustache covered past his top lip, waxed in the highest of fashion. One of his lapels held a pin, a black clover.

"What message? From whom?"

"Mr. Carson would like a word." His voice held barely above a whisper.

"With me?"

He nodded, and then spit on the ground.

"And where do I find Mr. Carson?" I asked.

"In town."

Every few words would cause him to wince. His leg trapped under the horse, likely broken.

"You deliver messages in the middle of the night with guns drawn?"

"Aye. When you weren't on the train, we had little choice."

He lied. They were here for another reason. They had come for the Old Man.

"What does Mr. Carson want?" I asked.

"He has a job for you. Something you can do for him."

"And why would I want it?"

He laughed, transitioning into a coughing fit.

"You won't. But you'll like the payment."

They had Aurora. He didn't have to say it.

"I'll find him then. He'll have need to purchase three pine boxes before he leaves." I raised the pistol as if to dispatch him.

He stared at me. There was no fear on his face, just a constant unbroken gaze. I thought of Wyman Baxter, the sick, twisted man who had hunted Molly and me through these very woods—the man who had killed Emeline's mother by the great oak. Their accents were worlds apart, but they could be the same person.

"Killing me doesn't get your daughter back."

I lowered the pistol.

"What do you know of her?"

A smile spread over his face. Anger built within me until it snapped. I leveled the gun and pulled the trigger. The round skimmed past his head. A trickle of blood poured down his cheek and a piece of his ear went missing. It wiped the sick look from his face—replaced by fear and rage. I leaned in, applying pressure on the horse. He winced—then moaned.

"Tell me," I said, leaning harder on the dead animal as he writhed beneath it.

"Mr. Carson would like to see you."

His jaw set hard, absorbing the pain. All the while he stared, defiant, enticing me to more violence. I raised the pistol once more.

"Joseph," Molly yelled.

I looked to her. As usual, she held my moral center. I de-cocked the gun, flipping it until I held it by the barrel. His stare remained unbroken. Maybe he reacted to the pain. I didn't care. I leaned on the horse to make him stop. Raising the pistol, I let it crash on top of his head. He went limp.

"We need to get the horse off him," I said. "Charley, get a team harnessed up. When we get him free, we'll take him to the jail, then send for Doc Herman."

Charley nodded and jogged toward the Old Man's cabin. A small barn lay just beyond it. Molly stepped closer and placed a hand on my shoulder. I brushed it off. I didn't like what I felt, and I didn't want it to spread to her, like a disease. From outside the meadow, the wolf began her howl. Even with all the noise, she hadn't run off. The Great Spirit sent her for a reason. She came for me—I had too long fed the other wolf.

Molly tried again, placing a hand on my arm. I put the pistol inside my belt and took the rifle from her.

"I need to find Mr. Carson."

CHAPTER FIVE

THE SUN ROSE over Essary Springs. It cleared the foothills and played with the little eddies of dirt as they lifted from the wagon wheels. Charley sat in the back with the stranger. I loaded him in the wagon without care of his pain, after we bound both his hands and feet. Partway down the road, he had begun singing some kind of Irish folk tune meant to annoy us. Molly grabbed him by the jaw and stuffed a rag into his mouth to force him quiet.

Approaching town, my anxiety set in. Although we had dispatched two of them, Mr. Carson would have more help. I steered the wagon around the edge of town, only diving onto Main Street when I felt certain we could make it to the jail. Charley opened the building while I stood guard outside with my Henry rifle. A few locals watched in curiosity. On a normal day, the jail held only the town drunks to sleep off the liquor before we sent them home.

Charley came back, and together we dragged the stranger up the stairs and into the cell. The sound of the metal locking in place felt reassuring when we closed the bars.

"We'll need to get Doc," I said. "Can you manage to round up some help, Charley? I'd like a few more guns here until we know what we're dealing with."

"The Hardeman boys should be back in town. That do?"

I nodded. Charley headed out to find them.

"What do we do next?" Molly asked.

"Once he gets back, I'll go to the hotel. That's the only place I can think to look."

"I'll go now," Molly said.

"It's not safe." I grabbed her by the wrist to stop her from leaving.

She turned, annoyed. Her emotions never strayed far from her face.

"I can handle myself, Joseph. I'll ask around. Nothing more."

I released my grip. She was right. I had to remind myself of all she had been through—the training with Pinkerton. She needed no protection.

"Will you let me know when the Old Man comes with the children?" I asked.

"I will."

Molly held out a hand and brushed it along my face. Then she opened the door to the jail and stepped out. The sun pushed through the doorway, falling on the man in the cell. He moaned, the rag still in his mouth.

As I went to sit behind the desk, the man writhed on the floor like a snake, making his way toward the metal bars, his hands still bound behind him. I felt in no mood to release them, even as he lay inside the cage—at least not until Doc Herman came. The man moaned, resting his head between two of the bars in the cell door.

Reluctantly, I stepped over to him and then squatted. He moaned again, indicating he wanted the cloth taken from his mouth. I reached in and grabbed a corner of the rag so he couldn't bite. I yanked it clear and let it fall into the dirt of the floor.

"What is it?"

He coughed. It progressed into a laugh—twisted and maniacal.

"What's your name?" I pressed.

"O'Malley."

"You're a little out of place, Mr. O'Malley. You should have considered that before you came."

"Aye, you think so? There are more of us than you."

I began to pick up the rag, wiping some of the dirt on the floor with the wet portion of the cloth. I intended to shove it back in his mouth.

"What does Mr. Carson want?"

O'Malley smiled. "Mr. Carson has a politician problem."

"That seems far from my issue."

"You're the one who'll be helping us though."

Hearing footsteps on the boardwalk, I looked to the door.

"We won't kill you just yet," he said, working my fear. "Not like . . ." He caught himself before he said too much.

"Not like who?" I asked.

His face could not contain his joy as the sides of his mouth upturned in a smile. I reached through the bars and grabbed the hair at the back of his head. Pulling his long hair, I slammed his forehead into the steel bars. His whimper built to a cough, and then into a low chuckle. I slammed his head again, this time harder.

"My mother? Is that what you meant to say?"

"She said you were a wolf." He began to bark, making fun as he built his chirps into a howl.

My hand found the knife the Old Man gave me. I pulled it out, thrusting the blade under his neck. He stopped.

"Are you the one?" I asked. He knew what I meant. "Tell me."

"A wolf?" he said. His voice strained, raspy. "More like a beat dog."

My knuckles were white on the handle. As a child, my mother called me *her wolf*. She told this man on purpose—as a message, like the dark wolf in the field the night before—another sign from the Great Spirit. My grip eased upon my knife. With so little pressure I could thrust it into his neck. The door to the jailhouse opened behind me.

"Joseph," the Old Man said. "What's happening here?"

The sunlight poured around his silhouette. I eased the knife back through the bars and then let his hair fall through my fingers.

"We need the county judge. I want this man hung," I said.

Grabbing hold of his lapel, I ripped the black clover pin from the fine cloth. I turned it over in my hand, and then stood. I picked up my Henry rifle from the desk and handed it to the Old Man. Emeline and Daniel stood outside on the boardwalk. They peered inside. I sheathed the knife and brushed past, leaving the Old Man to watch O'Malley. As I walked by, he placed a hand on my shoulder.

"Joseph—"

O'Malley began to bark, and then howl from his cell.

"I have to find Mr. Carson," I said.

I walked down the boardwalk, where O'Malley's voice no longer reached me. Charley hadn't returned with the Hardeman boys, and I had seen no sign of Molly. I waited until Charley came down the road, the two brothers in tow. They each had a shotgun or a rifle. I tipped my hat as they walked by, and Charley continued on to the jail.

Without Molly, I headed toward the hotel—the most logical place to find Mr. Carson. As I crossed the street, the dust kicked from my boots. I scanned the rooftops—nothing. O'Malley's warning that they outnumbered us made me ill at ease. He could have been lying, but I didn't want to take the chance at surprise.

The hotel had only six rooms, with one master suite. Mr. Parsons, the innkeeper, hoped to draw in the rich and famous as they made their way west. Essary Springs held little more than a small mark on the great rail lines, so most of the hotel lay empty. When I walked inside, I found Mr. Parsons behind the main desk.

"Sheriff, haven't seen you about town in a bit."

"Luckily, there's been no need, Mr. Parsons."

"Molly came by a little back. Are you looking for the same fella she asked about?"

I nodded. "You seen him?"

"Upstairs, in the master suite. This isn't going to cause trouble, is it, Sheriff? He paid cash for three nights."

"You can keep your cash either way," I said. "He's got plenty to spare. Did you see where Molly went?"

Mr. Parsons shook his head. "She asked on him and then headed out."

I stared toward the second floor. Darkness gripped the hall past the last stair. The sun from the main door only made it up a few steps.

"Is there anyone else up there? Anyone take another room with him?" I asked.

"He better be alone. There's a charge if extra people are in the suite. He called down for breakfast a while back—the boy is in the kitchen fixing it now."

"Breakfast for one?"

Mr. Parsons nodded. "Eggs and grits. Here's the boy now."

Behind me a small child with blond hair stood with a plate and a cup of coffee. Mr. Parsons had taken him in after his folks passed, kept him on as a houseboy to clean and cook if things got busy. They never did, but Parsons seemed fond of him. The boy looked to get by me so he could make it up the stairs.

"I'll take that up, son. I'm headed up there anyways."

I took the cup of coffee from the boy, and then started up.

"Sheriff, he'll be wanting his food, too," the boy said.

I shook my head. "He'll be fine." I didn't want to have my other hand burdened, but the coffee might come in handy as a scalding distraction.

I eased my weight onto each stair. It still made them creak. At the top, I found the hallway dark, as the boy had already turned the oil lamps off for the day. I stood on one side of the suite door, as far as the hall allowed. The knuckles of my free hand fell hard upon the wood.

"Breakfast," I called.

It took a moment, but then he answered.

"Come in."

I turned the knob and pressed into the room. A man, a decade older than I, sat at the lone table in the spacious suite. His balding hair scarcely covered his scalp, pulled across in a thinning comb-over. His portly physique betrayed his lack of physical exertion. A silk smoking jacket hung over his expansive body. I checked over my shoulder, scanning the room—nothing. The master suite meant more floor space, not more luxury. Little else adorned the room. The man looked at me, then to the cup of coffee in my hand.

"I thought you were my breakfast," he said.

I found his accent difficult to place. Not Irish like his man in the jail, but not of this land either. I walked over to him until I stood just out of reach. Then I upended the cup and let the coffee fall to the floor. As it splattered, he pulled his feet in to avoid the burning liquid. I put the cup down on the table, and then pushed the whole thing away. Grabbing the other chair, I set it in front of him. I drew my knife and let it rest on my knee as I sat.

"We need to talk."

"No, Mr. Foster," he started, "you need to listen."

He looked to the knife in my hand and then to me.

"I see Mr. O'Malley found you and delivered my message," he said. "May I ask where he is?" He folded the paper he had been reading and then reached to place it on the table.

"He's waiting for the county judge."

"And what would be the charges?" He looked to my chest where the silver badge clung to my shirt. "Sheriff?"

"Murder. And kidnapping."

"I see," Mr. Carson said. "That does sound serious. Perhaps you need to rethink your actions."

"How's that?" I worked the blade against my pants, as if wiping it clean.

"I have come with an offer. It is one that will benefit both of us. You wish to have your daughter back, and I need something in return."

"You admit that you have her?"

Mr. Carson leaned back in his chair, crossing his arms over his chest. He looked to the knife.

"I do."

"And my mother? You admit to that as well?"

He looked up from my knife, staring right at me.

"That was Mr. O'Malley. He thought you would only believe her, that you would not take us seriously unless we showed you that we were."

"Oh, I believe you, Mr. Carson. And that is why I'll have them build the gallows twice as wide so you can swing with your friend."

Mr. Carson smiled. Not the deranged smile of O'Malley. His held confidence.

"He's not my friend. And that would be unfortunate, especially for a small girl I know. You see, Sheriff, I work for men who are far less sympathetic than I."

"And what is it *they* want?" I asked.

"Your help. The Senate scheduled a commission hearing in several weeks. They will consider impeachment proceedings against our new president. You will convince them to move forward on the charges."

The suggestion shocked me. I had not expected it. They were attempting to depose President Johnson. His policies changed the nation—deconstructing the power the Barons had built while empowering the labor unions and ending tariffs on foreign goods.

"I assume you work for the Barons?" I asked. It was the only thing that made sense. The Confederation of Industrial Barons sent Mr. Carson. Or maybe I sat in front of one of the Barons himself. These were the same men who had trapped the Old Man in the White House, who had killed my wife and stolen my daughter—and now, the same men who had murdered my mother.

"We prefer to call ourselves the *Consortium*."

"And what role do I play?"

"You will testify that *you* killed Mr. Ward Hill Lamon. And that President Johnson ordered the killing to blackmail Mr. Lincoln into resigning."

Lamon had been the head of the Consortium—the critical link between the world of politics and the Barons. He had grown powerful, controlling Congress as the fighting in the South simmered.

"I am dead. No one will believe it."

"They *will* believe you, Mr. Foster. You just have to tell the story the way that we need, and all will be forgiven between you and the Consortium."

Mr. Carson's face did not betray if he knew the truth—that the Old Man had killed Lamon. It happened in Ford's Theatre as I tried to convince the Old Man to resign. Lamon had burst in with his henchman in an attempt to seize me. The Old Man had saved me from certain death, in the same spot where I had saved him from Booth's revenge. Afterward, Pinkerton used Lamon's body. He passed it off as mine—discovered in a barn fire in Virginia. We hoped in death that I would avoid the grasp of the Barons.

"And that's why O'Malley tried to kill Mr. Lincoln?" I asked.

If they eliminated the Old Man, there would be no one to refute what I had to say in front of Congress. The Old Man could never testify that he had killed Lamon. He could never tell how the Barons trapped him in the presidency to use as a puppet for their policies.

He did not answer. Instead, he deflected.

"If you come with me, and do as I ask, no one will bother you again."

"My daughter?"

"You get her back."

"How do I trust you?"

Mr. Carlson went to stand. "May I?" he asked.

I waved the knife at him. This man could do little to me. Even if he had a gun, I doubted he knew how to use it under stress. Knowing how a gun worked, and using it against a person, were different things. I had no fear of this man.

"I don't expect you to trust me," he said. "And, frankly, I don't care. If you want your daughter, you'll come with me. You've already faked your death to escape us. That didn't work. We'll keep coming. There is no more running, Mr. Foster. Think of Miss Ferguson. Think of the children you keep."

He made his way to the bed against the far wall. A set of clothes lay upon the bedspread. They were fine, matching the housecoat he wore.

"If I agree, I get my daughter before I see Congress."

"No," he said. "She can be at your side for your testimony. But you don't get her until you tell them how President Johnson stole the presidency."

"And Mr. Lincoln?" I asked.

"I'm assuming, since you are not here with Mr. O'Malley, that Mr. Lincoln is unharmed."

"If I agree to what you want, he remains that way—safe."

"For now," Mr. Carson said. "I suppose it is too much to ask that Mr. O'Malley return with us?"

"He'll meet the judge for what he did to my mother. I'll see him hanged."

Mr. Carson laughed. "He is more trouble than he is worth. You may have him, though I suspect he will find his way back. He always does."

Mr. Carson reached for his clothes. A small brass bell sat on the bedside table. He picked it up by the wood handle and rang it. The sound could barely have escaped the room. But the door behind me opened. Two men entered, each wearing a gray suit and a Bowler hat—like O'Malley. They were larger than me. One of the men held a set of irons in his hands. He looked at my knife.

"Allow me a minute to change, and we will leave," Mr. Carson said. "The train is waiting. And if you will be so good, place the irons upon your wrists."

The second man brushed back his jacket and pulled a shiny revolver—the same as the other men, with a long barrel not suited for the west.

"I thought we had a willing agreement. Am I to be kidnapped and taken to Washington?"

Mr. Carson had nearly finished dressing. "You get what you want, after we get what we want. Did you think I would be so foolish to leave you on my train without irons? If you want your daughter, put them on."

I looked to the two men. I had little choice. If I said no, they would kill me. I would have no way to protect Molly and the children then—no way to find Aurora. If I went with them, then

I had a chance. I had confidence in only one thing—running would solve nothing. If they found me here, they would find me anywhere. But I had no way to get word to Molly. I pulled the sheath for my knife from my pants and buried the blade in it. Then I placed it upon the table. She would find it and know I would never have left of free will without it. I took the irons from the first man and closed them on my wrists.

The two men walked me out, followed by Mr. Carson. We made our way down the stairs, where only Mr. Parsons' houseboy saw us leave. I nodded to him. He responded in kind. He looked to my wrists. As we walked past and outside, his footsteps fell on the wooden floor. He had run out the back.

Once outside, the men led me down the first alley and to the back of the hotel. I searched the street, but the morning hadn't broken the full grip of night. Only a few people were out. The ones who were, paid us no mind.

We walked down the boardwalk past the ticket counter. A woman stood, purchasing a ticket. A large hat adorned her head, obscuring any hope of seeing her face, though I recognized the dress. A single curl of her deep auburn hair fell from under the hat. As we walked by, I overheard her conversation with the stationmaster. She inquired about the train. The regular line would not come to town this day. This happened sometimes when a special came through. Extra passenger cars would pick up midweek travelers to offset the cost of pulling the special cargo.

In this case, a smaller train set upon the rails. The engine looked new, pulling a tender and three regular passenger cars. But the last car—the one in place of a caboose—caught my attention. It seemed as equally out of place as these men. The sides shone, though a layer of dirt and grime had built over its journey. The wood finish stood out. A bright green adorned the window trim, and the rails at the end were brass—polished. Red velvet curtains sealed the windows.

The men pushed me past this car, and toward the older passenger car in front of it. They opened the door and directed me inside. I took one last look out over Essary Springs, and then stepped onto the stairs. From the side of my vision, I noticed the woman from the ticket counter. She mounted the same steps into the car behind the engine.

CHAPTER SIX

6 MARCH 1874

THE TRAIN TO Chattanooga made slow progress. This part of the South had not seen reconstruction like the rest of the former Confederacy. It sat too far west—too rural. Most of the route came from old *strap rail*—steel plates bolted to wood planks. At times it forced the engine to a crawl, drawing out the first leg of our journey. I spent my time focused outside, watching the trees and the rolling hills. It wasn't until first light of the new day that we pulled into the main rail hub at Chattanooga. It wouldn't have taken me much longer by horse, if I rode light and fast.

Carson's men locked my irons to a chain bolted to the floor. It gave me enough room to lean against the side of the car and gather some rest. The metal cut at my wrists though, and they were sore by the next day. I had nothing to do but work the chain, stressing the screws that held it fast to the wood below my feet. Eventually, they would give.

My captors numbered only four. They kept to themselves at the front of the car playing cards, or sleeping. Each had the same accent as O'Malley—a grip of their Irish homeland that hadn't let go. They glanced to me and brought water when I called, but otherwise let me be.

On occasion, I caught glimpses of Molly through the door between the rail cars. She ventured in once, pretending she needed to stretch her legs. The men rose to challenge her. One invited her to stay a spell—his intentions less than pure. She talked her way out of the car, but let no sign of recognition cross her face— nothing to give us away.

Once past Chattanooga, the rails were better. The train picked up speed. We took on passengers in Knoxville, where fresh coal filled the tender and water for the boiler. I knew this line—a major route from the booming East Coast cities to the lure of the West. We would head into Virginia and then onward to Washington. Trains headed the other direction carried men filled with thoughts of glory and adventure. The tall tales that sold newspapers back east fueled their passions. My car remained empty. At each stop the men in the gray suits closed the shades so no one could peer inside.

As we moved farther north, the men played less at cards. They kept their voices low. I wasn't certain what changed, or why. They brought forth rifles—shiny Winchester repeaters that no one had ever fired. One of the men pulled the shade to the window between the cars. I saw no more of Molly. On occasion, the little silver bell would ring from the rear car. It barely rose above the clacking of the rails. Each time, one of the men got up from his post and disappeared through the back door. The noise of the steel wheels filled the stale air when the door opened.

"Mr. Carson would like you to join him," one of the guards said. He had returned from the last car. Pulling at the chain anchoring the irons at my wrist, he undid the lock holding me fast to the floor. The irons remained on my wrists.

We walked through the door, though I fought to keep my balance. I had sat for the better part of two days, as the length of chain did not allow me to stand. It seemed a small blessing that I no longer had need of the liquor. This time on the train would have passed as an eternity without it. The man opened the door into the last car and pushed me through. Inside, Carson sat at a dining table along one side of the car. He motioned me forward.

"You can remove his irons," he told the guard.

The man paused, and Carson motioned with his knife. He went back to cutting a piece of beef that sat on the plate in front of him. I rubbed my wrists as the guard removed the metal cuffs. Mr. Carson pointed to the chair across the table.

"You may go," he told the man.

A moment passed, and the man did not leave. Carson motioned with his knife again. The door behind me opened, letting in the rail noise. Then it softened once more as the man left. We were alone.

I stared at the plate in front of me. My stomach tugged. I hadn't eaten since we left. The knife at the side of the plate caught my eye. It sat in easy reach and appeared sharp enough to bury through Carson's head.

"I didn't get my breakfast the other day, so I thought I would return the favor." Mr. Carson took another bite of his steak. "Then, I realized my manners escaped me. I should be more hospitable. You must be hungry—eat."

A steak sat on the plate in front of me, and as much as my stomach asked for it, I kept my hands on my lap.

"You're not hungry?"

I stared at him, revealing no answer.

"You are a difficult sort to understand," he said.

"You hold me in irons, then invite me to dinner. What is there to understand?"

He smiled. "I figured by now the anger had passed, and you would use reason to understand your predicament."

"And what would I have figured out?" I asked.

"That you have little choice other than to help us, and with it we return your life."

From the side of the table he grabbed hold of a crystal bottle with many fancy cuts that reflected the light. He poured one glass of a dark brown liquor and then another. I could smell the alcohol waft from the glasses. I looked away as if to hold the temptation at bay. The inside of the passenger car held extravagant furnishings. The walls were wood lined, a deep stained mahogany. Skilled hands had fit the trim, and made the heavy red velvet curtains. Every brass fixture shone. A curtain separated the back half of the car, likely concealing bedchambers. This train represented the extension of the Barons' power.

He held out the glass. I made no effort to take it from him.

"I heard you liked your liquor."

"It dulls the anger."

Carson stared for a moment before diverting his eyes to the little bell at the side of the table. Then he summoned his courage and took a drink, downing the whole glass. He took hold of the other, holding it by his fingertips above his plate. His ring finger bounced against the crystal, sounding a soft staccato in the space between us.

"This will be over soon, I assure you. I am no more happy to be this far south as you are to head east."

"Yet you travel light for being so concerned. You must not be important to the Consortium."

Anger swept across his face, then vanished. He took a sip from the glass in his hands, and then continued tapping the glass.

"We all play our roles, Mr. Foster."

"And yours is errand boy?"

He smiled. "Tell me about the West," he said. "I have hopes to go there soon. In fact, I am to help lead an expedition this summer. We have new interests opening in the wild of the frontier. Perhaps I will become a cowboy and run a ranch."

"You wouldn't last."

"I would surprise you at how well I adapt. I would hunt and live from the land. In fact, this summer I shall eat buffalo upon the plains. It will be a raucous good time. I am well suited to the frontier."

"Is that what you hope to accomplish?" I asked. "To open up the West? Will you steal children from the Indians now that the rebellion is over?"

I referred to the Draft—the practice forcing children of former Confederates into northern factories. It held little more than punishment for continued resistance after the Great War ended, though the Barons loved the practice as a means to break the labor unions. Before the Old Man resigned, the Consortium received anything they wanted—even laws protecting the Draft. They controlled Congress so they could pass any legislation they desired, even over a veto from the president.

He paused, twirling the glass while maintaining his tapping. "Now that is an idea. I would wager that Congress would allow us to take the little savages and teach them a trade."

I looked to the knife beside my plate. I could reach it and plunge it into his fat belly before he reached his bell. He watched my gaze.

"I would be careful," he warned.

Our eyes met.

"Will I see my daughter again?" I asked.

His finger fell silent against the glass in his hand.

"Of course," he said.

Slowly, he began his steady tapping once more.

"And if I don't testify?" I asked. "What then?"

"Do not be foolish, Mr. Foster."

"What would happen to your Consortium if I do not testify?" I pressed.

"We will find another way. We always do."

The train slowed. Both of us looked out the window as the track took a bend. I couldn't tell exactly where we were, but we closed in on Lynchburg—the next stop on this line. It would be a short time to Washington.

"Maybe *I* will find another way," I said.

His eyes darted to the knife at the side of my plate, likely regretting his decision to invite me into his car.

"This is the easiest manner to have your daughter," he said. Though in his warning, his voice concealed rising fear.

"At what price to the nation?"

"*We* are the nation," he said. "*We* are the progress that will see us surpass Europe. Do not be foolish."

The train slowed further—the time between each click of the rails grew longer. He looked out the window, straining to see in front of the car.

"Maybe the nation needs another way," I said.

He no longer answered, distracted as the train came to a halt. All day we had stopped and started, allowing trains to pass on sections of rail that were not yet double laid. Yet outside the far side of the car a second set of tracks stretched as far as the eye could see. Something seemed amiss.

"Who do you work for?" I asked.

"I already told you." His voice strained, and he pushed up from his seat to look out the window.

I picked up the knife.

He turned to see me holding the blade. His eyes fell on the bell at the side of his table. He fixated upon it, as if it were the only signal he could give to his men. That happened to some when faced with fear, especially if they weren't used to the feeling. They would fire until their gun went dry and stand there dumbly still pulling the trigger. They never realized that it could still serve as a club—so fixated they were on the one use of the thing. This man forgot his own voice as he stared at the bell.

I plunged the knife into the steak on my plate, tearing off a piece of meat and skewering it with the tip of the blade. I held it up and then bit into the meat. He stood frozen.

"*Who* do you work for?"

"The Consortium has many members," he said. "It is a committee."

"There's always one person. Who is it?"

"It doesn't matter."

"It does."

"Why?"

"He will be the *second* one I kill." I rose from my seat.

Mr. Carson backed away. He glanced out the window again as if help would come.

"You are being foolish. You would sacrifice your daughter?"

"You don't have her. And if you did, you already killed her." I thought of what he did to my mother. Her words fell on my ears, her warning.

He looked to his bell. I picked it up and tossed it to him. His hands fumbled with the liquor glass he had been holding, dropping it as he caught the wooden handle of the bell. The glass shattered as it struck the floor. Staring at the broken shards, he rang the bell.

Nothing.

He rang louder, thrashing it until it sang a near continuous tone. I stepped forward. The door opened behind me. I didn't have to turn. The wind outside blew her perfume into the car.

Molly stepped into the car. She held one of the Winchester rifles, flanked on both sides by two men. Not the ones dressed in gray suits with the Bowler hats. These men had *Pinkerton* lapel pins on their dark suits. Each had one of the Winchesters. Behind them, another man entered the car. He looked older than last we met, but more vibrant—*Allan Pinkerton.*

"I had hoped to next see you two at your wedding," Pinkerton said. His slight accent lingered among his words. "Though it is always good to see you, Joseph."

"I was able to get that telegram off," Molly explained. "Though it had to wait until Chattanooga."

"This is foolishness," Carson yelled. "Your daughter will be lost. I cannot save her now."

I raised the knife, and as he cowered with his hands over his face, I lashed out with my free hand. My fist crashed through his hands, and the fat little man crumpled into a pile on the floor.

"I see you met Matthew Carson," Pinkerton said.

"Who is he?" Molly asked.

"One of the Barons," Pinkerton answered. "Though he plays only a bit part in their Consortium. He would like to move higher in the organization, but a lack of competence holds him back."

The little man lay unconscious on the floor.

"He doesn't have Aurora," I said.

"I would doubt it very much," Pinkerton answered.

"I know he doesn't. Though he wouldn't tell me who led the Consortium."

"I doubt he knows," Pinkerton said. "*We* don't even know. They've been good at hiding themselves, operating out of their factories in the Northeast."

Pinkerton walked over and picked a glass off the table. He wiped the rim clean and then poured a large serving of the liquor. Taking a sip he savored it, swirling the glass to smell the spirits. He offered it to me. I shook my head.

"More for me then, it's damn good."

"How do I find Aurora, if she's even—"

"We have time," Pinkerton said, cutting me off. "There has been a struggle between President Johnson and the Consortium. The Barons retreated to New York when the Old Man resigned. We have little influence in the North now. And with the president fighting impeachment, it will stay that way for a time."

"All I need is Aurora. I care not for these politics."

"I know, Joseph. I am telling you, we have a bit of time. They wanted you to testify in a few weeks. Mr. Carson was to bring you back and hold you in a safe house. I can take him, and the Barons won't realize for another week."

"How does that help us?" Molly asked.

"There's a factory," Pinkerton began, "in upstate New York. It's out of the reach for federal forces, until the politics settle. They have children there. We think it's among the last factories where they still hold them. Despite the Executive Order banning the Draft, they haven't given up all their free labor."

"And Aurora, she's there?" I asked.

"We think so. It's the safest place they could hold her. They own the police and the courts that far north."

"That's not good enough," I said. "If I only have a week, I need her before then—else I testify."

"No," Pinkerton said. "You cannot. No matter what. Even if you told the truth, it would mean Congress did not know everything about that night in the theater. They would hold President Johnson to task for it. We need more time to root out the corrupt senators, those who remain on the payroll of the Barons."

He stepped forward, placed a hand upon my shoulder, and looked right at me. He did this whenever he wished to stress a point, as if the physical contact alone drove it home.

"This is a fight for the soul of this country, Joseph. You gave us all another chance when you forced President Lincoln to resign. We mustn't go backwards now."

I shook his hand off.

"I will burn this country down to get her back," I said. "I've done my part and paid too much for it. I sacrificed her once before and I promised never again."

Pinkerton's face changed to the slight pink that rose with his anger. He nodded, an admission he understood what I meant—not that he agreed. From inside his jacket pocket, he produced a piece of paper. He handed it to me.

"I can't give you anything else," Pinkerton said. "You'll have to make your way by yourself."

"You won't send us with anyone? None of your detectives?" Molly asked.

He shook his head.

"I can't. It's a hornet's nest, and sending you with anyone would be kicking that beast. Right now the North is like the South during the rebellion, though controlled by the Barons, not the rebels. You'll have better luck alone—fast and quiet."

Molly gripped my hand.

"I'm coming," she said.

"I know."

She reached down and took something from her boot—the knife from the Old Man.

"The boy at the hotel—he brought it to me."

I pulled the blade from the sheath. Pinkerton stared at it, then at me.

"It's time to wake the wolf."

CHAPTER SEVEN

16 MARCH 1874

MOLLY AND I lay in the grass outside the factory, hidden by a thicket of young trees. This far north the air felt colder. The Hudson River flowed behind us, a half-mile back. We could run down the gentle slope to where a barge floated alongside a worn wood dock. The river formed a brown ribbon, emptying the northern lakes as it flowed toward New York City and then to the ocean beyond. It created an ideal site for a factory. River traffic could haul goods to the city, and from there, the industrial products of the Consortium could reach anywhere along the East Coast and the merchants in Manhattan.

We watched the factory, stalking it as a hunter might. Out of sight, we gathered what we could of the operation. As much as I wanted to charge in headfirst and find Aurora, drag her out of this awful place, I waited. Pinkerton's training stressed patience over action. Times like this, though, were hard.

It had taken the better part of a week to find our way north, especially this far into New York State. The train served our purposes most of the way, until we rented horses at a livery in Albany and rode from there. I wanted to stay off the rail lines, to mix our travel in case someone followed. I felt better with a horse beneath me, as a means to escape that was not tied to the trains.

The factory was not hard to find. The Consortium had placed it well outside the nearest of towns as a means to hide the children from the Draft. Only a series of long brick buildings marked its presence. One had a tall smokestack where they ran a steam boiler. Likely it affixed to an old-style beam engine. Even from where we lay, the sound of looms reached us. They crafted fine cloth in this place, for the suits of rich men. And for that they needed the smallest of fingers to thread the tight weave of the fabric. Mr. Carson had worn such a suit.

Once the sun began to fade, we moved from the trees. We closed in on the buildings, always mindful to keep some manner of grass between us as concealment. The building had meager windows. They were staggered between columns of red brick, painted white, then worn by the weather. The windows were dull from lack of cleaning. They offered little glimpse of the area within. A few men walked the grounds, each carrying a Winchester rifle and a sidearm. Their suits were dark and well kept, and they carried themselves in the manner of those who had been in the Army. My hopes for an easy trip faded. I had brought a pistol, but nothing more. A rifle would have attracted too much attention on the train. This far north the country had settled and no longer bore the wild character of the West.

Well past the point where my stomach rumbled for dinner, the doors of the largest building opened. A man and a woman escorted a line of children—all girls, their dresses a patchwork, mended time and again. The man led the first of them, with the woman at the rear. My heart beat faster until it's furious drumming plagued with my vision. I strained to see their faces, to match them to Aurora. But I was too far away. They disappeared into another building not far from the first. Smoke rose from a chimney and the smell of hot food fell over us. It made my stomach tug.

As the noise within the factory died, quiet descended. Men left the textile mill, in groups of two or three. They carried lunch pails as they walked a well-worn path toward a waiting wagon. From the smeared dirt upon their clothes and their heavy boots, these men worked the factory. They loaded into the wagon, and a moment or two later, the driver cracked the reins. It started toward Saratoga Springs, the nearest town. The factory had emptied—done for the night. But the men with the guns remained. We were in the right place.

"How do we do this?" Molly asked. "I counted three of the guards. Why would they need guards for children?"

"I'm not certain. Pinkerton said Mr. Carson owned the place, that *gentleman* we met on the train. Maybe we go through the front door."

"Is that wise?" Molly asked. "Besides the guards, I count the man and woman who led the children out, and maybe the cook we saw earlier. Even if we had rifles, we're outnumbered."

Earlier we had watched the cook, a fat man in a stained white shirt with an apron, berate and slap a small girl. She feverishly peeled potatoes and carrots, though not fast enough for his liking. It took all my restraint not to stand and beat the man.

"We could wait until they slept," Molly suggested. "That other building must be for the children. The man and the woman must stay in the house. Maybe the guards will leave. There's no room here for them to stay."

To the far side of the complex, past the dining hall, a little house sat back from the dirt road. Painted white, it had flower boxes under the windows and green handcrafted shutters. A bunkhouse stood next to it, though it looked not nearly as cared for.

"Do we want to wait that long?" I asked. "If we get caught at night, there is no doubt to our purpose."

"But the guards may leave. They tied their horses near the bunkhouse. Surely they can't stay the night."

I shook my head. I didn't know what course might be best.

"Joseph, do you think this whole idea is wise?" Molly asked.

"How do you mean?"

She stared toward the building as she lay next to me.

"I don't trust it. Pinkerton sent us with no one. Why?" she asked.

"He said he couldn't—not this far north."

"I know what he said, but I don't understand it. When I telegraphed and said we were on the train headed to Washington, he was eager to help. But he couldn't send help with us now?"

She looked away, pulling a long strand of grass from the patch that concealed our presence.

"You think it's a trap?" I asked.

"I don't know what I'm saying." She paused. "Why would they need three guards for children at a textile factory?"

"Why would Pinkerton betray us? What does he have to gain?"

Molly stayed quiet, spinning the strand of grass with her fingers. She tugged at the ends, fraying the strand and pulling it apart bit by bit.

"Molly?"

"He doesn't want you to testify. Isn't that clear? You heard him. Just by showing up alive to the committee, it proves President Johnson knew something. At the least it shows Pinkerton covered it up. He's better off with us quiet, and if not quiet, then . . ."

She didn't finish.

"After all he's done for us?"

"What has he done?" Molly asked. "Name one thing that did not serve his interests. I can't think of a thing."

I looked to the factory, then beyond to the dining hall. The girls were out of sight. As dusk dulled the day, the light of oil lamps lit the windows of the long building.

"He cares about us. He cares about the Old Man. He wouldn't walk us into anything."

Molly's hands stopped turning the strand of grass. She let it fall through her fingers.

"He whored me out. Is that what you mean by how he cares about us?"

Her face held no emotion—her eyes said everything. I wanted to look away, but I didn't dare. While I had been the Old Man's shadow, his last wall of defense from men like John Wilkes Booth, Molly worked different circles. Pinkerton found her as a young woman, after her family died down south. He provided a job, if one could call it that. She worked the social circles, letting men share her bed while they spilled their secrets—secrets she provided Pinkerton. He knew all the desires of the senators and other Washington power brokers.

Molly might be right. Pinkerton insisted upon avoiding Congress. His face reddened when I made mention of testifying. And then he sent us here. He knew where Aurora was, or claimed to. And gave us nothing more than an address. I looked over my shoulder. *Could it be a trap? Were there more than three guards?*

"Joseph," Molly whispered.

She gripped my arm. I had been looking to the river behind us, half expecting a boat to sail upriver with an army ready to descend upon us. I turned to where Molly pointed. A horse and its rider came down the dirt road at a steady pace. The rider wore a suit, though not as dark or as well kept as the others. But most important, I recognized him—one of Pinkerton's men from the train.

"Do we need more proof?" Molly asked. "We should leave. She's not here, Joseph."

I shook my head. Anger took hold, turning the taste in my mouth bitter. I wanted to lunge from our hiding place and rush him. I could run him through with my knife and send his lifeless body back to Pinkerton.

"We came all this way, we check first. Then we find Pinkerton." The taste strengthened—metallic, the mixing of anger and revenge. Before I had always kept it subdued with the liquor.

"But the guards?"

"We wait for dark, and I'll take them one at a time."

I grabbed hold of Molly's hand, and we slid backward from where we lay, letting more grass conceal our bodies. The sound of conversation rustled through the grass, though I could not make out the words. I felt like a boy again. I would lie in the fields, waiting for the wind to be just right before rising to take a deer without spooking it—more lessons from my mother. I owed her everything.

The men talked only for a few moments, and then the three guards rushed to their horses. They all headed in the direction of town. We had gone through there several hours earlier, and had stopped to buy provisions. I had asked for directions in the General Store, which now seemed a stupid thing to have done. Try as I might to blend into the background of life, a half-Indian this far north stood out. Pinkerton's man must have followed us—a smart move. We had taken a room in the local hotel and slipped out the back without notice. That ruse may have bought us time.

As the sound of the horses faded, one of the girls left the dining hall carrying a small basin of water. She walked a dozen paces from the door and threw the water onto the ground. The basin slipped from her hands. When it struck the ground it issued a loud metallic clang—the first noise to split the evening. Her brown hair caught her face as it blew in the wind. She looked older than some of the others—almost the right age. *Aurora?*

I stood. I couldn't help it. I needed a better view, to see for myself. I started toward her, stepping high to walk over the grass.

"Joseph," Molly hissed, keeping her voice from carrying over the wind.

I didn't listen. The guards were out of sight. I pushed through the grass like a boat would plow through high water. The girl saw me and stopped. She stooped to pick up her basin, holding it between us as some manner of defense. She backed away as I closed the distance, shuffling while locking eyes with me. Molly followed. Her dress brushed over the ground, making a rushing sound like the wind pulling through the grass.

I stopped a few feet from the girl. She wasn't Aurora. I reached into the pocket inside my jacket and pulled forth an old photograph. Pinkerton had given it to me—of Aurora sitting with Colonel Norris and his family.

Turning the photo around, I showed it to her—part explanation and part hope.

"Do you know her?"

The girl looked at me and then to Molly who walked up behind me. Her eyes fell on the photo, scanning it. Then she stopped and leaned closer, ever so slightly. She nodded.

"You know her?" I asked.

She glanced over her shoulder.

"Who are you?" she whispered. Her voice held firm to her southern upbringing.

I pointed at the picture of Aurora.

"I'm her father."

The girl stared. Her eyes filled, even as she fought the tears.

"No one ever comes here," she said. She held her voice low, almost to a whisper. "My father died in the war."

The door behind her flew open. A man stepped out. He looked to the side of the building.

"Get back in here, you wretch!" He called to the space toward the river. Then he saw us. He stepped from the door. "Who are you?"

The girl tried to step back. She fell, landing hard on her back. For the first time I noticed the chains that bound her feet. The metal chimed as the links fell against one another. Sores covered her lower legs where the irons fastened to the chains had dug into her flesh. No one had removed them in months.

"Joseph!"

Molly tugged on my arm. The man had closed upon us. He seemed no older than me, though balding and fat. Sweat covered his chest and stained his white shirt. In his hand he held a meat cleaver. He wore a bloodstained apron around his middle.

"Who are you?" He stepped closer, holding the cleaver and raising it shoulder level. "You're not to be here!"

He reached with his free hand, trying to catch my shirt or jacket. I swatted it away, pulling him off balance. He stepped forward to catch himself. Then he brought the cleaver down in a large arc. Stepping to one side, I snagged his wrist, though the blade of the large knife still struck my hand. Anger surged through me. I pulled my knife. Still holding his arm, I plunged my blade deep into his chest. Then I yanked his wrist down, pulling him close to look into his eyes. He stood for a moment, defiant. Slowly his weight pulled him toward the ground. He fought it, a hissing noise coming from his mouth. Glassiness overcame his eyes, and his body went limp. I twisted my knife free and pulled it out. He crumpled to the dirt.

The little girl pushed back on her hands and feet, away from me. Molly stepped forward and placed a hand on my arm, lowering the knife.

"Joseph, your hand." Her voice held firm and emotionless, easing my anger and bringing me back.

"He tried to . . ." I didn't finish. I stared at the cleaver on the ground.

"I know," Molly said.

She leaned down and tore a part of the liner to her dress. Taking the cloth, she bound my hand. It wasn't deep. I had held his wrist in check, but the edge of the wide blade still found a portion of my hand. When Molly finished, she gathered her skirt about her and kneeled, facing the girl.

"How many more adults are here?"

The little girl shook her head. She watched me as I inspected my hand and then leaned down to the dead man to wipe my blade clean on his apron. His eyes were open, staring toward heaven. I hoped he knew no peace.

"It's alright," Molly said, reassuring her. "We're looking for the girl in the picture. But first, how many adults are here?"

"Two more. Will you kill them?"

Molly shook her head. "We just want to find that girl."

"Kill them. Please," the girl said. "If you don't, they'll—"

A woman's voice called out from the other end of the dining hall. She rushed toward us.

"You there. What are you doing?" she demanded.

She stopped when she saw the dead cook. Blood flowed from his chest, turning the dirt under him into a thick red mud. I stepped past Molly and toward this woman, my knife still in my hand.

"James!" Her voice panicked. As I came closer, she yelled again. "James!"

A man ran from around the corner of the building, in the same direction the woman had emerged. He held a small wooden club in one hand, the kind that city policemen carried. A leather loop bound it to his wrist, and he twirled it as if used to carrying the weapon. He rushed toward me. As I walked past the woman, I pushed her down with my free hand. She fell backwards. I wanted time to deal with the man alone.

He saw the woman fall and stopped. The club swung in his hand again, and then his gaze fell upon my knife. He took a half-step back—he wouldn't fight.

"Drop it," I said.

With my jaw clenched, the noise came out like a hiss. I surprised even myself with the hatred it contained. He hesitated. As I took another step in his direction, he tugged at the leather tie and pulled the club from his wrist. He let it fall to the ground and held up both hands.

"Easy, easy. You've got the wrong idea, mister." His eyes darted in the direction where the guards had ridden off. No one came.

I stopped in front of him, ready to drive the blade through him if he lunged, or ran.

"Where are the keys?" I asked.

"Keys, for what?"

"The shackles."

His eyes darted to the little girl still sitting by Molly's feet. He knew what I meant. I reached out and grabbed him, pulling him by his shirt until he stumbled close. Only the knife stood between us.

"Joseph," Molly called out. Her voice held stern—once more directing me back from the edge.

"She has them," the man said, pointing at the woman.

I flung him toward the woman.

"Get them."

The man bent over and took a set of keys from the woman's hand. She had dug them out from some pocket on the front of her skirt. With a shaking hand, he held a key up for me. I took it and tossed it to Molly. The metal of the chains sang again as Molly worked the lock. I watched the man and the woman without turning.

"Oh my God," Molly said.

I turned to see. She pulled the shackle off the girl. It had cut deep into her legs, likely to the bone. The metal band had been too small for the girl's ankles.

The man started to push himself up, hoping to catch me distracted. He made it halfway to standing when I caught the movement in the corner of my eye. Rearing back, I kicked with all my might. The bottom of my boot fell across his face. He fell hard and didn't move. The woman screamed and dove toward him. I leaned in and dragged her by one arm toward Molly.

"Put them on her," I said.

I didn't have to tell Molly. She already worked the shackle around the woman's ankle. The woman began to struggle, until I towered over her. Then she stopped.

"They're too small," Molly said.

"No they're not."

I sheathed my knife and leaned down. Grasping with both hands I squeezed until the shackle closed upon itself. It wouldn't lock. I let it open, tore at the woman's tall bootlaces, and then ripped her shoes off. Then I tried again. Using all my strength, I managed to close the shackles. They latched. The woman screamed in pain.

I stood over the man. His chest rose and fell in regular intervals, making me wish I had kicked him harder. Molly gathered up the girl and spoke to her.

"Who else is here?"

The question mattered little. We had made so much noise that anyone else would have heard.

"At night it's just the three of them," the girl said. She stood, holding Molly's hand to steady herself. "But those men came the other day, the men with the guns. They've been living in the house."

"Be quiet, you little—" the woman said.

Molly bent down and her hand fell hard across the woman's face. The welt rose on her light complexion before Molly had the chance to rear her hand back again. The woman lifted a hand to shield herself. Tears ran down the woman's cheeks. Molly stood and reached to hold the girl.

The girl spoke to me. "Mister, that girl is not here."

"But you know her?" I asked again.

"She only stayed here for a time. Then they took her."

"Who took her?"

I started toward the girl, but as I did, she took a slight step back. Molly held her tight and shook her head, telling me to back off. I stopped.

"The Irish man. He took her. He had a lock of white hair over his forehead."

O'Malley. He had killed my mother and taken my daughter. I should have strangled him in the cell before I left.

"When?"

"A while back. They brought her here for a week, maybe a bit more. She wouldn't work, so they hit her. She broke one of the looms, and we didn't have dinner that night. Then the Irish man came for her."

"How long ago?" I pressed.

"Weeks," the girl said. "It had to be. The pastor comes every Sunday morning for a service, and he's been here three times since."

Three weeks. Well before they came to Essary Springs—before my mother made it to me.

"They took her with a rope around her neck and pulled her with the horses. They dragged her until her dress came off."

"No." I shook my head. "No." I couldn't hear it. I shook my head, trying to clear the image, but it clutched my mind.

I walked away, toward the dining hall. I pushed the main door open. A group of girls gathered by the window, cramped together to peer out at what had happened to their captors. They turned from me, frightened.

"Aurora! Aurora!" I stepped forward, pushing into the small swarm and dragged each one out as I checked them. I searched a dozen faces—some too small, some the wrong hair color—none of them were Aurora. They clung to one another as I stepped toward them, cowering like puppies who had too long been beaten by a cruel master. Some sobbed—others stood near emotionless as they watched.

"Joseph." Molly's voice fell so soft I could barely hear her. She came up behind me in the dining hall, placing a hand on my shoulder. "She's not here. I'll get the shackles off the girls."

I sat at one of the tables, my head buried on the hard wood surface. Molly worked with each girl, pulling the chains off as gently as she could. She had to coax each one out from the group in order to free them from the irons. They didn't trust us. It must have been unfathomable that escape was within their grasp. Most cried—their legs were so raw. A small pile of shackles built upon the table behind me. I stood and grabbed several sets, then walked out.

The woman who Molly shackled had crawled over to the man. Perhaps they were married. I didn't care. She cried out when she saw me coming, trying to protect him. He remained unconscious.

Taking the first set of shackles, I pulled at his boots to make sure I clamped them down on his ankles. I wanted his bare skin to feel the bite of the metal. The irons were too tight, but I positioned the shackle and then stomped down on it. His leg crushed as the metal clicked shut. The man bolted upright, screaming. I pushed him back down again. The woman reached out and pulled at my arm, trying to prevent me from getting the second shackle on. I backhanded her and she fell into the dirt. Positioning the second one came harder as the man writhed in pain. But I stomped until it, too, clicked shut. He screamed. The woman reached out to hold him. I left them like that and walked toward the factory.

Darkness hid the interior. With the sun setting, almost no light made it past the large barn-style doors. I pulled a lantern from the side of the door. Striking a match from a package that sat on a nearby shelf, I lifted the lamp to see inside.

The light fell to the back of the large room. There was no one else here. Stacks of fabric sat in folded piles after being removed from the large looms. Leather belts drove the machines, run from a single shaft at the back of the large space. I picked up a bolt of fabric. The fineness of the weave made the fabric smooth between my fingers. This would sell for a high price. Mr. Carson made only the best.

Molly walked behind me. It seemed a small comfort that I could always hear her approach. She reached for my shoulder.

"I'm sorry, Joseph."

I said nothing.

"We can look elsewhere."

"No," I said. "She's gone. O'Malley came for her here. You heard how the girl described him—an Irish man with a bolt of white in his hair."

"Maybe they have her somewhere still. We can find her."

I turned toward her.

"Not these men. I didn't tell you what they did to my mother. They cut her, like a surgeon would—to make her bleed slow. She barely made it to us. She traveled for days while they followed, like a hurt animal tracked to its den. They did it by design. These men have no soul, Molly. You heard how they came for Aurora, what they did. I don't even know where they buried her, if they bothered."

We were quiet for a moment. Molly tried pulling me close, but I resisted. I didn't want her comfort. I wanted the rage.

"I used to tell myself that death would be better for her," I said, "before she truly knew this world."

"What do you mean?" Molly held her voice low.

"When Norris took her, after I saved the Old Man, he told me I could get her back if I did what he asked."

"He wanted you to return and kill President Lincoln," Molly said.

I nodded. "I couldn't do it. I thought I would at first, but I couldn't. When I fled and headed west, I thought Norris would kill her. That would be better. He would do it quick, and she would never know all the pain in this life. Most of her time would have been happy, and she would be with her mother in whatever place lies beyond this world. But if I saved her, she would only have me. What life would that be?"

Molly said nothing. She gripped me closer. She could do nothing else and she knew it. Turning, she looked behind us. Some of the children had gathered at the factory door.

"What will we do with them?" Molly asked.

"Send them home," I said. "They are free, let them go."

"Some are so young, Joseph. They can't get there by themselves."

"We don't have time, Molly. I need to get to Washington."

"What for?" she asked.

"It's time to tell the truth—everything that happened. They took my daughter. They took my mother. I will make certain the Barons burn. I will make Pinkerton burn."

"After we take the children, Joseph. I won't leave them here. If we can't save Aurora, we can save the others."

I turned to Molly. She meant it. With her mind set like this, I could do nothing to change it.

She continued, "We'll take them with us to Washington. You'll need more proof."

Molly always saw the details. If we could get these girls to Washington, they could tell their own story. Surely that would end the Barons—to prosecute Mr. Carson for his role in the continuing the Draft. And he wouldn't go quiet. He'd tell all he knew if it meant less prison time.

"Get them to the barge," I said. "We'll float downriver. No one will expect us to travel by water. Have them pack what they have and gather food."

Molly pulled me toward her, placing her lips upon my cheek.

"Thank you. Let's do what good we can."

"Hurry," I said. "I don't think they'll be able to see the fire from the town, it's too far away. Though it's better we leave soon."

"What fire?" she asked.

I took the lantern and tossed it into the back of the factory. The glass shattered, and oil spilled out along the floor. The flames spread, lapping at the liquid.

"This fire."

CHAPTER EIGHT

31 MARCH 1874

I HAD WALKED in the halls of Congress before, always at the Old Man's side. It felt odd without him, as if I had no purpose in the place if I were not guarding the president. Molly kept me in her sight and with her followed the little girl from the factory—Anne. Her legs had only begun to heal, and she shuffled at times as if her feet were still joined by a length of chain.

We managed to deliver the other girls safe into hands that would find their parents. Even so, the experience left a hole with Molly. An old newspaper contact in Washington took the girls with the promise he would see them south. He wanted to publish their stories. And as a transplanted Southerner, he wished to see them returned safely home—the last remnants of the Draft. His ego would see it done, portraying himself as Moses to the last of the Draft children. The weakness he held for self-publicity meant I trusted him to this matter. And if I found any of them did not make their way home, I told him I would come for him. He believed me.

The congressional committee rooms were off one of the great halls. Our feet fell upon the marble, announcing our presence. I always hated that sensation. It went against everything my mother had taught me about walking soft and quiet. It felt like our shadows reached far ahead of us, letting everyone know that we approached.

Pinkerton sat on a bench away from the committee room. As we walked down the last stretch of marble flooring, he stood, rising to meet us. Two guards flanked him. It took all I had not to rush them all, to pull my knife and let it do all my talking.

"Joseph, do not do this. It is not too late to walk away—to go home."

Urgency filled him. He glanced over his shoulder to see who amongst the staffers took notice as they scurried between offices.

"You set us up! Did you think we wouldn't know?"

"I don't know what you're talking about."

He lied. I could see it in his face—in his voice.

"Don't do this," he pressed. "The republic cannot bear another scandal. Not as we're just ending the War and recovering."

"I'm done lying. And I'm done hiding," I answered. "The only way this ever ends is if someone exposes it all."

I tried to push by him, but he grabbed my arm and drew me close. The whiskey on his breath filled the space between us. Molly looked away. Her last words about him filled my mind.

"You would so jeopardize the president's image? Are you so selfish?" He held his voice low, though filled with anger.

"Which president?" I asked. "Mr. Lincoln is far from here. He's another man now. Or are you talking about President Johnson? Letting it all out will save Johnson, not doom him. This only hurts the Barons, and in that regard, I am eager to inflict any punishment I can. Especially if it brings you down with them."

"And you will tell them that President Lincoln killed Lamon? Is that your plan?"

He blocked the hall, his hand on my chest.

"I will tell them what I have to, that President Johnson had no part in the Old Man stepping down," I said. "That Johnson knew nothing about Lamon's death, and that he certainly didn't order it. But perhaps you are worried about your own role? You moved the body. You covered up Lamon's death and passed it off as me. And now you work with the Barons."

"I tried to protect you!" Then he looked over his shoulder as he softened his voice. "I only care about what's best for the nation."

I reached for Anne's hand to pull her forward. Stooping, I pushed her stocking down so Pinkerton could see.

"She's been in chains for years—taken by the Draft. No one returned her home after the Old Man stopped the practice. But you knew, and you did nothing. If you want what's best, then let it out so the nation can heal. I'll tell what the Barons did. I'll tell about the corruption."

"I can't rescue every child," he yelled.

"No, I suppose you can't. You couldn't even rescue mine. Or you wouldn't. That's why I'm here."

Molly took Anne's hand as she pulled us past Pinkerton. He didn't give way, but he didn't stop us. We walked down the corridor to the large mahogany doors of the committee room. When I pushed them open, Molly and the little girl entered first. I stood for a moment and looked down the hall. Pinkerton stared at me. His face hid his thoughts. We stayed like that for a moment, and then I stepped into the room.

*   *   *

My testimony lasted hours. A gasp rose from the audience when I said my name. The papers had told the story that I'd died, killed in a barn fire in Virginia after fleeing the capital. Pinkerton had worked to clear my name. But it had soon become obvious that the papers were complicit in the plan or had been duped. I suspected both, depending on whether the editors were personal friends of Pinkerton.

I told of saving the Old Man—how I threw Booth over the balcony to where he died on the stage of Ford's Theatre. After that night, I found my wife in a pool of her own blood. Colonel Norris' men had come for me—taking my daughter as consolation after my wife tried to fight them off. The faces of the men I killed when seeking Aurora flashed before me, though to some I could not even confess a name. Time and whiskey had worn the memories. I told them how Colonel Norris sent me to kill the Old Man as a condition to get Aurora back and how I couldn't do it. The Old Man had been a father to me. The panel of senators was shocked when I spoke of the Old Man's dreams. He predicted his own death to let the Great War end. I had saved him in the theater—denying his place in history alongside Jefferson. Somewhere, down deep, he counted it as betrayal.

The journalists murmured when I told of the Old Man's mistress and how he sent me to find her in the Deep South. The fact that the Old Man had a colored mistress and had fathered her child brought uproar. Pinkerton's words from the hall echoed in my thoughts. *Did I tear down the Old Man's reputation? To what end?*

Then I told them about Lamon and how he had sent his henchmen after me—Wyman Baxter and the Black Fox. Baxter executed the Old Man's mistress, before we killed him under the great oak tree. And, finally, I told of confronting the Old Man and my escape from Washington—how Lamon and his men cornered us at Ford's Theatre. As the story came out, I remembered each detail of that night—the deep red of the wallpaper, the hiss of the gaslights, the struggle in the state box, and how the Old Man pulled the trigger to save me—to save us all. Lamon fell, dead at our feet. I escaped, jumping from the state box to where I broke my leg on the stage below. Pinkerton found me in a tobacco barn in Virginia, where we passed Lamon's body for mine. It solved the mystery of Lamon's disappearance. President Johnson knew nothing of the affair.

When I had my say, they tried to dismiss me from the chamber. But I held my hand out for Anne, the little girl we brought. I stood her on the table. Pulling down her stockings I showed the room the legacy of the Draft—the legacy of the Barons. Some senators turned away, repulsed. Anger erupted in others, and it took little effort to tell which among them the Consortium had bought. The chairman brought his gavel down time and again to silence me. But the press had already rushed upon us. They shouted questions to the girl, about her family, about the factory—about the Draft.

The chairman stared through me as he gave up. The Consortium had bought him, his rich house paid for by the Barons. Hatred burned in his eyes.

"Sergeant," he yelled. "Get me Allan Pinkerton!"

Their plan to impeach the president would fail. It left Pinkerton as a consolation prize. I no longer cared. The newspapers would publish the story of the Barons now. I stood and reached for Molly. She gripped my hand, and we headed for the door with the little girl in tow. Reporters followed, shouting questions. The crowd spilled into the halls. We pushed through them to find open space. As we cleared the throngs of men chasing us, a few still a step behind, a man stepped off the wall.

"Mr. Foster," he said. "A message."

His accent caught me—the same as O'Malley. He held something. I stared at him as reporters caught us, all the while shouting questions. Some sensed the situation. The banter quieted. I took the velvet bag from his hand. I had no need to open it. I knew what it contained—a pair of thumbs—child's thumbs.

He reached out and grabbed me by the neck to whisper in my ear.

"It took her longer to die than your mother."

I dropped the bag and with both hands I grabbed his head. I pulled back and struck him, letting my forehead split his nose open. Blood splattered my face and all those who stood near. The reporters stepped back, letting the brawl have space to develop.

My fists found him again and again as I beat him. He crumpled. I reached down, pulling his jacket up and over his head to bind his arms to where he could not fight back. Holding tight to the cloth, my knee reared into him. As he fell, I peeled the jacket away and tossed it aside. Then strong arms grabbed me on either side and pulled me from him. A whistle sounded as the master at arms and several city police officers made their way to us. I scrambled to find the velvet bag I had dropped. The feet of fleeing reporters had kicked it across the floor.

The officers grabbed me, separating the fight. The man lay unconscious. They had to drag him to his feet. His face dripped blood and one of the men at his side pulled his head up by grabbing his hair. I hoped I killed him.

"Enough. Let him go."

Pinkerton pushed his way through the crowd, several of his men at his side. The officers holding the beaten Irishman began to ease him to the floor.

"Not him!" Pinkerton roared. He nodded toward me. "Him. Let him go."

The men at either side released their grip. I shifted my jacket and adjusted my shirt. Then I stood in front of Pinkerton. He had the velvet bag in his hand. I reached for it. The reporters formed an anxious circle around us. Murmurs of their conversation echoed off the marble floor.

"Is it . . . is it her?" he asked.

"You knew where she was. You could have gotten her any time you wanted."

"No," he said. "I couldn't. You don't understand it all, Joseph."

I took the bag from him.

"I understand this—what's in this bag, that's all I have to bury next to my mother. Someday we'll square up on this."

One of his men stepped forward—reminding me they were there.

"Not today," he said.

"You have other problems today." I looked around at the reporters. "But soon."

Seeing Molly in the crowd, I stepped away from him. She had the little girl with her. We pushed through the reporters and headed toward the daylight. Once outside, I took a deep breath of the early summer air. I had always loved Washington, but now I felt like I would vomit. I bent over and tried to regain my composure.

"Joseph. I found this," Molly said.

She looked over her shoulder. No one followed us. They had surrounded Pinkerton and were demanding answers. Molly held out a telegram.

"What is it?" I asked. I wiped my face. The tears were rage and pain mixed until they were indiscernible. I held tight to the velvet bag, sickened by it yet at once unable to let it go.

"When you threw the man's jacket aside. I found this in his pocket."

I unfolded the paper.

Give our gift to Foster.

It said nothing else—though it contained an address. I stared at the telegram, and then folded the piece of paper.

"We're going to New York. It's time to pay the Consortium a visit."

CHAPTER NINE

4 APRIL 1874

I COULD NOT compare New York to any place I had ever been. I had seen cities before—walked the dusty streets of Chattanooga and Memphis, felt the cobbled roads in Savannah, and lived in Washington. But this land felt like none of those places. I had no words to describe it. The age of this city meant it had collected many more ghosts.

A sea of humanity swarmed New York, overwhelming me. I recalled the time the Old Man and I went to Richmond during the war, right after the city fell. The city slaves surrounded him, reaching out to grab hold of his clothes. New York reminded me of that day, the closeness of it all, the tightness. The sounds of the wild never reached into the city, not even in Central Park. Without them I felt untethered, though I told myself all would soon change. In truth, none of my experiences prepared me. Streetcars rode iron rails, some inset into the cobblestones. Horses pulled them, making it nothing more than a glorified wagon on rails. They stopped for nothing.

The first day in the city we rented a room in a tenement house. The walls spanned barely farther than my fingertips fully extended. Molly hated the place. She had been happy in our small cabin, still smelling of pine pitch. But this space suffocated her. She couldn't step outside to breathe clean air. I had dragged her to the city when she had thought the whole affair finished. And giving up Anne to the reporter stirred her maternal feelings. Even though Anne headed home, she missed the little girl, and Daniel who waited for us in Essary Springs. In her mind we could bury Aurora with my mother, alongside the great oak tree after we returned home. But my heart beat differently. Drums of war filled my chest, and I would be satisfied only once we found the man responsible. And I had the address.

The families around us were immigrants, most from Europe. No one seemed to mind me, or the differences I held to Molly. The women who remained home in the day chased children around while finishing the chores. The men left early and returned late—dockworkers. They paid us little mind, though when they did, their attention focused upon Molly. She insisted on several new dresses. Each maintained a fashion too upscale for our tenement.

We took a couple days to settle, and once more I let patience dictate my approach. Pinkerton had trained me well. I knew better than to follow my emotions and kick down the door to the address on the telegram. We stalked the place several times every day, taking a long walk through Central Park so as not to appear obvious. It was a residential address with a brick façade and ornate arches. On the second floor the main windows set behind stone pillars cut into a small balcony. At the top of the building the façade extended skyward, like the fake storefronts out west.

Each time we walked by, I searched for lookouts—the same people sitting on benches or the same faces. Molly switched dresses before our evening walks so she might appear different than during the morning. The place always appeared the same, like no one used it.

"Could it be a ruse? Another means to conceal the Consortium?" Molly asked.

"I don't know. I would have thought we would see something from here. It's been days."

"Then we can go?" she asked.

I turned to her, yet said nothing. She knew the look on my face. I needed to end this, some tangible means to strike back. I had buried my mother, and my daughter had vanished. I had to know we would be safe when we returned home—some way to ensure the whole affair concluded. Killing the man behind this telegram seemed the only thing I knew to do. If he wasn't the head of the Consortium, pulling the strings on puppets like Carson and O'Malley, then he stood on the next rung of that ladder. When you went high enough, there was always one man. That would be how I ended it. I'd kill the monster on the top rung.

"What did the telegram from the Old Man say?" I asked. I tried to change the subject. She had picked up the note along our walk but had said nothing of it.

"They are settled and safe."

"And the judge? Did he make it yet? We'll be back to see O'Malley hung."

Whenever I closed my eyes, I saw an image of my mother on the doctor's table—her cheeks as pale as the sheet that covered her.

Molly said nothing. She had not answered my question.

"Did he say anything about the judge?" I asked again. We had walked past the address on the telegram and headed back toward the tenement house.

"No." Her answer came out clipped and she stared straight ahead. She held something back.

"Molly, what is it?"

I stopped walking and pulled her to face me. Her eyes watered. I had been so lost in the thought of what to do next, what step made our revenge, that I hadn't noticed the sadness upon her. She looked away.

"He's gone," she said.

"Who?"

"That man. The one in the jail."

"He escaped? The children?"

"They're safe. Mr. Lincoln moved them to town."

She looked away, refusing to meet my gaze.

"What is it, Molly?"

My other hand grabbed her upper arm and turned, trying to make her look at me. She refused.

"What is it?" I did not hide my anger. Over the last few days it had become easier to snap as the darkness gripped me tighter. "What happened?"

"Charley. He killed Charley."

I let go of her upper arm. Her hand covered her mouth as she turned from me. She wept silently into her gloved hand. I felt numb. The quilt of our life unraveled, the threads pulled out until the scraps of fabric fell at our feet.

"Molly, when? Did the Old Man say when it happened?"

"Maybe a week ago. I'm not . . . I don't know."

I looked back along the road. The address upon the telegram sat down a block on the opposite side. I wanted to take hold of Molly, but I couldn't. If I started to hold her, I would grab too tight, and then squeeze harder till neither of us could breathe. *This was not happening.* With every step, we were further away from the peace we wanted. Further from the patchwork of a family we had almost pulled together.

I let go of Molly's other hand and started toward the street. I waited for a streetcar before crossing the cobblestones. My patience had worn through. It felt invigorating. My heart beat in my chest, and I smelled the night air from back home. The rocking chair was beneath me as I sat upon the porch and listened to the wolf. If anyone lived in that building, I would kill them. I would feed the wolf of darkness and tear down the Consortium with my own hands.

I paused in front of the building. Other people strolled the street. The streetcars passed every few moments. Someone would notice if we went through the front door. Instead, I headed for a gate that led to the back alley. When I pressed against it, the metal door would not budge. But the faceplate to the lock looked more ornamental than functional. I waited for a break in the foot traffic, and then I used my knife to pry the metal plate off. Inside, the workings of the lock showed it to be a simple mechanism. With little effort, I pushed the bolt free with the tip of the knife. I opened the gate and stepped through. When I tried to pull it shut behind me, it caught. Molly stood on the sidewalk, holding the gate from closing. She pulled it open and stepped through with me.

We said nothing as we made our way along the alley. Windows from neighboring buildings faced our direction. I searched each one as we walked into a large courtyard. The back of the residence stood more plain than the front. Yet the façade maintained the fake pillars and arches over the windows. It also held a single door at the top of a steep set of stairs. I mounted the stone steps and rested my hand upon the door—locked.

Molly stepped up behind me. As she scanned the other buildings, I pressed my shoulder against the doorframe. It budged. I hit it again. This time the frame splintered, and the door swung open. I pushed it aside and stepped into a small hallway. Once there, I pulled my pistol and cocked the hammer.

We searched all three floors of the house, moving from room to room with haste. I pushed each door open and then cleared the closets. Molly even peered under the beds. We were alone. Rich wallpaper covered each room, and a polished banister flowed with the staircase up and down the floors. Clothes hung in the closet, expensive suits made from the finest fabric—the kind woven in a textile mill outside Saratoga Springs. We made a quick examination of each room until we came to the downstairs study. I opened each drawer of the desk and rifled through them. Molly searched the sitting room across the hall from the main entrance.

Despaired, I sat in the lush leather chair behind the desk. In the corner of the massive cherry desktop a crystal bottle sat upon an engraved silver tray, the bottle filled nearly to the top with a deep amber liquid—likely whiskey. I wanted to reach out for it, to take the top off for a smell. An ornate silver flask leaned against the bottle. I used to carry one just like it, to ward off the shakes or drive away the faces of the men I had taken off this earth.

"Joseph, do you know him?" Molly called from the sitting room.

I startled and stood from the chair. Outside, people walked along the sidewalks. Only the thin lace curtains hid our presence. I joined her in the sitting room, facing a portrait hanging above the fireplace. In the large oil painting a man in uniform sat upon an imposing leather chair. The uniform revealed a Union Army general, with a full beard, thick dark hair, and deep inset eyes. In his hand he held a pistol that rested over his other gloved hand.

"A general. Looks like the Quartermaster Corps."

I had rarely paid attention to the finer accoutrements that decorated officer uniforms. Generals of all types came to visit the Old Man during the War. But I had never seen this man.

"What do they do?" she asked.

"Quartermasters supply the troops—food, blankets, ammunition—that sort of thing. They make sure supplies reach the front, set contracts with the merchants and factories."

"The perfect man to run the Consortium?"

"I would say."

"You don't know him?" she asked again.

I shook my head. "From the letters on the desk in the other room his name is Dorsey—Terrell Dorsey." I held out a crumpled piece of paper. "I found this in the wastebasket."

Molly read the paper. I had done my best to smooth it flat. It had been a letter, started then discarded after the ink bottle left a ring at the top of the sheet—a round black mark that had been blotted in an attempt to salvage it obscured the name of the addressee.

"He's not in the city," Molly said.

"He has a summer house across the river. It doesn't say where." She handed the failed letter back to me.

"We can go then. There's no use in searching all of Connecticut," she said.

I let the paper fall to the carpet and walked back to the study. I pulled each book from the shelf, dropping them at my feet after skimming through the pages—searching for anything of use. I found nothing. I tugged out each desk drawer, looking underneath for anything tacked to the bottom or back. Nothing. Once more I slouched into the chair behind the desk. I didn't know what to do next. This house had been my last idea. Molly watched me from the other room as my head sank in my hands.

The darkness slipped further around me. It tugged on my heart, pulling the rage from deep within, howling like the wolf upon the field back home. I felt lost. My mother and daughter were ripped from me, even Charley. We should never have come. O'Malley should lie in a shallow hole, and I should have taken Molly and the children farther west. We could have lived deep into the far country where nothing would ever have reached us. Instead, I failed.

I stared at the crystal bottle at the corner of the desk. The liquor had always held off the darkness, pushed it away till I felt nothing. My hands shook as I reached for it, pulling off the stopper and letting it fall with a thud to the floor. From across the hall in the sitting room, Molly watched. Breathing deep through my nose, I pulled flavor from the open top—smooth. I held the glass, peering at perfection, a fine rye. Then I tipped it to my lips and took a long pull. At once my hands steadied, as if they anticipated what would soon reach them. The burn of the liquor as it went down warmed my body. My fingers felt alive. I took another long drink.

Molly walked into the room and put her hand on my shoulder.

"Joseph." She held her voice soft and low, as if scared to say my name. She reached for the bottle, but I pulled it back and took another drink.

"I can't do it, Molly. I can't . . ."

Standing next to me, she pulled me in, holding my head against her belly. She leaned over and placed her forehead against the top of my head. I pictured my mother, stretched upon the table under that sheet. I remembered the last time I had seen Aurora, a happy girl with a doll that wore a patchwork blue dress. Then I saw my wife as she lay dying. I had promised her I would find Aurora and shelter her from the evil of this world. My memory failed me—if I had meant those words or spoke them only as comfort to my dying wife before she met the Great Spirit. It mattered little. I had failed.

"I'm sorry, Joseph. I am."

Her hand ran through my hair, keeping me close.

"Can we go?" she asked.

I nodded.

We sat for another minute, and then she let me up. I stood, pulling the bottle along the top of the desk. I dragged a corner of the crystal to knock some of the papers to the floor. We stepped out of the study and into the hallway. I faced the portrait of the man, sitting in his uniform with his pistol across his hands. Stepping up, I threw the bottle at him, letting it arc through the air until it crashed into the portrait. The bottle ripped the canvas and punched through the painting. It broke against something metallic beyond. Molly looked at me, startled.

We approached the ripped painting. I took a footstool from in front of a chair and stood on it to grab the frame. Pulling on the corner, I knocked the torn canvas from the wall. Behind it, a safe sat in a space behind the portrait. It had a metal handle and a dial set into the door.

"Don't touch it, Joseph."

Molly tugged at me, urging me to step down. I switched places with her.

"You know how to open these?"

She shook her head. "But I used to see a senator who had one like this. He also hid it behind a painting. Bring me a light."

I rushed to the study where I found an oil lamp and matches. I struck one and lit the lamp before walking back. Molly held it to the place in the wall, letting the light fill the hole. I searched out the windows, pulling back the curtains to see if anyone had noticed us. Everything looked as before.

"What are you doing?" I asked.

"The man I knew with this kind of safe always reset it the same way. There are three numbers in the combination. If he had need to leave it closed for a long time, he dialed the first two numbers, especially in the summer. The tumbler would seize with humid weather. But you can always make it catch the last number."

"So how does that help? We still don't know the last number."

"He used to keep it open for a long time, too, and when he did, dust settled on the top of the dial. I only had to turn it to where the dust remained heaviest, then search a few numbers. With a bit of pressure on the handle and . . ."

Molly turned the dial slow—it clicked. The handle released and the door opened. She stood perched above me with a smile upon her face.

"What's in there?" I asked. She heard the urgency in my voice and spun back to the safe. At first she pulled out a stack of dollars and then a ledger. She handed me both.

I flipped through the cash and gave it back to her.

"We should keep it," she urged.

I nodded. I had no love for this man. He robbed others of their childhood so I thought nothing of relieving him from some of that profit. But I stood too engrossed in the ledger to care. Page after page of detailed transactions, deposits into the local banks and the like. He spread out his fortune, documented it to the penny—even the sources. It listed every factory, every bank in New York City, and some beyond.

"This has everything," I said.

"Everything for what?" Molly asked.

"Where the Consortium places all their money—every last penny. It all comes to this railroad—The West Shore Railroad. The textile companies, the steel companies, even the arms makers— they all pay this one railroad."

Molly stepped down from the footstool. Disapproval hijacked the expression upon her face.

"Joseph, we can't. They'll never leave us alone."

"You think they will if we just leave? After that testimony in front of Congress? After the newspaper articles are written? After the reporters track Mr. Carson and all his network?"

She shook her head. The realization of our position sank in. We needed to kill the monster or it would always nip at our heels.

"We lure General Dorsey from his hole," I said.

"And then what?" Molly asked.

"I kill him."

"Then we go home?" she asked.

An edge entered her voice. She wanted nothing more than to leave. And I wanted that, too. But I couldn't—not until we had some manner of protection. I needed some means to know we no longer had to watch over our shoulders all our lives.

"I promise."

I took the oil lamp from her, lifted the glass lid, and blew out the flame.

"You won't burn this house down?" she asked.

The smell of the burning factory rose from my memory. It would feel good to watch Dorsey's house engulfed by the lapping orange tongues. His home would turn into nothing more than smoldering ash and smoke. But I shook my head.

"Other houses are too close. I mean to kill the Consortium, and nothing else. And besides, we want General Dorsey to know we were here."

I walked to his desk while I fished through my pocket for the telegram that had his address upon it.

"You think he'll come back because you took his ledger?" Molly asked.

"No. We're going to take something *much* more valuable."

Molly searched my face, puzzled. I spread the telegram upon his desk. Picking up a letter opener, I stabbed it through the telegram, pinning the paper to the desk. Then I picked up the small flask that sat on the corner of the desk.

"We're going to take all his money."

CHAPTER TEN

7 APRIL 1874

OUR FIRST HEIST went easier than expected. So easy I thought for certain the cashier had raised the alarm in some manner. But the Consortium's henchmen did not swarm us. We escaped unscathed, amazed at the ease of the act. I felt a surge of confidence. Before we robbed the place, I drained the flask from General Dorsey's desk. It contained the same smooth rye he had in the crystal bottle. My hands felt steady, the first time in months. The warm feeling burned away the fear, easing the pounding in my chest. Molly noticed, though she said nothing.

We picked the first bank from the list on the ledger—the Murray Hill Bank on 3rd Avenue. In typical fashion, we stalked the location a day or so ahead. They had one guard, a fat old man who held nothing for speed against me. Molly stayed outside, concealing her pistol in the event I needed the help. I feared someone coming from behind, someone I had not noticed who might watch the bank. They would little suspect Molly, standing in a fine dress with a sun umbrella and a hat. She looked the part of the New York elite, not a criminal about to fleece the rich of their wealth.

The entire bank was comprised of a small room—a three-man operation. We waited until one left the office, hoping to keep the chances of an altercation low. Once at the door, it looked like no other bank I had ever seen. The banks out West had higher regard for security, with bars on the teller windows and cashiers who were well armed. This seemed more like a merchant's office. They seemed to have nothing to fight off a robbery—as if they were never robbed.

"They'll kill you," the cashier said as he lifted the countertop gate to let me back. Slowly he paced away from me. He wore a tight-fitting vest over a striped shirt and a short dark visor perched across his balding head. His guard lay slumped in the corner. I had locked the door and flipped the sign to say the bank had closed.

"Who will?" I held my pistol level, the hammer already cocked. My gaze fell to his hands, lest he try to thwart my effort.

"You don't know?" His expression turned. It seemed like I had robbed a church and should expect retribution from the Great Spirit. "No one does this. Not since . . ."

"Not since when?"

"Not since I can remember. You will regret it. They string up the whores who rob their gentlemen suitors. They punish the children who steal from the fruit stands. No one does *this*."

"Who?" I pressed.

"The Irish—they enforce everything. Who else?"

I stepped forward, pushing the man toward the back room.

"Open the safe."

"Don't do this," he pleaded. "They'll beat me, too. They'll say I helped."

"No, they won't. I won't take it all. You have twenty thousand in holdings from the West Shore Railroad. That's all I need. When they come to ask, you tell them whose money I took."

He shook his head, yet stepped backward into the room. The safe filled most of the back wall and had a huge dial and handle near the center of the steel door. I wondered if they kept the first numbers dialed into the tumbler.

"This defies reason, sir. You know who owns that railroad, don't you?"

"I do. He took something from me. I intend to extract what I may in return."

The cashier turned to the safe.

"I hope you have no wife or children. For they will never have enough of you to bury, so small they will cut the pieces."

I pushed the barrel under his jaw, forcing him to stand taller, though not quite on his toes.

"I had a daughter. And now I have not enough of her to bury. I had a mother. I had a friend who wore an Eagle's feather in his hat. They're all gone. We'll call this a down payment. Open the safe."

I lowered the weapon and pushed him into the large metal box. The safe door was massive, taller than a man and wider than my arm span. He worked the dial, only hurrying when I pressed my barrel against his neck.

"Please, I beg you. Take the money from another bank first. Don't make me the first."

I de-cocked the pistol and placed it back inside my waistband. Then I produced the knife. Men were always more afraid of the blade than the gun. It seemed a universal truth, as if the years spent in the dark ages had honed a fear of sharp steel. A pistol killed too fast.

"Open it!"

With the blade against his neck, he opened the safe. It took all his effort to tug at the door. I looked at the stacks of money, neatly counted and bound into packages. It occurred to me I had no idea how much paper I would carry forth from that building.

"Take it out," I said.

He pulled stacks of the money onto a side table, grabbing as much as he could in each hand and then returning for more. When certain he had it all, he counted—twenty bundles, each containing a thousand dollars. The stacks of printed-paper were more than I could carry.

"I didn't know it would be so big," I muttered. I had never seen so much money before. When I had been in the Union Army, they paid us in cash from large trunks. But even then they kept the contents out of view and well guarded.

Several canvas bags hung on the wall behind me. I grabbed one and poured the cash into the bag with the hand that held the knife. Then I thought better of it and pulled one bundle out. I held it out to him. His eyes wandered to it, not understanding.

"Do you have a family?" I asked.

"A wife and son."

"When they find me, either they die, or I will," I said, still holding out the bundle of cash. "Either way, they'll never know you have it."

He shook his head, but his eyes stayed trained on my hand.

"I could never face Mr. O'Malley without him knowing."

"O'Malley?"

"He's the only one that brings the West Shore Railroad deposits. He makes all their deposits around town. He leads the *Black Murphys*."

"Does he have a patch of white hair near his forehead?" I asked as I pointed with the tip of my knife blade.

"He does."

"When did you last see him?" I asked.

"Several weeks ago."

I studied his face—he didn't lie.

"Turn around," I said.

He turned, perhaps fearful I would kill him from behind. I leaned close.

"Remember this. Tell them Joseph Foster wants to talk. Until they come out of their hole, I will bleed them dry. And tell O'Malley, when next you see him, that there are no more prison cells where I send him."

With the heavy handle of the Old Man's knife, I struck the man at the back of the head. It was a quick glancing blow. He would wake with a tremendous headache, though he would live. Taking the packet of cash, the one I had held out for him, I leaned down and placed it inside his vest. They would never know he had it.

CHAPTER ELEVEN

22 APRIL 1874

MOLLY AND I moved to a nicer place. Not as upscale as she would have preferred, but I felt more secure with the switch in housing. Amongst the poor dockworkers, her appearance had been a liability—a white woman too well dressed. No matter how I cajoled, I could not get her to put on more country dresses. I still feared I might be easy to remember. In truth, the city contained such a mixing of peoples that for the first time I fit in. But Molly attracted attention. We found a more neutral abode, amongst the merchants along Canal Street.

That next week we struck two more banks. Word of our first robbery had not reached these institutions, at least not that we could tell. Both cashiers pleaded in the same manner, asking us not to rob them first. They knew not of the other hold-ups. Though they would have no luck concealing it once the Black Murphys came calling on the Consortium's money.

Pinkerton's former training guided our actions. I loved having Molly with me. Before, I had always acted alone—guarding the president and staying silent in the background. But now we worked together, watching each building for a day or two before making our move. When the time came, Molly stayed out front as both lookout and extra hands. These were small banks with rather meager holdings according to the ledger. Each housed a safe at the back and only one man to work security. Armed robbery did not fit among their worries. The Black Murphys guarded against it. From one bank we removed fifteen thousand dollars, and at the other just over thirty thousand. I came prepared, bringing a leather satchel capable of carrying the amount of money without notice. The canvas bag from the first bank had been too conspicuous, even for the market district.

After each robbery we walked the city. We scouted other locations while circling back to the address on Broadway—General Dorsey's house. The windows remained dark. It would take time for word to reach him, though I felt certain it would not be long. Still, the darkness meant disappointment. No oil lamp burned, no lights issued forth from the top floor past the fake stone pillars or the carved arches. I tried not to stare long—to neither reveal my interest in the place nor make my heart heavier. I reached inside my jacket and produced the flask, taking a long pull. Guilt filled me with every drop of the whiskey, but my hands shook even worse without it now, so long I had been dry. I couldn't drench a desert floor and then expect it to go back to desert without a fight. For now, I needed this demon—that's what I told myself each time I unscrewed the lid. *Just once more.*

"We must do something more dramatic," I said.

"Like what?" Weariness filled Molly's voice. She had grown tired of this idea to draw them forth. "I think we may have done enough."

I looked to her as we walked. She did not shift her gaze from the sidewalk.

"What would you have us do?" I asked.

"You know what I want, Joseph. I fail to see how any of this makes us safer."

"Because they will come for us if we don't find them first."

"Men always say that," she muttered. Her voice barely carried above the streetcars as the horses pulled along the steel rails. The smell of manure fell heavy around us. I realized that with the start of spring a thick air had moved in, suppressing the usual evening breeze.

"Do you want to sit in our cabin and wait then? Is that it? Until one night, years from now, they come again?"

"After your testimony, they have enough to worry about."

"If I were them, I would come. My testimony freed President Johnson from impeachment, but it might make our situation worse. They'll come for us when they can, unless we handle it first. You can't ask me to walk away. I'm doing this for us."

She stopped, facing me for the first time that evening.

"For us? We have a young child waiting. Or did you forget about Daniel? And Mr. Lincoln will not be able to raise that girl of his all the way—he will be too old someday. So there are two people who need us. And yet, we're across the country in this city because you can't take your mind from revenge."

She refused to look at me. Instead, she crossed her arms over her chest and watched the street traffic. A few people passed on the sidewalk, stepping around us. The gentlemen used walking staffs that clicked against the stones. I moved closer to Molly and lowered my voice.

"We should talk about this elsewhere." I looked around as I reached to take her arm. She wouldn't budge. "Molly, please."

"We would have been married already. Or have you forgotten?" she said. "Last month."

"Is that what this is?" I asked. She looked away. "You can't possibly believe I wanted this to happen—that I wanted my mother to show up dying at our doorstep just to delay our wedding? I will marry you here. Pick a church, any church."

I threw my hands to the air, motioning around. She glanced at me as I spoke, then looked away again.

"All we do is make it worse," she said. "We should let a sleeping bear lie. Stealing from them we ensure they chase us to recover their money."

"You've seen the ledger. General Dorsey controls it all. He's the man at the top. If we remove him, the system will crumble. That's how these things work."

"And then another will replace him, and they will still want their money."

"I don't think so," I said. "These men may wear fancy suits, control factories and politicians, but they're like any other street gang. They rule by fear, with men like O'Malley paid to scare all into submission. When the leader topples, the next in line will fill his shoes. But they'll spend all their effort consolidating power. We'll be gone by then, no longer a threat and no longer worth the time to pursue."

I thought about the velvet bag the man had given me after I testified, and the white sheet in Doc Herman's office.

"And I need this," I said.

I hadn't opened the bag. I didn't need to. It sat in the top dresser drawer of our small room. I couldn't bear to part with it until we made it home, to bury what I had left of Aurora next to her grandmother.

I turned Molly's face until she looked into my eyes. "They killed my mother and my daughter. They need to pay."

"A daughter you hadn't seen in eight years. *You* left her with Colonel Norris," Molly snapped. She meant it to hurt.

My teeth clenched. I had never wanted to strike Molly before, but anger surged through me. I dropped my hand from her face and let go of her arm. I leaned close, speaking as low as my voice would hold. "You *know* why I left her."

We stood like that a moment. Then I turned and walked on. I only made it a few steps before she joined me, a half-step behind. We walked a block in silence, then another. Streetcars passed in both directions. The city never slept, never ceased in the endless cycle of commerce. Even at this hour the bustle remained incredible.

Molly reached for my arm. "I'm sorry, Joseph. That was cruel. I didn't mean it in that manner."

I waited a moment, then reached over and covered the hand that had wrapped around my arm. I said nothing.

"Would it matter," she started, "would it matter if we had a child? And I don't mean Daniel. I mean our own, one that waited for us. Would you leave then?"

I stopped walking and faced her again.

"I don't know," I said. "Maybe. But we don't. I meant what I said. Pick any church, and we can be wed tomorrow."

She shook her head. "We'll wait until we get back. It won't be long, I'm sure you are right."

I took hold of her face and drew her close. Then I kissed her.

"I need this, Molly, I truly do. I don't want to spend my life waiting for them. And I need to make it mean something, to make someone pay."

She nodded. "You said we needed something more dramatic. What did you mean?"

"Merchant's Bank on Wall Street. It has the most Consortium money—a half-million."

"Joseph, you can't be serious. We checked that place. You saw how many guards were there. It has a vault, not one of these small banks with a safe in a back room. There are only two of us."

"I've been thinking about that. Word will get out this week. The money was good, but not enough to hurt the Consortium.

They'll increase the guards everywhere, maybe even put the Black Murphys to work. They'll start with the small banks. That's all we've gone after. Once they guard them all, we'll never get another chance. We have to make it big to draw General Dorsey out, and they'll never expect us to hit the largest bank they use."

We walked in silence for a time. My mind whirled, more convinced than ever of the possibility. It would awaken even the largest sleeping monster. I knew Molly thought of a means to dissuade me, even make me drop the whole idea of attacking the Consortium. It wouldn't work.

"Even if we forced our way into the vault, we couldn't carry it all," she said.

I pulled the flask from my pocket and unscrewed the lid—*just one more*.

"Don't worry." I grabbed her hand. "We won't need to carry it."

CHAPTER TWELVE

24 April 1874

MOLLY ENTERED THE bank first this time. No one had seen her at our other heists, so she remained in the clear. If they posted extra guards, then they would be searching for me. I imagined the island of Manhattan contained only one half-Indian—picking me from a crowd would be no matter. Instead, I pulled my hat low to cover my brow and waited a minute before entering behind her.

Merchant's Bank stood as a testament to the city's economy—enormous. Even the sound of my boots upon the polished marble floor disappeared into the vastness. I felt small, immediately regretting this decision. I scanned the room, then walked to a central island where patrons filled out slips of paper to hand to the clerk. Molly stood in line. She had worn a practical dress, but one that nonetheless fit a distinguished lady of the city. One hand gripped a leather satchel filled with cash—in the other hand she held a sun umbrella. From this distance her revolver remained hidden.

Patrons filled the lobby. By the measure of business in this bank alone, New York boomed. Most of the customers were men. They dressed in suits with Bowler hats in the style that O'Malley wore. They didn't bother to remove them once inside, not like out west. I thanked the Great Spirit. I hid under mine, though the wide brim might mark me as a foreigner to this land. I pretended to write upon a deposit slip as I waited.

Two men circled the lobby, casually looking to those who stood in line. They wore matching gray suits with black leather shoes that fell in regular intervals. They met in the middle of the lobby, spoke a few quiet words, and then proceeded past one another. Their jackets hung open and loose. I imagined both concealed revolvers. One looked in my direction as he walked by, but paid me no extra attention. They clearly guarded the bank. I let my hand fall from the handle of my knife. So far we went undetected.

I made my way toward Molly. A tall mahogany counter separated those waiting to deposit their money from the tellers. She stood in the line nearest a small door in the counter. It ushered patrons toward the offices in the back, and most importantly, to the vault. Standing in the right place I could see past the vault door. It stood perched open. A metal cage was the only thing blocking the cash held within from flowing into the lobby. Unlike the other banks, this place contained a large operation. A dozen tellers stood behind the polished wood, where rows of bars extended to the ceiling. The only means to the vault appeared to be through the small door, and then past the metal cage. From there, no other manner of escape existed. My hands shook with the adrenaline.

"I wish to see the head cashier." Molly's tone remained stern, unwavering in its demand.

"Ma'am, I am more than capable of helping you," the teller replied. He was accustomed to handling unruly customers.

"I have a rather large deposit, and before I decide to leave it with you, I require the head cashier. I have heard rumors from other banks, and I want to ensure the security of my funds at your institution. The head cashier, please."

The man looked at her. He wore no jacket. Probably by design, so the head cashier could ensure none of his employees were tempted to keep the transactions. He stared at Molly, uncertain of what to do.

"Ma'am, like I said before. I am trained to handle all your needs, if you—"

Molly cut him off, holding up one finger to command his silence. With her other hand she opened the leather satchel and let him look inside. She had stuffed it with bundles of cash from the other banks—nearly thirty thousand dollars. It amounted to an unheard-of deposit for a single woman. He stared into the satchel and seemed to understand. Nodding, he raised his hand and made eye contact with another man at the end of the line of cashiers. That man struggled down from a tall chair and adjusted his suit jacket as he walked toward Molly.

"Is there something we can help you with?"

He crowded into the cashier window and dismissed the younger man who had attempted to deal with Molly. He didn't notice me loitering within earshot as he brushed the few strands of hair on top of his bald scalp. The man had no fat upon his body, and it seemed he could slip out of the suit without undoing a button.

"I have a deposit, but one of significant size. I wish to see for myself that it will be secure."

"I'm afraid, ma'am, that we do not allow guests back past the cashiers for any reason."

"Nonsense," Molly countered. "As I stood in your ridiculous line, I witnessed several customers invited back. My business is sizeable." She held the satchel open for him to see. "This would represent a good-faith deposit only."

"I see," he said, peering into the leather case. "Those are established customers. Am I to understand you are new to us?"

"I am. I have taken my holdings from other institutions and wish to place them here. There have been . . . complications elsewhere." Her pause before saying the word *complications* gave it just the right emphasis. She switched roles so easily. Any other life would have left her acting upon the stage, and famous for it.

He looked to her and then conceded, motioning her toward the small door.

"Very well, ma'am. I will show you to my office, and we can discuss further. This way, if you will."

Molly waited outside the small door where I joined her. As he undid the latch, the head cashier looked up. His eyes locked with mine and then darted to the two men in the gray suits, walking the marble floors behind us. He knew of the other banks—the panic grasping his face gave him away. From inside my jacket I produced a photograph. I passed it through the metal bars at the top of the door. He stared at it.

"How did you get this?" He stuttered the words as he reached for the door to steady himself.

It had been a simple matter to figure out who held the position of head cashier. The day prior I paid a visit to this man's house while he watched the bank. It had taken only a moment to talk my way past the housemaid, with the excuse of leaving a package for the master of the house. His desk contained one portrait—of a young boy. I gave the silver frame to a poor boy upon the street. He could sell it for the price of the silver alone, enough to feed his family for a spell.

"No harm becomes your boy, if you provide us a moment of your time with no attention drawn to us."

We did not have his child, but he had no way of knowing and no means to discover our deception before we left. I looked behind me. The men in the gray suits took no notice of the happenings at the door. They were hired help, bored in their current employ, and forever walking the marble hall.

"Please, no," the man muttered.

I feared he might pass out, so I reached through the bars and pulled on his jacket to focus his attention.

"I have no interest in your son," I told him. "Take us to your office where we will discuss our terms further."

He nodded as sweat beaded upon his brow. With shaking hands, he pulled back on the deadbolt and turned the door handle. Opening it wide, he let both Molly and me pass behind the counter.

"He is a good boy, and all I have," he pleaded with me.

Molly placed a hand upon his arm. As usual, her touch contained the perfect amount of leverage. In this case, she was most delicate. "Nothing will come of all this if you lead us to your office."

The man fixated upon her, nodding as she interlaced her arm with his. She kept her voice low, forcing him to focus as she spoke.

"Is it this way?" she asked, nodding toward the back of the bank—several doors with frosted glass led to back rooms.

Without saying a word, he nodded. Molly escorted him toward the office doors. She made it seem effortless. Anyone who stood even a few paces away saw nothing unnatural. I followed a step behind.

Once inside the office, we closed the door behind us. The man struggled behind his desk, leaning on the large wooden surface. I pulled my knife, fearing he meant to reach for a weapon in the desk drawer.

"Dear God, not that. Please, I beg of you!"

"We will not harm you or your son," I said. "We come for a different purpose. If you give us no trouble, I give my word you will walk out of here tonight with nothing more than a story to tell your boy."

His eyes fell to the knife. "You were the one who stole from the other banks."

"Yes."

"They will kill you."

"The men you have out front?"

He shook his head. "No, the Irish."

"The Black Murphys?"

"Yes."

"Good," I said. "I need a word with them."

I looked to the door and then sheathed the blade. With the knife away, he appeared to calm. He spoke to Molly, perhaps as a means to ease his stress.

"What do you need?" he asked.

"You have holdings for the West Shore Railroad," Molly said. "We need them."

"Why do you do this? You know who these men are, don't you?"

I reached inside my jacket and placed the portrait of his son upon his desk. Then I pulled out the velvet bag—the one the man gave me after my testimony to Congress.

"What is it?"

He glanced at the bag and then to me.

"See for yourself." I held the bag out for him.

"Joseph—" Molly started to say something, but she stopped when I glared at her.

"He can take it," I answered. "He needs to know who he works for."

The man's hands shook as I placed the bag into his open palm. Carefully he tugged the bag open, holding it by just two fingers.

When he peered inside, he dropped it, holding both hands up and cringing. His eyes shut as he covered his mouth.

"Animal! Why would you keep those?"

My stomach turned. I had just violated what I had left of Aurora. Seeing the blue velvet again filled my mouth with a vile taste—bitter with anger. I took the flask from my jacket and unscrewed the lid. The whiskey felt warm as it burned on the way down.

"Joseph, not now." Molly reached to push my arm down. I pulled it away from her. I needed it—to feel numb. Tipping the flask back, I took a long pull.

The head cashier stared at me. For the moment he no longer feared me, he despised me.

"That's all I have left of my child. Those men you work for, they took her. And when I didn't do as they wanted, they gave her back to me like this."

I took the bag from the desk and closed the drawstring. The whiskey hit me. I was not as stable under its influence now, though the shake in my hands had calmed. I had been so long without it that the liquor seeped into all those little spaces that had dried out.

"You'll do this to my son?"

I looked to the desk, where the little boy in the picture stood stiff and tall.

"We don't have your boy. We just need your help."

The man's face eased. He looked at his son's image.

"You don't have him?" Hope clung to his voice.

"No. I would not harm a child. Especially like that."

Our eyes met. Slowly, he extended his outstretched hand across the desk. I placed the flask into it. He smelled the opening and tipped the container back, emptying it of its contents. A coughing fit took over as he pulled in the last drops. He thumped his chest to ease the cough.

"You can't take all the money. It's too much."

"Show me," I said.

He handed me the flask and motioned to the door. "This way."

Leaving his office, the noise of the bank flooded around us as if we had waded into a torrential spring creek. My hands were numb—my body slower. The liquor claimed its toll. We walked across the marble floor, behind the cashiers busy with their transactions. The head cashier raised his hand to someone—a signal. I reached for my knife, expecting our foray to end with the men in gray suits bursting through the small wood door. Nothing happened. He must have done this all the time, or it signified that all was well. When we reached the large metal door, he ushered us inside the vault where the cage door hung open.

Inside, the confined space smelled of cash—stacks and stacks of printed paper, worn with the sweat and the blood of those who had earned it. Several gas lamps cast the only light, pushing the shadows into the corners of the small room. Metal lock boxes lined both walls of the vault from floor to ceiling. The head cashier produced a key from a chain around his neck. He placed it into the lock of the safe against the back wall. Then he slowly spun the dial. The safe opened with a hollow clunk, a sound only the wealthy knew.

Once open, he stepped aside. Stacks of bound paper covered four shelves. There were even bearer bonds on top of a stack of corporate documents. I pulled these out and handed them to Molly. The rest comprised pure cash, bound, and stacked in neat piles.

"This is it?" I asked.

"This is their safe. They come once a week."

The holdings were enormous. I had never seen so much money in one place.

"I told you, there's no way to carry it out," the cashier said. "It would be obvious. You would never make it past the door."

I pulled the first bound stack out of the safe—a stack of hundred-dollar notes. All were crisp and new—blood money, the labor of children. I looked back out the vault door. Only a sliver of the lobby peered through. It blocked our activity in the vault. But it left me uneasy, as we could be set upon without knowing that anyone waited right outside.

"Joseph, we should hurry," Molly pressed.

"How many guards?" I asked.

"Just the two out front. Normally we have more."

"Where are they?"

"Sent to other banks. They didn't expect you here."

I searched his face. He didn't look away—he wasn't lying.

Reaching into the safe, I used my arm to sweep each shelf of bills onto the floor. I picked up a few and handed them to Molly.

"Unwrap the bindings and fill the rest of the satchel. I want all the bills loose."

I picked up several myself, tearing the paper that bound the stacks together. Then I shoved the notes into my pockets until they could hold no more.

The cashier watched us from a few paces back.

"Is the ceiling steel?" I asked. "Is there any other way out of here?"

The cashier shook his head. "It's an inch thick, riveted together all the way around—same with the walls. You would need dynamite to get through without the combination. That's why the Irish leave so much money here."

"Perfect."

Using my foot, I pushed the rest into a pile in the middle of the room.

"Joseph, we should leave," Molly pleaded. The worry in her voice pressed in upon me. She watched outside as her hands fidgeted with the satchel.

I stared at the pile. This would bring General Dorsey out of hiding. Taking this much from him would stir any monster from their slumber. And there was no going back. From inside my jacket, I took another container—a glass vial, the same size as the flask. It was stoppered with a cork. Pulling it out with my teeth, I dumped the clear liquid upon the bills. The smell of kerosene wafted through the vault. I stepped to the lamp that burned along one wall. Lifting the glass, I stuck a few hundred-dollar notes into the flame.

"You'll burn the bank down." The cashier appeared desperate. His collusion would be hard to hide at this point.

"No," I said. "We'll close the door after us. The flame will burn out when the paper is gone, or once it consumes the air from the room."

I dropped the bills. Instantly, the fire flashed in front of us. I had to back up from the sudden wall of flame that scorched the hair on my hands. Molly turned as the light in the vault burned bright and cast dancing shadows upon the wall.

"Go," I said, grabbing the cashier's arm.

We stepped into the bank, and the cashier and I pushed the vault door. When it shut, the clang of metal against metal rang louder than I anticipated. A few cashiers turned to stare at us.

"Walk us to the door," I said. I grabbed the cashier by the arm, starting him toward the counter where the others worked. A few watched now, uncertain about what unfolded behind them.

As we reached the door, I paused and let go of the man. Then I held out my hand.

"Just shake it, and then walk to your office," I said. I held my voice low so no one might hear. "We'll be gone in a moment or two."

He grasped my hand.

"I am sorry for your child," he said.

"So am I."

Molly and I pushed through the counter door and into the lobby. Some of the cashiers stared. Once the door closed, I couldn't tell where the head cashier went—if he followed our directions.

As we crossed the great sea of marble, the smell of fire caught up with us. I wasn't sure if it had been on my clothes as we left. I turned to look. Black smoke issued forth from the edges of the vault. It started as a small flow, curling and thick, congealing at the ceiling. There must have been cracks in the construction of the room, between the riveted steel plates. I grabbed Molly's hand to hurry her, but our pace did not go unnoticed. One of the men in the gray suits watched. He looked back to the vault, and then to us.

"STOP!"

The chatter of business and idle conversation ceased as if a wave crashed over the lobby. Patrons turned to look where the man yelled. He thrust back his jacket and pulled out a revolver. As he cocked the hammer, I reached into my pockets and threw fistfuls of the loose bills into the air. The nearby customers stepped back, trying not to get hit by the falling paper. Then they realized what rained amongst them.

All around us the crowd surged forward, scrambling to pluck the falling money from the air or off the ground. The man in the suit lost his chance. He pointed his pistol to the sky as he tried to push through the people. Molly grabbed my arm and urged me toward the main doors.

Before we reached the exit, the other guard came upon us. He encountered Molly first. She dodged his grasp as my fist caught him on the chin. He reeled, then fell upon the ground. I reached into his jacket and pulled out his pistol. Molly threw more bills behind me, making the scene all the more chaotic.

Behind us, the remaining guard fired into the ceiling. The report of the shot ripped through the jubilant patrons as they scrambled along the ground in search of the money Molly threw. The sound ricocheted off the marble. People scattered, fleeing the man with the gun. He searched the crowd, and as he did, I leveled the pistol in my hand.

I fired. My first shot went wide, and my next deliberately hit the pillar next to him. I never practiced with a pistol, and the tall pillar was easier to hit as a distraction. It sprayed marble chips into his eyes. As he covered his face, I steadied my aim and squeezed. I didn't see where I hit, but he fell backwards. People around us panicked, running from the sound of the shots. My ears rang and Molly pulled my free hand toward the door.

Once outside, the crowd on the street stared at the building. White stone stairs led to the door, with a crowd milling about on the steps. Molly and I dashed down the stairs. She continued to throw bills into the air. Those outside now rushed forward, collecting what they could. They met us in a wave up the marble steps. Molly threw the satchel into the air. It tumbled while traversing a great arc. Money fell upon us and scattered in the breeze.

We slipped away, making our escape to the edge of the crowd. As we brushed past the people, the pistol in my hand came loose by the rushing mass of humanity that crashed around us in an attempt to recover fortunes that littered the stone steps. As we cleared the edge of the crowd, we ran into a boy standing at the edge. He held a whistle to his mouth and blew with all his might.

But my attention drew to his hair—a white forelock fell across his forehead. As he faced me, his eyes widened. He blew harder upon the whistle. I saw a black cloverleaf pinned to his lapel.

I grabbed the whistle from his mouth, flinging it to the ground. I had no idea who he was trying to summon. He pulled back his jacket and stabbed forward with a knife. It was a small blade—though large enough it would kill if it hit the heart. It caught my hand and cut deep—a momentary sharp pain, and then nothing as it severed nerves deep in the tissue. He pulled the blade back and lunged forward. I caught his arm this time. Without thinking, I had already pulled my knife from its sheath. As he flung himself with all his weight, I pushed his arm to one side and pulled him close. He collapsed upon my blade. It plunged deep into his chest.

For a moment we stood like that. The world around me faded. I was in Ford's Theatre once again. I held Booth in my arms, my knife buried deep. His eyes faded as he saw the world beyond this—the one with the Great Spirit. They glassed over, staring at a place I could not see.

"Joseph!"

Molly pulled me back to the bank with the sea of humanity all around us. She pushed the boy from me. He fell backwards, sliding down several stairs. His eyes stared distantly at the sky, unmoving. Blood spurt from his mouth, forming a steady flow that dripped down the stairs. The white forelock danced in the breeze.

"Joseph, what have you done?"

We stared at the boy for only a moment, then Molly grabbed me by the jacket and pulled me through the crowd. They collapsed around us. Hands pushed past, fighting for the money that floated in the sky or had already fallen to the ground.

CHAPTER THIRTEEN

"HE WAS JUST a boy. It was only a whistle." Molly sat in front of me, stitching my hand.

I drank out of a large bottle, not even bothering to pour the liquor into the glass that sat on the table. She had been tight-lipped, and when she did speak, her words were terse.

"Then what did this?" I asked, motioning toward the deep cut in my palm. She didn't answer. "He had the pin. He was one of them."

"What pin? What are you talking about, Joseph?"

I took my hand back from her and stood. My jacket hung by the door. Inside one of the pockets, I still had O'Malley's pin. I handed it to her.

"What is this?" She clipped her words. I hadn't shown it to her earlier.

"The Black Murphys. I took this from O'Malley. The boy had an identical one."

"He stood right in front of us, Joseph. There was no pin on his jacket."

"It was there, Molly."

Though now I felt uncertain. The whiskey had made me feel so slow in the bank. *Had I imagined it?*

"Even if he had such a pin, you don't know what it means. Did you ask O'Malley what special meaning it hid? Maybe it signals nothing."

I shook my head.

"See? Even if this boy wore one, it could mean anything. Maybe he sold papers, and it was a symbol from the press or a charm for good luck."

"No." I shook my head. "No!"

"No what? You don't want to admit you killed a boy? You could easily have dispatched him without killing. You and that damn whiskey. Now sit so I can finish."

I eased into the chair and let Molly finish stitching my palm in silence. With my other hand I took a long pull from the bottle on the table next to us. Molly looked up and shook her head.

"There are plenty of Irish in this town, Joseph. Not every one of them works for O'Malley and his street gang. I'm Irish."

"He had a knife, Molly. He blew the whistle to summon someone."

"He blew the whistle because we tossed bundles of cash to the wind! He likely called to his friends. And then you grabbed his whistle and threw it aside. Any boy that grows up in this city has a pocket knife and would have lashed out just the same."

I said nothing. Instead, I took another drink from the bottle. As I held it to my lips, Molly swatted it. The bottle flew across the floor. The top half spun to a stop against the far wall while the bottom half shattered. My mouth bled where the lip of the bottle struck my lip, jamming my teeth. I sprang from the chair, knocking it to the floor behind me. When I reached for my lip, my fingers returned nothing but blood. Molly stared at me, defiant, her fists clenched and held at her side—she wanted a fight.

For a moment we stood locked in that pose. I half expected her to strike. In truth, I wanted her to. I wanted an excuse to hit back, to unleash the rage that built inside—over my mother, over

Aurora. Molly held her ground, pulling us toward the brink. Finally, I turned and walked to the door. I gathered my coat and looked back at her. She hadn't moved.

"Leave then!"

"What do you want, Molly?"

"I want to see Daniel and Emeline and Mr. Lincoln. I want to go home!" Her voice rose with each word until she shouted.

"They would follow us. We've done nothing to stop that. I'm keeping us safe."

"And it's a fine job you've done! You've ensured they follow us. But maybe that's what you wanted. You never intended to settle down. And now you have the perfect excuse. Go. Just go!"

I stepped toward her.

"You don't mean that. I told you to pick any church. When we're safe—"

Her hand flew, striking me across my face. It fell hard. My ear rang, taking me oddly off-balance. Between the whiskey and the blow, I stumbled to one side, only catching the table to keep me on my feet.

"Joseph—"

Molly reached to steady me. I lashed out at her, pushing her off and flailing with my arm, which struck her hard. She fell backwards. I stood over her for a moment, then headed to the door. This time I didn't look back as I stepped into the hallway and slammed the door behind me.

Despite the late hour, New York still thrived. Streetcars passed, filled with goods for the morning markets. They brought fish from the Sound, produce from Long Island, and industrial products from upstate. The smells changed at night—fish mixed with tomatoes and manure. I turned my face every time the horses passed.

The whiskey claimed my senses, and I stumbled on every lip in the sidewalk. I wandered without purpose. My pocket still contained several loose bills. I found the nearest tavern to spend them. I had no idea where I was, but I cared little as long as the whiskey flowed. I remember ordering a bottle and then sitting by myself until the place closed. The barkeep woke me by kicking the chair out from underneath where I sat. I stood and took a swing at him. I know he hit me at least once, and when next I woke, I lay out on the paving stones in front of the pub. I crawled to the gutter and vomited. The cold stones against my face were the last things I remembered.

The first light of day fell hot upon my jacket. I stirred and woke, uncomfortable under its warmth. My head throbbed, and my body still wobbled from the influence of the whiskey. I had drunk more than I ever remembered at one sitting. Before, I used the whiskey to numb the pain, pushing it away so I did not think upon it. But last night I tried to drown it—maybe to kill myself in the process. My heart pounded in my head, and the daylight dug like daggers into my skull. I stood and staggered down the street.

I returned to the apartment, easing the door closed behind me. I tried not to make too much noise, but then I stumbled and fell hard into the door. Pulling myself to my feet, I made my way to the sitting room. I didn't want to face Molly, so I lay down on the couch. Before sleep claimed me again, I remembered turning to my side and retching onto the floor.

When I finally startled awake, the day had faded. It was the image of the boy that had shocked me from slumber. He stood on a street corner and delivered papers, blowing a whistle and calling out the headlines. When I asked for a paper, he turned to face me, a forelock of white hair plastered to his forehead. He wore no pin upon his jacket. He handed me a paper—nothing else in his hands. I woke before I ran him through with my knife.

I opened the window to let in some light while I searched the apartment. Molly had left. Striking a match, I lit the oil lamp on the table. My stomach grumbled, but I wasn't sure what I could put in it that I might hold down. When I reset the glass over the flame and turned the knob to expose more wick, I noticed the note.

Joseph—
I will not fuel this revenge. I cannot be part of it when we do more damage to the innocent around us. It is folly and will result in nothing but damnation. Come home to me.
Molly

I read her words several times, sitting and letting them sink in. My stomach lost all interest in food. I stayed like that for a spell. I'm not sure how long. The shadows crept across the floorboards, sneaking toward me until I moved my foot from their path. I didn't know what to do next. Without Molly it seemed a different world. *Could I do this alone—kill Dorsey? And if I did, would Molly forgive me?* Or, I could find her, take the children and the Old Man, and disappear out West. We would go deeper this time, beyond the reach of anyone who might recognize us—start anew.

I began to pack the apartment. A few changes of clothes filled one bag. Molly had left a leather satchel filled with cash we took from the first few banks. It looked identical to the one we used at Merchant's bank where we showered the crowd with loose bills to make our escape. She had taken some of the money, but left a small fortune—enough to find our way free. Maybe she was right.

I had done enough damage to the Consortium, and the cycle we started might never end. The time had come to leave—to find Molly. She would get her country wedding and then we would disappear for good.

Before I left the apartment, I scanned out the window. I searched in both directions to where my vision failed. Then I leafed through the ledger again. If I took it, I might be tempted to use it, to inflict more suffering to the Consortium. Instead, I let it lie on the table as I closed the door. I pocketed the little blue velvet bag. I would bury it with my mother under the great oak tree.

Outside, night began its descent. Pain surged through my head with every heartbeat, and my stomach tugged when I breathed deep of the early summer. With each passing day the sun hung later and later. Eventually it surrendered, making way for the darkness. It felt fitting to leave the city as night fell—the end of one day, where darkness would usher in the next.

I had only walked a few blocks when the wind whispered. It sounded so real that I turned to see who had crept up upon me, my hand falling to my knife—no one. Yet my mother's tongue filled my imagination and spun off again before I made sense of it. Suddenly the dark felt ominous. It pressed in on me as I made my way. I searched over my shoulder, trying not to be obvious in my manner. A few times I changed direction, doubling back along the other side of the street. I searched the faces that walked behind me—nothing.

As the darkness settled deeper, something came with it. My mother had always been in tune with the world around her—as if it spoke a language she could hear and understand. Many times while leading groups of slaves upon the Underground Railroad, we had barely escaped. It was always due to her instincts. I suspected there was more to it, though I never understood her answer when I pressed the topic.

The city had eyes. That is the only way to describe how I felt. I stared at everyone's lapels, seeking out the symbol of the Black Murphys. My eyes strained to find the telltale white forelock of hair, as if it held some special link to O'Malley's men. Most people tipped their hats as they passed, or said nothing to me. I couldn't find the source of my discomfort, no matter where I turned to catch it.

Walking uptown, a gust of wind blew me into another passerby. I barely escaped with my hat, clutching it atop my head. I stopped at the side of the road and turned in a full circle. Behind me, a pair of men followed. They walked a few steps apart—far enough one might not suspect they were together. But they were close enough to still talk and make themselves heard. Each wore a dark suit and a black Bowler hat.

I started again, quickening my pace. They followed at a distance, and with each turn I had a few precious seconds to disappear. People still littered the roadways. Streetcars filled the road. I hoped the crowded streets made action by these men less likely. They would choose a location where few people could act as witnesses. I threaded my way through the crowd, using it as a shield—if only to their eyes.

The breath of pursuit pressed in upon my neck. I had felt this before. Someone shadowing me, only to jump to action when the timing favored their purposes. I needed to preempt them, to either strike first, or disappear. I made a turn toward Broadway, hoping to find a busier section of town. Then I noticed a small church on my left. Without hesitation I mounted the steps. If locked, I had doomed myself to an early confrontation—though I now held the high ground. I pulled on the door. It swung open.

I slid inside, pulling the door closed save a sliver to see through. The two men followed around the corner and stopped. They checked the traffic in all directions. The gas streetlamps were lit, which complicated their search—shadows flickered along the street. They split up. One ran down the far side of the street. The other turned slowly. I closed the door before he saw the movement. Then I locked it. A moment later, the door tugged. Then it stopped. They had moved on.

Inside, the church was empty. The pews sat in ordered rows, though their condition appeared much maligned for a Catholic church. I felt it as good a place as any, so I sat in the back row. If one of the men backtracked and figured out where I went, I wanted open space. This would work.

Opening Molly's letter, I reread it—several times. I wondered how far she had gotten. With a day's head start, she should have left the island, perhaps taking the first train that morning. A sickening thought gripped me—*what if they followed her?* I would have to find her to know for sure.

As I read the letter a final time, a hand fell upon my shoulder. It startled me, and I jumped to my feet. I turned with my hand on the handle of my knife, expecting to find one of the men in the dark suits. Instead, a priest stood in front of me.

"I meant not to startle you, son," he said.

His speech held more than a touch of the New York City Irish—impossible to tell if he came from the motherland or grew up amongst its descendants in this city. He appeared no older than I, though he carried far less weight. I always hated how religious men referred to me as *son*. It felt like my stepfather, though he had more right to the term after he married my mother. I eased from the handle of the knife, letting my jacket fall over my weapon.

"I'll just be going."

"No need. You must have followed me up the steps," he said. "I just came across the river and opened the church up for Mass this evening."

"No one else is here?" I asked. His face changed, and he took a step back. I had frightened him. "I mean no harm—I'm not here to rob you."

His face broke with a nervous smile, not convinced of my intentions. It filled his thin face. Nervously he brushed back his hair. It was coal black.

"I felt pursued, so I came in to sit a spell." As soon as I spoke, I feared I said too much.

"We are all pursued by sin and temptation. You are welcome here as a refuge."

I smiled—the first bit of humor I had found in weeks.

"Was something I said funny?" His tone implied he took offense at my response.

"No, not at all," I answered. "Sin and temptation follow me all the time. This was more physical, like the devil nipped at my heels."

"I see—that would be serious. The Lord will watch over you here. You may stay as long as you like. Will you sit?"

I nodded. I wished to give nightfall more time. I would let the shadows between the gas lamps envelop the street until I could hide amongst them. As I sat, he took the space on the pew right next to me.

"I am Father McElhenny."

"Joseph."

"A fine name. I'm sure you know. What ails you, Joseph?"

"Are you from here? The city?" I didn't want to get into my story.

"I grew up across the river in Brooklyn, at an orphanage there. I run the same one now. Were you an orphan by chance?"

"No. Although I guess you could call me one now—my mother recently passed."

"I am so sorry for your loss. Was she . . ." He didn't know how to finish what he asked.

"Indian?" I asked.

He nodded.

"Of the Miami people."

"I thought that might be the case." He looked over his shoulder. Then he lowered his voice. "You know they are looking for you."

His words pulled the breath from me. I bladed my body so I might draw my knife. My eyes darted around the church.

"No one is here. Let me explain." He reached to put a hand on my arm, but I pushed away to create more space. "It is not like that, Joseph. I am not in league with them."

"Who are you?" I pulled the blade slow, placing it as a barrier between us.

"I am a priest, what you see before you. I run an orphanage in Brooklyn. Those men, the ones who seek you out, they come to the orphanage sometimes. They recruit the impressionable and the vulnerable. I detest it."

Most men cannot look into another's eyes when they lie. They look away under the stress. His eyes never wandered. No deception crossed his face. Without breaking my stare and without lowering my blade, I reached into my pocket and took out the pin. I held it out to him.

"The Black Murphys," he said.

"You know them?"

"Unfortunately."

"How about Thomas O'Malley?" I asked.

"Most unfortunately."

"Tell me of him."

The priest looked to his hands, and then at the front of the church. His eyes never left the statue of Mary to the side of the altar.

"I knew him as a boy. We grew up together in that orphanage—the same I manage now. His parents were taken in front of him. He watched as his father was dragged off and beaten, and his mother . . ." He paused to look at me. "They raped her as he watched. Then slit her throat. The police found him sitting by her side in a pool of her blood. He didn't speak for weeks at the orphanage when they first brought him."

"Who were they?"

"The Bowery Boys—a street gang in the city. They hate the Irish and all Catholics. They cut a cloverleaf into her forehead as they left her to die. That's where he came upon the idea for the pin. They all wear one. No one dares cross a boy who joins the Black Murphys."

I thought of my mother, her body lying under that sheet—what O'Malley had done to her. Such pain so young distorts a life forever, twists until it surfaces in unexpected ways.

"He wasn't all bad," Father McElhenny said. "Not at first. He saved me from a beating once, then took me under his wing. He was older by a year or two, and I was scrawny in a way he wasn't."

"Yet you're not friends now?"

He shook his head. "We had different ideas of how to save souls. He thought forming a gang would protect the weaker among us. And it did. He held us together for years. But it led to violence. It seems this life always does. Thomas changed with it, from sheepdog to wolf. He no longer protects the innocent—he uses them. I went with the Church. If I shepherd even one boy through the orphanage without losing them to the Black Murphys, my savior will reward me for it. I'm afraid Tom chose darkness."

In an odd way I pitied O'Malley. Yet I would kill him when I found the man, for butchering my mother, taking my daughter—and Charley. I had almost forgotten the telegram from the Old Man. Charley counted among the dead, too. O'Malley was the wolf in the darkness.

"Why do they leave?" I asked.

The priest looked to me. From his face, no one had asked him this before.

"They're hungry—scared. We don't have enough food, nor clothes. And when they steal, they need protection. Revenge always comes for them."

"I've taken enough of your time, Father." I stood, sheathing my knife.

"You will leave?" he asked. "The city?"

I nodded. "This place is not in my blood. And I have a family to find—a family to save."

He held out a hand. I took it.

"What street is busiest at this hour?" I asked.

"Broadway, without question."

I made my way from the pew and toward the door.

"Joseph," he called out. "You have forgotten your bag."

He held the leather satchel. I shook my head.

"I left it on purpose. I have what I need. Save someone from the darkness."

Outside, the gas lamps cut through the dark, though they could only push it away so far. I stayed out of their light, preferring the shadows as I made my way west across the island until I hit Broadway. Every few steps, I checked behind me. There were enough people still out, though the foot traffic had eased considerably. Once I hit Broadway, I turned north. Molly had a day's head start.

Surrounded by many people, my nerves calmed. I blended in better, flowing with the crowd. I walked behind the streetcars as I crossed to the other sidewalk, checking if anyone followed. Molly and I had walked this area so many times. As I made it farther north, I recognized part of our daily stroll. My heart beat faster and my stomach tightened. A block farther and I stood in front of General Dorsey's house.

My mother always spoke on how life intertwined—one thing flowed to the next in ways we may never see or understand. The Great Spirit guided the world. I listened to my mother's stories yet never tried to understand. They were stories. Some meant to put me to sleep, others meant to summon courage when we most needed it. But this night, in this city so far from my mother's people and so long after she told me her stories, they made sense. The Great Spirit wanted me here.

Every window of General Dorsey's house burned bright.

CHAPTER FOURTEEN

I HELD TO the shadows as I pushed past the gate and down the narrow back alley. Passing each window, I peered inside—nothing. Yet someone had lit the lights and set them out, turning the entire house into a beacon that drew me in. I was the moth, drawn to this flame. I hesitated on the stone steps, but then climbed to the top and pressed against the back door.

With an easy push, the door swung opened. It revealed the hall that led to the front, the stairs, and the study. My heart beat in my head, and my hands shook. I had been dry all day, and the binge from the night prior left the worst headache. It had only begun to abate. I had the flask in my pocket, filled with whiskey. But I wasn't certain how my body would take it. Every bit of me wanted to turn, to leave this place and find Molly. All my training told me to leave, to make it to Broadway, and run north. But I stood firm. The city, the people, the closeness of it—they all dulled my senses, distorted them as if I stood in a carnival house. The wise move would be retreat, to watch from a distance and catch them in the open. But with each second, Molly drew farther away. I could still make it work. I drew my knife.

Once inside I set each foot down slow, listening to the floor as it shifted with my weight. Despite the light, no noise came from within. I hoped it meant they were upstairs and I might be able to catch the general in the bath or busy at work. One hand brushed against the wall while I made my way toward the study. I glanced upstairs as I passed the polished wood banister and then peered into the study. Nothing. I turned my attention to the sitting room where Molly had opened the safe hidden behind the portrait.

As I angled around the corner, moving slowly to bring each new sliver of the room into view, I nearly missed him. He sat in the high-back chair next to the fireplace, perfectly still. Our eyes met, yet he said nothing. He moved not in the slightest, as if he were stuffed and mounted to the chair. The white forelock fell across his forehead. My feet stopped, as if held to the floor by nails. I couldn't move, and my chest could only draw in small gulps of air. *O'Malley.*

"I've been wondering if it was mere folly to await your arrival," he finally said. His voice carried well in the house.

I didn't respond. He held his hands up from his lap showing me his palms.

"I have just come to talk," he said.

"What would we have to talk about?" My words barely cleared my mouth. I had been breathing in short swallows and it dried my tongue.

"The general insists on taking you alive. It seems that in you he has found another purpose."

"I don't intend to go anywhere with you."

He stood slow, favoring one leg. The other had set from where the horse fell upon him, though it appeared weaker. I noted how he moved.

"I was hoping you would say that." His hand pulled a knife from inside his waistband—the blade no longer than the one the boy had carried the day before. "If you came willingly, it would be that much harder to kill you."

I stepped back, checking over my shoulders. *Why would he be alone?*

"Oh no," he said. "I wouldn't bring anyone to ruin this. Do you recognize it?" he asked, edging closer and holding up the knife for me to see. "It still has your blood upon the blade."

I circled into the room until my back pressed against the small table facing the window. I kept my knife in front of me. Stitches held my other hand together.

"He was just a boy—a lookout," O'Malley said. "I promised my sister I would keep him safe. Instead, I will kill you with his blade."

"He was kin?" I asked. The boy must have worn a pin—I hadn't imagined it.

"My nephew. His father died in the War. Now my sister must grieve for her son, too. For this, I will cut pieces from you."

"Maybe you could carve a clover into my forehead, too?"

He stopped. His brow wrinkled, straining to make sense of what I had said, where I learned of such a thing. I wanted him off-guard, but it didn't last long. His face balled, turning red with rage. He sprang forward, though I had anticipated it. Stepping to the side, my free hand brought up a large book from the table behind me. I swung it and hit him across the head. He tumbled to the ground, yet stood before I pounced. He came up swinging, the small knife cutting a wide arc through the air. It tore into my jacket, slashing the fabric. My hands probed the cut—no blood.

When he came in again, I lashed with my knife. He cringed. I had cut his arm deep, though it merely forced him to switch hands. He ran full bore into me, both of our blades falling into the melee of tangled bodies. I found myself on my back, my arm and my knife trapped between us. A sick smile developed across his face.

His knife stuck half-buried out of my chest, above my heart. I breathed deep, gasping for air. No pain fell upon me—nothing.

I stared at the angle of the blade, straight into my chest. He laughed, further wrenching my hand between us. No matter how I pulled, the blade stuck fast. My white shirt darkened all around the knife in my chest. Panic gripped me. I had only moments left. My thoughts turned to Molly—she had left upset. *Would she ever know?*

He raised a fist and it crashed across my face. Then he reared up again, attempting to plunge the blade further into my chest. It wouldn't budge. He pulled up, but it wouldn't come free. A square bulge protruded through my jacket. The knife had buried itself in my flask. The darkness overtaking my shirt wasn't blood. It was whiskey. He twisted and pulled, but it only seemed to make the blade further stuck. I began to laugh—liquor had saved me.

As he let go of the knife, he pulled back as if to hit me again about the face. I released my knife handle. The blade remained uselessly trapped between our bodies. My hand slipped the trap, and I struck with all my might upon his leg. The color drained from his face. It still hurt. His fist fell forward but had lost its sting. Pushing off my chest, he tried to rear up again. But behind us, two men rushed into the room. One held a leather sap. He swung it wide, crashing it against O'Malley's head. He fell forward, his head striking mine full force. The thud echoed in my body, and the darkness collapsed upon me. When next I came to, the men were pulling O'Malley from me.

"Is he dead? The Indian?"

The other looked at my chest. The whiskey had spread, and from the position of the knife, he assumed I had died.

"You saw it—O'Malley killed him. I won't answer to the general for this. We'll bring O'Malley. Bind his hands."

One man started to tie up O'Malley as the other began to search my pockets. When he leaned over, I knew he would detect my breathing. So as he drew close, I snapped my eyes open. He startled. I used his reaction to buy me just enough time. I grabbed hold of his jacket and pulled him near. He wore a pistol on his right side, and my hand drew it from the holster. Cocking the hammer, I pulled the trigger. The concussion from the gun rocked my chest, but the bullet struck the man in the side. He fell forward on me as O'Malley had done, screaming in pain. I rolled to one side.

The other man still had both hands upon O'Malley. When he realized what had happened, he brushed back his jacket and made for his pistol. My thumb fumbled at the hammer, trying to gain purchase upon it to re-cock the weapon. The stitches Molly had put in strained until one tore through the skin. The man fired. The bullet hit, though it brought no pain. The other man on top of me stopped writhing. The bullet struck him in the head.

My thumb still fought with the gun. The other man cocked his weapon again and rushed toward us. He pulled his partner to one side, perhaps thinking he might still live and that his bullet had found me. As he pulled the body clear, I thrust the pistol up and fired. He did the same, shooting toward the floor. The bright flash blinded me, powder crashing upon my face. The smell overwhelmed my senses, and the taste of sulfur filled my mouth. The bullet tore through the side of my face. It skimmed along my cheekbone and ripped at my ear. I struggled to get the hammer back once more, but I needn't have worried. The man standing over me fell backwards. My shot had struck under his chin.

I pushed the body off and rolled to my side. My stomach heaved, and I doubled over for a moment as I tried to clear my gut. But I had eaten nothing that day. O'Malley lay on the floor a few feet away, his hands bound tight in front of him. I knelt, searching the floor for my knife. It lay a few feet away, so I crawled to it.

Once I had the knife, I walked over to where O'Malley lay on the floor. My chest still had the knife sticking out from the flask. I twisted at the handle, working the knife back and forth until it pulled out. Then I reached inside and produced the flask. It clanged upon the floor as I dropped it. All the whiskey had drained from it. I licked my fingers to get the last taste.

"Looks like your fortune has turned," I said.

O'Malley made a wild move for my legs. I stepped aside and kicked at his broken leg. He screamed in pain and turned on his side, doubling up so his bound hands could reach his leg. He threw up on the floor and then began coughing. I knelt down and grabbed his hair. I pressed my knife under his chin.

"I should have killed you in the cell," I said. The Old Man had stopped me—*at what cost?* He had killed Charley according to the telegram.

O'Malley's laugh started as a small chuckle—then grew. I pressed the blade under his throat, about to cut him open.

"We have her," he said.

"Who?" I asked.

He laughed, taunting me. So I reached down and grabbed his leg, squeezing with all my strength. It overpowered his laughter.

"Your woman."

I released his leg. "Molly? How?"

"The red-haired bitch. Irish women are hard."

"Where is she?" I asked. My hand went back to his leg.

"I told you, the general wants to talk. He'll exchange her for you."

"You lie," I said. Someone had seen Molly at the bank, or the head cashier had talked.

"She was upset at you. Upset you killed the boy."

I pushed back, then checked over my shoulder. No one came. He didn't lie. He couldn't have known what we fought over if they didn't have her.

"The general wants me, in exchange for her?"

"For both of them. That is his message."

"Both of whom?" I asked.

He gestured with his chin. "Look inside my jacket."

I studied his face, as if it might be some kind of trick. His expression didn't change, so I patted down the outside of his jacket. He had placed something in the inner pocket, though I couldn't tell what. Reaching inside, my hand found it. I pulled out a small velvet bag, the same size as the one I had with Aurora's thumbs. I feared the worst—*Molly*. Dropping my knife, I tore the bag open and upended the contents into my palm.

This time, a silver chain fell out, and with it, a delicate silver eagle's feather. My stepfather crafted it, one of a pair of earrings he made for my mother. He had been a fine silver artisan. My mother had split them, giving one to my wife years ago, the other to Aurora. This one had been missing since I lost my girl. I looked to O'Malley. He must have read the disbelief on my face.

"We didn't kill her. The general will trade you for both of them."

CHAPTER FIFTEEN

26 April 1874

STANDING NEAR THE edge of the lake, I forced O'Malley to sit in front of me. I had tied his hands in front and had looped a jacket over the bindings so no one would notice as we walked. I held another jacket, folded over a pistol in the event he decided to escape. I had no need though. I walked him toward freedom and he knew it. His best play was to sit and wait.

We stood just inside the cover of the trees, ensuring we hid amongst the blooming wildflowers. This was the middle of The Ramble—a wild expanse of Central Park. The web of trails that cut swaths through it only partly tamed the land here. This had been Molly's favorite place in the city. The Bow Bridge that crossed over the narrow portion of the lake made an excellent spot for the exchange. I would watch General Dorsey and his men as they approached from the south. The land on the far shore jutted into the lake, giving me a wide view. And the expanse of The Ramble provided enough ground where I might escape in case it all went poorly.

The land whispered here. But the words were dim, overshadowed by the gas lamps along the paths behind us. They hissed louder than the cicadas could fill the night. Only a few people dared stroll through the park at dusk, especially this deep. I had requested the meet over a telegram, not waiting for a reply. Instead, we came to the location early. They might try to trap me, place men on my side of The Ramble. But I left them only an hour to set upon the spot. It limited the general's options.

"You know they will kill you. And your woman." O'Malley finally spoke.

"Quiet." I leaned my knee into his back, forcing his head forward.

"There's no way out for you," he said.

I pressed the revolver into his head.

"I'll get you out of the city. You won't make it without me," he continued.

"And why would you offer such a thing?"

"So I can kill you myself."

"Since it seems I face certain death with either decision, I think I'll take my chances."

"But I'll make it quick," he offered. "General Dorsey will drag it out. He'll see to it the pain lasts."

"I have others to think about. Keep quiet."

"As soon as they cross that bridge and take you in exchange, they'll kill your woman and your daughter. Likely they'll do it in front of you. Come with me, and I will spare their lives."

I jammed the pistol into the back of his head. He spoke no more.

The other side of the bridge held open ground. The sound of horses' hooves hitting the hard stone paths echoed ahead of their arrival. Three carriages pulled out of the dusk, stopping in a row on the edge of the wide arc of light from the lamps. A series of men stepped from the first and the last carriages. They all wore dark suits and the Bowler hats that were so common here. Peering into the night, they spread into a wide formation. It made shooting them harder. These men were well trained—disciplined. Finally, the middle carriage opened and an older man stepped out. He held ten, or maybe fifteen years on me. His beard was finely trimmed, his clothes immaculate—every bit the match to his portrait. He paused while his feet steadied themselves on the ground. Then he reached back and held a hand into the carriage.

Even from this distance, I saw the woman had to be Molly. Her mannerisms were so distinct—how she held herself, even in a time like this. She took the hand, though from the stiff posture of her arm it seemed more formality than acceptance. Then she reached into the carriage and did the same—offering a hand to someone inside.

The girl emerged in the door of the carriage—*Aurora*. I had sought after her so long, yet I had not stood this close since the night they stole her from me. My chest tightened till I could only draw breath in small sips. The yearning in the pit of my stomach built—to run across the bridge and hold her, to scoop her up, to see her face. I strained through the darkness to see better, hoping Molly would drag her farther into the light. She wore a plain gray dress, with dark stockings. Together the general led them until they stood at the end of the bridge.

I went to take the last drink from the bottle, to quell my nerves and steady my hands, but thought better of it. I didn't want Aurora to smell the fresh liquor on my breath. I dropped it to the ground. It slid downhill until it came to rest near the water's edge. Pulling O'Malley to his feet, I dragged him out of the brush toward the path. It looked clear in all directions, though I figured the general had sent men in from the north to stop my escape. I had yet one card to play—the ledger and all the corporate paperwork that we took from Merchant's bank. I hoped it mattered as much to him as I suspected.

Prodding O'Malley forward, I headed toward the bridge. The cast-iron structure rose above the path. It wasn't until I stood on its crest that the general and his men came into view once more. Gas lamps lined the bridge, throwing circles of light to push back the darkness. We stood outside of one of those circles—O'Malley in front of me as a shield. I checked over my shoulder. No one approached. Molly stood next to the general, Aurora clutching her hand. The shadows danced over her, obscuring my view.

Slowly they started up the bridge. The general led the way, followed by Molly and Aurora, then one of his men. They stopped a few paces away, Molly behind the general. I tried to glance behind her to the little girl who grasped her hand. But she cowered behind Molly. The general held my immediate attention. He looked to the pistol in my hand.

"I hope we might conclude this business peaceably," he said. His voice filled with confidence—he had covered all avenues of escape.

"My hope as well."

"Then you accept my terms? A trade. You and Mr. O'Malley in exchange for Miss Ferguson and the girl?"

I nodded. "But they walk free."

"Of course," he replied.

"Yet you have men at the end of The Ramble to retake them." I said it as a statement of fact, as if we had seen his men already. We had not, though he would not know.

His face maintained composure. Through his beard the edges of his mouth upturned just a bit, enough to be noticeable.

"Are you a chess player, Mr. Foster?"

"No."

"That's a pity. If you were, I would call this check and mate. You might better understand your predicament."

"I don't play, though I've watched my fill of it. This game is not over."

"How so?"

My words intrigued him—which was my intent.

"I still have something you need. You can have it when I know *they* are safe."

"And what would that be?" he asked. It seemed I had amused him. "My ledger?"

"It means more than you let on."

"Replaceable—unfortunate, but replaceable. You don't get to my position without having duplicates."

"Then you won't mind when it's published?"

The confidence on his face slipped. The side of his mouth leveled—no longer amused.

"I left it in certain hands," I continued. "My testimony to Congress provided many friends in the Baltimore press. Having duplicates is one thing. But in the manner you went to protect it, I'm certain you would prefer if your business remained private."

"What do you suggest?"

"Your ledger will return to you, once I know them to be safe."

"And how will you know that?"

"A telegram. Molly will send a message that only she will know."

He studied my face for a time, quiet and pondering. The longer it went, the more confident I grew. I tried to see Aurora. The shadows still hid her.

"I will still have you," he said.

"It seems a small price."

I had the other documents and I might be able to parlay them into my own freedom. I wouldn't tip my hand too early in that manner. The general turned to the man behind Molly and Aurora. He nodded.

"Walk Miss Ferguson out of the park and escort her where she needs to go. Then report to me."

The man started to take Molly and Aurora past me. I pushed O'Malley toward the general and grasped Molly's hand.

"Joseph—" Molly began. I cut her off by raising my hand.

Kneeling, I looked upon Aurora for the first time. In the dim gaslight I found it hard to make out all her features. The shadows danced upon the bridge, buffered by the wind. I had imagined her face for so long, but when I closed my eyes, I always pictured the face of a child—three years old. Now she stood on the threshold of womanhood. She looked exactly like her mother.

"Father?" she asked, her voice timid.

I nodded but couldn't say anything. My throat tightened and my eyes swelled.

"You're not coming?" Her gaze darted to O'Malley.

"Not yet." I choked on the words.

"But you will?" Her southern accent held strong upon her words. So long had she lived with Colonel Norris in the Deep South. Even though he had kidnapped her after I saved the Old Man, he had treated her like his own family.

"I will."

"Miss Molly said you have Daniel. I so want to see him again." Once more she checked on O'Malley and the general, edging from them as she spoke.

"You will," I said. "Go with Miss Molly and listen to her."

When I went to grasp her hands, my fingers found the bandages. I stared. They bound the space where her thumbs were missing. Her glare at O'Malley was fueled by hate. I followed her eyes. His face twisted in the light—maniacal, a smile dancing in and out of view with the flickering light. He held up both hands, still bound at the wrists, and waved to her. She startled, pushing toward Molly. The general took hold of O'Malley's shoulder, pushing him toward the carriages. He said nothing, taking a step back to provide me a moment with my child.

I took her head in my hands and drew her close, kissing her forehead.

"I never stopped looking for you," I said. It was a lie, but one I needed to tell myself—to tell her. I had run when Colonel Norris sent me back to kill the Old Man in exchange for her freedom. I would explain when I could at a time when she might understand. "I'll never stop looking. I will come. Stay with Molly."

As the tears filled my eyes, I stood. If I held on to her any longer, I might not let go. It would only make things worse. I grasped Molly.

"Take care of her."

"I won't leave without you. I'll find you," she said. Her hand fell upon my face. I pulled it down and forced her to look at me.

"No, Molly. Leave now. Find the Old Man and don't look back."

"If I leave, they'll—"

"Take this."

I reached inside my jacket and produced the velvet bag with the silver eagle's feather. Inside, I had placed a note. It told Molly how to find the ledger and where to run.

"I need you to take her. I need to know she's safe—and loved. Send a telegram when you are free. Put in the name of the Old Man's daughter. No one else knows it."

She nodded but refused to look at me. Her eyes welled. I pulled her to me and kissed her. I would have held her like that forever, but her lips trembled, and I felt the eyes upon me. I pulled back, my forehead rested against hers. I pressed my pistol into her hands.

"Molly, forgive me."

Then I let go and stepped toward the general. He guided me down the bridge. I turned to see them one last time, standing in one of the circles of light. Molly held Aurora at her side.

She mouthed the words—*I love you*.

I turned and walked. O'Malley waited farther down the bridge.

"How many times have you broken that girl's heart?" he asked. "You should be ashamed, telling her that you'll see her again."

His hands were still tied, though he reached to where my knife was, and pulled it from the sheath. Flipping the blade toward himself, he cut the bindings loose. Then he looked at the knife, roughly formed from the old file.

"Is this the knife that killed Booth?" he asked.

"No."

"Too bad." He turned the blade over, letting the unfinished spots bathe in the light from the lamps. "I will still sell it as Joseph Foster's knife. I expect it to fetch a small fortune after you're dead."

CHAPTER SIXTEEN

25 May 1874

I LOST COUNT OF how many times the sun rose through the small window the prison afforded me. And how many times the cold moonlight made it past the bars. Day by day, my mood slipped, like sand that escaped my grasp with each movement. When they first took me, they placed a burlap bag over my head and bound my hands with irons. The carriage ride lasted only minutes. Then they ushered me into a boat. It rocked with each oar pull until they hauled me into the back of a wagon. The irons only came off my wrists when they shoved me into the cell. The door closed before I tore the bag from my head. I stood alone.

Darkness descended upon me. I knew nothing of Molly. I prayed to the Great Spirit that Molly and Aurora made it to safety. I fought to remember my mother's words from those many years ago. She always spoke to the Great Spirit to ask for guidance, praying for a clear path as we escaped the slave catchers on the Underground Railroad. My native tongue had fallen into such disrepair, though the sounds gave me comfort as they surfaced from my memory. Every day I would recall more as I focused. I remembered the time spent with my mother, ferrying souls from the Deep South toward freedom. Each memory brought a faint whiff of happiness. They reminded me of the white sheet upon the doctor's table, forcing me ever deeper into the darkness.

I fought, though it offered no relief. It was like wrestling with the impending nightfall that only the Great Spirit could abate. My hands shook. I took my last drink before crossing the bridge with O'Malley. Each time they delivered food, I begged for General Dorsey. I needed some word of Molly. Once I knew that she had reached safety, I could tell him of the other papers I possessed. Instead, the guards knew nothing, eyeing me as a lunatic who spoke gibberish. My one reprieve came several times a day when the sound of children found its way through the window. If I stood on the wooden bucket they left as a toilet, I could see the playground outside an old brick building. Nuns stood guard upon it, scolding those who became too carried away. Still, their laughter held hope, pushing back the darkness for a time. I needed all the help I could muster.

At night the cell turned cold. Nothing blocked the elements from the window. Not even the poor excuse for a blanket they left upon the stone floor. I huddled under it and dreamt of Molly. When I tried to picture Aurora's face, I only saw my wife, affixed with a disapproving scowl. I had failed her—failed Aurora. The darkness pushed in upon me once more.

The days wore on, blurring my mind. I stopped standing on the bucket to watch the children. Strangely, my hands ceased their shaking. I wanted no liquor. I floated in the world around me, with nothing and no one to anchor me to reality. I no longer abhorred my own stench. My only notice of the passage of time came from the emerging shadows of the early morning light. They lengthened along the floor until they fell upon the empty plate from the previous night's dinner. I had not touched it. The mice had devoured the beastly rations, chewing the side of the wooden plate. Even as the sun fell upon me, cold gripped my body. It held tight and refused to surrender. I would die here, dreaming only of Molly and the little girl I never had the chance to know.

Lost in that haze, I didn't hear the door open. Two men stood over me. One held a hand over his nose as he pulled me to my feet. The other kicked the blanket to the corner. They dressed in matching gray suits with dark leather shoes escaping the pleats in their trousers. Both wore black clover pins upon their lapels.

"He stinks."

"Just get him up."

They pulled me to standing and placed irons upon my wrists. I offered no fight. In truth, it took all I had to stand and walk as they pulled me down the corridor outside the cell. When I stumbled, they pulled me up by the irons, forcing the rough edges of the metal deep into my wrists. The pain felt good. I twisted them until they bled. At least I felt something.

"The warden wants to see you."

I had not the strength to resist. They escorted me upstairs, then down more corridors lined with stone floors. The hard leather bottoms of their shoes marked our progress, and the air hung thick from the burning oil lamps. My stomach pitched. This building had stood for years. I tried to follow our path, as if it would offer some means to flee if escape became an option. But I became lost. My edge had dulled.

At the end of one corridor, we came upon a double set of mahogany doors. One of the men knocked upon it, making a hollow sound that filled my chest. Someone called from beyond, and they pushed the doors open. Inside, we stood in a magnificent office. Windows filled the far wall, flooding the room with sunlight. I tried to raise my chained hands to shield my eyes. Daylight surrounded me, as if they had thrown me into an ocean of light.

"This is him? The one we're watching for the general?"

A man sat behind a great wooden desk. His obese body barely fit, though his clothes were well tailored. A woman stood in front of his desk—her back faced me. Long black hair fell over her shoulders. Her dark red dress, adorned in velvet and embroidery, bespoke of wealth.

"This is the man you were looking for?" the warden asked.

He stood, offering an outstretched hand, presenting me like a prize. The woman turned. My mind churned slow, not under-standing. Her hair was black, the dress extravagant beyond de-scription, but the face—*Molly*. I tried to piece it together, to unravel the scene. My mind could not process what I saw. I started to call to her, but I caught the look upon her face. She wished that I remained silent. She had some plan in mind, and my place was to understand it without asking aloud, else I might ruin it and place us all in further jeopardy.

"What have you done to him?" she asked.

I didn't recognize the voice. It was tainted with a trace of an Irish accent.

"We keep him in a special section of the jail, Miss O'Shea." The warden held the same city dialect as O'Malley.

O'Shea? The name meant nothing to me.

"I should say that you did. For what was he arrested?" She stressed it now, playing the part to these men. I didn't understand what the game might be. I looked around the room. *What had she done with Aurora?*

The warden glanced to his men before he spoke.

"He is a special case. Stole from some powerful men, and they wish to make an example of him."

Molly turned from me and stared at the warden—a mixture of disbelief and condescension. It would coax him to say more.

"He is no simple thief," the warden said. "You are sure this is the man?"

Molly turned again. This time she walked toward me. The men at my sides let go as she neared. When she reached me, she stopped, as if on inspection. My stench must have battered her senses as her nose flared. She fought for composure, placing a gloved hand over her mouth as the men had done in my cell.

"Don't say anything," she ordered. Her tone remained cold, yet her accent slipped enough that I might perceive it. She played to these men and warned me at the same time. "I thought you might be different, but you were like the others—after my father's fortune. Though you didn't want to spend it. You sought only to destroy him."

She looked so different, even acted strange. She'd dyed her hair dark, and satin gloves of the highest quality covered her hands. She behaved as an heiress might—like all those born into wealth and distinction.

Molly turned from me and walked the few short paces to stand in front of the warden. Once more he sat back in his seat and watched.

"You didn't tell us the nature of your relationship." He tried to make sense of what had transpired in front of him. "I assure you. This man will stand trial for those robberies and will be hung."

"Yes, yes. I know well what he did. They will try him for the robberies to discredit his words in front of Congress."

"I see you know the story."

"I do. I have not been the . . ." she paused, "the ideal daughter. I intended to hurt my father, but I will not see his fortune pulled down around him. You do understand how all this would look if it were known, of course?" Molly asked. "I am not a young woman, and my father has for so long hoped he would find a suitable match for me."

The warden nodded. "I see. And your father is—"

Molly cut him off. "Martin O'Shea."

He nodded again. "Of course." He didn't know, but fear overcame his curiosity.

"I trust you can keep this discreet?" Molly asked. "Incidents like this develop their own legs, as they say. I have already disappointed my father, but I am his daughter. You would be wise not to disappoint him. You are not kin, and he can be a hard man."

The warden nodded, still perplexed by the interaction.

"I'm uncertain what we can do for you, Miss O'Shea?"

"Do you attend Mass, sir?"

"My wife ensures I make it each week," he said, pointing to a crucifix upon the wall opposite the windows.

"Then you must understand—my child will not be born a bastard." She turned from him and looked into my eyes. Her voice lowered, losing the accent. For a moment only Molly and I stood in the room. "I am with child."

She was not acting. Her face softened. She fought the smile that came upon it, but managed to hide it before the others noticed. Her words struck me in the gut. I wanted to grasp her, to pull her close and cry—tears of joy and pain. At the same time I wished to shrink away—to return to my cell and fade into the stones. *She was with child? My child.* And suddenly I understood. She couldn't leave without me as I had asked. She wouldn't. She planned an escape, playing the role of some heiress whom I had seduced and wronged. Though I couldn't see what came next. We could not risk a flight from the prison—we'd never make it out the gates.

"I see," the warden said. He smiled, seemingly figuring out what took place before him.

"So you understand my reluctance in coming here today?" Molly pressed.

"Yes, I can appreciate the predicament. Of course, with the trial these things have a way of coming to light." He maneuvered for position, hoping to extract concessions from Molly. But she came ready for such a tactic.

From inside her purse she removed a stack of cash—crisp bills bound together by a paper binding, from the proceeds of our bank heists. She placed it on his desk.

"My father can compensate you more than I am able."

The guards at my sides stared at the money. Their body language shifted, leaning toward the warden and his desk. The warden didn't take his eyes from the pile of bound paper. His hands reached for it. He grasped the bills and let them shuffle between his thumb and forefinger.

"So what is it you require, Miss O'Shea?"

He looked up, though he held tight to the money in his hands.

"A wedding. I need a priest."

"You wish to marry . . . him?" He pointed toward me with the stack of cash.

"I may be forced to give up my child to an orphanage, but I will not condemn a baby to eternal damnation."

"We can find you a priest." The warden held up his free hand and motioned toward one of the guards. "We'll have one here within the hour."

"And a Catholic church," Molly said. She angled for a means out of the prison. For a place less guarded. It was audacious and clever.

The warden paused. "I'm afraid that will be out of the question. We cannot permit this man to leave the building. We will bring a priest here for you."

"My father would only see this done in a church. And no self-respecting priest would perform a ceremony honored before God without one."

Molly reached into her purse once more and placed another stack of cash upon the warden's desk. Her free hand held another she had yet to surrender.

"It would be shortsighted, sir, to walk away from the retirement my father would provide. In this affair he will have his limits, so the less people in the know, the better it will be for all involved. He will provide for those you say have need of it."

Molly turned to look at both men holding me. She made certain to look into their eyes. With her gaze she told them they would be paid. A clever move. She toyed with their greed, buying their silence. Fewer people involved would only serve to further line their pockets.

"There are a few churches nearby. I suppose it would not hurt to acquiesce to your request, Miss O'Shea. I do not want to disappoint your father."

"Then you would have made a better daughter to him than I."

The warden laughed. Molly placed the third stack of cash upon his desk. One of the men at my side shifted with the interaction. The other cared only for the money.

"Sir, might we need to talk to Mr. O'Malley?" the man said.

The warden held up his hand. "Look at him. Take a good look!"

The man shifted once more. I slouched my shoulders and stared toward the floor.

"He can't go anywhere. We'll bring him to St. Marks."

"In two days," Molly said. "I need time to prepare."

"Time?" the warden asked. His voice filled with doubt, perhaps suspicious about the ever-changing request.

"My father is traveling from Washington. He wishes to be here. And I believe you wish him present as well." She reached down and tapped upon the cash.

The warden nodded. "Two days then."

Molly looked to me once more, though she turned quickly. She had acted well.

"Make certain he is washed and has fresh clothes."

CHAPTER SEVENTEEN

27 May 1874

THE CAGE AROUND me became unbearable. I had sat for weeks, losing the will to do anything other than drift toward oblivion. But now, all had changed. Seeing Molly made the cell small, the air tight. I paced. Standing on the bucket, I could again look out toward the children. I ate the pitiful meals when they brought them—gaining what strength I could for when they returned.

When they came, they brought me to a room with a hot bathtub—the same two guards as before. It took minutes to lower my body into the scalding water. I had slept so many nights on the hard stone slab that the cold remained barricaded in my body. Even when they pulled me from the water, I had not warmed. My fingers felt slow, teased by the glimmer of warmth. The guards offered a change of clothes, and I gladly pulled them on. They held nothing to the finery that Molly had worn the previous day, but they would do.

That night I waited, washed and alive for the first time in weeks. Night came through the window, but it did not bother me. The weather had turned, transforming the cool air with the first hints of warmth. I closed my eyes as I sat upon the stone slab, thinking of time spent in our little cabin. I rocked back and forth, sitting once more in the rickety chair the Old Man made for us. The breeze blew through the prairie fields, and the moon fell bright upon the great oak tree. Off in the distance the wolf called to the wild things.

Around me the children ran, cutting deep paths through the grass. I longed to see Emeline and Daniel again as they chased one another from cabin to cabin. And Aurora. She would run after them, when finished helping Molly with the chores. I would know her for the first time. Though when I thought of holding her, of taking her by the hands and whirling her through the grass, I remembered the bandages. The white of the cloth that wrapped over her palms—the same color as the sheet over my mother. The call of the wolf became louder. She was hungry.

Daylight came, and still I sat upon the slab. When they opened the door, I stood. They didn't need to haul me to my feet. I walked between them, my hands bound in irons in front of me. They left no chain to get around their throats. It didn't matter. Molly had some manner of plan, and I would wait for it to play out.

They led me down long corridors, past other doors with bars in the small windows. Oil lamps burned and the smell singed at my throat. I savored it. With the pain, life surged through me again. I held my palms level. They didn't shake. The stint in the cell had dried me better than my time in Tennessee. I had asked for none of this. If the wolf came, I had not called her. But I would let her wreak havoc upon them.

Outside, daylight burned. I tried to lift my hands to my face to block it while my eyes adjusted, but the men pulled my arms down to escort me. They were nervous here, scanning in all directions. They worried someone might see us on the short walk across the courtyard to the church. They feared their own people. Their jackets still held the black clover pins of the Black Murphys, but greed drove them. Their group could break—money was the wedge.

The transition inside the church came as a harsh adjustment. The glare of the sun stayed with me as bright green spots plagued my vision. Again, I wished to rub my eyes, but my captors would not allow it. Molly stood at the front of the church with a man dressed in dark robes—Father McElhenny. He was the priest I had left with the bag of cash. He stared as the guards pushed me forward.

My heart felt like it might tear from my chest. I glanced around us, but I saw no one who might come to our aid. The warden sat in the first row of pews and stood when I approached. He nodded toward the priest.

"Let's get this going," he said.

"Wait," Molly ordered. "We are still early. My father will be here."

The warden seemed nervous, as if he regretted this decision. He nodded, then studied me. I diverted my stare toward the ground, only daring to steal glances toward Molly. She wore a different dress this day—a deep sapphire blue. Though she still held herself composed as any heiress might. Reaching into her purse she produced a timepiece. After opening the face of the watch, she regarded the time, and then made a production of closing it.

I so wished to talk to her, to have her tell me of Aurora. But I bided my time. My heart beat faster with each passing minute. Whiskey always made this kind of thing easier, dulling the nerves. I stared toward the floor and closed my eyes, thinking back to the prairie grass and the sounds of the night. When the door at the back of the sanctuary opened, it startled me.

He stood in the doorway a moment, framed by the sunlight that streamed past his wide shoulders. Though his face escaped my vision, I instantly knew whom Molly had summoned to play this role—Pinkerton. I also knew how hard it must have been to ask this man for help. He stepped into the church with two men at either side. The warden walked toward them, pointing to one of his guards.

"I said nothing of an audience," he called out.

Pinkerton met him halfway down the aisle, his men staying close and flanking their employer. They wore dark suits. From how they bladed and protected their sides, they brought weapons with them. Pinkerton spoke. His accent fell upon the wooden pews and the marble floor. Only scraps of the conversation reached us. Pinkerton dismissed his men. They walked back the way they came. Pinkerton held open his jacket to show he concealed no weapon. He wore a fine tailored suit of thick wool. He had also upgraded his wardrobe to play this part.

Escorted by the warden, Pinkerton stopped in front of Molly. He embraced her, leaving a kiss upon her cheek. She remained cold and rigid—her feelings for him fit her role. The awkward distance painted her all the more as the disgraced heiress of this powerful man. He turned to me; his face held a neutral pose.

"This is the man, my dear?" He spoke to Molly.

"Yes, Father."

Pinkerton looked me up and down, as if laying eyes upon me for the first time. After our last encounter, I knew not what to expect. Molly had been right. He had used us for so long to his purposes, even grooming me as the Old Man's bodyguard because it fit his needs. He still placed his notion of loyalty to the nation ahead of us. That much we could count upon. But the fact he came to New York, where his safety was not guaranteed, counted for something. I couldn't be sure what it meant.

"And what are the chances he leaves your prison?" Pinkerton addressed the warden.

The warden smiled. "None. After the trial, he will swing. If it were up to me, we'd have buried him already, but General Dorsey wishes a more public display. He stole a large sum from the wrong men."

"It's not the money," Pinkerton replied.

"What is it about then? No one steals from General Dorsey."

"It's about the president. They wish a public display to discredit his testimony." Pinkerton stared at me while he said the last part.

"I'm surprised you're here then," I answered.

He diverted his eyes, avoiding my glare. Instead he looked to Molly.

"We've all made mistakes. Some are easier to fix than others."

His face softened, and something reflected in his eyes. Perhaps I imagined it, assigning meaning to something that had none. But now he seemed the man I had known before.

"Shall we?" Pinkerton motioned toward Father McElhenny.

"Sir, before we start there is a small matter . . ." the warden started, unsure of how to make his request. "What I mean to say is, we've assumed considerable risk for the sake of your daughter."

"Yes, I appreciate you looking after her honor in such a manner." Pinkerton looked to Molly. "I wished she had the same regard for our family name."

"No, sir, I think you misunderstand—"

Pinkerton cut him off. "I understand. You seek recompense for your efforts."

The warden appeared puzzled.

"Money. You want payment for your efforts," Pinkerton clarified.

"Yes. Though I meant not to be so blunt."

"Of course you did." Pinkerton's voice rang with annoyance. He played his part well, comfortable with the subterfuge—like Molly. "Once we finish here we will retire to your office and discuss further."

"Certainly, sir." The warden nodded to his two guards. The one who still held my arm released it and stepped aside. "Get on with it," he said to Father McElhenny.

The priest appeared anxious. Sweat beaded upon his forehead. One of the drops broke free and rolled until it launched itself off his eyebrow. He wiped his forehead. His hands were not steady. They shook the leather-bound Bible he held.

"You understand, this is most unusual," the priest said.

"Get on with it." The warden's tone held cruelty, as if he spoke to a broken dog.

"I am just uncertain where to begin. Normally we would have the opening prayer, readings, the gospel, a homily—"

"The Rite of Marriage. Start there. Will it suffice?" The warden looked to Pinkerton, who nodded.

"Very well." Father McElhenny began to open the Bible, but then stopped. "Please rise." He looked out at each of us. "We are all standing, I see." He stared to the cover of his Bible again, but it remained closed.

"My dear friends, you have come together in this church so that the Lord may seal and strengthen your love in the presence of the Church's minister and this community. Christ abundantly blesses this love. He has already consecrated you in baptism and now he enriches and strengthens you by a special sacrament so that you may assume the duties of marriage in mutual and lasting fidelity."

He adjusted his collar as he looked to the warden, then Pinkerton. He had been nervous when I first met him in the city, a meek type of man. Though his temperament now seemed excessive. With every few words he looked to the warden, or the two guards. I imagined he stared at their black clover pins.

"Joseph and Molly, have you come here freely and without reservation to give yourselves to each other in marriage?"

He looked to Molly. She nodded her consent. But when he locked eyes with me, he immediately looked away, toward my wrists. It seemed ridiculous to ask if I stood freely before him while so bound in chains. If he had only known the truth, it might have eased his nerves. Standing across from Molly, no manner of chains changed my desire to stand here with her.

"Will you love and honor each other as man and wife for the rest of your lives?"

"As short as they might be?" the warden added.

Pinkerton glared at the man. The warden shrank back a half step under the withering pressure of Pinkerton's stare. Father McElhenny's voice continued to falter. Though he pressed on as if he never noticed the exchange.

"Since it is your intention to enter into marriage, join your right hands, and declare your consent before God and his Church."

Molly reached out and took both my hands. In this entire ordeal, I hadn't truly looked at her. I feared what I might find there. But her grasp was warm and firm. Her thumbs caressed the back of my hands. She forgave me. I fought to maintain my composure. Even after everything, she still stood here—still with me.

"I'm sorry," I whispered.

"I know."

"Joseph, do you take Molly to be your wife? Do you promise to be true to her in good times and in bad, in sickness and in health, to love her all the days of your life?"

"I swear it, Molly."

"Molly," Father McElhenny continued, "do you take Joseph to be your husband? Do you promise to be true to him in good times and in bad, in sickness and in health, to love him and honor him all the days of your life?"

"I always have," she said.

"You have declared your consent before the Church. May the Lord in his goodness fill you both with his blessings."

Father McElhenny looked to the warden. A strange determination came across him. The warden sensed it, too.

"What God has joined, men must not divide."

Molly's hands shifted, still grasping mine. I only noticed when the first shackle came free from my wrist. Then the other—she had a key. Father McElhenny opened his Bible. The book contained a carved-out compartment, and within it a small Colt's revolver. Molly grabbed the weapon, pulling the hammer back and leveling the barrel upon the two guards.

The warden stepped forward, pulling back his jacket. He had a small revolver in a holster along his side. I grasped the chains in the middle, and swung them at him. The iron cuffs that had held my wrists struck him across the face. A tooth flew from his mouth, and he spun before falling face-first upon the marble floor. His fall made a sound as if I had dropped a watermelon upon the floor. I rushed to retrieve his weapon.

As I pulled it from his holster, the guards looked to one another. A man's intent always plays across his face. These men wouldn't be taken like this. They had too much to lose, especially if O'Malley discovered they had freed me from my cell. Even with the deception, they were dead. I tugged at the holster, attempting to free the weapon.

"Molly—" I yelled.

The first guard pulled his pistol with a speed that surprised me. The men that came with O'Malley when they sought us out in Tennessee had no gun skill. But this man was trained. The sound of the shot echoed in the church. It bounced off the marble in the sanctuary and crashed into the beautiful stained-glass windows. It deadened my hearing, and the flash from the muzzle brightened the space in front of us for but a moment. Then a second flash filled the church. Molly fell, with Pinkerton on top of her.

I threw the chains toward the man. He raised both hands to blunt the impact, pausing his onslaught. My other hand freed the warden's pistol. I pulled back upon the hammer as I presented the gun. Firing at the man, I hit him once—then twice. He fell.

The other guard stood on the far side of Molly and Pinkerton. He had half-drawn his weapon when he stopped, frozen. I held my gun upon him, staring him down while desperately wanting to get to Molly.

"Molly!"

She didn't answer.

Then the door at the front of the church opened. Pinkerton's two men stepped inside and began shooting through the open door—other prison guards were coming. The fire from Pinkerton's men deafened the room. We had only moments. Out of the corner of my eye, I saw the guard going for his gun. I pulled the trigger, and he sank to his knees, the barrel of his gun still in its holster. Then he fell forward upon the marble floor.

Setting my gun aside, I rushed to the floor. Pinkerton trapped Molly, lying on top of her. An ashen color had overtaken his face, and he fought for breath. I pulled Molly out, and searched her—nothing. She roused as I held her face. Grasping the back of her head, we looked at Pinkerton. He bled from his chest.

"I always hated this city," he muttered. "Go, Joseph. Take her."

His words scarcely made sense over the gunfire at the front of the church. I knelt beside him.

"I'll get you up," I urged.

"No. Give me the gun." He held a hand out for the pistol. "Give it to me, Joseph."

I tried to pull at him.

"Damn it! Let go of me." His voice came out raspy.

Blood pooled at his side, spilling forth from his wounds. He wouldn't make it much longer.

"Give it to me, Joseph. I owe you, son."

Another barrage of gunfire broke out. One of Pinkerton's men lay upon the floor. The other struggled to reload his gun. Prison guards breached the door of the church. I handed Pinkerton my pistol. Then I reached over him to retrieve a weapon dropped by one of the guards. Pinkerton took that gun as well.

"Prop me up. I'll cover you. Just get Molly. Find the Old Man and look after your daughter."

I grasped his hand for a moment. I couldn't leave him like this.

"Joseph . . . damn you. Either you go now or we all perish. I won't make it." He looked to his chest. "My mother always said I needed to spend more time in church."

I hesitated as Molly struggled to stand.

"Forgive me, Joseph." He raised one of the pistols toward the door and fired. "Go! I'll send regards to your mother for you."

I pulled Molly to standing, only stopping long enough to recover the other revolver. It was still partway in the holster of the fallen guard. Father McElhenny urged us around the back of the altar, toward a door.

"Take the stairs. It leads out back, then to the street," he said. He tried to take the pistol from my hand. "I'll stand with him."

I resisted for a moment, not letting him have the gun.

"I am tired of all they take from us," he urged.

I let go of it.

"Go with God, my son. And don't die on your wedding day."

Molly pulled my hand. I followed her through the door and to the stairs. Looking back, I managed one last glimpse of Pinkerton. He remained propped in front of the altar. Swearing at the men who fought their way toward him—firing a pistol from both hands.

CHAPTER EIGHTEEN

10 JULY 1874

THE FIRST SIGHT of Fort Laramie brought relief to all in our group. The white buildings of the fort sat perched on a slight rise, overlooking the place where the North Platte River met the Laramie before they both flowed toward the mighty Mississippi. We had walked and ridden along the trail from Independence, Missouri, for over a month. Each night we camped out under the stars. Molly had heard rumors of Oregon, or possibly California. They swirled in her head until she became drunk with the possibility of a fresh start. She dreamed of peace and happiness. We had tried my method of disabling the Consortium—cutting off its head to make the monster falter. I had failed. If Molly had listened to me and fled as I asked, I would still sit rotting in their prison, or worse. So now I followed her plans.

The Old Man had found us a guide for the trip across the Oregon Trail. Or rather, the guide found us. The man latched on with a keen sense of interest as our paths crossed. In general, I held him in low trust. He went by Jim Bridger—a man pushing into his seventh decade of life, yet full of spark and constitution. His skin was worn and leathery, and wispy white hair fell under his battered hat. He had been out west and back so many times that his feet wore their own path, leaving him wiry thin. I found it hard to hold any confidence in his stories. Each seemed more grandiose than the next. But he got on well with the children, especially Emeline, drawing her out of her shell. For long spells he sat in the wagon next to the Old Man, spinning yarns of fascinating geysers and unforgettable peaks of solid granite. If his experiences matched his bragging, then I conceded to the Old Man that he would be of use.

The fort itself sat upon the north shore of the Laramie River. The men who built it nestled the structures onto the wedge of land above the North Platte River. The water there flowed from the wild country above us. No stockade separated the buildings from the prairie, nor those who ventured upon it. The buildings stood in the open. Molly gazed upon them longingly. The magic allure of the West still called from beyond the fort, but its song had faded. Fort Laramie held safety. It was a place where we could camp and rest before deciding upon the next leg of the journey. And Molly could use a rest, perhaps a real bed for a few nights. Her pregnancy had started to show, with her dress tighter at the sides.

Other campsites speckled the land surrounding the fort. Wagons were parked nearby and horses picketed or turned loose to graze. We had followed the waning tide of wagon trains that flowed toward the plains. Most emigrants jumped off the Oregon Trail in the spring. They wanted to reach the mountains before the snows trapped them in the passes. Even with the lateness of the season, plenty of traffic worked the trail. There were Mormons who hoped to find the southern route, Swedes and German immigrants who might stop part way and tease a living out of the plains, rough French trappers who traded amongst the Indians for furs and provisions, and a steady flow of miners who had heard tales of the yellow metal that filled the Black Hills. Several tipis stood upon the grass in a cluster—their shape unique among the other camps. I stared toward them, hoping for some glimpse of the people there. They would be the first I had seen of Indians in the West. An ancestral curiosity tugged at me, though I fought the urge to walk over to them.

Aurora grabbed my hand and stood facing the Indian camp. She had to grab hold by cupping her fingers into her palm. I was getting used to the feel of it, though each time it made me burn with anger. I would kill O'Malley if we ever crossed paths.

"Do you think those are Grandmother's people?"

I grabbed her around the shoulder to pull her close.

"I don't know how to tell. There are many tribes who live upon the plains. And more were forced here."

"Should we talk to them?" she asked. "Do you know the language?"

I shook my head. "What little I remember came from your grandmother. I think they have a different tongue here. I doubt they would understand me."

Aurora watched, drawn in this time by the voices of children carried upon the wind. They darted in among the tipis, playing a game—the same as our children.

"Aurora, will you see how Molly is feeling?" The Old Man had come up behind us.

He handed Aurora a blanket. The wind had picked up, and we hadn't yet pitched the tent. He gave her a chore to give us time to speak.

"I've been thinking," the Old Man began, "that this place might be right to stay for a time. Molly grows more uncomfortable, and I'm not sure any of us can stand the children cooped in that wagon much longer."

"How long were you thinking?" I asked. For this journey I had let the Old Man and Molly dictate the direction, always under the advice of Mr. Bridger. He claimed to know the land.

"Through the winter." The Old Man turned to face me, gauging my reaction.

"We would have to build then," I answered. "I wouldn't want to venture a winter upon the plains in just a canvas tent."

The Old Man shook his head. "I was thinking of the fort. They have billeting and a surgeon for when the baby comes. The trail is no place to give birth, especially in the dead of winter. Perhaps in the spring this whole affair will have blown over and we can return home."

I looked to the fort, considering the Old Man's suggestion. From where we stood the buildings looked pristine, well maintained. A large flag flew over the parade ground. It reached above the roofs and tugged in the wind.

"I doubt they will let us stay. I imagine they only house the soldiers and their families. And even then, only those of the officers."

The Old Man pulled the wide-brimmed white hat from his head. He had used it in crossing the wild grasslands of Kansas. I had insisted on it as part of his wardrobe change. He traded his suits for homespun shirts and trousers of thick wool. One morning before our trip, he emerged without a beard. So long had it been a symbol of him that I could have passed him in the street without so much as a glimpse of recognition. Now, from behind his back, he pulled out his top hat. In an instant, he seemed himself again—the man I had guarded so many years ago—the man who had led the nation and then became mired in his office by the Consortium. Even without the beard he seemed presidential.

"Mr. Bridger knows the commander here. He believes if we ask, the major would grant quarters for the winter."

I nodded. Molly would want to press forward, but I could convince her to hold out until after the baby arrived. It held the best plan for our survival, especially as we were so late upon the season.

"Good," the Old Man said, laying a hand on my shoulder as he turned to walk away. "For I have already sent Mr. Bridger to arrange our meeting. He says the commander here is a good stout Union man, so we should have no trouble."

Molly fell into an uncomfortable sleep after we staked the tent. I prepared a light dinner for the children. They were more interested in darting to the edge of our campsite to see the Indian children across the way. When they spied each other, both parties dove back behind their tents with squealing voices—a game that seemed to tire none of them.

Aurora had the same curiosity that pulled at me. Perhaps the stories my mother shared with her had piqued her interest. Or maybe it came from somewhere deeper—some distant link to our people from long ago. Save her dark hair, she retained little that might betray native heritage. Her mother's skin, when mixed with mine, had washed Aurora even paler than I. With another generation any sign of our native origins would be lost to the ages. Time would only leave stories whispered around the fireplace on cold winter nights.

Mr. Bridger came back with an escort of several soldiers. They were anxious to see if his tall tale of having Abraham Lincoln amongst their midst held true. The lieutenant did not recognize the Old Man until he had perched his top hat in its rightful place. Once he did, he snapped to attention with a military formality rarely required on the plains. We left Molly napping and Aurora in charge of the children. The Old Man, Mr. Bridger, and myself climbed the hill to the fort.

The major stood at attention and greeted us warmly when we stepped into his office. He had not believed Bridger, either. The shock on his face betrayed this fact. He stammered at his words, then motioned to the chair across his desk. Bridger and the Old

Man took seats, while I stood behind them. The major paid me no attention—once more relegating me to the background. I rather enjoyed it, as I observed without having to join the conversation. They started by talking about why the Old Man traveled so far west and where we planned on heading. I didn't like the probing questions from the major. He wanted to know the size of our party and if we had need of an escort. The Old Man responded in a vague manner. He remained noncommittal to everything save the request for lodging.

"We have no open quarters, sir, but if you give me a few hours we'll clear out an officer's billet for your party."

"That would be most agreeable," the Old Man answered. "And please know that I hold it not for myself, but we have a woman along who is with child. She will need the comforts that a tent upon the prairie cannot provide. Tomorrow morning would be a fine time. Our companion is napping and likely asleep for the night. You do have a surgeon at camp?"

"We do, sir. I will make him available to the lady. Does she require immediate assistance?"

The Old Man shook his head.

"We are months from her labor. However, his services would be most appreciated in checking on her from time to time."

"A request I am happy to honor," the major replied. "Can you stay for supper? I am afraid we have already dined, but I am happy to have the cook make something to your tastes."

The Old Man shook his head. "We have children to attend to. Perhaps tomorrow after we have settled in our new accommodations?"

The Old Man rose from his seat. The major and Mr. Bridger stood with him. As I stepped to the door, a soft knock sounded on the thick wood. I opened it just enough to see out, as I would have done in years gone by when protecting the Old Man. A soldier stood at the door and held a telegram.

"For the commander," he said.

I took it from his outstretched hand, glancing at the note. I read it without appearing obvious—another trick Pinkerton had taught me. Turning toward the major, I handed it to him.

Hold them at Laramie. I have men riding from Sherman Barracks.

Fear surged through me, though it could have meant anyone. The hot breath of pursuit pressed against the back of my neck. I tried not to let it show. The major read the note, glancing up and folding it over. He looked straight at the Old Man as he looked up. The Old Man noticed it, too.

"I hope all is in order. Not grave news?"

The major shook his head. "Just word from the Yellowstone Expedition. They left from Fort Rice last week," he lied.

"Who is leading that?" Bridger asked. "I've heard nothing about an expedition to the Yellowstone."

His voice held some remnant of jealousy. No doubt he wished to have been asked for such an expedition, as it held the prospect of being quite lucrative.

"It's to open a route for the Northern Pacific Railroad. They need to finish a survey along the north shore of the Yellowstone River. They're bringing a huge troop column—nearly two thousand men, with cannon and cavalry."

"And who's in charge?" Bridger pressed again.

"General Dorsey," the major said. "He has Custer and the 7th Cavalry with him."

I fought to catch my breath. It had to be the same Dorsey who led the Consortium. Mr. Carson, the fat man on the train with the brass bell to call for help, had spoken of leading an expedition.

I hadn't considered that again, thinking Carson merely bragged and had no substance to his words. It must be the same expedition. The major folded the telegram over again and placed it in a desk drawer away from any prying eyes. He glanced to the Old Man who walked to the door. The major never looked at me, perhaps assuming I couldn't read.

"We've taken enough of your time today," the Old Man said. He grasped the major's hand.

"First thing in the morning, sir. I'll have quarters ready for you."

"That would be most accommodating. I appreciate your hospitality, Major."

I held the door for the Old Man, and we started out into the darkening night sky. Bridger stayed behind a moment. We could hear him asking if the expedition headed to the Black Hills. No doubt his thoughts turned to the gold men claimed they found there.

The Old Man looked straight ahead, then placed a hand on my shoulder.

"Sir, we can't stay here." I said it as quiet as my voice could manage.

At first I wasn't certain if he had heard me. Before he answered, he adjusted his hat and looked toward the last rays of the setting sun.

"I know."

CHAPTER NINETEEN

11–18 JULY 1874

THAT NIGHT THE Old Man and I huddled together after the others slept. Bridger occupied his own tent. His snoring reached us as we sat around the embers of the fire. Though we had traveled for more than a month, upon riverboats and endless days across the plains, we seemed never to have had a time like this—alone.

"I never told you that I was sorry for my testimony to Congress. I never meant it to hurt you."

"Don't be, Joseph." He looked to me. "You did what was right."

"But it changes things."

The entire country now knew the story of his colored mistress and their child. The papers wrote of how the Consortium killed his woman and how he embraced his daughter. Emeline slept in the tent with Molly. There was no mistaking her lineage.

"It does. But it lifted a burden. Instead of a whole nation, I now only need to watch over one little girl. I'm not certain which shall be easier."

I looked back to the fire. Despite his words, I hoped he would not hold it against me. He rested a hand upon my shoulder.

"I am sincere in this, Joseph. I feel no trespass against me. Did you know that some papers likened me to Jefferson?"

With those words my guilt dissolved. He had always aspired to match Jefferson. No doubt the papers referenced the rumors that Jefferson had a colored mistress of his own and children with her. But the Old Man loved the comparison. All was forgiven between us. And he did appear much relieved. He walked like a young man, strength returning to his body. Even his disposition had lightened considerably, more than it had back in Essary Springs.

"Where do we go now, Joseph?"

The Old Man steered the conversation back to the practical. We had more pressing issues. I thought about it for a moment, weighing the options.

"If we flee farther west, they will overtake us. Sherman Barracks is along the Missouri, I believe. I'm not certain how long we have."

"Well, if we cannot stay, and we cannot continue, and we cannot return home, then we have little choice," the Old Man said. "We have only two directions."

"They will expect us to turn south," I answered. "It's warmer, and no one would willingly head north into Sioux country."

"Then we go north," the Old Man said.

"You could stay," I suggested. "Keep Emeline and the other children here. I suspect they want us, not you. And they couldn't harm you, not without exposing the Consortium."

The Old Man shook his head. "I will not leave your side. It is my turn to watch over you. And neither of us have Mr. Pinkerton to rely upon any longer."

I nodded. "Then we should pack and move now, get a few hours in before dawn."

"We'll have to wake Bridger," the Old Man said. "We'll need him."

"Can we trust him?"

"We can trust his love of gold," the Old Man said. "We'll tell him we wish to rendezvous with the expedition, then head north to Fort Benton. The Mullan Road extends west there, over the Rockies and to Washington. We could get Molly to the fort before winter."

After I woke Bridger and explained, it took less prodding than I anticipated. The Old Man had guessed his intentions. Bridger wanted to head north—toward the expedition. In fact, as we packed he kept talking about the Bozeman Trail and how it held the best route over the Rockies. He had been to Fort Benton and described it as utopia. He neglected to say anything of the hostile tribes north of the Platte Valley, nor the packs of wolves that followed wagon trains along the trail. His tall tales were renowned.

I woke Molly gently. She took the news better than I expected. While the Old Man and I tore down the tent, she remained tight-lipped and prepared the children. We broke camp in under an hour and took extra time to arc wide of the fort. I wanted none of the sentries to know we had left. It seemed the major had not posted a watch to ensure we remained camped along the Laramie.

We rode hard the first day, and then into the next, only stopping for a few hours of sleep upon the prairie. Bridger came alive at the prospect of the journey, though he kept drifting to the rear of our group and searching behind us. When I asked him for the cause of this behavior, he dismissed it as old habit. In truth, I watched to our rear as well, fearing that the major of Fort Laramie had sent soldiers in pursuit.

When we stopped each night, we did not bother to unpack a tent. The weather stayed fair, and I placed the children under the wagon in case it began to rain. By the third day, we approached another fort on the Northern Platte River—Fort Fetterman. We waited until dark and then made our way around it. Bridger never asked why I pressed the pace, taking more than twenty miles a day. He even helped us around the fort, ensuring we were out of sight of the sentries. With another day, we turned onto the old Bozeman Trail. It calmed my worry as we headed north. Dorsey's men wouldn't expect this. The trail had been off-limits to white settlers since Red Cloud's War five years earlier. But Bridger knew the trail, and he spoke the languages. He insisted he knew Red Cloud personally, and that the tribes would be hunting in the east toward the Black Hills.

Bridger's paranoia played on me now, too. I watched the horizon behind us, even as we disappeared into the prairies to the north. Bridger seemed to slow our pace, constantly watching the hillsides to the west and the rolling grassland to the east. He wished to stop often and rest the horses. We followed his lead. Resting the animals assured we had them in case the need arose. Whenever I stared behind us, no one followed.

As the mountains loomed, Aurora became excited. She would stare at them, pointing to the outcrops in the foothills while telling me she saw sheep, or wolves. My eyes could never find them. My favorite times were sitting next to her while driving the wagon.

"What are those called, Father?" she asked, pointing to the north and off to our left.

"I don't know."

"How about those?"

This time she pointed to the east. I shook my head.

"Those are the Black Hills," Bridger said, pulling his horse alongside the wagon. He had been watching them as they drew closer with every day we spent heading north.

"The *Paha Sapas*?" she asked.

I drew the wagon to a stop and stared at her. I had heard those words before. The vision of my mother lying under that white sheet came to me. She had pulled me close and said the same words—the ones I didn't know. I let my mouth form the sounds, repeating them to Aurora.

"*Paha Sapas?*" My mother's voice echoed in my head. Those were among her last words.

"The Black Hills, Father."

"Where did you hear that?" I asked.

"Grandmother. She said if we were in trouble to head to the *Paha Sapas* and find her people."

"You never told me this before."

"I thought you knew," she said. "Grandmother told me that her father was *Man Walks Alone*, from Chief Šóta's lodge."

My mother had rescued Aurora from a small farm in Georgia, where Colonel Norris had secreted her away. During the journey home, she confessed our family history to Aurora—more than she had ever admitted to me. She was not full Miami Indian. Her father had come from a great Oglala Sioux lodge on the plains. I started the wagon again and looked toward the hills. I had never heard the name Chief Šóta before. Molly had been lying in the wagon behind the seat. She reached up and held my arm. Aurora held the key to where we should go. I released a deep breath, and with it the tension I had carried since Ft. Laramie. We were on the right path.

After a week of plodding over the overgrown trail, we finally heard the telltale rush of flowing water. Bridger urged us upstream to a place we could fjord the Powder River. The spot he chose led us down to the water. With the horses pulling the wagon, we had no trouble diving into the river and dragging the load up and across the far shore. From there we headed east. As the sun set, we came upon the remains of Fort Reno, an old outpost along the Bozeman Trail. After the war with Red Cloud for control of the Powder River Valley, the Bozeman had closed. Red Cloud's warriors harassed the retreating soldiers all the way to the Platte River. Then they burned the forts along the trail. But there were ruins here, enough to pitch a tent against and have a hard wall at our backs. And the children could use a few days off, not to mention Molly. In truth, it would be nice to have fresh fish for dinner.

Fort Reno sat on a finger of land that stretched into the Powder River. Fire had consumed much of the structure as Red Cloud's warriors swept south. But some elements resisted the blaze. Part of an adobe building remained, though the walls were black with soot where the fire scorched the hardened clay. The ruins of several blockhouses dotted the corners of the fort. They stood like old footprints preserved in dry mud. Outlines of rectangular buildings sat amongst the ruins, burned to the bottom logs. They were likely storehouses or garrison buildings—impossible to tell once so consumed by flames.

We unloaded the wagon near the adobe structure and pitched the tent inside the old building. The children dismounted from the wagon and searched for relics amongst the burnt ruins. Molly gathered wood to make dinner. It would be too late to head to the river for fish, but at first light, I planned on taking Daniel and Aurora to teach them. I felt certain fish aplenty lived just under the surface of the rough water. We would bring back a surprise for Molly, who had grown tired of the corn meal and salt pork with beans.

Unpacking the wagon, I picketed the horses nearby. I gave them enough room to eat in their feedbags. Then I started the fire to put on coffee and warm the corn meal.

"We'll stay here a few days?" Molly asked as I worked.

I nodded. "I don't think they'll risk coming up the Bozeman after us. Too many rumors of Indians nearby."

"Why are they still after us? Is it the money?"

We had bags of it left, enough to live comfortably when we arrived in Oregon or California. Still, I thought it unlikely the Consortium pursued because of the lost cash.

"We have nothing else."

"The ledger," Molly answered. "And those other papers. Do you think they are important?"

"We could show the Old Man. He might know better than us. I can't see why. General Dorsey didn't seem interested in the ledger before."

"Maybe that was on purpose," Molly said, "so we wouldn't know its importance."

I turned to the fire as the children came up. They had found a few arrows. Some still had the fletching of feathers near the nock—where the string fit. I held one in my hand.

"Are they old?" Molly asked. Her tone became concerned.

The wooded shafts had aged in the sun and warped with the rain.

"Yes. Though the arrowheads are long and made of iron."

Mr. Bridger and the Old Man neared the small fire. They had been scouting the river.

"There are boats still along the water, 'bout a mile down along the shore," Bridger said. "The Sioux must have missed them when they burned the fort. We could take them downriver."

He reached for one of the arrows, examining it as he spun it about the point of the iron tip.

"The river flows east," I said. "We head north."

"I just thought it might be easier on the little lady to float on down the water, rather than stay in that wagon the entire time."

I studied his face.

"Or heading east gets you closer to the expedition?" I asked. "The Powder River empties into the Yellowstone, doesn't it?"

"Make no mind of it then," Bridger said, trying to distract us from his intent.

I wanted to be nowhere close to Dorsey and his expedition.

Though I tried not to reveal our need to stay clear of the soldiers venturing into Indian country from the east.

"Are the boats water-worthy?"

"We found them under oilcloths," the Old Man answered. "Seems they are in good enough shape, sheltered from the weather as they were."

"And how is the river here? No rapids or falls?" I made sure to look at Mr. Bridger as I asked the question.

"Not this time of year," he said.

"The water might flow slower in July, but doesn't that mean the rocks are higher?" I asked.

Bridger nodded.

"We'll stick to the wagon," Molly said.

Bridger tipped his hat toward Molly. "Yes, ma'am." Then he walked toward his tent to begin fixing it for the night.

"I don't trust him," Molly said. She held her voice low.

"As long as he thinks there's something in it for him, he won't abandon us. And we'll need him if we encounter the Lakota. None of us know the language."

"We could offer to pay," the Old Man suggested. "We haven't talked about that."

"It might be best. Can you work out a sum?" I asked.

The Old Man nodded. "Let me talk to him."

As he walked away, I helped Molly to her feet.

"I'll round up the children. It's getting late, Joseph. Let's eat and get them to bed."

I kissed her on her forehead. She leaned her head against my chest and clutched me for a moment.

"I don't like this place," she said. "It feels wrong—the burned-out walls, the old fort, Mr. Bridger. It all feels wrong."

"It will be fine. We all need the rest. Just a few days, and then we can move."

"Just a few days." Molly brushed past me and made for the direction of the children's voices.

That night the air turned cold, as if it flowed from the distant mountains and followed the river. Even in the tent the ground tugged at me, pulling the heat from my body. It might have been the proximity to the river, but I understood what Molly meant now. This place felt different. The trail so far had energy about it, something familiar, though it escaped my memory. My mother would have said the ancestors spoke. But I doubt they would have recognized me—a half-breed who lived in the white man's world. Yet something about the country appealed to me. It called me forth and drew me north into the plains beyond the Bozeman. I just couldn't figure what held the attraction.

As I lay in the tent, the howl of a wolf echoed over the hills. They had followed us all week, singing us to sleep while marking our progress upon their land. But this night, it was just a single wolf. With dawn only an hour away, it seemed an odd time of night. Even the song seemed different. I waited for the others to join in. They did not. Every other night we had heard the serenade of the pack. This was different, and it bothered me.

Slowly I sat up and pushed the covers off, trying not to make any noise that might wake Molly or the Old Man. The children slept well, but Molly grew restless at night. I grabbed for my jacket, hanging on a tent pole, and walked outside into the night. The moon hung bright overhead. Bridger's snoring issued forth from his tent.

I walked toward the horses, picketed a short distance away. They stirred, but didn't seem spooked. The howls continued to echo in the hills. I wondered how this wolf became separated and what its song meant. Then I spotted her, up on the slight rise that led toward the river and the fort, amongst the sagebrush. She

moved fast, white and lean. Stopping, she leaned back and continued her homage.

I closed my eyes and let it wash over me. I breathed deep of the
night. Then as suddenly as it had started, she finished. I searched
for her. She scampered up the incline, running as fast as she dared.
The horses kicked the ground. I walked to the first of them and
placed my hand on his nose. He twisted his head and pushed me
away. Then he stamped the dirt, scraping at it. The others did the
same.

I strained against the night so I might hear what they did—
nothing. Not satisfied, I moved to the wagon and stood upon
the empty seat. The canvas cover blocked part of my view, but
I scanned the trail we rode in upon. The moonlight fell bright
here. Off in the distance a thin snake of dust built and reached
skyward. I strained to see better, then turned my head to listen.

Riders.

CHAPTER TWENTY

I FLEW INTO the tent, throwing back the flap. The moonlight bathed the interior, falling in a wedge that framed Molly on the bed. She roused.

"Molly, get up. Get the children." My voice came out loud, not hushed as it should have been. She sat upright. I grabbed my Henry rifle and a satchel that contained my extra ammunition. Then I pulled the covers off the Old Man at the other end of the tent.

"Joseph, what is it?" he asked. Sleep still gripped him.

"I need you. They're here."

I ran back outside to wake Mr. Bridger. He met me at the door of his tent as he pulled at his suspenders.

"What is it?" he asked. He already had his rifle in his hand.

"Horses. They're coming."

He eyed me solemnly. "Who is coming?"

"Men with whom none of us would wish to exchange words."

The expression upon his face told me he heard the distant footfalls of the horses.

"Perhaps they travel like us."

"At this time of the night? Upon the Bozeman?" I asked. "Not likely."

"We can wait and find out."

"This is not the time," I said. "These men have not pursued us to talk."

"Who are we running from?" he asked.

We hadn't explained it to him—on purpose. I paused, thinking of what to explain as I looked over my shoulder in the direction they would appear. The Old Man walked over.

"Evil pursues us. There is no other way to describe it," he said. His voice remained calm as he cocked the lever of his rifle to load the first round.

"You told me nothing of this," Bridger exclaimed. "What men?"

"Railroad men," I said. "They wish us for their purposes, and I intend not to be taken."

I ran to the wagon, which still contained our supplies. The distant hill opposite our camp echoed the heavy horse footfalls. We had only minutes.

"I'm not paid for this," Bridger said.

"They'll kill you, too," I replied. "For sport."

"Then I want double."

My grip turned white upon my rifle. Even at a time like this, he angled for himself. In some manner I knew it to be fair. We had told him nothing about possible pursuers.

"Fine. Get the horses ready."

Molly arrived outside the tent, pulling clothes onto the little ones. She hadn't taken the time to put on her own dress. The moon caught the white of her undergarments.

"How long, Joseph?"

We paused to listen. I stared at the horses. None were bridled. The wagon harness hung limp. We'd never get them moving in time.

"Where were the boats?" I asked the Old Man.

"You can't be serious?" he asked.

"I am. Get Molly and the children moving toward the water."

I ran to the wagon and pulled out the other satchel—the one that contained the ledger and all the corporate paperwork. I kept the papers inside bound in oilcloth to keep dry. I would not leave it to be reclaimed so easy. If this held the key to why they pursued us, then it might be our only means of escape.

Halfway down the bluff, I caught up with the others. Molly hadn't time to don a dress, and I knew what manner of mood that would bring forth in her. It mattered little for the time being. I picked up Daniel and held Aurora's hand. The Old Man carried Emeline. Bridger followed behind—ever slow. At a time like this, he felt like an anchor. Every few steps I turned back toward our camp, certain they would stand perched above us. We were in the open, dropping below the high ground. If they chose, they would cut us down as we ran. The fully stocked camp might buy some time as they stopped to check the tents.

We reached the river in a frenzy. Despite the colder air of night, I had soaked through my shirt. Scrambling along the bank, we found the boats. There were four, lined up and turned over to prevent the seasonal rains from filling their hulls. Each had a wide flat bottom, meant to navigate across the rapids of the Powder River. The Old Man and I righted one and launched it into the water.

We placed the children in first. Then I helped Molly settle into the bow. Together the Old Man, Bridger, and myself pushed the boat into the water. We splashed without care for the noise—escape within our grasp. As I handed a set of oars into the boat, the snap of a bullet flew over my head. A moment later the echo of the shot bounced off the hills on the other side of the river. Another fell on us—then more. The river splashed, issuing forth a small tower of water at each place a bullet ripped into the current.

Several men stood on the high side of the bluff. A few formed a firing line, while others raced toward us. I pushed the boat further into the water.

"Get their heads down!" I pointed toward the children.

Mr. Bridger and I took the oars. We pulled, forcing the boat into the current. As the water caught our vessel, I realized we had left the other boats upon the shore. I grabbed my rifle from the bottom of the boat and handed my oar to the Old Man. I took aim at the overturned boats we left along the river, struggling to hold their wooden hulls in my sights.

"You won't hit them from here," Bridger yelled over the report of my rifle. He thought I fired at the men on top of the bluff.

"I'm trying to hit the boats."

It took him a moment, but he realized what I meant. He handed the other oar to the Old Man and pulled his gun from the bottom of the boat. We both took aim now, emptying our rifles upon the darkened shapes still under the oilcloth. Once empty, we couldn't reload in the pitching current. I prayed to the Great Spirit that some of the bullets had found their mark. The holes might make the remaining boats leak if not outright unworthy for the river.

The gunshots from the bluffs died as our boat floated out of range. We turned our attention to the river. The current tugged at us, and we flowed downriver faster than any horse could keep pace upon the shore. I took stock of what supplies we managed in the escape—almost nothing.

Molly sat in the bow, clutching all three children—despondent. She wouldn't catch my eye. This had been her plan, to flee west. And yet we hadn't escaped the Consortium. They pursued us still. I had managed to keep the two satchels—one with my ammunition and one with General Dorsey's ledger.

The Old Man pulled at the oars, keeping the boat aligned with the middle of the river. He couldn't prod the vessel any faster and still steer us free of obstacles in our path. I strained to see the water ahead. Here the river flowed faster than I anticipated, the power of the water coursing beneath us. Though at my feet, the boat was losing the fight against the water. It trickled in from somewhere along the hull. These boats had baked in the sun for years, without anyone to repair or patch any cracks. I reached with my hands to bail it out.

"Pull the water out!" I yelled.

Molly looked down and began grabbing handfuls to throw over the sides. The children helped as well.

"How long can we last like this?" she asked.

I scanned the bluffs, where the men would come with their horses—nothing. Ahead and to our right the sun began to rise, turning the horizon gray.

"Stay at it," I said. "We need to keep this boat together as long as we can. Let's get as far downriver as we might make."

Mr. Bridger joined in our futile attempt to keep the water out. He pulled his hat from his head and filled it. I followed his lead and used mine as well.

I kept watch along the shore, expecting to see a column of riders at any moment. After bailing for a time, I sat up. We had at least pulled even with the seeping water, but I needed a moment to catch my breath. With the early sun, the river behind us came into view.

"Joseph—" Molly pointed behind us. "There's a boat."

"Where?" I turned to scan upriver.

Sure enough, two boats headed after us. We must not have hit them well enough, or they managed to patch the holes and launch the old vessels. We were at a straight section of river. If we could see them, they knew we were just ahead. Our only fortune came in the nature of the river. It held plenty of twists and turns, and we would be out of sight in short order.

I traded places with the Old Man, pulling on the oars with all my strength. He used my hat and scooped up the water lapping at our feet. In rapid succession we hit several rocks, low in the water. The boat groaned, yet held together. But the water filled faster. The life of our vessel faded fast.

Around each turn I checked over my shoulder. They closed. The gray masses in the boats became individual men, though I could not make out faces. Occasionally, they took a shot. The bullets sailed harmlessly over our heads or ricocheted against the banks. Their boats pitched in the current as much as ours. We held our fire.

"Is there a good place to beach the boat?" I yelled to Bridger. I hoped he knew this portion of the river. My thought was to flip the craft and use it as cover, surprising them as they came upon us after a bend in the river. We could take a few of them with steady aim.

"It won't matter much longer," he replied. "The rapids up ahead will take us."

"What rapids?"

"I've never seen it this low," he answered. "In the next few turns there are rapids with a big rock shelf. It drops over. This boat won't stay together."

"You're the one who wanted to take the boats." Molly mentioned Bridger's suggestion earlier that day. In her frustration she lashed out. Without a dress her mood only soured.

"This boat won't last, not over those rocks. If there was more water—"

"Tell me where," I cut him off.

He pointed ahead.

"Point it out when we're upon it. When we're out of sight, we'll pull the boat to the shore."

He nodded and continued to bail water. It had risen above our ankles, and the boat slowed. When I pulled at the oars, it no longer surged. Now it seemed we floated down a river of molasses while our pursuers floated atop fast-moving water.

"This turn," Bridger yelled.

The noise of the water rose. We fast approached a monster from which there would be no escape. The Old Man grabbed an oar, and as we rounded the bend, we both pulled with all our strength to bring the boat to shore. It beached itself in a shallow sandbar without any form of cover.

Frantically, we pulled the children from the boat. Then I threw out the rifles and the satchels. Even with the Old Man and Mr. Bridger, we couldn't flip the boat over to use as a barrier. Too much water anchored it to the shore. I took one look at Molly and then grabbed the Old Man's arm.

"Help me push it back in the water."

"But, Joseph, we need it—"

"No! Help me get it back in."

The Old Man and I pushed at the stern, throwing our weight against the half-submerged boat. It lumbered back into the current. I stepped into the water and then hopped into the back of the boat. Molly locked eyes with me for but a moment. I turned to look behind me. They weren't yet in sight.

Forcing my weight against the oars, I pulled hard. The boat moved, dragging itself into the fast-moving water. Again and again I thrashed with the oars, while peering ahead into the foaming river. The water percolated with such furor against the large boulders that it threw a fine mist into the air. A bullet flew past me. They were close. Then one hit the boat above the waterline and blew out a section of plank. Hot pain from sharp metal tore into my leg. At least a portion of the bullet struck me in the calf.

I stopped pulling with the oars. I had nothing left to do. The water rose too fast in the boat. And the current held me in its grip. I threw the oars to the bottom of the boat where they floated. Then I searched the shore. There had to be a place to bail out.

As I drifted into the mist, I found what I sought—a sandbar with several large boulders. I hurled myself from the boat and into the water. The current dragged me under. I fought, flogging the river in an attempt to reach the sandbar. My fingers caught upon a rock outcrop. I grabbed hold. No sooner had I held it than the water tore me free. But it changed my trajectory. I rammed into another large boulder and flung onto the edge of the sandbar. The breath completely knocked out of me, the current had ripped the boots from my feet, and my fingers bled. But I was alive.

I lay on that sandbar as voices drew forth from the mist. Men yelled, calling out the location of the rocks in the current. The first boat passed. Once they were out of sight, a sickening sound of splintering wood rose above the turbulent river. The next boat came so close I could have leapt into its hull if I had the energy. None of the men saw me, save the last one, the man at the oars. He stared, not even bothering to reach for a weapon to fire. He had no time. I recognized the hat upon his head—a gray felt Stetson with an eagle feather—Charley's hat. A white forelock of hair hung underneath it, plastered against his forehead. *O'Malley.*

The boat disappeared into the mist. As it passed, everything stood still. It was like the noise of the river had been swallowed. Nothing else existed except for O'Malley and me staring at each other in the midst of the raging water. Then, in an instant, the sound crashed back upon me. His boat disappeared into the whiteness. The splintering of wood rose above the rushing water, followed by screams piercing the mist-laden air.

I waited a moment. Nothing else followed. There were no noises of man—just the continual rush of the water wearing down the rocks. I struggled to my feet. I studied the sandbar, choosing the upriver end to plunge back into the water. This time I faced the shore. The water moved much slower on this far side, and I made it to the shoreline with little struggle. Crawling on my hands and knees, I ventured to stand and walk back toward Molly and the others.

I stepped slow along the shore, amongst the sagebrush and the jagged rocks. My calf bled. I pulled a small piece of metal from it, and the blood poured down my leg until it mixed with the river. The fragment hadn't gone deep. It would heal fast. Up ahead, voices rose above the water. Around the bend, I found Molly clutching the children. The Old Man and Mr. Bridger stood motionless, facing the shore. When I neared, they saw me, yet no one came to my aid. Even Molly remained stoic. I clutched my side and stepped among the rocks, stumbling closer.

"Joseph—" Molly's attention remained fixed upon the bank of the river.

I stopped to look. Six men stood on the embankment above us, leveling rifles in our direction. Paint decorated their faces in lines of vermillion and black. Each had at least one eagle feather in their braided dark hair.

The Lakota had found us.

CHAPTER TWENTY-ONE

EVEN IF WE had wished to make a stand, we had little means to resist. The Indians had the high ground. Their party numbered at nine. Each carried a Henry repeating rifle—likely taken from battles with soldiers upon the plains. I had no breath to fight and no boots upon my feet. Mr. Bridger held his rifle above his head, indicating we came in peace. They approached cautiously. Several came down the embankment toward us. One at a time, they took our rifles. They claimed my satchel with the ammunition, but threw the other upon the ground when they saw it contained only the ledger and papers. I picked it up as we climbed the riverbank.

When we all assembled on top of the embankment, their leader sent two of his men downriver. I assumed they searched for survivors from the other boats. Molly stayed near me, while Aurora gripped my hand. The warriors spoke to me as if I might understand. Mr. Bridger tried to explain.

"They want to know if you're Lakota," Bridger said.

"My mother came from the eastern tribes."

"But your grandfather was Oglala," Aurora said.

She disappeared behind my back as the men shifted focus to her. Bridger spoke to them.

"You cannot speak Lakota?" he asked me.

I shook my head.

The one in charge stepped before me. He stood so close that when he spoke, his breath fell upon my face. Bridger translated.

"He is Yellow Knife. They were scouting for soldiers when they found us. Now he will take us to his village council, and the chiefs will decide our fate."

He motioned to the endless expanses of prairie in front of us. Nothing upon those rolling hills broke the light of the sun. No obstacle marred the horizon for as far as my eyes could discern.

We walked for the better part of the day before making a crude camp along a lightly treed creek. The heat of the afternoon rose with each step until I thought we had entered an oven. The grass steamed under the unrelenting pressure of it. For the most part, the warriors were silent. When they spoke, their voices stayed low. Yet they always watched us. Only Bridger could understand. Several times he engaged Yellow Knife. These men were Hunkpapa Sioux, from the village of Rain-in-the-Face—a prominent chief upon the plains. They had tracked O'Malley and his men after they crossed the Platte River.

Without shoes, my feet bled badly by the end of the first day. Molly remained tight to my side throughout. Both Aurora and Daniel clustered around her. Before we fled that morning, Molly had the good sense to pull on shoes. Aurora walked beside us, her curiosity building. She watched these strange men, recording their every word and action to memory. Little by little, the fear lifted from her. She ventured to walk on her own, though never more than a step or two from the safety of my side. Daniel acted more hesitant, while no daylight separated Emeline and the Old Man.

Yellow Knife appeared the eldest amongst his party. His long dark hair parted in the middle. He fastened it with rawhide strapping behind his head in a ponytail. The others wore their hair in a similar manner, or in two long braids to either side. They fashioned antelope skin into leggings, each adorned with beads along the side seam. All but Yellow Knife wore a loose-fitting tunic, also made from antelope or deerskin. Yellow Knife had a wool jacket of a cavalry officer, another spoil of war. It must have been hot in the July sun, though he likely wore it as symbol. Each of his warriors had at least one eagle's feather braided into their hair—a reward for a brave deed facing their enemy in battle. Yellow Knife had four.

We headed due north. Their village camped at some point between the Powder and the Tongue rivers. When the walk proved slow, Yellow Knife ordered Molly and the children to the horses. At first Molly refused. She had never ridden bareback before, and she feared falling and injuring the baby. But she relented when I walked at her side. Yellow Knife took an interest in her, trying to use sign language. Mr. Bridger told him we were married and she expected our child. He pretended to ignore her after that exchange. I felt certain they had never seen a white woman with red hair. They pointed to her and reached to her hair when it blew in the wind.

Late in the day, the two scouts returned to the group. They had counted several coups—killing the men from O'Malley's party. Mr. Bridger heard them discuss it that night. One had killed two white men, but they remained perplexed. These men wore uniforms, yet not those of soldiers. They dressed in gray. One of the scouts returned with a Bowler hat, the kind O'Malley and his men wore. He also had fixed one of the pins to his own shirt—a black cloverleaf. The victory that day included a rifle. It was a new Winchester model, polished and carved with intricate designs. I had seen one like it before, on the train car that kidnapped me from Essary Springs, the one with Mr. Carson—a pretty firearm meant for hanging over a mantel, not for life upon the plains. I was certain there were others, though they had been lost to the river. The two scouts also returned with scalp locks, taken from the dead men. They proudly displayed them for all to see, and reveled in Molly's disgust. None had the telltale white forelock.

We moved across the prairie the next day, and my feet continued to bleed. From afar the grassland appeared as a waving sea, soft and beckoning. In reality, the rough grass cut the bottoms of my feet. Yellow Knife and his warriors never once bound our hands, nor threatened in any manner. We couldn't escape, nor would it have been wise to make such an attempt. On our first break in the day, Yellow Knife produced an extra pair of moccasins from supplies strapped to his horse. He held up my Henry rifle, and then brought it to his chest. Then he handed me the moccasins.

"He wants a trade," Mr. Bridger translated.

I nodded, the intent obvious enough. I held no position to refuse. With my feet bleeding upon the harsh grass of the prairie, I felt it a fair trade. The moccasins fit tight, but were a welcome relief as we plodded onward through the rising sun.

"What do we do after we arrive?" the Old Man asked. He had walked up next to me, carrying Emeline upon his shoulders.

"We ask for permission to cross. Maybe for horses."

"Though we have nothing to trade?" the Old Man replied.

"We can warn them of the soldiers. Perhaps they will not know that General Dorsey leads an expedition from the east."

"They have scouts," the Old Man said. "If the columns are as big as the major at Fort Laramie claimed, they will know."

Late in the afternoon we saw the first signs of cooking fires. Plumes of darkened smoke lifted along the horizon. They looked like the smoke of a steamer ship over the swells of an ocean of grass. We managed our first view of the village only after we crested the final hill and headed toward a large creek.

Tipis broke the plains landscape, spread in concentric rings around a common area. Horses were picketed away from the village, some tied in groups, others held behind a crude corral. From the distance, the village looked miniature. It resembled a model— the kind I had seen in Washington where artists re-created great battles. If not for the distant cries of children and the barking of dogs, I might have thought myself back in Washington, looking at one of those miniatures. Yellow Knife paused on this hill. He knelt and looked out over his village. I couldn't tell if he admired the view, or if the practice held some greater meaning. Perhaps he told lookouts we had arrived. Or maybe he prayed to the Great Spirit that he had returned safe—with trophies.

When we made our way forward, the calls went out. A village crier made our presence known. Children came from everywhere to stare at the strangers. Women stood near the entrances of their lodges as we passed. Some wore cradleboards on their backs carrying infants. Others tended to the fires beside their lodges. They examined each of us, but Molly garnered the most attention. They stared at her and spoke to one another. Many of them quieted when they noticed me, perhaps thinking I spoke their language.

Yellow Knife led us through the village, stopping in front of a lodge with a cold cooking fire in front. He spoke to Bridger.

"He wants the women and children to remain here. This is his lodge, and he will have them fed. But they must remain inside. His mother will come with food and clothes for your wife. The rest of us will meet Rain-in-the-Face and his council."

I turned to Molly, but before I said anything, she clutched my arm.

"Do not leave me here, Joseph."

Her eyes held fear. This had not been what she planned when she sought to escape across the plains. Aurora and Daniel realized it. Daniel clung close and tight to Molly. The Old Man stepped forward. He labored a moment to put Emeline on the ground. The girl did not fully grasp what happened around her. She held her father's hand.

"Perhaps they will allow me to stay with the women, and you and Mr. Bridger could meet with the chief. My days of politics are over, and I suspect they might trust you more, Joseph. Here, I am the fox in the henhouse."

Mr. Bridger started to translate, but Yellow Knife cut him off. He nodded as if he followed the conversation. Then holding open the flap to his lodge, he stood aside so we could see. It stood empty, with little in the way of possessions. A cold hearth filled the center of the space, and several piles of buffalo robes sat around the edge of the lodge. He must have been a bachelor or else a widower who had not claimed another wife.

"There's no one inside, Molly," I pleaded. "And Mr. Lincoln will stay behind. Please, we'll need to talk to the chief to figure a means north."

Molly let go of my arm, her hand sliding down until it stopped at my wrist, and then let go. I grabbed hold of it and pulled her to face me. My other hand held her head. Drawing her near, I kissed her.

"I will never leave you." My hand fell to rest on Aurora's head. I looked to the little girl. "Or you."

I motioned to Yellow Knife. He had watched us speak. I began to suspect that he spoke English yet hadn't let on. With a nod he started toward the large cluster of tipis, leading the way. Aurora followed the Old Man into the lodge. Molly stood outside and waited until we disappeared into the maze of the village.

Yellow Knife's lodge had been on the outermost ring. Perhaps he held low status, though I suspected it signified something else. He wore the soldier's jacket. And with so many feathers to mark his courage, the position of his lodge might have been born in practicality. He could rise to defend the people at the slightest provocation. Whatever the reason, it meant we had to traverse the entire village. A gaggle of children and dogs followed. The little people ran ahead and appeared at every turn. They giggled to themselves, stalking our progress. Mostly they wore the same kind of clothes as the warriors—deerskin frocks and buckskin trousers. The dogs showed less fear. They nipped at our heels until we kicked them back.

At the heart of the village we came to a grand common area and a great lodge. It measured several men tall with two cooking fires out front. The door opened toward an expansive common area, and Yellow Knife motioned for us to remain outside. He ducked inside the flap, leaving Mr. Bridger and myself waiting.

Some of the children started to test their bravery. Amongst them the boys dashed by, daring to hold out a hand to touch one of us. They would run off howling with delight, to encourage their friends in the exploit.

"They're practicing for the days when they become warriors," Bridger said.

I ignored his comment. We had more important things to focus upon.

"How much do you know about this chief?" I asked.

"He's your age, maybe younger. Fought against the Army with Red Cloud over the Bozeman Trail. He helped burn out the forts when the soldiers withdrew."

"Can you broker our way north?"

"Maybe."

"What will it take?" I asked.

Before he could answer, Yellow Knife appeared. He motioned us inside.

As I crossed the threshold, the dim light forced my eyes to strain. A small fire smoldered at the center. Most of the smoke floated to the opening amongst the poles at the top of the lodge. Enough remained to sting my eyes. They watered, leaving my vision blurred. The walls contained paintings—of hunts and battles. Across the fire sat five older men on a mound of buffalo hides. Yellow Knife pressed on my shoulder, indicating I should sit. Bridger settled next to me.

One of the men spoke. After a few words, he fell silent. This had to be Rain-in-the-Face. He looked a few years older than me, though a guess at his exact age escaped me through my tears and the poor light. He wore his hair in braids. They fell over the front of his chest. Other men lined either side of him. They dressed in elaborate deerskin shirts. Rain-in-the-Face wore a vest made from two columns of bone. They were threaded together and tied behind his neck. He also had a ring on the little finger of one hand. I had never felt so out of place.

Bridger spoke more excitedly than he had earlier when dealing with Yellow Knife. I didn't know what he said. He motioned behind us. Rain-in-the-Face took his time, considering Bridger's words. Then he spoke slowly. Nothing was rushed.

"What is he saying?" I held my voice low so only Bridger could hear me.

When I looked behind me, Yellow Knife stood by the door. The flap behind us opened, letting in the deep orange light of the dying day. Another warrior entered with it, then let the flap fall. He stood by Yellow Knife. The two of them spoke in low voices.

Bridger turned back to the chief and council and started talking again. This time, almost pleading.

"Will they grant us safe passage north?" I asked. I studied Rain-in-the-Face, trying for some idea of his thoughts. He remained stoic.

As Bridger began speaking again, a sick sound filled the lodge, as if a melon had struck the ground. Bridger slumped forward. I caught him before his face landed in the ashes. Spinning in my seat, the warrior who had just entered the lodge stood over Bridger with a short club in his hand.

I started to stand, pushing Bridger to one side so he wouldn't fall into the fire. Yellow Knife held up his hands, motioning me to be calm. Then he spoke, his accent heavy, but his English rang true.

"The chief wishes to speak without this *dog*."

He spit at the ground as he said the word *dog*.

I looked to Bridger. A trickle of blood matted his hair and ran along the side of his face, but he lived. The other warrior pulled him from the ground. I eased back to sitting, angled in my seat to watch both the chief and Yellow Knife. My breathing eased though my heart raced as if it might escape my chest. The other man gripped Bridger's legs and pulled him from the lodge. With his body half-outside, the flap remained open. I witnessed them bind his hands before they pulled him wholly outside.

"What's happening?" I asked. I looked to the chief, then Yellow Knife.

Yellow Knife sat next to me.

"I will talk for the chief. He will say the words, and I will say them to you."

I nodded. Rain-in-the-Face spoke, and Yellow Knife translated.

"Many winters ago Blanket Bridger set upon our Arapaho brothers with the soldiers led by Star-Chief Connor. The Army attacked them at their camp. They burned the village and left the people with nothing except the clothes they carried. We will send Blanket Bridger to our Arapaho brothers. Their council will make of him what they will."

"Are you certain?" I asked. "We met him upon the trail. He said he spoke Lakota and would guide us north. He told us nothing of the Arapaho."

The chief spoke to the council while Yellow Knife and I waited. My heart raced, certain I might be dragged outside at any moment.

"There are those who remember him from that night. They saw him lead the white soldiers right to the camp. He had married one of their women, hunted their land, and shared their food. They knew this man. And yet he turned upon them. We will let the Arapaho deal with him."

I wanted to offer an argument to save Bridger, but in truth, I barely knew him. He might have done these things. He led us for money, so I felt we owed him little for his past transgressions. And seeing him dragged from the lodge showed how our situation might turn. I decided to stay calm and talk my way out.

"Why do you come?" Rain-in-the-Face asked. "This is Lakota land. By the treaty Red Cloud signed at your Fort Laramie, no white men may come upon this land without permission."

"We seek permission to go north. We travel to Oregon."

"With the settlers and their wagons?"

I nodded.

"Then why come this way?" he asked. "Stay south near the forts."

I wasn't certain how to answer. Yellow Knife and his men had watched O'Malley's pursuit of us north along the Bozeman. There would be no way to deceive them on that point.

"We were pursued by men. The ones you killed along the Powder River."

"Because you carry the Great Father?" Rain-in-the-Face asked.

The wind came out of me, though I tried not to let it show. He spoke of the Old Man. I had said nothing of it.

The chief continued. "Blanket Bridger tried to sell your Great Father for his own freedom. Those were the words he spoke as you sat there. You don't speak Lakota?"

I shook my head.

"But you are *Métis*?"

I looked to Yellow Knife. I didn't understand. He thought for a moment, then brushed his arm, and then brushed mine.

"You are part of the people, and part of a white man," he said.

"Yes."

"I am *Métis*," Yellow Knife said.

I looked closer. There seemed to be no white man to him. He appeared more native than me—although if I had the clothes to match my moccasins and hair to braid, I might pass as Lakota.

"What will you do with us?" I asked.

"Why is the Great Father here?" Rain-in-the-Face demanded.

"He is no longer the Great Father."

This created a stir among the council. They spoke to each other, leaning in as if they had to keep their voices silent from me. I understood nothing they said.

"He is the one who met Red Cloud in the great city in the East?"

"He is."

"And he is no longer the Great Father?"

I shook my head.

"The Great Council had no faith in him?" Rain-in-the-Face asked. For the first time his voice held some emotion.

I didn't understand. Yellow Knife saw my confusion and attempted to explain.

"There is a Great Council in the Father's city. Many men make the council. Red Cloud explained this to us."

"Congress," I answered, understanding what he meant. "No, Congress did not make him stop being the Great Father. He no longer believed he could lead the country. Evil men forced him to do things. By leaving, he stopped them."

After Yellow Knife translated, the men opposite us had a long discussion.

"Who are these men?" the chief asked.

"They are the ones who pursued us. The ones Yellow Knife's warriors killed along the banks of the river." I paused. I had almost forgotten about Dorsey's expedition. "And more come from the north and the east."

"How many?" he asked.

"Two thousand soldiers march across the prairie to survey for the railroad."

"Railroad?" Yellow Knife sounded out the word.

I didn't know how to explain it. So I drew two parallel lines in the dirt with cross-hatching to represent the wooden rail ties. Then I made the noise of a steam engine.

"The iron horse."

"Yes," I said. "The iron horse."

"We have not heard of these men," Rain-in-the-Face declared. "You lie to make our warriors go north to meet these men, while your soldiers come from the forts in the south."

"No," I said. My voice stayed firm. "They are coming from the north, from the forts along the Missouri River. You may ask the Great Father." I pointed behind me, out the lodge. My voice sounded like Bridger, pleading for our safety. I had nothing else to force a bargain.

The chief scoffed, shaking his head. "The Great Father and his people have lied to us with every word they make. Why would I believe him now?"

He spoke in a more heated voice to Yellow Knife, who responded and began to stand.

"You will come with me," Yellow Knife said.

As I stood, the chief and his council remained sitting along the back of the lodge.

"What will become of us?" I asked. I turned to the chief, hoping to plead our case further.

"He will take you to Tatanka Yotanka," Yellow Knife answered. "Together they will decide. Come."

He led me through the door of the lodge. Dusk claimed what remnants of daylight remained. The tipis glowed with the small fires inside, reflecting shadows on their inner walls. Even the dogs had found somewhere to sleep.

"Where is he taking us?"

Yellow Knife thought for a moment, seeking the words from his memory.

"Chief Sitting Bull. He is now the Great Chief of all the Lakota, and some Cheyenne and Arapaho are with him. And the Miniconjou. He has bound the people together to fight the white men and his Army when they come to our lands."

I stopped Yellow Knife, holding him by the arm.

"I'm not lying about the Army coming from the east."

He searched my face. "You will tell it to Tatanka Yotanka. He will decide."

I followed Yellow Knife through the camp. He knew the path he walked, the trails of beaten grass turned down by the children. This camp had only been here a few days, yet the grass lay matted to the prairie. The dirt had not yet worn through.

As we neared his tipi, Yellow Knife quickened his pace. He sprinted the last few yards. Muffled screaming came from within the lodge. Yellow Knife pulled back the flap and stepped inside. I followed.

Inside, the Old Man sat lashed with rawhide strap to one of the poles at the side of the tipi. The children were similarly bound as was Molly. She had a welt above one eye, and a scrap of clothing shoved into her mouth. I ran to her and knelt, working off the bindings. Yellow Knife freed the Old Man and handed me his knife. I cut Molly loose.

"Bridger," she said, gaining breath after having the cloth in her mouth. "He took her and the satchel."

I spun, searching the inside of Yellow Knife's lodge for Aurora. She was gone.

CHAPTER TWENTY-TWO

I FLEW FROM the tipi into the night beyond, scanning in every direction. Slowing my breathing, I listened for sounds of escape—a horse's heavy footfalls, or the noise one would make fleeing through the grass. I heard nothing. The heat of the day had died, and without it, the wind picked up. The noise it made flowing through the ocean of prairie eclipsed all else.

Yellow Knife emerged from the lodge. He began to trace the area, tracking the trail that Bridger would have made. As he searched for the signs in the grass, two warriors ran to him. They spoke in excited tones until Yellow Knife sent them off.

"He took a horse and headed south."

"How?" I asked. "I thought you had him." Anger rushed through me—and desperation.

"The warrior who took him left him in his lodge with his sons. He slipped his bindings and clubbed both boys over the head. Come."

Yellow Knife pulled me around the tipi to show the tracks and where they led.

"He took a horse, and then came here." He looked out toward the horizon. "They went there." He pointed into the distance.

The moonlight cast upon the land, bathing the hills in a bluish haze. It caught the grass, an uneasy ocean in the calm before a storm. In the distance it became impossible to know where the sky ended and the grass began. I started down the path, hoping to make the next rise to see before us where Bridger fled. Yellow Knife grabbed my arm.

"Wait."

One of the warriors brought forth several horses. This man's body language showed he was upset, jerking the horses rapidly toward where Yellow Knife and I stood. As he started to mount one of the horses, Yellow Knife pulled him down. They yelled at one another for several moments. Finally, Yellow Knife pushed the other warrior back and led a single horse to me, holding it by the bridle.

"This is my war horse. He is swift and true."

The brown and white blotches in its coat glistened under the moonlight. It had no saddle, only a bridle made from horsehair.

"Go. Bridger makes his way south. His horse carries two people, you should catch him by the rising sun."

"I'm going alone?" I asked. "What about him?"

I pointed to the other warrior.

Yellow Knife shook his head. "He wishes revenge for his sons—the ones that Bridger beat when he escaped. But they are not dead. This is your fight."

I looked to the tipi, then to the horizon.

"I don't know the plains," I said.

Yellow Knife shrugged. For some reason, he wanted me alone.

"At least give me my rifle."

Yellow Knife thought for a moment, then returned to the tipi. When he emerged, he had a war lance in his hand. It had a worn iron tip, with leather wrapped around the top, tassels cut into the skin there. Beads decorated the bottom in an intricate design.

"He has no gun. You have no gun."

He seemed happy as he said it. Anger surged through me. At a time like this he denied me a weapon. But I did not argue—time slipped through my fingers. Bridger made his way farther into the prairie with each moment.

"His path is easy, until the wind blows it aside. You must hurry."

I took the lance and slung myself onto the horse. I hadn't ridden bareback since childhood. As I steadied myself, I turned the horse in the direction of Bridger's trail. Yellow Knife grabbed hold of the bridle.

"This is my horse. If you do not return, I keep your woman."

Now I understood why he gave me no gun and why he let me leave in pursuit of Bridger. Yellow Knife dropped the bridle and swatted the beast upon its rear. It took off faster than I expected, and I nearly dropped the lance. I hoped he hadn't lied—that he told the truth when he said Bridger had no weapon. I would only know once I caught him.

As the horse cut through the prairie, I forced him to slow to better see the path. The wind had already beaten it back. At times I stopped and wheeled the animal in all manner of direction until I found the bent grass once more. When I found places where the wind had wiped the trail clear, I dropped to the ground and felt for the heavy footprints of his fleeing horse.

He cut into the hills and then up and over others—not a straight line. He assumed someone would follow. As the trail became fresh, I slowed my approach. I didn't need him to hear, and from the manner of his flight, he searched for pursuers.

Finally, the prairie relented. In the moonlight a silhouette appeared against the night. The dim light framed him against the distant hills. It held for only a brief moment, though long enough for me to set course and race after him. As I did, the long howl of a wolf filled the distance between us. They were upon the prairie this night, and nearby. My mother's story came to me. Tonight I wouldn't care which wolf I fed. When I caught Bridger, I would tear him to pieces. I had lost Aurora too many times to see her gone once more.

I spurred the horse with my bare heels while holding it tight with my thighs. The moccasins held fast to the beast, and I found it easy to keep it quiet. As I pulled atop of the first rising hill, I made out the trail again. Bridger had disappeared in the ocean of grass, though now he rode near. Descending, I caught movement out of the corner of my eye. A dog-like shape ran near us, aligned in our direction. Then another appeared. More ran on my other side. They closed in, running so close I could touch one with the lance had I the inclination to try.

The horse startled with the wolves. I tried to keep it running toward Bridger, but it sensed the carnivores closing around us— an entire pack pushing through the high grass. They seemed to dance through it, almost effortless. Some were dark. Some had light-colored fur. Their coats caught in the moonlight, forming on our lead as if infused with a common purpose. I had no time to figure their intent.

As we crested over the next hill, we had closed the distance. Bridger saw us. He checked over his shoulder, pushing his horse on faster. The wolves broke from our pursuit, vanishing down a cut in the hill. They blended into the grass until they were beyond view. I pushed to the crest where I had seen Bridger, no longer worried to discipline my noise.

At the top of the hill I pulled hard on the bridle. The horse halted so abruptly that it nearly threw me over its head. I righted myself, using my legs to stay steady upon the horse. Aurora stood by herself in the small valley. I saw no sign of Bridger. She looked to me, relief upon her small face, her dress torn from one shoulder.

I wanted to run to her, but I hesitated. Instinct held me back. Over the hill to the east the wolves howled, one louder than the others. I spun the horse, looking in all directions in case Bridger came upon us. *Had he left Aurora as a means to facilitate his escape? Or had he used her to set a trap?*

"Father! Father!"

She waved her hands. Gathering her skirts in her hands, she waded uphill toward me. I started the horse toward her. As soon as I turned my head, the footfalls fell heavy behind me. I wheeled the horse hard, faster than expected. The shot rang through the thick air. The flash from the rifle left me near blinded.

My horse faltered, falling onto its haunches. I managed to roll from him. Luckily, I was not fastened into stirrups or mounted high upon a saddle. At first I thought Bridger might have struck the horse, but it immediately struggled to get on its feet. I held it down by the bridle, using its body as a shield. Bridger rode down the hill, working the lever of the repeating rifle as he jostled upon his horse. Rising to my knees, I thrust with the lance as he came past. The iron tip and the shaft pierced his horse's neck, sticking fast in its head. It reared backward, kicking with its front feet until it fell sideways. Bridger tumbled down upon the hillside.

I sprung to my feet and charged. He sat dazed, his rifle lost amongst the grass. The receiver shone in the moonlight and caught my attention. I bent over to pick it up. Slowly, I racked the lever and stepped toward him. The spent shell casing ejected, making the rifle ready.

Bridger pushed back on his hands and heels. The satchel with the ledger and the corporate papers was slung across his chest. He shook his head, then focused on me. As I walked toward him, he scrambled backwards. Fear played across his face. He stared at me, then at the rifle, then back to me. He kept pushing backwards until we stood near the top of the small hill.

"I wouldn't have hurt her. I just needed her to get clear," he screamed. "You know what they planned with me."

"Did you do it?" I asked.

"Do what?"

"Along the Tongue River. Did you lead the Army to the Arapaho camp?"

"They were attacking the mail routes and the telegraph lines."

"Did you do it?" I asked again.

"I found them if that's what you mean."

"How many women and children died? How many did you kill?"

He didn't answer.

I raised the rifle and shot. The round dashed by his head and crashed into the grass beyond. It kicked up dirt.

"How many?"

"They're savages!"

I raised the rifle and fired again. This time to the other side. He held up his arms over his head.

"Savages?"

I racked the lever again, letting the next shell into the chamber. In the distance the wolves howled, filling the night. They closed in upon us. Below the hilltop they moved through the grass, creeping toward our position at the top. They made their way around both sides. I had never known wolves not to scatter at the sound of gunfire.

Bridger looked behind. He saw them, too. They darted amongst the grass, creeping closer.

"You burned the village, left them with nothing."

"Yes, yes! We burned the village."

"Because they cut the telegraph wires?"

"And they raided the wagon trains," he pleaded. "They're savages." The volume had drained from his voice, betraying a loss in confidence.

"These wagons they raided. Were they crossing Arapaho lands?"

He said nothing.

"You burned all they owned. You left their dead upon the plains. And you call *them* savage?"

The wolf pack had surrounded our position. Behind us Aurora had caught my horse and held the bridle. She clung to the animal. From where she stood she couldn't see the wolves, but she could hear them.

"Father!"

I turned. Bridger had managed to pull himself to his feet. He lunged toward me. But I had the rifle held upon him. Instinctively, I pulled the trigger. The bullet plowed into his leg. He buckled and fell backwards. Then he struggled to stand again. When he managed to stand partway, I stripped him of the satchel. Then I kicked him upon his chest, flinging him to the prairie floor. He lay staring at me.

"I'll make us both rich," he pleaded. "I'll split the money with you. Just give me the satchel and the horse."

I stopped.

"Why would you want the satchel?" I asked.

He said nothing as he looked back. A large wolf had worked itself close, just a few body lengths away. It rocked back and forth on its front feet—waiting. It did not fear us. And somehow, I did not fear it. Something in its manner spoke to me. They weren't here for me, and they weren't here for Aurora. These wolves were one with the prairie, and they knew Bridger. The Great Spirit had sent them.

"Who?" I asked. "Who's paying you?"

"General Dorsey."

The name fell hard upon my ears.

"That's why you were so eager to join us. It wasn't coincidence. You sought us out."

"Yes."

"And that's why you didn't hesitate to take us north upon the Bozeman. You left a sign somehow, that we had taken the trail north—a sign for O'Malley and his men. And how you stalled as we rode—you waited for them to catch us."

He had turned his focus upon the wolf. It growled, low enough to carry on the night.

"He'll make us both rich."

"Did you see my daughter's hands?"

He shook his head.

"I saw you take notice," I spoke through clenched teeth. "General Dorsey is the one who took her thumbs. You think he'll pay me to return his ledger?"

He said nothing.

"Why does he need it?" I asked.

"I don't know," he said. "They paid me to get it back—and to kill you. But I'll let you live. I'll tell him you're dead. Just give me the satchel."

"You'll *let* me live?" I asked. "I'll kill General Dorsey myself. You have other worries."

A howling echoed amongst the grass. It built slow. The wolf behind Bridger crept even closer. Bridger lashed out to fend off the animal. It dropped back, but didn't turn tail to run. It had a dark coat, almost as dark as the night sky itself. It locked eyes with me.

I understood. It wanted Bridger. As I lowered the rifle, Bridger struggled to stand. Another wolf came upon the crest of the hill. It stood guard like a sentinel behind Bridger.

Bridger lowered his head.

"Make it fast," he said. "Kill me or bring me back. Don't leave me here."

He tried to lunge toward me again, forcing the issue. I raised the rifle and shot. It hit his other leg, right above the knee. Bridger fell backwards, screaming in pain, clutching his thigh. I turned from him and walked toward Aurora, stopping only to pull the war spear from the dead horse. The wolves waited, staying just out of reach of Bridger. They snapped as they came near, encircling the crippled man. He pulled at the grass and screamed in their direction.

I put Aurora onto the horse, then pulled myself up. As I took the bridle in my hands, I stirred the horse forward. The wolves had sealed off any escape for Bridger.

"Father," Aurora said. Her voice came out weak. I took her head and turned her from the sight of the man on the hill.

"Don't watch."

I dug in with my heels and pointed the horse back to the village.

The sun rose above the horizon as we returned. It cast incredible hues with the first light peering over the horizon. This land held such magic—and ferocity. Despite the early hour, the village pulsed with activity. The tipis were already torn down. The women and children packed the poles and buffalo hides, readying for a march. Dogs barked, and men broke down the horse corral and made the ponies ready. The village was on the move.

Molly met us when we arrived. She had transformed. If not for the hair—the deep unmistakable auburn—I might have ridden past her. She had exchanged her undergarments for the dress of a Lakota woman. Beads adorned the front of the thin deerskin, which swept down her legs to just above her knee. Her boots were gone. In their place were high moccasins wrapped around her calves—the same that every woman in the village wore. Her hair hung over her shoulders, no longer pulled back. The two braids angled across her chest. And for the first time, the baby showed. Under her looser fitting dresses she had hidden it well, but in these clothes she couldn't disguise the growing bump at her belly. She would never pass for native, especially in contrast to all these women. But it was as if the clouds above had parted and the sun cast only upon her.

"Do you like it?" she asked.

Before I answered, Aurora had slid from the horse and landed in front of Molly. The fear of the night before appeared to escape her. Or the trauma of previous events had steeled her against it.

"Oh, Molly," she said, reaching for Molly's braids. Molly bent to meet her. "Could you do mine the same?"

Molly gave her a kiss, then turned to me. She grasped me so tight I thought I might lose all my wind.

"I didn't know what happened to you."

"I'll explain," I said. "But first, where is the Old Man?"

"The Old Man?" She said it to poke fun, as she always hated that term for him, thinking it much too informal. It seemed to grow on her.

"With Emeline, over there."

He was helping to put tent poles onto a horse travois—a kind of drag sled using two crossed poles attached to a horse.

"What is it, Joseph?" she asked. Her voice turned soft and she spoke low so Aurora could not hear. The girl liked to sit and listen to the adults, absorbing all they had to say.

"General Dorsey paid Bridger to track us. That's why he joined with us so eagerly and guided us north upon the Bozeman. He left some kind of signal for O'Malley to follow."

"That's how they found us?"

I nodded.

"They paid him to bring back the ledger."

"Why?" she asked.

"I don't know. We've both looked at it. I can't make any sense of the value of the thing. When we did the exchange with Dorsey in New York City, he said he cared nothing for it. But it contains something, and whatever it is, there's value to it. I'll have the Old Man look at it. Perhaps he might decipher the meaning and why Dorsey craves it so."

I started toward the Old Man, but before I reached him, Yellow Knife found me. His face betrayed his feelings—upset I survived through the night.

"My horse."

He held his hand extended to take the bridle. I let him have it. It took all I had to keep my anger in check. I held the rifle for him to see.

"You told me he had no gun."

"Give it. You won it on my horse, it is mine."

Again he held out his hand.

I held out the horsehair bridle. As he clutched it in his other hand, I reeled back with my free fist. I let it fall hard upon his face. The sound came out dull and hollow. He crumpled to the ground. With the impact his eyes rolled back in his head, and one foot contorted behind his back. Some of the warriors hurried our way. Two started to lunge toward me, but a third stopped them. He pushed them back screaming until they settled. When he turned, I recognized him. He was the man who brought the horses the night before—the one with the sons who Bridger had injured in his escape. He looked to Yellow Knife on the ground, then to me. With a small nod of recognition my way, he turned and escorted the others back toward the village.

I watched them leave, then I took the war lance Yellow Knife gave me and broke the shaft upon my knee. I dropped the pieces upon his limp body and walked to Molly.

CHAPTER TWENTY-THREE

22 JULY 1874

THAT DAY WE traveled until the sun held high in the sky, scorching the earth and all who walked upon it. The hot, moist air made everyone's temper all the worse. The entire village stopped along a creek to make a meal, though we had farther to go until we rested for the night. The heat bore overhead, like an insufferable weight pressing upon us with no reprieve. At times the wind blew. It provided a moment of relief. All those in sight turned their faces toward the moving air and whispered thanks to the Great Spirit. My shirt had soaked in the first mile of our walk. The village marched in a single column, trying as best to disguise their numbers. It stretched a mile ahead of us. We walked at the end with only Yellow Knife's warriors acting as a rear guard for the village.

When we came to a stop, I sat Molly under a small tree to give her some shade. The Old Man finally opened the satchel and took out the ledger. He looked through the pages, studying each for a few minutes in between glancing to Emeline who rested at his feet. The ledger fascinated him, and with it, I hoped he saw what we could not. As we sat fanning ourselves, Rain-in-the-Face approached with Yellow Knife. The welt over Yellow Knife's eye had grown and darkened.

Yellow Knife spoke for the chief. He refused to look at me. His voice remained stiff. The ambush I paid him with my fist held only a small means to repay how he set me up. My anger had subsided, but his remained.

"Rain-in-the-Face wishes to know what happened to Blanket Bridger."

The chief motioned for us to sit as I stood to greet him. When he settled before me, I told the story. I wasn't certain how much Yellow Knife translated and how much he left out. In this, he held me at his mercy.

"He is dead?" Yellow Knife asked.

"Yes."

"You are certain?"

"The wolves tore him apart. His screams filled the night behind us—they were hungry." I looked to Yellow Knife as I said this, then continued. "If you don't believe me, ask my daughter. She heard it as well."

The chief sat for a moment, his face flat until Yellow Knife translated. He looked to Aurora, lying next to Molly with her head on Molly's lap. Her hands rubbed the bump at Molly's belly. Without her thumbs she let her fingertips swirl in small circles. Rain-in-the-Face smiled. He spoke to Yellow Knife.

"I am to tell you that I did not know Blanket Jim Bridger had a rifle. No one told me. And I should not have sent you alone," Yellow Knife said. "I should have sent my warriors."

For the first time he looked at me. His emotions remained hidden, and I ventured to hold mine from my face as well. This was hard for him. The chief had clearly chastised him for his actions.

"You are to have two horses from my stock. A reward from our Arapaho brothers," Yellow Knife continued. "Use them for your wife and the children. We have a day more before we come to

Tatanka Yotanka's village. There you will tell him the story about the soldiers to our east, and about Blanket Jim Bridger. He may grant you passage through our lands."

The chief stood. I nodded, the only gesture of thanks I could offer. Molly would welcome the news of the horses, making the journey that much easier. As the chief walked away, Yellow Knife remained for a moment.

"I will find you horses. When we stop, the chief will have a tipi for your people. But you must agree to stay with the village and not try to flee on your own."

That evening, Rain-in-the-Face made good on his promise. He even sent one of his wives to us with food. She showed us how to pitch the tipi. Though the poles reached little above my outstretched hands, I struggled with the construction. The women normally made camp while the men scouted, hunted, or set watch. It amazed me how they managed to place the poles and stretch the thin buffalo hides to make the lodges. I failed again and again until the chief's wife took charge.

Inside, we laid several buffalo skin robes upon the ground making a crude bed for Molly and the children. The Old Man stayed in the lodge with us as well. He corralled the children while we made camp, and once finished, returned to the ledger. I wanted to ask what he had found, though I let him read on, as the dwindling daylight would be precious. I would ask once the sun had set.

The summer hunts had been good to the Hunkpapa. They reaped fresh buffalo hides to reframe the tipis for the winter. They used only hides from the cows, as the thick skin from the bulls was too heavy for the poles. Even with the new skins, the tribe would cut fresh poles when they made their way to the Black Hills—unless Sitting Bull believed our story about the expedition encroaching upon his territory.

We ate the dinner the chief's wife prepared—a light stew made from dried buffalo meat. Molly did not tolerate it well, and lay down after just a few bites. The Old Man and I, along with the children, devoured the rest of the meal. We were ravenous after the long walk. I watched Aurora navigate the bowl with no thumbs. She never said anything about her deformed hands. Somehow she found a means to accomplish everything, even if, at times, it appeared awkward. She lifted the bowl to her mouth and tipped it back until empty. The thought of more miles ahead made my stomach tug. When we finished, we settled the children. Soon they were fast asleep. The walk had worn on them as well.

"We should talk about the ledger," the Old Man said.

"Have you found anything? You poured over it at each stop."

"It holds an amazing story, Joseph. I see why General Dorsey is so keen to have it returned."

He reached for the satchel, which lay near the tipi entrance. As he began flipping through the ledger, I placed more wood on the fire and stoked the coals so we might have some light.

"It begins here," the Old Man said, turning to a page and pointing to some entries. "I didn't understand at first, but it makes sense with everything I saw when in the White House."

"Those look like entries to pay companies," I replied. "From the West Shore Railroad."

"They are," the Old Man exclaimed. "But they're so much more. You see, during my second term, Dorsey incorporated the new railroad. But they own nothing—no cars, no engines, no track. They're a holding company, investing in many other companies. All these entries, they have states listed. At first I thought they were investing in business there, until I saw this."

He flipped through several pages until he arrived at the middle of the book.

"This entry, the one that's scratched out, this one is the key!"

"I don't understand," I said.

"The recorder made a mistake here. They started to record a name, and, in fact, they wrote the whole name and then crossed it out. It says *Barlow*. Then he replaced it with *New York*. Francis Barlow was the Secretary of State for New York State. You see? These are not corporate investments; they're bribes—kickbacks."

I looked closer. Every northern state had an entry—some had several. It even listed the banks where the payments were made.

"And this," the Old Man said, pointing at entry after entry, "all these are to the US Senate—the Great Council."

"They're all bought. But we knew that," I said.

"Yes, of course. We knew, but we never had proof. We never knew exactly who was paid what, and how to track it. Now we have it. This is a map, Joseph—a map of the corruption the Consortium spread. Once we follow it, the system unravels. Almost every senator from the northern states is listed."

He pulled out the corporate documents that we found in the last bank we robbed.

"These names are the senators on the committee who tried to impeach President Johnson. They're given stock into the new Northern Pacific Railroad."

"That's the railroad General Dorsey is surveying, the one he leads the expedition for?" I asked.

"Exactly!" the Old Man said. "But it gets better, Joseph. He doesn't care about the railroad. He's using it to bribe the senators to remove President Johnson."

"Then why go to all the trouble of the expedition?"

"Because of this."

The Old Man brought out the last of the corporate paperwork. It was an incorporation document for the Black Hills Mining Company.

"What does it mean?" I asked.

"Dorsey made this company, his name is on the deed. I never paid it much mind when I was president. I refused to sign away mining rights to the Black Hills. They asked for an exception to the Laramie Treaty of 1868, and I never granted it."

"The one Red Cloud fought for?" I asked. The war closed the Bozeman Trail. It had shuttered the old forts along the Powder River, including Fort Reno where we found the boats.

"Yes. We agreed to relinquish claim to all the land between the Rocky Mountains and the Missouri River, including the Black Hills. But miners snuck in and found gold. All of it rumors, of course. At least I held it as nothing more. I denied the mining company access to avoid another Indian war. But I never knew the Black Hills Mining Company was the heart of Dorsey's Consortium."

"So they don't care about the railroad? It's a ruse?"

The Old Man shook his head.

"They'll need the railroad to get the gold out, at least to the steamboats along the upper Missouri. And if I remember the treaty correctly, the government can build roads north of the Yellowstone River. But eventually they'll need to lay track to the south and into the Black Hills."

"So Dorsey means this expedition to provoke a war." I spoke into the fire.

"I think so," the Old Man said. "Why else would they be so heavily armed? The major at Fort Laramie said the 7th Cavalry joined columns of infantry—nearly two thousand men. They're spoiling for a fight to push the Sioux from the Black Hills."

I stared into the fire. Night had fallen heavy upon us, and I poked at the embers with a stick. I liked how the shadows danced upon the ground. In the distance the wolves began their song. They seemed to follow close to the village, always nearby. A few dogs joined in the nightly howl—their wild instincts not yet bred out.

"We have to bring this to Sitting Bull," I said.

"We will. Though it is better you do the talking, my friend," the Old Man said. "I long heard rumors that Sitting Bull was upset with the Great Father over the Santee uprising. That nasty business in Minnesota."

I remembered it well. I guarded the Old Man during that time. He had even asked my council, as if I had connection to that different land because of my mother's people. Early in the Civil War, supplies never made it to the Santee as promised. Too much was diverted to the war effort—and into the corrupt pockets of the Indian agent at the agency. The Santee starved. Unable to bear it any longer, they revolted. When soldiers finally broke the rebellion, they found the Indian agent dead, his mouth stuffed with grass—revenge for telling the starving Sioux they should eat the grass. The Army sentenced over three hundred men to death, yet the Old Man halted the executions until he reviewed each case.

"You issued clemency for most of those men," I said.

"But I sentenced thirty-three to hang. Sitting Bull won't have forgotten." He held the ledger. "Can you explain this for me? There is no use if the messenger overshadows the message."

I took the ledger, feeling the leather cover. This book held the proof we needed, and perhaps with it, the means to buy our passage north. It would free us.

"Then I am off to bed, Joseph," the Old Man said. "That is, if this howling might subside for a time. Please speak the words of your mother and ask them to quiet down."

The Old Man stood, placing his hand upon my shoulder. Slowly, he stooped to pull back the flap to the tipi, and then disappeared inside. I stayed next to the fire for a time, listening. In the distance, other wolves joined. One by one, they would give way, letting their howl fall upon the hills only to rise again. I found it mystifying. I closed my eyes and breathed deep. With the smell of the grassland, I remembered home—Essary Springs. I longed to return. Perhaps one day we might.

As I absorbed the night, I startled when a hand rested upon my shoulder. Molly leaned upon me. Holding her hand, I helped her sit.

"You're getting quieter," I said.

"Did I catch you this time?"

"You did."

"It must be the shoes. I rather like them. I don't know if I can go back to the others, especially if my feet continue to swell like this."

"Did the wolves wake you?" I asked. Even the lone wolf in Essary Springs bothered her. Now she had to contend with an entire pack.

"They're growing on me."

We sat for a time. She leaned close, wrapping her arm around me. I kissed her upon the top of her head and smelled her hair. The scent of her soap had vanished, replaced by the smell of smoke, and grass, and the lingering flavor of tanned deerskin.

"Did you really see wolves when you went after Bridger?" she asked, finally breaking the silence.

"Yes."

"Aurora told me you did, but I thought she made it up. They attacked him? You heard it?"

I nodded, but said nothing. She could feel my body rock in answer to her question.

"I worry about her, Joseph. She told me the story with no care, as if it didn't bother her."

"She's seen so many things," I said. "So had you by her age, and so had I. This world is cruel—she'll need to see some of it to survive, to know what people are capable of so she's ready for it."

"I don't forget," Molly said. "Life is both beauty and terror. I just wish she wouldn't go through the bad as we did—that we could spare her of it."

"Maybe we can go home once we finish here."

"And give up Oregon?" she asked.

"Or maybe the Lakota would allow us to stay. The Consortium would never find us here."

If I was truthful, there was an allure to the life here. Maybe it was my ancestors signing across time. I could feel them somewhere behind me, and part of me felt like this could be home. Molly was quiet, but her body tensed.

"Is it that terrible?" I asked.

Molly was a point of interest in the village. The women would steal subtle glances as often as they dared, while their husbands sometimes would stand not ten paces away to watch her. At times it took all her strength to hold her composure.

"No, it's just . . ." Her thought faded.

"It's not our world," I offered. She nodded.

"It's not my world. They would never accept me, or Aurora."

I thought of Yellow Knife—how he lived on the outskirts of the village.

"I don't think they would ever fully take me in, and according to my mother, I am part Lakota."

"We need a place where we all belong. Our family is so different."

I had never really appreciated what we had in Essary Springs. The mountain folk there accepted us without question, never once raising suspicions about our odd pairing. I couldn't recall anyone even asking about it.

"We should go back to Tennessee. There's nowhere else like it."

"Will we be able to?" Molly asked.

"Maybe. The Old Man deciphered the ledger. He understands why they've chased us. It maps out all the bribes from the Consortium. Even if Dorsey had another copy, he wouldn't want this one to get out. If anyone followed the money, they'd understand it all."

"What will we do?" she asked.

"Tell Sitting Bull tomorrow. And then find a way to make the ledger public."

We were quiet for a time, listening to the wolves. The howling grew closer, with a lone song rising above the rest. It couldn't have been more than a hill or two away in the sea of grass that surrounded us. Molly shifted so she could face me.

"I don't care where we go, as long as we find safety."

I nodded, though I stared into the dying embers. They danced where the wind hit them.

"I mean it, Joseph. I will not lose this baby."

I turned toward her and found her hands. I saw her eyes start to water.

"Is there something wrong with the baby?" I asked.

She shook her head but didn't look at me.

"Molly."

She looked up.

"No, Joseph."

"You're sure?" I asked.

"I am. It's just . . ." Her voice faded and she tried to shift back to face the fire. I held her hands and didn't let her turn away from me.

"It's just what?" I asked.

She stayed silent for a moment, and then looked at me. She fought, but a tear rolled down one cheek. I let go of one hand so she could wipe her face.

"What is it?" I pressed.

"I lost one child already. I won't lose this one. That's all."

"With us?" I asked. I thought perhaps she miscarried and never told me.

"Before us. It wasn't your child."

"You never told me."

She shook her head.

"She was so little. I only held her a few moments before they took her from me. I never even named her."

I didn't understand. She had never said anything like this before.

"Who took her, Molly? When did this happen?"

She looked at me—her eyes now hard and defiant. A flash of anger replaced the sadness. It burned away the tears.

"Pinkerton."

"Pinkerton?"

"He said she went to an orphanage, that it was best for both of us. I could do my job, and she would have a life. I never had another chance."

I found her free hand again and brought both of them to my face. I kissed them between her knuckles.

"You never told me this," I said again. I didn't know what else to say.

"I've never had anyone to tell before. I've never had the comfort of feeling safe with another person. With you I have no need to measure my words."

I held her close, not knowing what to say. She breathed deep, as if a weight had lifted from her soul. All along she knew how losing Aurora tortured me. She understood in a way I never knew.

"We won't lose this baby. No one will take it," I said.

"You promise?" she asked.

"I do."

No one could ever promise such a thing with certainty. She knew it as well as I. But she needed to hear it. I needed to hear it. I held her like that until I thought she slept. The fire died beside us, and out on the prairie, among the tall grass, the wolves sang to one another.

Suddenly Molly pulled away and grabbed my hand. She pulled it to her belly.

"Do you feel it?" she asked.

The baby moved, kicking against her belly below where she placed my hand.

"Your son likes the wolves, too," she said.

CHAPTER TWENTY-FOUR

23 July–3 August 1874

WE TRAVELED FOR more than a week with Rain-in-the-Face's village, heading north and west. Each night held the same routine, though I became more proficient in raising our lodge with each stop. A small cadre of women always gathered to watch—in part to stare at Molly. Raising a tipi counted among the work of women, not men. They enjoyed my struggle, and even more, they were interested in Molly. Some came near and tried to talk, using sign language where the words failed. Aurora fast picked up Lakota and made good as an intermediary. The other children of the village walked with us now, talking and playing with Daniel and Emeline.

It amazed me how these people accepted our presence, though we were prisoners of a sort. They would receive no such treatment in kind from white men. That's not to say they held no prejudice. Yellow Knife and the other *Métis* were not equal in stature. I suspected this accounted for the four feathers in his hair.

One morning as the sun rose high, we came upon a bluff that overlooked the Yellowstone. The river flowed in spectacular fashion—meandering when wide, yet fierce where it pinched in the narrow passes. To the north, a great village spread upon the flat land of the opposite shore. My mind wandered to New York. I thought back to its crowded streets and avenues—the noise and congestion. In this peaceful place I realized that the clatter of the city served only to insult the ears. In contrast, the scene before us seemed pulled from a painting and placed in our path. Smoke rose in thin ribbons. The only movement came from darting children as they played among the lodges and the stirring of horses fenced in the corral.

Yellow Knife rode down the column of humanity, seeking us out. He brought two fresh horses, holding their bridles behind him. When he found us, he turned them around and pulled them alongside.

"You and the Great Father are to come with me. Rain-in-the-Face wishes you to tell Tatanka Yotanka of the white men to our east. You must tell the story, and we will see what he chooses."

I helped the Old Man onto one of Yellow Knife's horses, and I mounted the other. Unaccustomed to riding without a saddle, the Old Man clung precariously to the beast. He had ridden almost none of the journey so far, preferring to let the children hop on and off the horse as they tired. The exercise did him good, making his legs as strong as a young man's once more, or so he claimed. The lure of the West touched him as it did Molly. It held an intoxication so great that it tugged an ocean of humanity westward, like the moon to the tides. To his credit, his stride had opened, falling with the gait of a younger man. He seemed ageless upon this adventure. For too long the weight of the presidency had preyed upon his soul.

Yellow Knife led us to the Yellowstone, crossing it at a place where the river rose to the shoulders of each horse. Halfway across they lost their footing and swam with the current. Once their hooves found the riverbed below, they pulled us to the far bank.

Entering Sitting Bull's village, we were met with much curiosity. The children swarmed Yellow Knife and shouted questions—he ignored them. They pointed and laughed at the Old Man and myself. The women stopped their chores and stood to watch, and a pair of warriors halted our approach. Yellow Knife spoke to them in low flat tones, and they fell in step behind us as escorts. Throughout the village the criers ran two steps ahead, announcing our presence. I couldn't tell if they heralded us as honored guests or if fate would dictate a different path.

The center of this village held the same open structure. Sitting Bull's tipi occupied the most prominent position. His lodge stood as the tallest I had seen, with elaborate paintings and designs on the outside. Yellow Knife entered first, while the Old Man and I waited outside. The Old Man placed his hand upon my shoulder.

"Who would have thought we would one day stand here together?" he asked.

He enjoyed this moment, while I felt my heart might race from my chest.

"Today I stand behind you," he continued. "I rather like this change in our circumstances."

Before I answered, Yellow Knife stepped from the flap in the lodge. He beckoned us inside. The Old Man held the flap to let me enter. Behind me he stooped through the threshold. The Lakota were significantly shorter than the Old Man. Though in truth, he towered above most everyone. Similar to Rain-in-the-Face's lodge, each panel of the tipi held paintings depicting great hunts or acts of bravery. A fire blazed in the middle, and despite the heat, I no longer minded it. After my time with Rain-in-the-Face and his people, the smoke no longer teased my eyes. And I paid no mind to the scent that lingered upon my clothes. It had become part of me.

On the far side the council ringed the fire—eight men in total. Rain-in-the-Face sat near the middle, and to his left, Sitting Bull. He sat on buffalo skins stacked high upon the ground. Above him a war bonnet with eagle feathers floated, somehow suspended from the poles of the tipi. I could not tell how they did it, but its placement left no mistake of who led the village. Sitting Bull wore his hair like Rain-in-the-Face. Two braids fell over his shoulders and onto his deerskin shirt. Wrappings of rabbit fur, or some other unfortunate animal caught upon a hunt, held them together. A single eagle's feather emerged from behind his head, and his eyes held an unwavering focus. His brow furled toward us. No hint of emotion crossed his face.

After our time with the people of these plains, I had become tempered to the way of the Lakota. They preferred thought to speech. Conversation never began in a hurried manner. No matter how great the chief or how pressing the issue, no one demanded a rushed answer. In this regard, I took comfort in the silence. I preferred not to push the matter at hand.

Sitting Bull leaned forward and pulled a twig from the fire, the ember at the tip burning bright orange. Using it, he lit the bowl of a long pipe. The smoke rose into the space between us until it mixed with the ribbon of gray that rose from the fire. Then he passed the pipe to me. I grasped the end—fearful I might drop it upon the flames. Taking a deep breath, I pulled the tobacco into my lungs.

Immediately I coughed. The tobacco singed my throat. The council laughed—low and to themselves. Sitting Bull turned his gaze toward them, and the noise quieted. I passed the pipe to the Old Man.

After it made the rounds across the entire council, Sitting Bull grasped the pipe once more. He took another pull from it, then held it in his hands. As before, Yellow Knife sat behind us and translated.

"Rain-in-the-Face tells me you wish to travel through our hunting grounds to the forts in the north. He also says you have brought us the Great Father," Sitting Bull said.

I nodded, preferring to let our silence build. I hoped it lent gravity to our claims, making me seem as reserved in manner as the Lakota.

"This is the same Great Father who brought Red Cloud and Black Kettle to see the Great Council? The same Great Father who killed women and old men at Sand Creek, then sent Long Hair Custer to attack Black Kettle at the Washita? The same Great Father who pushed the Santee from their lands and made them live on the Crow Creek?"

I looked to the Old Man—he feared this most. The conversation would become about him, not about what came next. Sitting Bull might not believe what we had to say, that an expedition hunted the Lakota for the yellow metal concealed in their hills.

"I am that same Great Father," the Old Man began. "These things you say are true, though not all were done by my word. And I am no longer the Great Father."

As Yellow Knife translated, the council murmured to itself for a few moments. Then Sitting Bull held up a hand.

"Are you saying your children did these things without your permission?"

"Some of them, yes. I did not order the attack at Sand Creek. When I heard of it, I removed Colonel Chivington."

I served as the Old Man's bodyguard when he heard of the Sand Creek massacre. Colonel Chivington led his Colorado militia in an attack upon a village of the Cheyenne and Arapaho peoples. Some reports claimed more than a hundred died. At first the

paper heralded it as a great victory upon the plains. Then the survivors' stories found their way to the press—women and children
comprised most of the dead. The Old Man's anger emerged un-
checked when he heard. Chivington could have aided in the fight
against the Confederates. Instead, he inflamed tensions upon the
frontier. The investigations and tribunals went nowhere, mired in
politics. And the Old Man had a war to run. He wished to send
Chivington to the trenches outside Petersburg—to let him fight a
real enemy. But even his powers as commander in chief had limits.

"Did you hang Chief Chivington as you did the Santee?"
Sitting Bull asked.

The Old Man started to answer, then stopped. He looked to me.
His eyes fell to the fire and they did not rise to meet Sitting Bull.
In all my years with him, I had never seen him back down from
a conversation. Even when talking to captured Confederates, he
never faded or withdrew from an argument.

"No," he answered, his voice weak. "In the end I could do little
to Chivington without the blessing of the Great Council."

"But you did not kill Chief Chivington."

The Old Man shook his head.

"And for that you are no longer the Great Father?" Sitting Bull
asked.

The Old Man looked to him.

"That is not the reason," he said.

"Then why?"

"I lost faith. The Great Council became corrupt and no longer
represented the people. I could not support it."

Sitting Bull sat for what seemed an eternity. He reached for
another ember from the fire to relight the pipe.

"Why did you come then?" Sitting Bull asked. "All that seems
to follow the white man is death to the Indian. We took your
hand as children do with their father, and at every turn you still

take from us. The Great Spirit—*Wakan Tanka*—told me that all the lands belong to him. No people may own them. He told me I am to tell this to the white people when they come to my council."

The Old Man nodded. "I am afraid that my people see the land different than the Lakota. If no one owns it, they mean to take it."

"Do you want us to settle and raise crops as your people do? To keep the buffalo in fences as your people keep cattle?" Sitting Bull paused, taking more of the tobacco from the pipe before continuing. "If you stake a horse to one place, he will not grow fat. He will eat all the grass he can reach, and then he will starve. It is the same with the Lakota. We roam the prairie because we are free and happy. When we settle down, we will grow pale like the whites and then die. Is this what you have come to ask? To tell us how to live on *Wakan Tanka's* land?"

The Old Man shook his head. He looked to me, then across the fire with steeled resolve.

"We came to ask permission—permission to cross your land and head north. But now we come to warn you."

"Warn us of what?"

"A great expedition has started in the east. They have several weeks upon the trail by now. They seek a fight, to start a new war."

The council talked for a moment. They spoke fast, with emotion entering into the chatter. Sitting Bull held up his hand to quiet them.

"Our scouts tell us nothing of this in the east. Why would they come?"

I ventured to speak, desperate to give the Old Man some relief from the questioning. My voice faltered at first—filled with smoke. But then I started again.

"Miners found gold in the Black Hills. If these soldiers can provoke a war, they will take the *Paha Sapas* from you."

Sitting Bull and his council turned their attention upon me. The Old Man breathed deep. Perhaps he felt relieved I finally took the conversation from him.

"The white man goes crazy for the yellow metal. There have always been miners. We will take care of them ourselves."

"But this is a large expedition," I pleaded. "Thousands of soldiers head this way."

"So you wish me to take my warriors and ride toward these soldiers? Perhaps you lure my warriors away so our village would be full of women and old men like the one at Sand Creek. Then your soldiers could ride from the south."

"No," I said. "We want you to avoid these men—to move south of the Yellowstone River. They survey the land for a railroad to the north. If you don't attack, they have no provocation to turn south upon you."

Several of the other chiefs leaned toward Sitting Bull, or discussed with Rain-in-the-Face. The village was currently on the north side of the Yellowstone, in the path of the survey team and the columns of infantry marching toward it. The Old Man and I were enveloped in our own world as the council discussed. I looked to Yellow Knife. His eyes locked in a glare though his face remained stoic.

Finally, Rain-in-the-Face spoke, disrupting the council debate.

"The white man's medicine may be stronger than ours, and his iron horse rushes over the buffalo trail. But what you ask is that we run. Even before your army arrives, you think the Lakota are cowards who will scatter like children."

Those around Rain-in-the-Face quieted. They wanted to hear our response. To imply cowardice among the Lakota would get us both killed. It would also force the warriors to meet the army headfirst. As I struggled for what to say, the Old Man spoke.

"We know the Lakota are not cowards. Look at how Red Cloud fought. We don't want you to lose all that he gained in his treaty. We ask that you avoid these soldiers until I can go to the Great Council and show them what these men do."

"And why would they believe it? You are no longer the Great Father," Rain-in-the-Face said. The others murmured their consent. He had a point.

The Old Man fumbled with the satchel, tugging at the latch that held it closed. When he opened it, he placed the oilskin bound ledger upon the ground in front of him. Slowly, he unwrapped the cloth. Then he held it for all to see.

"They might not believe me, but they will believe this."

Yellow Knife translated. The chiefs didn't understand.

"This book shows why these soldiers are here," the Old Man continued. "It is like . . ." He faltered for words, searching for some manner to bridge the cultures. "It is like your paintings."

He spun his hand around the tipi, indicating the artwork upon the animal hides.

"This book contains the story of these men and how they come to rob the gold from the Black Hills," he said. "The Great Council may not believe me, but they will believe the stories here." His palm fell upon the book for emphasis.

The council discussed in low voices. Sitting Bull listened. Finally, he held up his hand to speak. But before he started, the shouts of the village crier reached us. I had no idea what message the crier heralded, yet alarm rose in the faces of the council. Sitting Bull nodded toward Yellow Knife. The younger man dove from the tipi. A moment later he returned with another warrior.

Hurried words passed between them. The council became agitated. They no longer spoke in hushed tones. Instead, the debate raged. Sitting Bull stood. He spoke to Yellow Knife.

"It seems the words you spoke were true. The soldiers have come. The village will move, while the warriors face the bluecoats. Come."

Yellow Knife held open the flap to the lodge. The Old Man rebound the ledger in the oilcloth and secured the satchel. We followed Yellow Knife from the tipi as the chiefs readied their plans.

"What will they do?" I asked Yellow Knife.

"The warriors will attack and give the village time."

The Old Man and I looked to one another. We were too late. This would be the seed of war that General Dorsey needed.

Behind us, Rain-in-the-Face exited the tipi. He grabbed me by my upper arm and pulled me close. Then he spoke to Yellow Knife.

"The chief will lead the warriors into battle against your soldiers," Yellow Knife said. "Your people will stay with the village."

Rain-in-the-Face spoke again, gaining more purchase upon my arm. Yellow Knife nodded.

"To ensure your people do not flee, *you* will come to battle with us."

CHAPTER TWENTY-FIVE

3–4 August 1874

I FOLLOWED YELLOW Knife and Rain-in-the-Face. We rode through the darkening prairie along the north side of the Yellowstone River. They refused me any weapons, so I rode into battle with nothing more than my clothes and a bladder filled with water. Dusk had settled, and with the darkness, the pace slowed. Finally, we stopped to sleep for a few hours. When daylight broke it became easier to find our way. Even in this ride to the emerging battle, I saw how different the Lakota fought. They kept no unified leadership. Most looked to Rain-in-the-Face as the eldest amongst the warriors. Yet each man held to the group more from pride and respect than any military formality.

A young Oglala warrior led us to the place where we slowed the horses, quieting our approach. They called him Crazy Horse. According to Yellow Knife, his bravery had fast become known throughout the Lakota peoples. The day before, he had been part of a group hunting along the south shore of the Yellowstone. They were searching for buffalo near the Tongue River when the columns of troops came into view. His warriors remained behind to track the invaders while he swam across the Yellowstone and then rode to warn Sitting Bull. His companions kept a vigil all night, tracking the cavalry as they moved out at first light.

Walking the horses, we approached a stand of cottonwood trees along the northern bank of the river. Crazy Horse's hunting group had secreted themselves amongst the trees and high grass. They watched the cavalry as they took an early morning break. We followed and picketed the horses in the floodplain at the far edge of the trees. Once more, the heat of the day built above us. However, the Great Spirit provided cool air from the river. On occasion a fine mist blew on the breeze and reached my face.

I followed Yellow Knife and Rain-in-the-Face through the cottonwood stand. We crawled the last few body lengths to lie in the high grass along the far side of the trees. About a mile distant, two groups of cavalry soldiers milled about. They served as sentries. Other soldiers lay in the open grass. Some slept, while others explored the river, setting lines to fish. A mile or two farther to the east, a large hill rose from the prairie, breaking the skyline. The infantry would descend from that hilltop. These soldiers were a mounted advance for General Dorsey's infantry. At most, the marching soldiers could only be a few miles in arrears.

Behind us, Oglala, Hunkpapa, Miniconjou, and Cheyenne warriors trickled in. Sitting Bull had sent out a call for reinforcements. They had left their camps hours after us and rode through the night. They wore war bonnets and painted their faces. The Cheyenne placed crow's feathers in their bonnets, while the Lakota used the feathers of eagles. Most had stripped to the waist in preparation for battle. They came in groups of three or four, filtering down the river. They moved silently between smaller clusters of cottonwoods so as not to concede the surprise. I lost count after seeing more than a hundred warriors arrive. When I tried to number our adversary, I had no better luck—most stayed out of sight, napping in the tall grass. My best estimate came from counting their horses. They numbered in equal parts to the warriors assembled around us.

We waited like this for hours. The heat rose as the sun climbed ever higher. Rain-in-the-Face wanted more warriors before attacking. He moved between groups, devising a plan and securing their allegiance. As the sun approached its peak, excited shouts came from the direction of the soldiers. A small group of warriors crawled through the grass. They had hoped to reach the place where the cavalry had picketed their horses, to spook the animals. It would trap the soldiers on foot. But the sentries spotted their approach.

The song from a bugle fell upon the open expanse of grass before us—*Boots and Saddles*. I had heard the cavalry practice in Washington during the War. Our surprise had been spoiled. The bugle echoed amongst the trees. It called the soldiers to sprint to their mounts and ready for battle. With luck, the noise wouldn't travel far in the hot thick air. The infantry might be unaware that a battle commenced in the valley before them.

The soldiers mounted in haste—obviously well disciplined. They formed into a neat triangle. Their leader and three others rode in front, followed by a row of twenty horsemen. Farther upriver the balance of the troops held in reserve. The Lakota scouts who had tried to spook and scatter the horses pulled back, albeit slow. They lured the cavalry forward, to bring them within range of the warriors. In the initial moments their plan appeared to work. The scouts retreated, and the lead group of four soldiers galloped after them. After pursuing for nearly a mile, the cavalry halted. The scouts responded and stopped just short of rifle range. Then it started again. The cavalry chased, and the scouts fell back. This game continued, with one group edging away to draw forth the other. But the soldiers must have recognized this tactic. They had seen it before or been warned by veterans of earlier conflicts on the plains. So before they came within range from the trees, they halted for good. Their leader wore a bright red shirt. His long blond hair extended from under his hat. He signaled to the woods, perhaps asking our intent.

"Long Hair Custer," Yellow Knife whispered to me. He lay to my side, his rifle at the ready. "He killed Black Kettle at the Washita River five winters ago. The Cheyenne will not stand for him here."

This was an Army bought by the Consortium, and General Dorsey had found the very best among the cavalry. He likely paid Custer a handsome price to participate in this expedition. Yellow Knife had barely finished his thought when a terrible cry came forth from the trees around us. Cheyenne warriors recognized Custer. Some had been in the village during his attack against Black Kettle. Now they mounted their ponies and dashed from the woods. Most were well armed, holding Henry repeating rifles. Others rode forth with only war lances in their hands—arrows and bows strapped to their backs. Custer spun his horse and fell back. The twenty troopers behind him dismounted and formed a skirmish line.

The Cheyenne closed fast upon Custer and his advance guard. But the soldiers who had dismounted rose from the grass and fired a volley—then another. It broke the attack. The warriors reeled and spun toward the grove of cottonwoods. None seemed injured and none fell from their horses. Custer collected his men and withdrew downriver toward another stand of trees. Rain-in-the-Face ordered everyone to the horses. We had to attack Custer before the infantry arrived.

As Yellow Knife and I emerged from the far side of the cotton-woods, the full force of the sun fell upon us. Before, the trees had shielded us as we lay in the grass and watched the cavalry. But now the full intensity beat upon our backs. To make matters worse, we rode away from the river in an attempt to surround Custer and his men. The cooler air near the river gave way to heavy thick air rising from the scorching green grass of the prairie.

Custer's cavalry raced in front of us and made it to the stand of cottonwoods along the river. They disappeared amongst the tall trees and behind some sort of depression formed by the raging water during flood season. Their position provided a natural barrier, and I could no longer see them except when the occasional smoke issued forth from their rifles. Rain-in-the-Face directed his warriors to fan out opposite the cavalry. He remained in the open directing the attack, while all about him the bullets flew. Yellow Knife and I watched from a safe distance further back as the Lakota extended in a wide ring from the riverbank on the west edge of Custer's cottonwood grove, to the east. As the river trapped the soldiers to their rear, Custer's only retreat would be to brave the rapids and swim—or fight his way through us.

While I stood next to my horse near the back of the Indian lines, I recognized Crazy Horse—the warrior who first brought the news of the columns of soldiers. He directed the attack from the vanguard, seemingly impervious to fear. He raced amongst groups of warriors and shouted directions. No bullet found him, though I was certain the soldiers practiced their best aim upon him. I watched until Crazy Horse disappeared at the far end of the Lakota lines, then I surveyed the rest of our surroundings. The hilltop behind us worried me. It lay upriver and extended to our north. I tugged on Yellow Knife's jacket to get his attention.

"The infantry will come from there." I pointed. "Are there scouts up there?"

Yellow Knife looked to the hilltop and then beckoned to Rain-in-the-Face who had ridden back to our position while directing the attack. The chief listened while Yellow Knife spoke, but he didn't seem concerned, too preoccupied with the current fight. He didn't even glance back to the high ground. His attention was drawn to the warriors in front of us. Most had dismounted, and now they crept closer to the cavalry, using the tall prairie grass as concealment. It was hard to see how far they had advanced, as the grass shielded most of my view. Instead, I gauged the progress by the amount of gunfire.

After the initial engagement and the chase to the cottonwood stand, the fighting fell into an uneasy equilibrium. It was only interrupted when the warriors crept too close and the soldiers needed to fend them off. Crazy Horse and his men could not break through, though Custer and his soldiers were unable to flee. Even though surrounded, Custer had the better position. He had time on his side, and from what I could tell, a better defensive position. The stand of trees sheltered his men from the blazing heat, while the sun bore down directly on top of us. Custer's soldiers even had water at their backs to refresh themselves. They only needed to wait until the infantry crested the hill and trapped us upon the prairie.

Even with the intermittent gunshots, the smell of powder burned my nose. It wafted across the battle, carried on the wind, and settled in pockets amongst the high grass. As the fighting stalled, the individual nature of the warriors began to show. One at a time they stood and charged Custer's lines, running back after making a daring dash and drawing rifle fire from the soldiers. I regarded the acts as sheer stupidity. It might earn them another feather for bravery, though it risked eternity with the Great Spirit.

And to make matters worse, it played into Custer's hands, exposing where Lakota hid amongst the grass and how close they had managed to low-crawl toward the soldiers.

Obviously frustrated at the progress, Crazy Horse rode back to speak with Rain-in-the-Face. The younger man's expressions showed his dismay as he pointed back toward the soldiers hidden amongst the trees. I listened but understood nothing, though Yellow Knife followed the conversation intently. Their words turned heated until Crazy Horse rode off. I couldn't tell which man had won the argument, or what it had been about, though a short time later the prairie in front of us began to smoke. Several warriors ran along the front of the Lakota position with bundles of tall grass in their hands, each consumed by orange tongues of open flame. They were setting fire to the prairie.

As the flames caught, the rising heat fell upon us in unbearable waves. The sun already punished us enough, soaking our backs with sweat and grime. With the unrelenting heat, I had already drenched my clothing.

"What are they doing?" I asked.

"They make smoke," Yellow Knife answered. "To make the bluecoats blind."

"But the infantry!" I pointed back toward the hill. "They'll see the smoke."

Though the grass was still green, thick black smoke rose from the field of battle. It wouldn't take long before it lifted above the hilltop to the north. Any approaching soldiers would see it from miles away and know something was amiss. Rain-in-the-Face, who sat atop his horse nearby, became interested in my hand gesturing. He looked back to the hilltop, then interrupted us, speaking to Yellow Knife as he pointed at me. They talked for a few moments before Yellow Knife mounted his horse and gestured for me to follow.

"Come. The chief wants us to go with him to the hill. He wishes to see the marching soldiers. If you are right and they are close, we will have to leave."

I pulled myself atop my horse and followed Yellow Knife. A few warriors joined us, along with Rain-in-the-Face. As we waded through the thick grass on top of our horses, I anxiously watched the ridgeline towering above us. I hoped the infantry was still miles away. Despite my worry, it was a blessing to be riding once more. The wind had long ago died, and the gentle breeze as we rode became a welcome relief from the stifling heat. I took a long pull from my water bladder, letting excess water drench the front of my shirt.

As we neared the bottom of the hill, we steered the horses toward a steep buffalo trail that led to the top. Just as we were about to drive the horses up the incline, the lead warrior cried out. Ahead of us we found an amazing sight. Three white men descended the same trail from high on the ridge. They weren't soldiers. At least they wore no uniform. Their focus trained on the ground so as not to tumble down the steep path. Incredible as it seemed, they had not seen our party. The fighting continued more than a mile away, and while the prairie smoked, the sounds of gunfire sounded like a gentle popping in the distance. Even when the report of a rifle fell to our ears, the scarcity of the shooting made it sound like a buffalo hunt, not a battle.

Rain-in-the-Face motioned us to some tall grass. We dismounted, and one of the warriors grabbed our horses by the bridles to pull them closer to the river and out of sight. The white men coming down the trail pointed toward the distance. Smoke lofted above the crest of the hill, and they watched it almost as much as they trained their eyes to the trail in front of them. They never saw where we hid in the grass at the bottom of the hill.

When they reached the level ground, Yellow Knife and another Lakota lunged forward. They grabbed the reins of the first two white men, controlling their horses. Both warriors fired their rifles, nearly planting the muzzles of the guns in the bellies of the two riders. One of the white men slumped forward in his saddle, while the other rolled off the side like a sack of potatoes.

The third man trailed further behind—so far, in fact, no warrior had managed to grab hold of his horse to control him. From his posture he had spent little time in the saddle, and when the shots rang out, he froze. I recognized him—*Mr. Carson*. Even from this distance I recalled him sitting across the table from me while we traveled on the train. I wondered if he still had his little bell.

Startled, he jolted upright in his saddle, losing all grip upon the reins. The horse bolted under the noise, bucking and running the rest of the way down the buffalo trail. Carson remained strapped into his stirrups, the only fact that saved his life. Despite the thrashing, the horse did not throw him to the ground. Instead, his bulbous body remained attached by his feet. His hands flailed in the air as his hat blew across the grass. None of the warriors fired after him, not even as he raced by us a few arm's lengths away. Even if they had managed to raise their rifles, their laughter precluded any chance a bullet would find its mark. His horse bounded out of sight, following the level ground of the riverbed and fleeing east along the river. Within a moment, Carson had disappeared around a bend. His hands raised above his head while he screamed in terror.

Yellow Knife handed me the reins of the two captured horses. I finally had a horse with a saddle to ride. I made a quick inventory and realized I should jump on the brown mare. She had a pair of pistols mounted cavalry style on either side of the saddle horn.

Rain-in-the-Face already made his way up the buffalo trail with renewed determination, walking while he held the bridle of his horse. He coaxed the animal ever onward over the steep terrain, perhaps realizing my fears were well placed. These three men we had just encountered were obviously not sent to rescue Custer, but the infantry couldn't be too far behind. If they came before the Lakota had finished off Custer and his soldiers, then the warriors would be fighting on two fronts. Behind us, the smoke continued to reach toward the clouds. The fires had not ignited the entire prairie as I expected. Instead, the green grass captured the flames into small pockets. Yet the smoke held thick, and the fighting had started once more. Staccato gunfire reached our ears. The sounds of the fight urged Rain-in-the-Face to pull harder upon his horse.

I was last in line, and even then, I only made it halfway up the trail when a bugle call interrupted our climb. It came from over the top of the hill—we were too late. Yellow Knife turned to me. My face must have held the same fear I saw upon his. Rain-in-the-Face reversed course, pointing his horse downhill. His manner held calm, but excitement contorted his face. We pulled ourselves onto our horses, but the poor animals went slowly to avoid slipping and sliding on their haunches. I did not fancy lying under a large horse as she slid to the bottom of the valley.

Once we made it to the prairie floor, the first soldiers came into sight above us. Rain-in-the-Face hesitated, watching them. As I stared with him, a patch of blue moving toward us caught the side of my vision—a single soldier. He rushed from the path where Mr. Carson had flailed upon his charging horse. The sun glinted off the bugle emblem upon his campaign hat, the sign of the infantry. Still at a good distance, he knelt and raised his rifle. Just as the white smoke rose from the breach of his gun,

I pulled Rain-in-the-Face backwards. The chief tumbled to the ground. The bullet struck the chief's horse in the side. The animal reared upward, and collapsed as it came down on its front legs. The trooper anxiously reloaded—a breech-loading carbine. I pulled one of the pistols from the pair mounted to my horse, and dug my heels in. My horse charged. I had never been gifted with a pistol, but the Great Spirit guided my shot. I fired before I reached the soldier, and the man in blue rolled backward upon the grass.

I hurriedly turned the horse and rode back toward my companions. Rain-in-the-Face stood, filled with rage. I had thrown him from his horse—a great insult. Yellow Knife screamed something and pointed in the direction of the soldier. The chief stared. Then his face softened. He understood what had happened. With his horse dying upon the prairie floor, I reached out and pulled him onto the back of my horse. The chief had to sound the retreat before the infantry surrounded his warriors. With a last glimpse to the hillside above us, I followed the others who galloped toward the Lakota lines. My horse, now burdened with two, lagged behind.

Sitting behind me as we rode, Rain-in-the-Face held his war lance high. He signaled the warriors as we rushed toward them. Behind us the vanguard of the reinforcements—more cavalry— swarmed down the hill. They were close. Their stubbly faces were covered with the same grime that marred my own. I held up my hand as we galloped past, hoping to distract them. A few troopers lowered their rifles. I wore the clothes of a white man and rode upon one of the captured horses. They must have figured me for one of their own.

However, amongst their lines one man stood apart. He didn't wear the blue uniform of the cavalry, or of a soldier. Instead, he wore all gray with a Stetson hat with a single feather perched upon his head—O'Malley. He had survived the river and found the expedition. His eyes locked with mine, but by the time he dug his spurs into his horse, we had already made it into the first of the fires. The smoke obscured our retreat.

As we reached the back of the Lakota lines, Rain-in-the-Face bounded from my horse. He ran among the warriors, directing their withdrawal. From somewhere he found an extra horse, and he galloped off down the Lakota position. With Rain-in-the-Face riding behind them, he forced each group of warriors to peel off and retreat. I could see he hoped Custer would not sense the hasty withdrawal.

Though it came too late, Custer discovered the ploy. I watched as Custer's cavalry broke through the wall of smoke just as their reinforcements rushed down the hilltop and flooded the plains behind us. Stirring my horse to a run, we were all in full flight. I pushed hard until I made it to the initial stand of cottonwoods, and then continued upriver. Yellow Knife rode right behind me. Every time I turned, the man in the red shirt—Longhair Custer— stayed at the front of his troops, pursuing us while he raised a carbine and shot. Slowly the heavier horses of the cavalry fell behind. In this open terrain they held no match for the nimble Indian ponies. As we continued three or four miles upstream, the chase ended.

Rain-in-the-Face continued to yell instructions as we fled. Groups of Indians broke off the main force and rode off on their own. The tactic neutralized the cavalry's purpose in pursuit. It reminded me of the long drawn-out fight with the Confederates. They would attack and melt back into society. In this case, the Lakota and the other Indians headed into the prairie. Each left to their own means in finding the village.

I rode with Yellow Knife and Rain-in-the-Face. The chief's anger at me had vanished. Yellow Knife spoke with him as he pulled alongside my horse, slowing our pace to no more than a hurried walk. He took out his knife, and gathering up the long tail in his war bonnet, he cut a feather loose. He held it out to me, using his free hand to grasp mine. I accepted the gift. Yellow Knife rode alongside as I stared at the feather.

"The chief says that you are a true warrior. You proved yourself today. He will tell the story of your deeds himself at the war council tonight."

CHAPTER TWENTY-SIX

8 AUGUST 1874

THE OLD MAN and I sat huddled over the fire. We kept the flames low, so cavalry scouts would not spot the light. The village had been on the move for four days, never staying in the same place more than a few hours, even at night. The people knew the stakes. They moved with a solidarity of purpose that I had never experienced before, not even during my short time in the Army. Rain-in-the-Face sent scouts behind us every night, and warriors rode as a rear guard all day. Sitting Bull believed us now—about the soldiers, about the gold in the Black Hills, about everything. We raced along the northern shore of the Yellowstone to where the Little Big Horn River joined.

Sitting Bull intended to cross in the morning, upriver from the confluence of the two rivers. The Yellowstone would narrow, making it passable for the children and all the horses hauling the travois. It was also the farthest point north in our travels. From there the village would escape into the great expanse of land to the south, holding the prospect of war at bay. As such, it seemed a good place to depart the village if we were to make an attempt. I longed to stay with the Lakota, yet I desired not to have a baby born while on the run. And it would be even worse if war loomed on the eastern horizon.

"We could make Fort Benton in a few days," I said. "Maybe a week."

"You don't think the Consortium would look for us there?" the Old Man replied.

He had a point. Even if the telegraph cables did not extend to the northern territories, express riders delivered mail between the forts. General Dorsey could have sent messages. If he sought us out along the southern route to Fort Laramie, it stood to reason he relayed messages to the other forts upon the frontier. And the presence of the Old Man made us easy targets.

"I supposed we could double back and head east with the ledger," I said.

The Old Man nodded, one hand rubbing the stubble that grew upon his face. He hadn't shaved. His old beard started to claim its rightful place making him more distinguished.

"I've been thinking about that, Joseph. You could carry on with Molly, and the children . . ." He paused, ". . . and I could take the ledger. I still know powerful men—journalists who would cast light into the darkest recesses of the Consortium. With the information here they will destroy the corruption. Surely that is the only way to kill this beast."

"Would that make us safe?"

He shook his head. "I thought we were safe back in Tennessee . . . and then they came." He stared into the fire. "Poor Charley. If not for us . . ."

He didn't finish the thought. I searched for some words to comfort him, though he spoke the truth. There had to be some manner of escape to finally break free of General Dorsey and his Consortium. If I had killed Dorsey in New York City, I wondered if they would still have pursued us. Perhaps the ledger held the best promise of all.

The Old Man continued, staring into the fire. "A woman came to see me two days ago, while you were gone for the fight. She brought a boy with her, who spoke some English. She had heard the *Great Father* had come to the village and she wanted to meet me. She had been with Black Kettle at the Sand Creek."

He stopped. I had only seen him hold back tears a few times in all my years with him. I feared his old melancholy would grip him, as it had after the death of his son. He held his head with one hand, not letting me see his eyes.

"Soldiers gunned down her daughter at Sand Creek," he said. "When I asked how old the girl was, she pointed at Emeline." He rocked for a minute. "The worst part of it, Joseph, was that she brought me food. She had seen me and thought I was too tall and skinny."

"You didn't order that attack," I offered.

"But I did nothing," he said. "I ordered an investigation, I removed Colonel Chivington from command, but nothing else. We were so mired in our great war, fighting the Confederates. The whole affair made me angry. I thought of it as a distraction, one more thing to deal with while our army fought in Vicksburg, and Richmond. I should have sent Chivington to fight in the trenches. To hell with Congress."

The Old Man stood, using my shoulder to rise to his full height.

"She brought me food, Joseph. How do I tell her that I did nothing to punish those who killed her daughter?"

"We were still at war," I said. "You couldn't do everything."

It sounded weak, but I needed to say something.

"Thank you, Joseph. I know you mean well, but you did not meet her."

His voice lowered. I hadn't seen this kind of sadness in him since the War.

"Do you remember Black Kettle?" he asked.

I nodded.

The chief had come all the way from his prairie home to meet the Old Man. He arrived with another chief—Lean Bear. They toured Washington. And both held such fascination with me. I was an Indian who guarded the Great White Chief—the Great Father. The Old Man presented them with peace medals to share their great friendship with the nation.

"At Sand Creek, as Chivington attacked, Black Kettle flew a giant American flag, Joseph. He flew it with a white flag underneath—a symbol that he remained our friend. I heard those details during the investigation into Chivington. And still I never sent him to the front like he deserved."

He leaned on me. Without looking I gripped his hand. It shook as he wept, causing his whole body to rock. I let him work it out without saying a word. I held fast upon his hand, not letting it go. When finally, he eased, I turned toward him.

"I should have done something, Joseph. I used our Great War as an excuse. The Devil makes such gains when no one watches. It was my job to watch, and I failed."

I tried to think of words to ease his anguish. But my mind held still. Nothing could erase that past.

"I need to rest these old legs, Joseph. This week has been hard on an old man like me. Do you wish me to douse the fire?"

I shook my head. "I'm not much for sleep yet. And Molly turns awful at night with the baby. I will take care of it when I retire."

The Old Man held my shoulder, squeezing it before letting his hand slide off as he walked away. He lifted the flap to the tipi and let it fall behind him. This had been the first night we erected the lodge all week, as the evening sky threatened to storm. Now it appeared clear.

I stared at the fire, watching the embers dance. The night had turned cool, and the smell of horses wafted over me. I closed my eyes and listened, longing to hear the wolves, though they seemed not to be nearby. The night held still and ominous.

I startled as a voice broke the quiet—Yellow Knife.

"Tatanka Yotanka would like to speak with you," he said.

I turned to see both Yellow Knife and Sitting Bull. They had sought me out. I stood to greet them, but Sitting Bull gestured me to sit. He joined me across the fire, while Yellow Knife sat by my side. I listened to Sitting Bull speak. His words never rushed. They flowed from him as if they were song. At times Yellow Knife struggled to find the translation. Yet he always managed the right meaning.

"I did not believe you when you brought the Great Father to us," Sitting Bull said. "We did not have scouts to the east. The buffalo herds were small this summer, and the Crows from the north invaded our hunting lands below the Yellowstone. Our warriors were busy defending the land. The soldiers came last year, and so I thought it would be some time before they returned."

I nodded, showing him I listened.

"I no longer trust the white man. He comes from a different place over the great ocean, and does not understand the way of the Great Spirit upon this land. He is a child who kills and does not eat. We take the buffalo when we need the meat to live and the skins to make robes and the winter lodges to stay warm. The white man uses his guns and kills many buffalo and antelope. He leaves the bodies to rot upon the prairie. And now you tell me these men come to take the *Paha Sapa* from us, to dig up our ancestors to find the yellow metal they crave."

I stared into the fire. Everything he said held truth. I didn't know how to help. Molly slept behind me. I thought of the children with

us, how I would best account for their safety. I had to ask Sitting
Bull to release us. As much as I wished to stay, to understand these
people and to know where I came from, I owed my family.

"As you said, we spoke words of truth to you," I started. "The
Great Father has a book, the one we showed you. If I can take him
to the Council in Washington, he can speak of that book. They
will believe him. Maybe they will turn back the soldiers."

Sitting Bull changed the subject without acknowledging my
words.

"Yellow Knife told me what happened with Blanket Jim
Bridger. How the wolves did not attack you."

I nodded.

"And Rain-in-the-Face told of your deeds at the war council.
You saved him upon the prairie and killed a soldier. He said your
mother's father was an Oglala warrior. A man from Chief Šóta's
lodge."

I nodded again. "That is what my mother said. Her father was
sent to unite the eastern tribes as they were driven west."

"Chief Šóta was an important man among the Oglala. I did
not know this when Rain-in-the-Face first brought you to us. The
Great Spirit sent you back to us, but I did not listen to your words."
He paused. "Your mother came from those eastern tribes?"

"She was from the Miami people," I answered.

"And your father was a white man?"

"Yes," I said.

"And he raised you in the white man's world?" Sitting Bull
asked.

I shook my head. "My mother never spoke of him. All I know
is that he raped my mother. After he finished, she killed him with
his own knife. If he were alive, I would want nothing of him. My
mother raised me."

Sitting Bull nodded. "The people here call you Two Wolves."

I looked to Yellow Knife, not completely understanding. Sitting Bull continued.

"You come from the white man and the Indian. You are *Métis*, but also Lakota. The Great Spirit sent you back to us for you stand with a foot in both worlds."

"My mother told a story about two wolves that live inside each of us." I touched my chest with my palm as I spoke.

Sitting Bull nodded. "I have heard this story. My Cheyenne cousins tell something like it. Each of us decides which wolf to feed, and each can decide to fight for good or become wicked."

"Is that why you came?" I asked. "To see if I would fight or if I lied for the white man?" He must have had a more important reason to seek me out at night and not summon me to his lodge.

"I came to find your intentions, though I do not think you fight for these men who attack us. Do you wish to leave us?"

I nodded. "My wife will soon give birth. She wishes to return to her people before the baby arrives."

"Do you think this is not your fight, Two Wolves?" Sitting Bull asked.

"I hope there is no more fight," I answered. "I hope the soldiers will not pursue once we cross the Yellowstone. You must avoid a new war until I can get the Great Father to speak to the Council. That is the only manner in which I may help you."

"You sound like Chief Red Cloud," Sitting Bull replied, his tone now dismissive. "You know of him?"

"A little."

"Red Cloud went to meet the Great Council, and then he went to another great city. When he returned to us, he told of the white men. He said he had seen more white men than blades of grass upon all the prairies. He said the whites would keep coming. They

TJ TURNER

would run out of space in their villages, and soon they would take our lands. Red Cloud said the only way for the Indian to survive would be to make peace with the white man and sign his papers."

My stomach turned at his words. "There is no manner in which you will stop all the white men who will come."

"Then you are like Red Cloud," Sitting Bull said. His hands fell hard upon his knees, making them clap. The noise split the night. "The white people put bad medicine over Red Cloud's eyes. They made him see everything and anything they please. They put the same medicine over you."

I had hoped that Sitting Bull believed my message—General Dorsey intended to start a war to justify seizing the Black Hills. Now it didn't seem that way.

"You mean to fight?" I asked. "You're not fleeing the soldiers?"

Sitting Bull shook his head. "The Great Spirit gave me this land. No one but the Great Spirit can take it from the Lakota. And he will, if I do nothing. He will give it to the white man if I sit and watch it happen, if I sign his treaties and do not fight. If I do that, I do not deserve this land."

"You can't win," I pleaded. "You haven't seen the cities to the east. You haven't seen how many men they have, or the weapons they'll bring."

"A vision came to me on this march. Soldiers fell from the sky like grasshoppers. They fell into our camp, and the Great Spirit spoke to me, saying, '*I give you these because they have no ears*'. The white man has never listened. They sign the treaties with the Lakota, and still they come into our land. We asked the soldiers to take the miners from the *Paha Sapas*, and they did not listen. Now they will fall into our camp, and we will strike them so they hear us. Then the Great Council will listen to the Great Father about his book. But only after the Lakota force these men from our land."

I thought about the march from the past two days. Sitting Bull had sent scouts to watch the cavalry and the infantry columns. They returned each night bragging on how they taunted Custer's cavalry. I figured it for the bluster of young men, anxious to earn feathers for brave acts. But now I understood. He ordered them to taunt, drawing the cavalry forward. The infantry could never keep pace with how fast the village moved.

"You haven't been retreating," I said. "You're drawing out the cavalry."

Sitting Bull smiled. "We used to call Long Hair Custer by the name *Hard Backsides*. He chased the Lakota and the Cheyenne far across the prairies—farther and harder than any soldier before. He is a fierce warrior, but this is also his weakness. He will chase too far, and he will fall into our camp. They will come, just as the Great Spirit revealed to me, because they have no ears."

Even with Sitting Bull's large force of warriors, he knew he couldn't fight the cavalry and infantry at once. The first fight two days ago served only as a blocking action—to give the village time to pack and move. Now they kept just enough ahead that it lured Custer out, beyond the protection of the infantry. It seemed a gamble, hoping to have enough time to fight one force before the other arrived.

"You think that defeating Custer and his cavalry will make the other soldiers retreat?" I asked.

"It will make them listen—and fear the Lakota. Then they might honor the treaties they signed. And then I will release you to go east with the Great Father to talk to the Council. We need one more day of travel. Then Long Hair Custer will be far from the *big-talking* guns that travel with the marching soldiers."

I looked to Yellow Knife.

"Big-talking guns?" I asked.

Yellow Knife searched for the right words. He spoke to Sitting Bull, and they gestured between themselves. They meant the guns pulled by the horses.

"Artillery?" I asked. "Cannon?"

"Yes, cannon," Yellow Knife answered.

"How many do they have?" I asked.

"There are two. They pull them with the marching soldiers."

"We need to capture those guns," I said. "If we take them, we can use them against Custer."

"No one here knows how to make them fire," Yellow Knife said.

I looked to Sitting Bull. "Before I served the Great Father as his life guard, I served as a soldier in his army. I stood upon the walls of his city, and they taught me how to use the cannon. If we can get them, I will show you."

Sitting Bull listened to Yellow Knife translate. For the first time emotion crossed his face—confidence.

"How well do you remember your mother's story, Two Wolves?" he asked.

"We feed the wolf we want to grow," I answered.

Sitting Bull leaned close, even though he sat across the smoldering fire. He shook his head.

"No. There *are* two wolves in each of us. They will always fight, but they need each other. One does not exist without the other. We only find true peace if we feed *both* wolves. And this is the land of wolves."

CHAPTER TWENTY-SEVEN

10 AUGUST 1874

THE NEXT DAY as the village crossed the Yellowstone, Sitting Bull showed his cunning. For the entire flight along the river, the Lakota had moved in a manner that betrayed their presence. They left tracks from the travois thirty rows wide. Villagers dropped items during the march. Personal things that made the retreat appear to be in panic. They abandoned moccasins, buffalo hides, and even stores of coffee they had traded with the mountain men who braved Lakota territory. These items cluttered the path, drawing a line for the cavalry to follow. I had figured it meant the villagers lightened their load to flee faster. But Sitting Bull meant it as deceit.

The village stopped laying the trail when we reached Little Big Horn River. Where the two rivers met, the water flowed too deep to cross so the village unhooked the horses from the travois. The women carried the long wood poles on their shoulders. They headed upriver above the Little Big Horn leaving no trace upon the land. They dropped nothing and left no marks upon the grass. The warriors grouped the horses together and drove them north, up the bluffs in single file. Once they were about a mile inland, they circled in a wide arc to join the women. The rushing water of the Yellowstone sat low above the Little Big Horn. The village crossed the river there and then headed east. They crossed the Little Big Horn below where the rivers merged. Once they were opposite the camp of the night before, they hooked up the travois, and turned south. In this manner, Sitting Bull made it appear that the village crossed the river at the deepest point. The cavalry could not venture the crossing here. Sitting Bull meant it to mire Custer in a position vulnerable to attack.

The village moved miles beyond the river to shield it from sight. Rain-in-the-Face deployed his scouts up and down the southern shores of the Yellowstone, while the warriors assembled upon the bluffs overlooking the river. The women, children, and those too old to fight moved on with the village. Sitting Bull would give them a day to march south before he attacked. He wished for a buffer in case his plan didn't work. And with their families at their backs, the warriors held a grim determination. The day delay also gave Sitting Bull time to send word to nearby Miniconjou, Oglala, Sans Arc, and Cheyenne camps for reinforcements. My role would be risky, but simple. I would try to take the cannon and then turn the artillery upon advancing infantry. Then the Lakota might stand a chance against the cavalry alone.

"Joseph, this isn't our fight. Please stay with me," Molly pleaded when Yellow Knife came to fetch me from the marching village. He and his small band of warriors would escort me across the river. Aurora sat with Molly upon a horse, while Daniel walked and held the bridle ahead of us.

"Sitting Bull will let us go if we help. In fact, he'll send escorts all the way out of the territory. And we need this, Molly. We can't keep running. I want us somewhere safe when the baby is born. The soldiers will eventually catch the village, and then none of us will make it. We need a proper midwife for you."

"I feel I won't see you again—"

I didn't let her finish her thought. I reached out to hold her.

"Come back to me," she said. Her tears were hot upon my cheeks.

"I will make certain he returns," the Old Man said.

He had ridden up on his horse and eased Emeline to the ground where she took her place by Daniel.

"No," I said. "I need you to stay with Molly and the children. And later you will need to take the ledger to Congress."

The Old Man shook his head. "I will not run, Joseph."

"I'm not asking that you do," I said. "We all have our part. Mine is here. Yours will come next."

The Old Man held an old Sharps rifle in his hand. He placed it across his lap as he sat upon his horse.

"I didn't tell you the whole story with the woman who came to see me." He looked to the weapon in his hands. "The boy she brought, the one who could speak English—he was her son. They call him Yellow Sparrow because his hair is so light. And his eyes came from his father—the soldier who killed her daughter. When the soldiers attacked that day, this woman ran to her tipi. The soldier followed. He caught her inside the tipi and raped her. But he didn't see the rifle. When he was done, she managed to get hold of it. She shot and killed him."

I stared at the rifle in his hands. It had been the same with my mother, though she used a knife to kill the man who had been the other half of my creation. I met the Old Man's eyes. He needed this.

"You'll have to shoot at soldiers," I said. "Do you think you can do that? They are our people."

The Old Man shook his head.

"I've read that ledger. These men who march against us aren't our people. This is an army for hire, paid for by Dorsey. They may wear the uniform, but they are patsies for the Consortium. We need to stop them."

I could do nothing to prevent him from coming, and I didn't wish to stop him. He had to feed his own wolves.

"I'll give the ledger to Molly for safeguarding." He handed the satchel across the horses. Molly accepted it and looped it over her shoulder.

I leaned in to kiss her. Then I kissed Aurora upon the forehead. She knew everything that happened yet I deciphered no emotion upon her. I worried that she had seen too much in this life to ever be a normal little girl—one who could go to school, fall in love, raise a family, and be immune from the terror in this life.

I dragged myself onto the horse that Yellow Knife brought for me—one of his finest war ponies. I took the rope bridle in one hand while the other clutched Molly. Her fingers slid through mine as I pulled away.

"Do not worry, Molly. It is my time to look out for him," the Old Man said.

As we rode away, I turned to see Molly and Aurora. The girl had tears in her eyes. Somehow it made me feel better—perhaps we all needed less healing than I thought.

We rode with Yellow Knife to the bluff high on the southern side of the Yellowstone and joined the warriors gathered there. After we picketed the horses, we crept upon our bellies to the ridge. The cavalry had moved in, finding the tracks the village laid. To Sitting Bull's credit, he had been right. Custer sent a scout across the river, swimming without a weapon or horse. The soldier came ashore right next to Rain-in-the-Face's men. They were concealed in the low scrub brushes, hidden amongst the rocks. Never once did the scout see them. Instead, he found the tracks of the village and then swam back to Custer on the far side.

Two sandbars parted the water at this point in the river. Custer's men made it through the shallows and onto these little islands. But there the game changed. It might have been a quarter mile to the far shore, but the water flowed deep and the currents were strong. Time and again the cavalry tried to cross, only to have their horses revolt and turn around part way. If Custer had thought clearly, he might have sent his scouts farther upriver in search of a better crossing. But he seemed intent on proving he could cross at the same location where Indian women and children had managed. Perhaps Sitting Bull's vision held true—these men had no ears, and maybe no eyes. The trap had sprung.

As we watched, the rear of the cavalry arrived, bringing a large herd of cattle. It seemed a funny addition to this light-armed unit. The cattle surely slowed down the cavalry, though I guessed they worried about finding adequate numbers of buffalo or antelope.

"Where is the infantry?" I asked. Sitting Bull had sent scouts miles downriver.

"Many hours from here."

"If Custer moved those cattle with him, the infantry won't be far behind—maybe not far enough. We should go now."

A terrible thought gripped me. *Had Custer understood what Sitting Bull planned? Did we fall prey to his trap instead?* Perhaps he did not send scouts along the river on purpose. Maybe he did not wish to cross the river. He would make it look like he attempted the crossing where Sitting Bull chose, but instead he lured us back. I pulled on Yellow Knife's arm.

"It's a trap," I said. "He wishes us to cross. The infantry is close."

Yellow Knife studied my face for a moment. Then he crawled to Sitting Bull and Rain-in-the-Face. They were discussing the plan with another young war chief—Chief Gall. They spoke for a few minutes. When the voices became heated, Yellow Knife pointed in our direction. Sitting Bull locked eyes with me and then turned his attention back to the cavalry. Yellow Knife crawled back.

"We go now," he said

"Did they listen?" I asked.

"We go and find where the marching soldiers camp. We will see if you are right."

The Old Man and I crawled back to the horses as Yellow Knife's warriors gathered around him. He had fifty men, designed to be the element that crossed the river to lay in ambush for the artillery. As he spoke, he kept his voice low so it would not carry on the wind. I doubted that Custer's cavalry could have heard even a war cry over the rush of the river, but we needed to maintain our surprise if the plan had any chance.

"You should stay," I said to the Old Man. "Things have changed."

"I promised Molly I would see you back in one piece. And I promised Mochi, the woman I told you about, that I would ride her rifle into battle. I will not turn back if you will not."

"Well then," I said. "We had better go. I may need saving."

CHAPTER TWENTY-EIGHT

YELLOW KNIFE LED us upon the exact route we took the day before. We crossed the Little Big Horn, and then rode upriver on the Yellowstone until we could wade to the opposite shore. The water still held the sting of winter, as it rose up over the bellies of the horses and met our feet. Even here, the current pushed us along the riverbed until the horses recovered their footing. After crossing, we rode with as much stealth as the pace allowed. We traced a route inland until we reached the top of the bluffs—well out of sight of the cavalry. Yellow Knife kept us a mile or more behind the soldiers. We even traveled through gullies in the bluffs in case Custer had posted sentinels.

When the sun rose high above us, we made our way toward the river. Once again, we used the runoff gullies formed during the rainy season to disguise our approach. When we were close, we picketed the horses. Several warriors remained behind, and the rest inched closer to the edge of the bluffs. Yellow Knife divided his force, ordering a dozen warriors about a quarter mile farther east along the ridge. They would wait his signal. There they found a gully that flowed toward the river. It made a perfect funnel to attack if the infantry rushed to reinforce the cavalry. We found a similar coulee, or gulley, and lay on either side of it. From our position the cut in the bluff formed a small valley. A man could jump from one side to the other if need be. It made a tight funnel to stream toward the riverbed, which could be our undoing. But it also provided an element of surprise.

Below us, and to the west about a mile, the cavalry still struggled to cross the Yellowstone. I figured it for a ruse. When the infantry came into view to our east, I felt stronger about my suspicion. They were maybe three miles downriver, but moving in our direction. They appeared as little dots along the river. From this distance the position of the cannon escaped me. Yellow Knife retreated from the edge of the bluff, to mask his location from the cavalry. He lifted a war spear to the sky. It signaled Sitting Bull across the river.

The first sign the battle had commenced came from Custer's camp. Little white puffs of smoke lifted skyward where the men kneeled. Moments later, the distant crack of the rifles fell upon our ears as we lay in the burning sun. I welcomed the breeze that flowed over the bluff, though it was too weak to dry the back of my shirt.

Lakota warriors at the opposite shore of the river began to fire. The bullets fell to the center of Custer's formation. They had crept to the waterline, concealed in the sagebrush. Boulders provided cover near the river. Even with the distance we heard them yell taunts back and forth with the Crow Indians of Custer's scouts. One by one, warriors swam with their horses across the river. Sitting Bull had decided to press the attack on Custer's side of the river.

It appeared to be a dangerous maneuver. As the warriors drifted downstream, they put themselves in the middle of the two groups of soldiers. The cavalry was to the west, and infantry marched to the rescue from the east. The cavalry couldn't see the warriors as they crossed and landed on the riverbed upstream from our position on the bluffs. The Lakota had stripped to the waist and held their rifles high over their head as they crossed. The cold water must have felt a welcome relief against the stifling air.

As the sounds of gunfire echoed across the river, the infantry doubled their efforts. Dust from their feet and wagons rose upon the horizon. A small wagon train with a light guard of cavalry approached well ahead of the marching columns. Horse teams pulled two Rodman guns—wheeled cannon that would change the fight. At the very least we needed to destroy the wagons and perhaps sink the guns in the river. At best, we could capture the cannon and use them against Custer. I tugged on Yellow Knife's arm to gain his attention.

"We need those guns."

"I go with the other men." He pointed to the warriors he had placed farther downriver. "When they pass, we come behind. You come from the front."

He motioned toward the warriors crossing the river.

"They will protect your backsides from the cavalry. It is all how Sitting Bull planned."

He scrambled across the small coulee, and then crouched as he ran the short distance to his other men. I turned to the Old Man.

"I want you to stay high in the terrain," I said.

"I'm coming with you, Joseph."

"That's not what I meant. I want you to stay high in this gully and use the rocks as cover. That Spencer rifle is better from a distance. You'll be able to cover us as we go in. Don't worry, you'll give that rifle plenty of revenge this afternoon."

I slid into the gully with a dozen of Yellow Knife's warriors. They each carried Henry rifles—repeating weapons that fired sixteen rounds fed from the tube below the barrel. I hoped they brought their good shells. They had a tendency to pull the bullet from the casing and remove powder—stretching it to last longer.

But it made the bullet slower. So slow that in some battles the lead balls struck men and never even broke the skin.

The small wagon train approached Yellow Knife's position and then passed. A guard of four cavalry rode with it, and two men sat in each wagon. Behind them, several horses pulled the cannon. Yet the front of this small unit gave me pause—I hadn't expected it. General Dorsey rode atop a beautiful white horse. He wore an impeccable uniform, as if the heat bothered him not in the least. A spotless white-brimmed hat covered his head. His pants and jacket gathered no dust. Next to him sat the fat man from the train, the one who had escaped us in battle the day before—Mr. Carson. He perched awkwardly upon an equally plump horse. Sweat beaded upon his face and rolled into his eyes. Removing his hat to mop his forehead, his nervous manner caused him to fumble with it and drop it upon the ground.

I raised my rifle to get the first shot upon the general. Putting pressure on the trigger, I stopped. Another man galloped from behind the cannon—the devil himself—O'Malley. I beckoned to the Old Man, who scrambled by the warriors to where I squatted concealed behind a boulder.

"What is it, Joseph?"

"You see the man with the hat? The one with the feather?"

The Old Man peered from behind the rock.

"Isn't that Charley's hat?" he asked.

"When we rush, I want you to kill him first. Make certain he's dead," I replied.

As I turned back to survey the scene below, O'Malley stared right at us. Even with the distance I swore he locked eyes with me. A grin came upon his face, as though we had arrived at the moment he so long had wished. Without breaking my stare from the evil below, I spoke to the Old Man.

"Tell Molly I love her."

He didn't have time to respond. Yellow Knife's warriors flowed from the gully behind the cannon. They yelled their war cries as they rushed from shelter and attacked. Shots rang out, and the light cavalry guard spun their horses to face the advancing Indians to their rear. The soldiers fired, and some of the warriors fell—yet O'Malley didn't break his glare. We stayed like that a moment, locked in our own space. Then he screamed, kicking his stirrups. Horse and rider rushed toward us.

I lifted my rifle and fired. After working the lever and loading another round, I rushed down the gully. The warriors at my back followed, running toward the now stricken artillery unit. On the far side of our position Yellow Knife had overrun the cavalry and taken the cannon. The remaining cavalrymen had dismounted to hide amongst the boulders. They kept up a constant rate of fire, but Yellow Knife and his warriors crashed in amongst them. I ran along the shore, stopping once to take a shot at O'Malley. I had him in my sights, yet as I pulled the trigger the report of the Spencer sounded behind me. O'Malley's horse crumpled, throwing him forward and into the waterline. The Old Man had missed, and with it my shot sailed over O'Malley's head. I pressed forward, reaching his bellowing horse.

I scanned up and down the river, but O'Malley had disappeared—as if he melted into the thick air, or swam from the battle. I had no time to search. Running toward the artillery, I reached it as the soldiers from the wagons beat back the warriors. They fired their pistols, dropping Lakota warriors all around them. General Dorsey held fast in the middle of the foray and shot from his horse. I raised my rifle and fired again.

The rifle lurched in my hand with a small popping noise. I had one of those rounds, where the Lakota had removed powder.

They had removed so much that the bullet didn't clear the gun. Running toward the general, I flipped the rifle around until I held it by the barrel. He saw me coming, swinging around on his horse. Leveling his pistol, he fired. The ball struck my leg, but I fought to stay upright. The burning swelled my anger. I swung the rifle with all my might, striking him in the middle of his chest. It knocked him from his horse. As I took a step in his direction, intending to crush his head amongst the river rocks, my leg buckled. It sent me sprawling upon the ground.

My vision pulled in from the edges of my eyes, and I fought to hold on. I lost sight of the general. Sounds came muffled, as if I were far away, or my head was underwater. Pulling myself forward, I reached the edge of the river. I grabbed a palm full of water and pressed it upon my face. The cold of it brought me back. All at once, the sound of the battle crashed upon me.

"Now you die!"

I spun to my back. General Dorsey stood above me. He pulled the hammer back on his pistol, cocking the weapon to fire. As he pulled the trigger, I cringed. The sharp sound of the hammer echoed as it fell upon an empty cylinder—no shot. Dorsey stared at the weapon in his hand. There is no sound louder than a gun that fires when it shouldn't—or one that doesn't when it should. I gave him no time to figure it out. Kicking with my good leg, I caught his knee. He stumbled and fell backwards onto the edge of the river, sending out a mist of water as he crashed around the river rocks. Rising up on one elbow, I threw myself on top of him. My hands fit around his throat and I squeezed. His face turned red as he flailed at my hands, then tried to gouge my eyes. I turned my head to avoid his outstretched fingers. He kicked behind me. Then his hand rose up and struck me about the head. He clutched a river rock, and the sound echoed like a wooden thud. I crumpled, feeling the water from the river wash over me as I lay half-in and half-out of the flowing river.

I found myself on my back staring into his face once more. He rose above me with his pistol, gripping it by the barrel as he used it like a club. When he slammed it down trying to strike my head, I grabbed hold of his wrist and blocked his strike. I used my grip on his arm to pull myself to a seated position and tried to strike his face with my head. But he pushed out of reach. My head spun, and slowly my grip upon his wrist lost its strength. With a sudden jerk, he pulled his arm free and raised the pistol high above our heads.

"Now you join your mother!"

But before he could drop his club upon my head, blood splattered across my shirt and General Dorsey arched forward. The report of the Spencer rifle rang out above the noise of the raging river, and a hole burned through Dorsey's chest. Behind us both, the Old Man held the Spencer rifle. The taste of iron filled my mouth as Dorsey's blood had splattered my face. The bullet hit him in the back and went straight through, striking me in the shoulder. My arm collapsed, and a moment later General Dorsey fell flat upon me. His face struck the hard river rocks over my other shoulder.

"Joseph! Joseph!"

The Old Man ran along the river line. He dropped his rifle and hauled Dorsey's limp body from atop me. As he pulled the dead man, I caught sight of the glazed eyes. A trickle of blood stained his teeth crimson. I looked at the devil himself—dead.

I pushed to one side. "Where's O'Malley?"

I searched in all directions as the Old Man propped me up. The battle continued a few hundred feet behind us, though only a few soldiers remained alive. One of the cannon stood intact, but the other lay on its side, a wheel splintered and the horses that pulled it lay dead in the riverbank. Yellow Knife still directed the fight. He rushed one of the remaining soldiers and clubbed him over the head.

Then before I could yell a warning, O'Malley rose from between the wagons. He appeared like a beast, able to spring forward in the manner of a large cat. In his hand, he held my knife—the one the Old Man gave me—the same one O'Malley took from me in New York City. O'Malley rushed forward and plunged it into Yellow Knife's back. Then letting go of the handle, he grasped Yellow Knife around the throat, turning him into a shield. Firing his pistol, he dropped two warriors, then another. I grabbed the Spencer rifle from the Old Man and tried to aim. As it fired, the kick of the gun knocked it from my grip. My shoulder screamed with pain. The bullet that killed Dorsey had taken a gash out of the side of my arm, though it missed any bone. But the wound was still raw, sending my shot wide.

O'Malley spun in my direction, still holding Yellow Knife. When he pulled the knife out of his back, Yellow Knife screamed with pain, and blood issued forth in a froth from his mouth. O'Malley howled, like the noise the deranged make before they die. Using the knife, he cut a feather from Yellow Knife's hair. Yellow Knife fell to his knees in front of O'Malley—his eyes focused on a different world.

Then the Spencer shot again. The Old Man had plucked it from where I dropped the rifle. O'Malley spun. My knife sailed through the air. The bullet struck him in the shoulder or chest. He fell, but then popped back up, still gripping the feather in his hand. Grabbing a nearby horse, he swung into the saddle and rode off, holding the feather high in the air above him. The Old Man fired again, yet O'Malley kept riding, toward the advancing infantry.

"Help me up," I said.

The Old Man said nothing. Instead, he bound my leg wound. He had ripped a section of his shirt and wrapped it hard upon my thigh. The pain forced me to double over. I vomited upon the ground.

"Help me up," I said again.

"Joseph, you're in no state—"

I cut him off.

"Get me up. We need to get these guns working, or all is for nothing if the infantry arrives."

The Old Man picked me up. Together we hobbled toward Yellow Knife. I used the Spencer as a crutch, pushing off the ground with every step. When I reached Yellow Knife, the life drained fast. Letting go of the Old Man, I lowered myself. I gripped Yellow Knife's head and forced him to look at me.

"We have the guns," I said.

"Make them speak," he answered. A hand reached out and grasped my wrist. His eyes lost focus. Then he snapped back for a moment. "He took my feather, Two Wolves."

"I'll get it," I said. "I'll find him."

He nodded. His strength faded.

"Tell my story at the war council tonight, Two Wolves. I want you to speak for me." His grip released, and his head slumped to one side. I let it down onto the ground.

Around us, a group of warriors gathered. There were only a few left.

"Get me up." The Old Man hauled me to my feet. "Get me to the gun. We need to spin it around. The powder and the shot will be in the wagons."

The Old Man guided me along the rocky ground to the one functional Rodman gun. When we reached it, I found a body underneath rolled into a ball—Mr. Carson. As I kicked him, the man sobbed. One of the warriors pulled him to his feet and looked set to slash his throat when I grasped his arm.

"No!" I gestured toward Carson's head and pointed to the approaching infantry. The warriors wouldn't understand what I said, so I had to gesture and try my best at sign language. "He knows of their plans. We'll keep him alive, for now."

As I said that last part, I looked at Carson. He cowered. I passed him to the Old Man and started working on the guns.

The warriors helped me spin the cannon. The infantry was well within range, and marching in our direction—maybe a little more than a mile away. When the Indians emptied the wagons and brought me the wooden crates, I split them open and began to load the gun. They watched as I rammed gunpowder into the bore. Then I placed the shot inside. I raised the back of the bore with the elevating bar until it held true upon the advancing troops.

The infantry marching toward us had no idea we had their artillery. They kept their hurried cadence until they reached a point along the river that forced their number to pinch together. We had the perfect shot.

I motioned for all to cover their ears.

CHAPTER TWENTY-NINE

FOR MORE THAN an hour we kept pressure on the advancing infantry. Though we fired the cannon less often than the soldiers would manage, they never came near to recovering the big-talking gun. As the sun faded overhead, the sounds of battle with the cavalry intensified behind us. We fired round after round, resorting to grapeshot when the soldiers ventured close. I worked with a small team of Yellow Knife's warriors until they could load and fire themselves. The Old Man helped. When we finally stepped back and let the Lakota take over, black powder smeared our clothes. We were in sore need of baths.

Only once did the soldiers try to work their way around, heading up the bluff to flank us on the high ground. Several warriors scaled the hill and called for help across the river. Within minutes more Lakota swam across the Yellowstone on top of their ponies. They galloped up the hill, through the gullies that we had rushed down to trap the artillery. The flanking maneuver never reached us.

The Old Man finally led an effort to get the other gun working. They swapped a wheel from one of the wagons for the broken one on the Rodman gun. It took the better part of an hour, but they managed. Spinning the cannon, they pushed it toward the sounds of gunfire upriver and toward the cavalry at our backs. The horses were all dead, at least the ones that had been bridled to pull the artillery. I limped to one of the downed horses and began taking off the bridles. Some of the Lakota helped me, understanding what we hoped to accomplish. The language barrier seemed not to exist as the bullets flew. They summoned extra horses from the men who had scaled the bluffs. In short fashion we had the necessary power to haul the cannon forward, including the ammunition wagon.

While the one gun fired on the infantry, Sitting Bull sent more warriors to repel the marching soldiers. The Old Man and I helped with the new cannon. We walked next to the horses, urging them toward the din of battle that raged ahead. I pushed the horses as hard as I dared. None had ever been bridled in this fashion, and thus the cannon made slow progress. But after a couple miles we came to a spot where the river bent. We could see the fighting with the cavalry up ahead.

The main body of warriors had now crossed the Yellowstone. They held low ground along the southern riverbank, nestled amongst the rocks for cover. In their position they kept the cavalry from fleeing to the southern shore. In contrast, the soldiers sought shelter at the base of the bluffs. But the Lakota and their allies had also seized the high ground above the soldiers. They fired down upon the stricken cavalry. Even to the west, on the far side of Custer's position, the soldiers were trapped. They had established a blocking force at the bottom of a gradual climb. But more warriors held the high ground there, too. The cavalry had no avenue for escape. We hurried the horses to get the gun ready.

As we prepared the cannon, it became clear our position held the only route the cavalry might flee, though it would have to be a fighting retreat. Except for the blocking force to their west, the soldiers had grouped into a tight formation. They used the bodies of their fallen horses as a means to shield themselves from the warriors. In the middle of the scrum, a single man issued orders. Occasionally he lifted his carbine to fire. His long hair flowed under his hat, falling onto a bright red shirt—Custer.

The rhythm of the battle ebbed and flowed. As we set the cannon, the firing seemed to stop. Everyone reloaded, and both sides assessed the standoff. Quiet descended around us. I kicked the rocks at my feet to ensure I hadn't gone deaf. Custer scanned in our direction. Perhaps he gauged the timing to make a break, or he sought in vain for the infantry that might yet come to his rescue. He pointed at us, yelling some manner of orders. Yellow Knife's warriors made ready on the Rodman gun. I worked the elevation lever until the bore would place a shell in the midst of the soldiers.

Custer must have seen the cannon—perhaps thinking that General Dorsey had come to his rescue. With the firing stopped, he stood and studied our position. Other men rose to look as well. To my amazement, Custer ordered a group of his soldiers to their feet. When they rose, they held musical instruments, not rifles. Their music fell over the field—coronets and alto horns. Everyone fixated on the scene, so unbelievable in the midst of the killing and the smoke. The tune was not the reticent song of an army about to surrender, or the sound of a bugle calling for maneuver. Instead, the wind carried a marching tune—the *Garryowen*. He meant it to inspire. Custer had not given up.

I had long read the stories of this man, whose mythos I figured could only be matched by his bravado. His battlefield heroics during the Civil War counted among legend. But the nation also knew him from the battles he waged against the plains Indians. Newspapers heralded him as a hero. And women swooned over the dashing man they saw in the sketches or tintypes. In the stories he brought his Army band for campaigning. In the midst of battle, they played to mesmerize the enemy and inspire the troops. He planned to charge.

"Ready—" I called out.

The man in red pulled his horse from the mêlée surrounding him. On my right the Old Man leveled the Spencer rifle, bracing it against the wheel of the Rodman gun. The soldiers were so far away that only incredible luck would have placed the bullet on target. The Old Man pulled back on the trigger until the gun jumped. Custer mounted right as the bullet found him. He swung in the saddle, reacting to the impact. Then he righted himself, clutching his leg. But otherwise he remained untouched. Pulling a pistol from his holster he fired it into the air. The smoke stretched skyward before the shot crashed among us. Kicking his horse, he charged.

The other soldiers followed. The men on the far side of Custer's position, the ones in the blocking force, mounted what horses they had. They formed into the attack, abandoning their far flank. Our position held their only means of escape.

"Fire!" My voice cracked as thirst plagued at me.

The Rodman gun kicked. I had loaded it with a shell as we hoped to hit the men comprising the blocking force. We really needed grapeshot to stall the charge. The shell sailed over the heads of the charging cavalry. It slammed into the position the blocking force had just occupied. Dirt flew in the air and did little more than scare the Lakota on the far side of the fighting.

"Reload! Reload!" I screamed to the warriors around us.

However, the men who brought the gun upriver had not yet manned a cannon. Frantically, I limped to the front of the gun and began to ram gunpowder down into the breech. Around me, the warriors discharged what they had left in their rifles. They fired into the charging cavalry. I looked to the bluffs to our north, imploring the Great Spirit to send reinforcements. Nothing broke the skyline above us save the grass that blew on top of the bluff.

I shoved a canister of grapeshot into the barrel of the cannon and slammed it home with the ramrod. As I pulled it out, the Old Man yelled, "Joseph, get down!"

I fell flat upon the ground. The cannon fired, spewing shot toward the charging cavalry. A horse fell, and several soldiers crashed upon the ground. Custer remained untouched. Strong medicine protected him. In some manner he had avoided all the grapeshot coming from the gun. I had no time to reload.

The man in the red shirt raised a pistol in one hand and took aim in our direction. Smoke rose from the barrel, but with the thundering of the horses crashing upon us, I heard nothing. Each of the soldiers fired from horseback. The sounds of battle came to me muffled again. My vision narrowed. As I pushed up to my hands and knees, the sharp pain in my leg brought back focus. Sound came rushing in—the report of rifles, the hooves of the horses, even men screaming. The Old Man lay on his back behind me, blood pouring from the front of his shirt. I screamed at him, but he didn't move. I scrambled, crawling around the wheel of the cannon. Over my shoulder they closed. I would never make it before the cavalry overran us.

My eyes focused on the red shirt—Custer—still on horseback. He raised his pistol, somehow managing to keep it steady even as his horse raced over the rocky ground. I stared down the barrel of the weapon. I could do nothing more than wait for the smoke to rise and the bullet to slam into my body. Instead, Custer bucked. His gun fired, though the weapon jerked upright where it would only hit the sky. In the middle of his chest an arrow had buried to mid-shaft. I looked to the ridge above. Warriors streamed down the steep slope. They would swarm the remaining cavalry.

As his horse ran past our position, Custer fell from the saddle. His body landed hard upon the riverbed next to me. He fought for breath as he looked to the sky. His hat had blown off his head and his golden hair blew in the breeze. Slowly, he turned toward me.

"Who are you?" he asked. A hacking cough rose from him. His eyes lost their focus like Yellow Knife's.

I crawled to him and grabbed a lock of his hair to pull upon. Jerking his head, I pulled him back from death's call. He stared into my eyes, fighting for every moment upon this earth.

"Two Wolves." I gave him the name the Lakota used.

"It wasn't supposed to be like this," he said.

"Black Kettle said the same thing as you shot him down."

I didn't know if my words held truth, but I wanted him to hear Black Kettle's name in his last breaths. Anger flashed upon his face—then it softened. The Great Spirit took hold.

I dragged myself to the Old Man. When I reached him, he still breathed. A lone bullet had struck him high in the shoulder, like my injury. When I put pressure upon the wound to stem the bleeding, he awoke.

"Damn it, Joseph, that hurts." His voice sounded parched.

He looked to me and started laughing. He struggled to catch his breath, but he could still speak.

"I suppose you know exactly how this feels. We are a pair, you and I. Molly will be glad to see the both of us."

As we lay there, Rain-in-the-Face descended through one of the gullies in the bluff. He walked to us. The shooting had completely stopped. When I looked to the east, the other Rodman gun no longer fired. Behind us, only the remnants of the cavalry remained. Lakota warriors walked among the dead and dying to collect what they might—rifles, ammunition, the jackets of fallen soldiers. The battle had died.

Rain-in-the-Face stood over Custer, holding a bow in one hand, with a quiver of arrows over his shoulder. Most of the warriors rode into battle with both rifle and bow. It was either tradition, or a means to stay in the fight if the rifle jammed. The fletching of the arrow in Custer's chest matched those in Rain-in-the-Face's quiver. He said something to me, pointing to Custer. I didn't need to speak Lakota. I understood. I had saved him a few days earlier. Now he had saved me. He picked up Custer's pistol. Another pistol remained in a holster on the dead man's belt. Rain-in-the-Face handed me one, taking the other himself.

"Help me up," the Old Man said.

I struggled—first rising to my knees, and then pushing off to stand. When I reached my feet, I helped the Old Man. We stood together, surveying the scene before us. Custer and his entire 7th Cavalry lay dead. Behind us the infantry had sounded full retreat. General Dorsey was dead on the ground behind us. Then I remembered Yellow Knife.

"We should go to the village and get these injuries of ours cleaned," the Old Man said.

"Help me get Yellow Knife," I answered. "We need to bring him home."

The Old Man and I walked downriver toward the first Rodman gun. I stumbled upon my one leg until the Old Man handed me the Spencer rifle to steady myself. As we walked, we collected a pair of Indian ponies that had wandered loose and strayed near the river to drink. Some warrior had dismounted and left them upon the battle. There would be many such horses to find today.

Near the first cannon, the warriors still collected supplies from amongst the dead infantry. They had taken the ammunition wagon and loaded the abandoned rifles and cartridges. They even took the rucksacks of the soldiers and their canteens and mess kits.

Anything might be of use to get the Lakota through the winter. Or it might be used to barter with the traders and mountain men.

They had even kept Mr. Carson alive and that surprised me. The fat man had lost his hat. He sat bound with rawhide to a broken wagon. He blubbered on about mercy as I neared. We would take him. The Old Man might need him to testify. His will had broken and he would likely tell all he knew.

When I reached where I had last seen Yellow Knife, his warriors had already picked him up and gathered him over his horse. I stopped them to see the man once more. Only three feathers were woven into his hair now. I prayed to the Great Spirit that the killing of the day was not in vain—not just Yellow Knife, but all the warriors and soldiers. As I prayed, I looked to my feet. There amongst the river rocks lay my knife—the one the Old Man gave me back in Tennessee, the one O'Malley had taken from me in New York, and the same knife he used to kill Yellow Knife. I bent down and picked it up.

As I turned it over in my hand, I had a sudden impulse to throw it into the river. I raised it as if I would throw it away. But I remembered Sitting Bull's words: *We only find true peace when we feed both wolves.* The knife had no fault in any of this. I lowered my hand, feeling the rough handle. Then I tucked it inside my belt.

I steadied my horse to picket him to the wagon to better deal with Mr. Carson. The Old Man grabbed hold of my shoulder. At first I thought he stumbled, so I reached out to grab hold of him. Instead, he pointed to the far side of the Yellowstone. High upon one of the bluffs a man sat upon a horse. He surveyed the destruction below.

With the setting sun I found it hard to see, but I knew who it was. He saw us, too. He wanted us to see him. With a quick turn he kicked the sides of his horse with his spurs—no Lakota rode in that manner. He dashed out of sight.

"Quick," I said to the Old Man. "Get me upon this horse."

"Joseph, you're in no state—"

"Get me on!" I strained to pull myself up. "He's headed for the village."

CHAPTER THIRTY

THE HORSE PLUNGED into the cold water of the Yellowstone. Instantly the current tugged, dragging us downstream. If I had more time I could have ridden upriver past the Little Big Horn, but time counted as the one thing I lacked. We struggled in the current. The wet coat of the Lakota horse became slick. I gripped tighter to the animal so the water would not wash me from its back. If I fell into the river, I had little chance to survive with the state of my leg and shoulder.

When the horse found his footing, I hugged him around the neck—part relief, and part as thanks. He eased us out of the water, testing each step before he bore full weight upon it. At the far side I turned around and held Custer's pistol above my head. The Old Man raised his rifle. In my haste I had not considered the weapons I brought. I should have taken the Spencer rifle, but now I had no time to head back across. Taking stock of the situation, I rolled the cylinder on the pistol—three shots left. And I had my knife.

I urged the horse up the far shore. We found one of the gullies that led to the top of the bluff. Near the top I dismounted to coax the horse up, holding the bridle and speaking in calm tones despite the steep terrain. This animal had never been subject to a saddle. He had never trained in the cavalry, yet he performed flawlessly. The Lakota were phenomenal horsemen. They rode in the midst of buffalo herds or on raiding parties against other tribes who incurred upon their land. They did not need saddles to control their horses. The rider and beast were closer, knowing what each other needed, and worked together. I hoped I might coax this one all the way to the village in such a manner.

Sitting Bull had sent the women and children south, providing standoff from the fighting. It seemed a wise move, but I didn't know exactly where they were. Maybe they followed the Little Big Horn—hopefully on this eastern side of the river. I held the bridle with one hand while my weak side gripped the pistol. Once upon the top of the bluff and under firm footing, the horse took off on me.

I gripped as tight as I could with my wounded thigh. The one time I looked down to it, fresh blood stained my trousers. The Old Man had bound it tight, but with all the effort of the day I likely worked it too hard.

Daylight fell fast, with the sun making a brilliant display of the horizon. It cast hues of red and orange, almost blinding to look toward. I rode into it, knowing I would hit the Little Big Horn before turning south to follow the river. I also searched the prairie. The grass hills rolled into the distance, giving up no sign of O'Malley. But the land held a rough nature here, with small peaks and valleys. O'Malley could have ridden in any number of little gullies and I would never have seen him.

The horse raced as fast as I could hold on. He sensed the urgency, knew that we had to find the village. Perhaps he guided us there by scent, or instinct. Maybe he could hear the river ahead. He led us to a small creek that flowed north toward the Yellowstone. From the size alone I judged that it could not have been the Little Big Horn. We crossed the creek and continued west.

Only a few miles later, I knew my choice to be a good one. We came upon a much larger river. In the valley below, the village had set camp. They had pitched the lodges, and the smoke from dozens of cooking fires climbed into the darkening sky. I urged the horse onward, pushing him hard downhill.

Once in the village, a pack of barking dogs greeted me. They continued to follow the horse as I rode to where Yellow Knife's lodge should have been. Molly would have placed our small tipi in a similar location. The village retained the same character whenever it moved. As I made it to the place, I jumped from the horse and pushed open our tipi flap—no one.

I rushed outside. A few lodges over, I heard a woman singing. I didn't know the voice, but it sounded like a prayer, as if she begged the Great Spirit to bring her husband home from the fight. I pushed toward the lodge as fast as my leg could carry me. Dusk had settled, and darkness would only hinder my search for O'Malley.

As I approached the lodge, a woman opened the flap. She likely heard the footfalls of the horse as I rushed into the village. She took one look at me and then beckoned someone from inside the lodge. A moment later, Molly rushed forth from the tipi.

She gathered me up in an embrace, almost knocking me upon the ground. As she pulled back, she read my face. Then she stared at the pistol in my hand.

"Joseph, what is it?"

"Where are the children?" I asked. My voice cracked. My mouth had filled with dust.

"Daniel and Emeline are inside. I sent Aurora to the river to gather water. Why? What is it?"

"O'Malley," I said as I turned toward the river. The setting sun had almost disappeared. "How long ago did you send her?"

"Ten minutes, maybe more. She complained of thirst, so I told her to fetch it herself."

"Are there weapons here?"

"I don't have any, Joseph."

"Show me," I said. "Where did she go?"

I grabbed Molly by the hand and dragged her toward the river. We stood at the top of a short bluff, with maybe a thirty-foot slope down to the water. Despite the dying daylight, a small shape knelt down by the river.

"Aurora!" I yelled.

The girl stood and looked my way.

I waved. She dropped her bucket and ran toward us. No one else stood along the river. Scrambling up the rocks, she headed toward the embankment. Relief coursed through me. I breathed deep, held it, and then exhaled. The pain in my shoulder made me laugh. I had found them all. O'Malley had likely ridden south, escaping the carnage that fell upon General Dorsey. We were free.

"What is it?" Molly asked. She had stepped behind me, wrapping her arms around my neck.

"My shoulder, and my leg—they hurt."

I turned into her to wrap my arms tight about her body.

"And that's funny?" she asked.

"No. It's just—"

I didn't finish my thought. Behind us, a man stood watching. Dusk concealed his face, though one arm hung limp. Alone and in this wilderness, death would claim him—he must have known it. He came for one thing, making him more dangerous than ever.

Molly didn't turn. She read my face, knew what the tightening grip upon her back meant. She released her hold upon me. Lowering her hands, she took Custer's pistol from me in a manner that O'Malley could not witness.

"I could have shot you in the back," he said.

"Why didn't you?"

"Because you need to watch them all die first."

He thrust his pistol forward, firing in the direction where Aurora climbed the embankment. The round struck something, but in the dim light the muzzle flash blinded me. I froze. Time stopped. I stood in the woods of Essary Springs when Wyman Baxter cornered us by the great oak. Helpless, I watched it unfold again. Baxter turned his gun on Emeline as the little girl lay in the grass. Before he could fire, the Old Man's mistress— her mother—dove in front of the shot. I could do nothing. The bullet hit her in the chest, with the blood welling upon her breast, staining her dress.

A gunshot pulled me back. Molly pushed me aside, turning to face O'Malley. She had used the bulge at her belly to hide the pistol. She didn't aim. The gun kicked in her hand. The muzzle flash lit the night. O'Malley grinned. Molly had missed, but her thumb fought for the hammer, cocking it in place. She fired again. He crumpled to one knee—struck in the lower leg.

The ringing in my ears dulled his laugh. With the injury, he had slipped from reality. He existed in a place where only the insane dwell—there would be no stopping him until he died. He raised his pistol toward Molly, and I charged. I would not fail her as I did the Old Man's mistress.

O'Malley rose on his good leg and dove toward me. We collided, falling to the ground. He tried bringing the pistol to my head, but I pushed it to the dirt. As he pulled the trigger, the hammer fell and caught the web of my hand between my thumb and forefinger. I screamed with the sudden pain, but wouldn't let go of the pistol. With the gun useless, he tucked into me hard and rolled. We tumbled side over side, still clinging to one another. When we hit my bad shoulder, I winced in pain, almost letting go of the gun. Then we fell, still locked together until we landed with a splash at the edge of the river. My head came to rest looking up at the sky while I laid in a few inches of water.

Above me Molly screamed my name. The cold from the water took the wind from my lungs. We had plummeted down the embankment to the riverbed below. I reached out to find him—nothing but empty night. Then in the rising moonlight, I caught the glint from the pistol. He stood above me, limping forward on one leg. He held the gun out at arm's length.

Pulling the hammer back, the cylinder indexed to the next round with a distinct metallic click. Still he said nothing. His laugh consumed him. He struggled to stand over me until he straddled my waist as he aimed down upon my head. Slowly pulling the trigger, his first shot landed on the right side of my head, kicking water over my face. I flinched and reached for my face. He fired again on the other side—still laughing. Then I caught movement from the corner of my eye.

Aurora swung her bucket, gripping it with two hands so she would not lose it. It struck O'Malley's pistol, knocking the gun from his hand. The weapon flew across the river and landed in the water. Distracted, he lashed out at her. As he did, I grabbed his bad leg causing him to fall on top of me. He screamed as all his weight came crashing down upon my chest. It knocked the wind from me, and I sucked in water. The impact threw us both deeper into the river with the current tugging upon us, and his crushing weight forcing my whole head underwater.

I thrashed for a moment, panic gripping me as I tore at his hands. I couldn't breathe. He sat on top of me and forced my shoulders down, driving my head deeper into the riverbed to keep my head under the rushing water. My shoulder burned, and only muffled sounds reached me with my ears submerged. The water distorted my vision, but even so, I saw the delight upon his face.

I tried bucking him off my chest to no avail. My muscles slowed. The cold from the water seeped in, through my clothes. I lay in molasses, and each time I thrashed my lungs burned worse with no means to replace the air they craved. A peace came over me. It eased the struggle. My fingers slipped from his clothes and my body began to relax. He pushed down even harder.

Then one of his hands let go, shielding his face. The sound of ricocheting rocks rose from the river. He ducked and another echo came forth from the water. He reached next to my head until he found a stone, throwing it toward the riverbank. When he reached into the water again, I grabbed hold of his wrist. Startled, he tried to pull back. I held on as tight as I could, though my grip slipped until I held only his thumb. With his other hand, he pushed me harder into the river, moving his hand until he held me by the throat. As I shifted under his weight, something jabbed my back—my knife. My free arm reached for it, still tucked into the small of my back.

I shifted again, managing to get onto my side just enough to pull the blade out. With every movement, I fought the cold peace descending over me. Yanking his thumb downward, the bone broke, yet still I held firm. Then I thrust upward with the knife, severing his thumb in one swift motion. He fell back, releasing me. I lunged up and out of the river, catching my first breath of air, sucking it in as deep as I could make my lungs fill. Then I pulled back with the knife and buried it into his side.

The noise of the fight came back all at once. He screamed, holding his wounded hand. Blood flowed down his wrist. He buckled on his side where I left the knife. Letting go, I pushed on top of him, switching positions. With my full weight, I held him under, gripping with both hands around his neck. He kicked, but this time, he held much less strength. I pulled my knife from him, and prepared to plunge it in once more.

Molly yelled above. Aurora screamed from the shore. She held a river stone in each hand, barely gripping them without thumbs. She had hurled them at O'Malley as he drowned me. A stunned look came over her face. I followed her stare to the water. In the low light I only saw my own reflection, and a hand holding myself underwater. Startled and repulsed, I let go. O'Malley lay there, his head stayed underwater. I sat up, and then pushed backwards to get off him. He didn't move. From under the water, he stared into the night sky—lifeless. Then the current caught his body. It pulled him into the river and the water dragged him along with the current. He bobbed as he went over the rapids.

Slowly I rose to my feet. Molly called from above, but I could only cough—water still deep in my lungs. Aurora rushed to me, holding me up and letting me lean upon her. When we stepped to the shore, I realized I still held O'Malley's thumb. I tossed it into the water behind me. Aurora walked me to the edge of the bluff. As we took the first steps to climb back up, I stopped.

At my feet lay an Eagle's feather. I picked it up. It still held a lock of Yellow Knife's hair, bound by a strap of rawhide.

CHAPTER THIRTY-ONE

25 AUGUST 1874

THE OLD MAN and I sat in the dark of Sitting Bull's lodge, across from the war council. It had been a fortnight since the defeat of the cavalry. I had slept much of it, recovering for the journey south to Ft. Laramie. Rain-in-the-Face had only just returned. For the past week he had led a large number of warriors to harass the fleeing infantry. They followed what was left of General Dorsey's army until all were well clear of the *Paha Sapas*. In typical fashion, the Lakota attacked time and again. They drove fear into the dismounted soldiers, forcing them to drop their gear as they tried to escape. The soldiers finally mounted steamboats sent up-river as resupply. Lakota scouts watched until the last of them had stepped off the prairie grass.

Rain-in-the-Face returned a triumphant hero, along with other warriors like Crazy Horse and Chief Gall. Sitting Bull had masterminded the trap. With it, he cemented his position as leader of all the plains Indians. He credited the victory in no small manner to our efforts to secure the big-talking guns. The village now had two of the weapons, though powder and shot would remain scarce.

Sitting Bull drew deep from his pipe before passing it. The tobacco remained the same, yet he called this one a peace pipe.

The immediate threat had sailed downriver, but we all still faced a growing storm. Despite the celebrations, Sitting Bull understood.

"We will send an escort to bring you to the old forts along the Powder River, where you first met Yellow Knife. After that, you may find your way along the road to the fort at Laramie." Sitting Bull spoke as he passed the pipe around the circle.

We no longer had Yellow Knife to translate. Instead, Yellow Sparrow, the young boy whose mother gave the Old Man the rifle, conveyed the meanings of the chiefs. His English came out less refined. He had learned by speaking with the traders who traveled through Lakota territory.

"I will take these books to the Great Council," the Old Man said. "I will tell them what has been done here." He held the satchel that contained the ledger and all the corporate papers.

"Will you talk to the new Great Father?" Sitting Bull asked.

"Yes."

"Will it be enough to stop a war?" Rain-in-the-Face asked.

I didn't know if he wanted to stop the war. The last week had seen such success for the Lakota. But Rain-in-the-Face had never been east. He couldn't understand the ocean of people who would crowd onto the prairie as the nation expanded.

"I cannot make promises," the Old Man replied.

"But you will try," Sitting Bull insisted.

"I will."

"When you meet the Great Council, tell them we will not allow anyone to destroy the buffalo. Or take the *Paha Sapas*. We expect the Great Council to honor the treaties that Red Cloud and the other chiefs signed. There will be no war from us unless they break their promises again."

Custer's cavalry had been wiped out—long-hair Custer among the dead. Much of the infantry were also lost, but enough escaped to tell the tale of the battle. The story likely already circulated in Washington. Maybe even among the other cities in the east. Custer would rise as a martyr, and the next campaign season would see a larger force head up the rivers. We had time to avert a disaster, though not much.

The Old Man felt confident that luck had shone upon us—though I credited the Great Spirit. One man had survived Custer's command, though not a soldier—Samuel Barrows, a reporter from the *New York Tribune* who traveled with the expedition. When the Lakota went to collect the cavalry's equipment, they found him. He had suffered a wound to the leg, and had been unable to escape behind Custer's final charge. So he hid under a fallen soldier, hoping the Lakota wouldn't uncover him amongst the dead. But when they found him, he was lucky. The warrior who pulled him from the pile of dead soldiers had seen how we saved Mr. Carson. Based on that example he spared Barrows as well.

Barrows had survived the long march with General Dorsey from the Missouri River, the first conflict along the Yellowstone, and finally Custer's arrogance in placing his force so far forward of General Dorsey and his infantry. Since that time, he had spent his days talking to the Lakota. He heard the stories of Sand Creek, the Washita, and a dozen other conflicts that no one bothered to name. He saw the bullet wounds in the women, the children who were maimed and survived. These were not the primitive beasts he had written about in his earlier stories. Before this expedition, he had translated from the cable dispatches. He had never sat around the fire, listening to the people, hearing the Lakota firsthand. The stories he had written in his newspaper articles all crumbled. The victors wrote the history, and now he knew it needed revising.

But the true evidence that swayed Barrows' opinion in favor of the Lakota came from General Dorsey's diary. The warriors had hauled in a wagon after the infantry fled. At first the wagon seemed more a work of art than a means of travel. Nothing of its sort had ever ridden across the plains before—the personal conveyance of the general. The finest workmanship crafted everything from sleeping quarters in the back, to plush velvet seats, and even the finest in steel spring suspension to soak up the travel over the prairies. When the warriors stripped it of anything useful, a journal lay among the effects. Dorsey never counted on being captured, let alone defeated. He must have thought his diary safe, but with the journal even Mr. Carson's testimony paled in comparison. The general confessed his sins from beyond the grave, written in his own hand. When combined with the satchel of documents and the ledger that the Old Man still safeguarded, the information would ruin what was left of the Consortium and any influence it still maintained. Half of the Great Council would resign for their corruption and greed, as the public would see how the Consortium bought their votes. Some in Congress would feel the cold stone floor of a jail—steel bars impeding their view out narrow windows.

The air inside Sitting Bull's lodge was laden with the smoldering fire, though my eyes no longer watered with the smoke. The Old Man took a deep breath from the pipe, and passed it to the council. Six of the Lakota war chiefs sat with us, including Rain-in-the-Face. One by one each of the chiefs enjoyed the tobacco.

The flap to the lodge opened behind us casting a long sliver of daylight into the dark. A few of the Lakota warriors had helped Mr. Burrows fix General Dorsey's wagon, and a full escort of Lakota warriors had readied their ponies to bring us south. The time had come to leave—to go home. The Old Man and I stood as Sitting Bull showed us out of his lodge, while Rain-in-the-Face followed us outside.

The Lakota had no use of the wagon, which would only slow their travel upon the plains. The travois worked far better, never becoming mired in the mud from the spring rains. We loaded General Dorsey's wagon with our scant belongings, the children, and the two captured white men. Mr. Barrows needed more time to heal before he could ride, and we dared not let Carson have a horse. He had been well looked after for the past week, but held as a prisoner of the Lakota. If we untied Carson for even a moment, he would try to escape, and the prairie would swallow him whole.

Before I mounted into the wagon, Sitting Bull pulled me aside with the young boy as translator. We stood next to the glorious wagon with the sun in our eyes.

"Do they have wolves where you go?" he asked.

I thought of sitting on my porch at night, hearing the lone wolf sing.

"There is one. She comes from the mountains and sings at night."

"Then when the Great Spirit sends you such messages, listen well. That is the song that sings you home. The Great Spirit may bring us to the same place again one day."

"I would like that," I said.

He held his hand out the way he learned from the white traders. I grasped it. Then I climbed into the wagon with the others. The Old Man sat next to me. He wore Charley's gray Stetson hat, which still had the original feather, and with it, Yellow Knife's feather.

"We will do our best with the Great Council," the Old Man said.

In his usual reserved manner, Sitting Bull spoke slowly. His voice carried so all in the wagon could hear.

"I want you to ask the Great Council something for me," Sitting Bull said.

He paused only long enough to see the nod from the Old Man.

"When I was a boy the Sioux owned the world. The sun rose and set in their land—they sent ten thousand men into battle. Where are the warriors today? Who slew them? Where are our lands? Who owns them? What white man can say I ever stole his land or a penny of his money? Yet they say I am a thief. What white woman, however lonely, was ever captive or insulted by me? Yet they say I am a bad Indian. What white man has ever seen me drunk? Who has ever come to me hungry and left me unfed? Who has ever seen me beat my wives or abuse my children? What law have I broken? Is it wrong of me to love my own? Is it wicked for me because my skin is red? Because I am a Sioux? Because I was born where my father lived? Because I would die for my people and my country?"

He paused before finishing.

"Ask them this for me."

CHAPTER THIRTY-TWO

2 SEPTEMBER 1874

A WEEK LATER we arrived at the remains of Fort Reno, where we had camped before fleeing in the boats. Our tents had blown down, likely taken in some storm. The old wagon sat there still, though the horses were long gone. O'Malley must have stampeded them onto the open prairie to prevent our escape—the wolves likely had a welcome dinner. Molly became most excited about finding her luggage intact. The men who pursued us were in such flight to make our capture that they never sorted through the bags. Molly pulled out her dresses, a bit of luck, as she required looser-fitting gowns. Her belly had grown larger though we still had months left. And neatly hidden below the clothing, the last assets of the Consortium—the money we had taken in New York.

That night we camped under the stars. I sat up most of the evening as the children and Molly slept. The Old Man and I took turns watching Mr. Carson. He itched to escape. In truth, I worried what role he might have in all this. His confidence grew as we reached farther south, as if he might make some play to run. I gazed upon the night sky, so rich with little lights that lit the heavens. In the distance the wolves sang to one another.

The next morning our escort of six warriors returned north. They had said little to us, as we had no means of translating. We used sign language when we needed, and it worked well enough. They guaranteed our safe passage to within grasp of Fort Laramie. We had several days' travel before we reached the Laramie River, but on occasion settlers or trappers made it this far up the Bozeman. It would be better if we traveled alone from this point. One of the warriors had been with Yellow Knife that first day they captured us upon the Powder River. He said something to me in Lakota before he rode away. The only words I recognized were *Two Wolves*—I imagined he wished us well.

With the sun still low upon the new day, we broke camp. I wished to get as far as we could before the heat overwhelmed us. We could take a break when the sun hung directly overhead, and then push again until dusk. Without the warriors I felt exposed, though the real danger would come with the forts in the Platte Valley. The commanders there might have received telegraphs about the fighting up north. We planned to avoid them, even Fort Laramie. Instead, we struck out for the Missouri River. Most of us would head home as the Old Man made his way to Washington.

The trail became smoother past Fort Reno. Even though it had been years since Red Cloud's war and closing of the Bozeman, ruts from the wagon wheel still cut deep through the grass. We followed these, and for the sake of my leg and Molly, I thanked the Great Spirit for delivering this wagon. The springs took much of the rough ride as they soaked up the bumps and eased the jostling of wagon travel.

With each mile, Carson became more talkative. His worry seemed to leave him as the warriors rode away. We kept him tied, at least with his wrists bound together to dissuade any surprise from the little man. I expected none. He had the courage of a chipmunk coupled with the body of a potbelly pig.

During our midmorning break I untied him so he might relieve himself. I dared not venture far with him as he pissed into the wind.

"Do you think they will believe you?" he asked. "Is that your plan? To make lies about General Dorsey and his great plans for the West?"

He still spoke of the general as if he were alive.

"Your Consortium is dead," I replied. "It died with Dorsey."

"You think he was the only one that knew the operation? There are others."

"And we have all their names—most telling, their trail of money."

As he finished, buttoning his trousers, he turned. He craned his head, searching for the others. They were out of sight. The Old Man was ushering the children into the wagon with Mr. Barrows' help.

"If you let me free," Carson suggested, "I will make you a rich man."

"I am a rich man," I replied. "I have all I need—my wife, my daughter, our family."

"Then think of them," he said. "If you help me, I promise I will never harm them."

Molly placed a hand on my shoulder. It startled me. After her time with the Lakota, she walked much quieter.

"What's going on?" she asked.

"I think Mr. Carson is threatening us," I answered.

"I offer opportunity, that would benefit all of us," he said.

Molly's voice remained flat, betraying nothing.

"What opportunity?"

"That I will protect you."

"I think you've seen we don't need it," Molly answered.

"Oh, you're wrong—so wrong. Though I don't expect a woman to understand."

Molly stepped forward. Her hand fell sharply across his face. Even though she towered over him, he reared back as if he meant to strike her. I drew the pistol from my holster—Custer's gun. Cocking the hammer, I leveled it upon him. His hands dropped, edging away from us.

"You're making a huge mistake," he yelled. "When we return, I will tell what you did. How you killed General Dorsey by shooting him in the back. How you used the savages to kill good Christian men. I will be a hero! And no one will believe you. Do you think that even with Mr. Barrows the nation will believe a half-breed? I will rebuild the Consortium and then I will find you!"

As he finished, we remained silent. He had worked himself into a frenzy, almost breathless, his face red. I lowered the gun, letting the hammer ride forward with my thumb.

"He may be right," I said to Molly. "Maybe we should let him go."

"Yes!" Carson said. "You see the logic. I am a powerful man."

"Joseph . . ." Molly turned to me.

"He is a powerful man, Molly. Perhaps we should let him go."

I stepped toward him. He eased away, his eyes darting around me.

"What was it you said back in the train?" I asked. "Do you re-member? It was months ago."

He shook his head. His eyes stared at the pistol in my hand.

"I think you said you would be well suited to the frontier—that you could hunt and live off the land."

He appeared puzzled, not knowing what I meant.

"Do you know how to use this?" I asked.

I held up the pistol. He nodded.

"Good."

I opened the cylinder and pulled out the bullets. I gathered them into my pocket. Then I closed the cylinder with a snap and handed the unloaded weapon to him, holding it out by the barrel.

"What is this?" he stammered.

"It's a gun, Mr. Carson. So you can hunt and live off the land."

"What?"

I turned and started walking back to the wagon. Molly came with me. Behind, Carson followed, still unsure of what transpired.

"You're leaving me?" he asked.

"You asked that we set you free. You're a powerful man—I wouldn't want to upset you."

"But, but . . . you can't leave me. Not here. I meant at Fort Laramie or in St. Louis."

"We're not going to Fort Laramie or St. Louis," I answered.

"Where are you going?"

"We're going home. And now we've let you free. You promised to keep us safe, remember? I expect you to honor it."

Molly and I had reached the wagon. I helped her up.

"But you can't leave me here!"

"We can, and we are," I said.

As I turned to get into the wagon, he tugged on my shoulder. I spun toward him, pulling my knife. With a single movement I held it under his neck. He let go of my jacket and stepped back.

"I'm done with you," I said. "I'm done with your Consortium. It's over—all of it. And we have no need of you. You asked to be free, and now you are. Go."

I lowered the knife, still keeping it high enough so he would not try to rush me. I pointed to the prairie behind me. He turned to look. The horizon remained unbroken, filled with only an ocean of rolling hills. His eyes fell to the pistol in his hand. He sank to his knees.

"You have to leave me bullets. Give me bullets," he pleaded.

I fished in my pocket until I found a single round. I held it up.

"I'll leave you one, but not here. A mile up the road, I'll leave it with a canteen."

"One bullet? How can I hunt with one bullet?"

"It's not to hunt with," I said. "At night, when the wolves track you, you'll be glad I left a bullet."

I turned and walked to the wagon. Climbing in, I settled next to Molly. I saw that The Old Man had watched the exchange, too. With a flick of my wrist, I started the horses. When last I looked back, Mr. Carson still stared at the gun in his hand.

After we crested several hills, I stopped the wagon in a valley. I untied a canteen and placed it in the wheel track where Mr. Carson was sure to find it. Pulling a bullet out of my pocket, I looked at it, turning it over in my hand. I bent to place it on top of the canteen, but then thought better of it. I placed it back in my pocket and mounted the seat next to Molly. Then I started the wagon once more.

"You're not leaving it for him?" she asked.

I shook my head. "He might shoot a wolf."

From behind us in the wagon the Old Man spoke.

"Well, Mr. Barrows, it appears you are the only survivor from Custer's last stand."

CHAPTER THIRTY-THREE

14 APRIL 1875

THE OLD MAN stood next to me under the great oak tree. Spring had blessed us, appearing in full force. The sun rose strong that morning, and as it arched ever higher, it burned away the crispness in the air. Birds sang, the wind fell soft among those gathered on the field in front of us, and Aurora held my free hand. I knew peace.

Somewhere out of sight the baby cried. From his wavering voice I could tell Molly held him, bouncing his little body up and down until he settled. She stayed hidden, still superstitious that I could not see the dress until the ceremony started. I knew better than to argue over such things.

We stood quiet for a time. The Old Man received a telegram that morning—a rider rushed from Essary Springs through the mountain trail. He had not revealed the contents, perhaps not wanting to intrude upon the day.

"Good news or bad?" I finally asked.

He smiled. "Good."

Mr. Barrows had released a series of stories. They exposed the Consortium, laying out all the dirty details—the flow of money, the web of corruption that spiraled into the Congress, the links to the railroad, to General Dorsey, and even details behind the Draft.

The last story covered the battles on the Yellowstone plains, and how the Consortium hoped to use them to steal the Black Hills and the gold that lay underneath. Between Mr. Barrows' reporting and the evidence the Old Man provided to Congress, the country reeled. Federal prosecutors gathered the evidence and started the trials. The first senators to fall were the minor players. They pled to deals—saving themselves. Then they testified against the more powerful and implicated their colleagues. The Consortium had existed as a vine, strangling the essence of democracy. Once exposed, anyone connected to their corruption was torn from office and cast aside. Democracy was a garden, and the Old Man the reluctant gardener.

"The President signed the Bill," he said as his hand stroked his beard. He had allowed it to grow back to full strength. "And the impeachment effort failed—by a single vote."

He had stayed in Washington for some time over the winter, only returning a few weeks earlier. He cajoled those still in power and untouched by the scandal. They formed a protection act for the Lakota and other tribes. It mandated troops to guard against incursions into the territory. The forts would still exist across the southern Platte Valley. They would protect the Oregon Trail. Other forts would remain on the eastern side of the Missouri River. But the land between the Rockies and the Missouri would be set aside for all time.

"No war then?" I asked.

He nodded. "We did that much."

"But will they be safe?"

His hand stopped and fell from his beard.

"I fear not forever," he answered. "There will be much pressure to expand. Every year it will grow worse." He sounded far away, his thoughts elsewhere.

"For a time then," I offered.

He broke the stare that pierced into the distance.

"Let's hope it is a long time."

He looked over my shoulder and smiled. The sound of the baby nearing meant Molly stood behind me. I dared not look or else incur her wrath.

"Joseph," she said. "Take your son. I cannot settle him."

"But I should not see you," I teased.

The Old Man suppressed a smile—then placed a hand upon my shoulder.

"If my memory has not failed me, I believe you are already married. After your time together, I think you are due some luck."

He spun me by the shoulder until I faced Molly. She looked incredible. Her hair fell upon her shoulders. Fresh wildflowers were woven into the braid that crowned her head. Her dress glowed—a beautiful cream color that created a perfect match to her complexion. And I loved the little ways her mouth curled when she smiled—the wrinkles that had not been there years ago when we first met.

"What is it?" she asked.

I shook my head, taking the baby from her. He eased into my shoulder, quieting with just a few small cries.

"It's not fair," she said. "He settles so easy for you."

I reached out to hold the side of her face. With everything we had been through, Molly had never been more beautiful. I pulled her close. My lips found hers.

"I will wait with the guests," the Old Man said.

He left us, walking down the short aisle formed by the guests who sat and waited. The Old Man took his place in front of them all.

Molly looked over the small crowd, then to the baby in my arms.

"I thought I would not have to hold a baby as I walked down the aisle," Molly said.

"You're not—I am. And would you have it any other way?" I asked.

She shook her head. Aurora leaned into Molly, clutching at a hand. Even without thumbs, she could hold tight. Molly bent and kissed her on top of the head. Then Molly took my hand. Her voice was soft as she pulled Aurora near.

"We should all be together. Are you ready?"

I looked past her. Three neat graves lay under the great tree— the Old Man's mistress, my mother, and Charley. My mother lay in the middle. How very much I wished she could be here.

"She's watching, Joseph, you know that."

I nodded.

"I sometimes wonder—" I fell quiet as I looked upon where my mother lay.

"Wonder what?"

"Every place has its price," I said. "One way or the other, you always pay for peace. Do you think we've paid it yet?"

Molly looked over her shoulder and then back to me. Her hand gripped mine, interlacing our fingers. She squeezed, turning me to face the Old Man. As we took our first steps together, she leaned close.

"We've paid our fair share in this land of wolves."

AUTHOR'S NOTE

THE AMERICA THAT MIGHT HAVE BEEN

FOR THOSE OF you who have read *Lincoln's Bodyguard*, you know the story of Joseph Foster and Molly Ferguson is not only historical fiction, but also revisionist history. I set out to answer the question: *What would America have looked like if our greatest president had lived?* And the answer was far darker and more dystopian than I had at first imagined. However, by the end of that novel, History corrected this revised timeline, bringing the nation back to the course we all studied in our high school history classes. *Or did it?*

As *Land of Wolves* opens in March 1874, we find Joseph and Molly almost a year after the conclusion of *Lincoln's Bodyguard*. They are living in the foothills of Tennessee, with the Old Man— Abraham Lincoln. But Joseph's daughter, Aurora, has yet to join them. Joseph and Molly have delayed their wedding to wait for her arrival, but as the weeks pass, they realize something has gone awry. Their worst fears materialize when they discover her disappearance is linked to the revenge of the Consortium—the Confederation of Industrial Barons who have kept the flames of conflict alive after the Civil War in order to amass great wealth.

In *Land of Wolves*, the Consortium wishes to see President Johnson impeached. Andrew Johnson did, in fact, follow

Abraham Lincoln in the presidency, taking office after Lincoln was assassinated. However, in *Land of Wolves*, Johnson becomes the president after Lincoln *resigns*. And he is faced with the same set of circumstances he dealt with in real life—the struggle of Southern Reconstruction, where he pits himself against Congress and the military authorities. In our nation's actual history, Congress did impeach President Johnson in a struggle over the role of the military during the Reconstruction era—in particular, over Secretary of War Edward Stanton. In *Lincoln's Bodyguard* and in *Land of Wolves*, this struggle still exists. Congress wishes to keep military control over the former rebellious Southern states so the Consortium can maintain cheap labor for their factories through the Draft. Many of those serving in Congress are little more than paid spokesmen for the Consortium—not unlike today's world where the influence of corporate money controls our nation's politics. As President Johnson intervenes in this process, upholding the Old Man's Executive Order abolishing the Draft, the Consortium seeks to have him impeached. As *Land of Wolves* concludes, we discover that Johnson has narrowly avoided conviction in his impeachment trial by a single vote. In actuality, President Johnson missed conviction by a single vote in the Senate on May 16th, 1868.

Believing that his daughter has been killed, Joseph heads to New York City to exact revenge upon the Consortium. During this period of the Second Industrial Revolution (1870–1914), New York City is an important hub for commerce. The head of the Consortium, General Terrell Dorsey, uses New York as his base of operations, hiring street gangs as enforcers. This resonates with actual history. During the era of the late 19th century, New York City experienced an epidemic of gang violence. The gangs facilitated and profited by everything from robbery and murder, to prostitution and turf wars. While the character of General Dorsey is fictional, it's not a far stretch to imagine a former Quartermaster of the Army would head the Consortium, and that New York would be an ideal location to base his new operations—away from the turmoil in Congress even as he controls representatives and senators to do his bidding. New York also provides a safe haven, with gangs like the Black Murphys who enforce the will of the Consortium. The Black Murphys of the novel are loosely based on the Dead Rabbits, an Irish street gang in New York City at the turn of the 20th century.

After fleeing New York City, Joseph and Molly follow the call of the West to escape the reach of the Consortium. Just as the Second Industrial Revolution is under way, so, too, is one of the largest movements of humanity across North America—the great migration westward across the prairies. Joseph, Molly, the Old Man, and the children join this journey, traveling along the Oregon Trail to Fort Laramie. Along the way, the infamous Jim Bridger joins their party. Like Abraham Lincoln and a few other characters, Jim Bridger is a man ripped out of history. Although known as a great frontiersman, he also bears some responsibility for a dark period in American history—the Indian Wars.

On August 29th, 1865, Jim Bridger led a group of scouts during the Battle of Tongue River. Bridger guided soldiers under Brigadier General Patrick Connor—Star Chief Connor as the Lakota called him—to attack an Arapaho village, killing over fifty Indians—most were children or elderly. They burned the village, leaving the Arapaho with nothing more than the clothes upon their backs and the few horses they used in their flight. During the raid some of the villagers recognized Bridger as a man who had hunted and trapped with them, even marrying one of their women. So while in reality Jim Bridger lived until 1881, he meets an untimely death in *Land of Wolves* as a means to rectify his involvement upon the Tongue River that day, even if only in the literary sense.

And so the novel moves squarely into the land of the Lakota Sioux. The Lakota are an indigenous people who live upon the Great Plains of North America. French traders and trappers introduced the term Sioux. They used it referring to a confederation of seven related tribes who speak the Lakota language: Brule, Oglala, Sans Arc, Hunkpapa, Miniconjou, Black Feet, and the Two Kettles. While the term Sioux would have been commonplace during 1874, used by the white settlers, soldiers, and frontiersmen, in most cases I refer to the tribes by their proper names out of respect for these great nations who still inhabit the plains today.

When Joseph and his party travel north from Fort Laramie, they do so upon the Bozeman Trail. This path cut right through the Powder River Valley in Lakota territory and was closed in 1865 after a protracted conflict between the United States and Red Cloud—a war chief of the Oglala. Red Cloud's War, as it became known, ended with the Treaty of Laramie in 1868. This established the Great Sioux Reservation, covering the lands west of the Missouri River in South Dakota. The treaty effectively closed the Bozeman Trail, blocking the path miners used to travel north through the Powder River Valley and into Montana.

As Joseph, Molly, the Old Man, and the children travel along the Bozeman, warriors from Rain-in-the-Face's Hunkpapa Lakota tribe capture them along the Powder River. Rain-in-the-Face was a Hunkpapa war chief involved in many battles upon the plains, including the Battle for Honsinger Bluff, the Battle for Pease Bottom, and even the infamous Battle of the Little Big Horn. Some accounts claim that Rain-in-the-Face personally killed General George Armstrong Custer, a claim that Rain-in-the-Face himself both made and retracted during his life.

After their capture, Joseph and the Old Man see life upon the plains as the Lakota face pressure from settlements on their eastern front, travelers who traverse their lands on the way west to California and Oregon, miners who chase rumors of gold amongst the Black Hills, and survey teams of soldiers who scout routes for a transcontinental railroad. Eventually Joseph and the Old Man are transferred into the care of *Tatanka Yotanka*—Sitting Bull.

In their first encounter, the infamous plains leader of the Lakota challenges the Old Man over the treatment of the Santee Sioux. This is a reference to Little Crow's War, when in August 1862, the Santee Sioux could no longer tolerate treaty violations against them. Their people had been forced onto reservations as the Indian agents assigned to oversee the reservations pocketed money and goods meant for the Santee. In addition, the Civil War diverted much-needed supplies away from the Santee. They were left trapped and facing starvation. After several months of conflict, the US Army subdued the revolt, and established quick trials condemning 303 men to death.

President Lincoln personally reviewed each case, pardoning all who had engaged in warfare against the US government. But he did confirm the sentences of thirty-eight Santee Sioux men who were found guilty of murder or rape against civilians. They were put to death on December 26th, 1862, in what remains the largest mass execution in United States history. The remaining Santee were removed from their land and relocated to the Crow

Creek Reservation on the Missouri River. Of the 1300 Sioux who were brought there, less than a thousand survived the first winter. Game was scarce, the soil was barren, and the water unfit to drink.

In 1863, a young Lakota warrior from the plains, when visiting his Santee Sioux cousins who were forced to live on a reservation along the Missouri River, heard the story of how their land was taken by white settlers. This left an indelible impression, and with it he realized it would only be a matter of time before those settlers pushed westward. If he wanted to keep that land in the hands of the Lakota, he would have to do something to stem the tide of settlement streaming from the east. That warrior was Tatanka Yotanka—Sitting Bull.

At the finale of *Land of Wolves*, we play witness to a series of battles along the northern banks of the Yellowstone River. These battles actually occurred, taking place between the Lakota and soldiers supporting the 1873 Northern Pacific Railway Survey party, which sought a route for a transcontinental railroad. In fact, some of the very personalities that play a role in the novel were involved in the survey. For instance, George Armstrong Custer led the cavalry during the 1873 expedition. In addition, the newspaper reporter Samuel Barrows also traveled with the expedition to document the journey for the *New York Tribune*. I did make one notable personnel switch for this portion of the novel. In reality, Colonel David S. Stanley was the expedition leader, though I conveniently replaced him with the fictional General Dorsey for purposes of the story.

George Armstrong Custer was a larger-than-life personality upon the plains. He was known throughout the country as both a Civil War hero, as well as a warrior during the Indian Wars upon the plains. His reputation has changed with the times, and today invokes a mixed image. However, he was a major protagonist during the August 4th, 1873 Battle of Honsinger Bluff—this is the battle highlighted in Chapter 25 of *Land of Wolves*. During this scene we see the battle play out in as close detail as I could extract from historical sources. This includes the siege of Custer and his cavalry along the Yellowstone River and the death of Dr. Honsinger—the expedition's veterinarian.

The final battle of the novel (Chapters 28–29) is also based upon historical events. The Battle of Pease Bottom took place on August 11th, 1873, and represented another conflict between Custer and Sitting Bull. I took some liberties with the depiction of this battle, mainly with the death of Custer. Historically, Custer's last stand came on June 25th, 1876 at the Battle for Little Bighorn, known to the Lakota as the Battle of Greasy Grass. Instead, I elected to have Custer fall during the Battle at Pease Bottom several years earlier. This sets up the situation where the Old Man can return and argue in front of the Great Council—Congress—for increased protections for the Native American nations. I did, however, let the battle play out mostly along historical lines. Custer did become trapped along the river, unable to cross. Sitting Bull did attack Custer across the river, and Colonel Stanley did charge ahead to rescue Custer, pushing his artillery ahead of his infantry columns. In addition, Custer brought his band to battle with him, just as I depicted in the novel. At the height of the battle, just before Custer charged the Lakota, he instructed his band to strike up the "Garryowen"—a popular song of the time and an Irish tune that Custer appears to have favored in motivating his troopers to fight.

When Custer falls at the final battle in *Land of Wolves*, the Old Man can plead with Congress to honor the treaty obligations signed with the Lakota and other Native American nations. Clearly, this is not the course that our nation played out for the Lakota and other peoples. Instead, the conflicts with Native American tribes continued until the United States claimed most all the land of the plains, restricting Native Americans to small reservations where it was impossible to continue their way of life. Even though *Land of Wolves* ends with hope that the outcome in this revisionist view of history may be kinder for the Lakota, even the Old Man is unconvinced he has done anything more than buy them a little time.

The quote at the end of Chapter 31 is truly from Sitting Bull. It bears repeating:

When I was a boy, the Sioux owned the world. The sun rose and set in their land—they sent ten thousand men into battle. Where are the warriors today? Who slew them? Where are our lands? Who owns them? What white man can say I ever stole his land or a penny of his money? Yet they say I am a thief. What white woman, however lonely, was ever captive or insulted by me? Yet they say I am a bad Indian. What white man has ever seen me drunk? Who has ever come to me hungry and left me unfed? Who has ever seen me beat my wives or abuse my children? What law have I broken? Is it wrong of me to love my own? Is it wicked for me because my skin is red? Because I am a Sioux? Because I was born where my father lived? Because I would die for my people and my country?

—Tatanka Yotanka

My research for *Land of Wolves* drew from many writers and historians, but for additional reading I highly recommend the select few sources listed here. These books offer a glimpse into a tumultuous period in our nation's history, revealing stories that in some cases we might prefer to forget. However, understanding our past, even the very darkest corners, is the only way we might avoid repeating the mistakes of those who came before us.

Bury My Heart at Wounded Knee by Dee Brown
Jay Cooke's Gamble by M. John Lubetkin
Crazy Horse and Custer: The Parallel Lives of Two American Warriors by Stephen E. Ambrose